Susan  2/04

MW00780633

House
of Illusion

House
of **Illusion**

Velda Johnston

Five Star • Waterville, Maine

Five Star First Edition Women's Fiction Series.

Published in 2001 in conjunction with
Spectrum Literary Agency, Inc.

Set in 11 pt. Plantin by Al Chase.

Printed in the United States on permanent paper.

Library of Congress Cataloging-in-Publication Data

Johnston, Velda.
    House of illusion / Velda Johnston.
        p. cm.—(Five Star first edition women's fiction series)
    ISBN 0-7862-3086-X (hc : alk. paper)
    1. Paris (France)—History—Siege, 1870–1871—Fiction.
    2. Women—France—Paris—Fiction. 3. Prostitutes—
    Fiction. I. Title. II. Series.
    PS3560.O394 H587 2001
    813'.54—dc21   2001045054

House
of Illusion

Chapter 1

1870

Even though she had been working at Madame Theraux's establishment for several months, Jeanne-Marie still was awed by the luxury of the establishment. She was not yet used to the silky thickness of the Aubusson carpet across which she moved, young and slender in her maid's uniform, but with a certain delicate roundness—of cheek and bosom and hip—which had reminded some of Madame's customers of paintings by that new young artist, Renoir. She still felt dazzled by the huge crystal chandelier, shedding radiance over the well-dressed assemblage, the men in formal clothes, the women in the narrow evening gowns which, by decree of the fashionable dressmaker, Worth, had replaced the graceful crinolines. She even liked the feel of the sterling silver tray, laden with champagne glasses, which she carried through the crowd, offering wine to anyone whose glass was empty.

She knew it was wrong to enjoy her employment here. If Uncle Claude and Aunt Therese, that grim peasant couple who had raised her, knew of how she was supporting herself and little Marcel, what would they think? What would her own mother think, that gentle, pious creature she scarcely remembered, if she knew that her daughter was employed, in any capacity whatever, by a brothel keeper? But Jeanne-Marie would not dwell on that. Better to pretend that this assemblage was what it appeared to be, a private reception for ladies and gentlemen.

She offered the tray to a tall, plump man with graying brown hair, a beard, and a monocle. "Thank you, my dear." He spoke French with some sort of accent, Swedish or German, perhaps. With one hand he lifted a glass from the tray. With the other he pinched her rosy cheek.

She smiled, not in the least offended. After her highly unpleasant experience with her first employer here in Paris, it was good to work in a place where men, content with cheek pinching, did not try to bed her. Men did not pay Madame Theraux's one-hundred-franc entrance fee in order to go to bed with parlor maids. They came here to purchase the favors of the evening-gowned women in this room, women with the appearance and carriage, if not the speech, of young duchesses.

As she turned away from the man with the monocle, her gaze fell on the young American lady, Mademoiselle Maggie MacNeil. She sat alone on a small red velvet sofa, shoulders bare and gleaming above her black dress, dark hair drawn back from her face into a knot of curls at the nape of her neck. Perhaps because no one sat beside her, her face did not bear the bright smile expected of Madame Theraux's young ladies. The gray eyes, set wide apart under brows like dark wings, had a look of sadness, and at the corners of her mouth there was a slight, bitter downturn.

In Jeanne-Marie's opinion Mademoiselle MacNeil, with her great gray eyes and perfect features, was by far the loveliest woman in the room. It was strange to see her alone. But perhaps this evening she was being reserved, so to speak, for some especially important gentleman. Jeanne-Marie moved forward and extended the tray of champagne glasses to Mademoiselle MacNeil.

"No, thank you, Jeanne-Marie," the girl said in her American-accented French. A smile warmed her face.

Jeanne-Marie liked the American. Many of the girls here, as if believing that their gowns actually had transformed them into great ladies, assumed a haughty air with the establishment's servants. Mademoiselle MacNeil did not. Moreover, something about the American touched the French girl's sympathies. She sensed that Maggie MacNeil had suffered a childhood as poverty-stricken as her own and perhaps even bleaker.

Jeanne-Marie moved on, offering champagne to men of several nationalities and almost every age, and to young women who ranged in coloring and origin from a pale blond Swede to a brunette from Martinique who was said to have a dash of African blood. Every one of these women was expensively perfumed, beautifully groomed and gowned, and ornamented with jewels, which, although in many cases only paste, added to her attractiveness. But Jeanne-Marie did not envy them the life they led. True, during her first days in Paris as a very young widow with an infant son to support, she had sometimes feared that she would have to surrender her body as the price of keeping her job in some factory or shop. That had not turned out to be the case, but even if it had, she would not have thought of herself as a whore, or harbored an intention of becoming one. How awful it must be, night after night, to allow men, for a fee, to make use of one's body.

She had almost completed a circuit of the room now. Her footsteps slowed. Just ahead, seated on one of the several high-backed sofas in the big salon, was Mademoiselle Diane Gautier with a thin, nervous-looking man of about forty beside her. Jeanne-Marie did not like Diane Gautier. In fact, she felt repelled by her.

The little peasant girl could not have said why. Certainly

9

there was nothing unpleasant in Diane Gautier's appearance. If there had been, she would not be a part of this assemblage. Tall, with reddish blond hair, eyes of a shade somewhere between green and hazel, she had the features of a Greek goddess—broad brow, aquiline nose, rather wide mouth, and a jaw line perhaps a little too firm. No, Jeanne-Marie could not define why she disliked any contact with Mademoiselle Gautier. She only knew that she did.

Approaching the sofa, she held out the tray. The nervous-looking man glanced up, smiled slightly, and shook his head. The blond woman looked only at the tray. Without a pause in what she was saying, she reached out and took a glass.

Little as she liked the woman, Jeanne-Marie did not feel that Mademoiselle Gautier was being deliberately haughty. The way she had taken a glass without even a glance for the one who offered it had seemed quite natural. She had the air of someone who had grown up thinking of a servant as not quite a person, but rather a creature whose only purpose was to open doors or proffer trays.

The tray was empty now. Jeanne-Marie left the salon and went down a hallway to refill the tray with more champagne from the butler's pantry.

With a thickening figure, henna-dyed hair, and a face still handsome at fifty-odd, Madame Theraux stood in a corner of the salon, talking with one of the establishment's more frequent clients.

"Then you feel no doubt, my dear Baron, that France will win the war?"

"None whatever, Madame Theraux." Middle-aged, coarse-featured, and with shrewd little eyes, Baron Foulon appeared typical of the businessmen to whom Louis Napoleon had granted patents of nobility during the last few years.

"But they say Bismarck has made the Prussian army into a

formidable force." Privately, Madame Theraux felt that the French had been fools, several weeks ago, to declare war for no better reason than an "insulting" statement the Prussian leader, Bismarck, had released to the world press. Probably, she reflected, wily old Bismarck had deliberately set that little trap, and had been delighted when the excitable French stumbled into it. To her it did not seem surprising that they had. In her business, she had long since ceased to be surprised by the folly of men, Frenchmen included.

"Just the same, Madame, I expect the French to triumph. The war should not last more than a few weeks."

Just long enough, she thought, for corrupt businessmen like Baron Foulon to make a pile selling shoddy goods to the army. The thought brought her no sense of indignation. She long since had become too cynical to experience moral outrage, even of the patriotic kind.

"The Emperor himself will leave shortly for the front to command our troops against the Prussians."

The Baron managed to say it almost, but not quite, with a straight face. Everyone knew that poor Louis Napoleon, weak and self-indulgent nephew of the great Napoleon Bonaparte, could command nothing. Anyone could influence him. Court hangers-on like the Baron. Women like the Empress Eugenie, who had gained her title by refusing to go to bed with him until, maddened by frustrated desire, he had placed a ring on her finger and a crown on her head. And he had been equally compliant with the Paris mobs who, earlier in this summer of 1870, had surged into the streets demanding that France punish the Prussians for their "insult."

"I had not heard that His Majesty intends to lead our forces." Her gaze slid past his shoulder and lighted upon Helene, a red-haired girl from Marseilles whose voluptuousness, her employer noted, was turning to fat. Madame suspected that over-indulgence in wine as well as food was responsible for that. And more than Helene's figure had suffered. She was losing the manners which Madame had managed to pound into the girl's rather thick head over several weeks of coaching, manners designed to turn farm girls and factory workers into reasonable facsimiles of young gentlewomen.

As she did to each new recruit, Madame Theraux had said to Helene, "My establishment is not selling just the use of female bodies. It is selling romance. Or call it illusion, if you like. If they choose to, my clients can feel that they have not come to a brothel. Instead they have paid their hundred francs for the privilege of attending some fashionable function, a benefit, perhaps. In such a setting a man can feel that the young lady he chooses will accommodate him, not because of the money he will pay her, but because she finds him irresistibly attractive."

To emphasize the difference between her establishment and other brothels, Madame Theraux had chosen not to provide rooms for her clients and girls. For the hundred-franc entrance fee, she furnished only this resplendent meeting place. It was up to the client to provide accommodations where he and the girl he had chosen could bed down, just as it was up to him to decide upon the amount of the "gift" he would bestow.

Madame Theraux demanded no part of those gifts. The hundred franc entrance fees enabled her to maintain this fine house on Paris's Left Bank, provide the fairest of champagne and caviar for her clients, pay each girl a modest weekly stipend, and still make a handsome profit.

She frowned. Helene, in her pink brocade dress now straining at the seams, had responded with a braying laugh to a sally made by the man seated beside her. Yes, Helene must be dismissed.

Still apparently listening to the Baron, she glanced swiftly at Maggie MacNeil. The American girl sat alone. That was Madame's doing. Tonight a Very Important Personage was expected to inquire for her. His equerry had made it known that afternoon that the Personage would seek the company of Mademoiselle MacNeil, just as he had once before. And so Maggie had been instructed to tactfully discourage any other man who tried to sit beside her.

Maggie MacNeil, unlike Helene and many of the others, was capable of behaving with tact. As she often did, Madame wondered just how it was that the American girl was even in Paris, let alone part of the company in this luxuriously furnished salon. Oh, she knew that Maggie, like most of the young women here, had been born to poverty. The day she had accepted Madame's offer of employment, Maggie had said matter-of-factly that she had been raised in a New York slum. It was also obvious that she had emerged from her early years with emotional scars. Her face, in repose, held a melancholy tinged with bitterness.

But there was more to the girl, Madame felt, than just the usual whore's history of impoverished and unprotected early years. Something or someone had helped her to rise above her background, if only temporarily. Someone must have helped her refine her slum-bred manners and cultivate her native intelligence. Although she had come to Paris only a little more than a year ago, she already spoke fluent and not too heavily accented French. And she undoubtedly was the only one of Madame's girls who read the daily papers, not just the scandal columns, but also the political news, including Victor Hugo's fire-breathing patriotic editorials.

Well, whatever her past history, Madame was glad of Maggie's services. A girl who could so please a future king that, months later, he again would seek her out, was indeed an asset to the establishment.

"And they say that when she gives parties she strews the floor with orchids and dances the can-can naked."

The Baron had begun to talk of Cora Pearl, one of the "*grande* horizontals," women far too rich and powerful, as well as too selective in their lovers, to be considered mere harlots.

"Yes, I have heard that she does." Madame knew that the Baron had already made an assignation for later in the evening with Dorothe Dupres, a vivacious little brunette who was the illegitimate daughter of a woman who, twenty-five years earlier, had worked in Madame's first establishment, a much smaller house on the Right Bank. Madame wished that the Baron would take Dorothe to wherever he intended to bed down, instead of standing here while he spouted stale gossip and talk of that foolish war.

Her gaze, again sliding past the Baron's shoulder, found the young woman who called herself Diane Gautier, and who told everyone that she was the daughter of a railway clerk in Nice. Again Madame frowned. Oh, not that Diane, like plump and noisy Helene, threatened to become a liability. With her cool good looks and regal carriage, Diane had become an instant attraction, especially for men who like a touch of arrogance in a woman.

But that was the trouble. Her arrogance. Madame long had been acquainted with the factors—impoverished background, plus bitterness or laziness or some other innate or acquired character trait—that inclined girls toward whoredom. But none of them, not even the few who managed to become well off, ever achieved the cool arrogance which Diane possessed right now, at what must be an early point in her career.

During the months Diane Gautier had been part of this establishment, more than one man had commented to Madame about the young woman's remarkable resemblance to a certain Englishwoman, who was the daughter of an Earl and the wife of a Baronet. But of course it was no more than that, a remarkable resemblance. For one thing, Diane's French bore no trace of an English accent. For another, Madame had read somewhere that the titled English woman in question had left more than a year ago for a long tour of the Middle East, perhaps with the view to publishing memoirs similar to those of Lady Hester Stanhope. And anyway, why should an English aristocrat choose to be part of a Paris brothel?

Madame Theraux did not know why Diane had become a harlot, and not knowing made her uneasy. No, more than uneasy. Afraid.

The fear did not arise merely because she was puzzled over Diane's origins. There was a quality in Diane that the older woman found vaguely alarming. Or perhaps it was a lack of something, an absence of human feeling that every other woman in the room, no matter how frivolous or how hardened, possessed to a certain extent.

In short, Madame Theraux sensed that the tall young woman with the red-blond hair might be capable of anything.

Madame Theraux wished she could dismiss her. But her business sense revolted at the thought of dismissing a girl her clientele found so attractive.

The thin, nervous-looking man seated by Diane said, "Do you know that you look very much like a lady I glimpsed at a large party two years ago in London? Her name was Lady Howard or Hatworth or something like that. You look enough like her to be her twin."

As always at moments like this, Diane said composedly, "Yes, I have been told I resemble this Englishwoman. The

15

wife of a Baronet, is she not?"

The architect nodded.

"And I know that it is true that I resemble her. I have seen her photograph in a magazine."

"Why, come to think of it, she even has the same first name! I did not actually meet her at that party, but I am sure that I heard her friends calling her Diane."

She smiled. "Yes, that is her name. I thought it would be amusing to change my name to Diane."

"Then it isn't your real—"

"No, I was christened Claudette. What's more, after people began to tell me of how closely I resembled this Englishwoman, I changed the color of my hair. People told me that she was a Titian blonde, so I became one too."

"The color appears very natural indeed," he said gallantly. "And very becoming."

"—have laid down five dozen bottles, just in case the war makes it difficult to bring in supplies from the provinces."

The Baron was boasting about his wine cellar now. "Very prudent of you," Madame Theraux murmured.

She saw old Pierre, the porter who had been with her for twenty years, approaching across the rich carpet. He whispered in her ear.

"Do forgive me, Baron," she said. "Someone I must greet has just arrived."

She moved swiftly across the room to the foyer. When she came back into the room, she was accompanied by a rather stout man of about thirty and a taller and thinner one of perhaps thirty-five. The plump man wore a wig and avoided looking around the room as Madame led them straight to the sofa where Maggie MacNeil sat. At their approach, the girl got to her feet.

Madame Theraux said, in heavily-accented English, "Monsieur Warren, you recall Mademoiselle MacNeil, do you not?" On his afternoon visit, the same equerry who accompanied him now had told Madame that on this trip to Paris, His Highness was using the name Warren.

"I remember with pleasure," the plump man said, and sat down on the sofa. Madame Theraux and the equerry moved discreetly away.

Mr. Warren smiled at Maggie, and she smiled back. As much as she could bring herself to like any of the establishment's clients, she liked this man, who one day would be King of England. But he would not reign as Albert, the papers said, even though that was what members of the royal family called him. He would take the throne as Edward the Seventh.

Careful not to use his title, Maggie said, "I am delighted to see you again, monsieur."

He laughed. "I thought I had best visit Paris again while I still could. It is said that the Prussians may soon try to draw an iron ring around Paris."

"In that case, the war surely will be brief."

"How so, mademoiselle?"

"A siege would not only mean keeping the French inside Paris, it would be keeping the rest of the world out. And any Frenchman will tell you that the world would never will allow that!"

He laughed. As he had discovered at their first meeting, this young woman was not only beautiful, but could turn a wryly-amusing phrase.

"Let us hope it will be short." He paused. "No doubt this is your first experience of war."

"No. There was our American Civil War."

"Oh, yes. The war which ended about five years ago. Didn't you tell me that you were born and raised in New York

17

City? There was no fighting there, surely?"

She said, after a moment's hesitation, "No, no actual battles."

But there had been the Draft Riots. Thousands of men, including the father she had not seen for some time, battled the police and soldiers who were trying to force them into the Union Army. Hundreds of them, including her father, had been shot or clubbed to death. Because her mother was too drunk to get out of bed that day, thirteen-year-old Maggie had gone down to the West Forty-Seventh Street Police Station to identify the remains of the man who had sired her.

But one did not talk of such matters to any client, especially one who was also the Prince of Wales.

"I can stay only a few minutes," he said. "Against my better judgment, I agreed to spend part of this evening at what I know will be a very dull reception. But I am staying, during my visit, at a rented house in Passy. Will you join me there at eleven tonight?"

"With pleasure."

"Splendid. There will be a carriage waiting for you outside this house at ten."

Across the room, the woman who called herself Diane Gautier thought, with amusement, "Why, there's Cousin Bertie!" Somehow, despite the vigilance of his redoubtable mother, the Queen, he had managed to slip his leash again.

They were not first cousins, of course, but nonetheless cousins. Their common ancestor was fat George the Second. The young man seated with Maggie MacNeil at the other side of the salon was descended from fat George's eldest son. Diane was descended from one of George's daughters.

She thought of how he might cross the room to say, in an astounded tone, "Why, Lady Harding!" If that happened, she would say blandly, as she did to anyone who broached the matter, "Yes, I know. I am supposed to resemble some Englishwoman."

But, of course, nothing like that would happen. In the first place, Bertie would be to discreet to draw attention to either himself or her in a place like this. Also, he was too nearsighted to see across the salon. And in the third place, all his attention was directed to that American girl with the Irish name.

The architect said, "That man who came in only a minute or so ago. Wouldn't you say he looks like the English Prince of Wales?"

Diane followed the direction of his gaze. "Does he? I could not say. But it isn't likely that he is the Prince of Wales, is it?"

"No, I suppose not." He took a watch from his waistcoat pocket, glanced at it, and then replaced it. "It is getting late." He paused and then said, in an awkward rush, "I have an apartment not far from here on the Boulevard St. Germaine. Would you accompany me there?"

Why, he was actually blushing. That confirmed the guess she had made about him when he first sat down beside her. Men who possessed the sort of sexual preferences Sacher-Masoch had written about almost always felt embarrassed by their predilections. What was more, such men instinctively sought her out.

"Of course," she said.

Chapter 2

At ten o'clock Maggie MacNeil stepped from the foyer into a cobblestoned courtyard flooded with moonlight so brilliant that one, quite literally, could have read large print by it. A closed carriage was waiting. Through that blue-white brilliance she rode along a winding street, past fine mansions that already were old when the Sun King reigned at Versailles. As the carriage drove over one of the Seine's many bridges, she looked to her right. As always, she felt moved by the sight of the Isle de la Cite, riding the moon-sparkled water like a gigantic ship, with the Cathedral of Notre Dame as its superstructure.

On the opposite side of the river the carriage continued on past the long arm of the Louvre, past the palace of the Tuileries where Louis Napoleon and his empress held their shoddy court of profiteers, sharp-dealing lawyers, and ladies with brand-new titles and shopworn reputations. She rode on past the arcaded shops on the Rue de Rivoli. When the carriage entered the vast Place de la Concorde illuminated by the mingled glow of the full moon and flaring gas lamps, she saw that even at this hour a company of National Guardsmen were drilling. In this prosperous neighborhood, of course, the company of guardsmen had chosen and paid for their own uniforms. Looking like actors in a light opera, they marched up and down in their pantaloon trousers, heavily braided coats, and red fezzes. Beside them marched their company *cantiniere*, or mascot, a pretty girl with a ceremonial water canteen slung over her shoulder and a fez perched at a rakish angle on her red curls.

The French sense of style, Maggie thought. It extended to everything. Greengrocers, for instance, displaying their wares in shop windows, arranged bunches of grapes and cherries as carefully as if they had been emeralds and rubies. And now the French—with bravura music, dashing uniforms, and pretty girls—were imparting a sheen of theatrical glamour to this unnecessary, and perhaps tragically fated, war.

Even though Maggie had never visited the Paris slum of Belleville, she had heard that there were also local companies of guardsmen who spent much of their time drilling, no doubt with much of the same dash displayed by these well-off young men in their expensively-tailored Zouave uniforms. But in Belleville the men wore shoddy, government-issued uniforms, and drilled with sticks rather than rifles on their shoulders. It was not that the government could not afford to give them rifles. It was afraid to, lest those half-starved men, sooner or later, turned their guns on their betters.

As she rode on across the vast square, where less than a hundred years ago the blood of thousands had dropped from the guillotine onto the stones, she felt an inward shiver. If the French won their war, all was well and good. Those slum dwellers, who for some unfathomable reason were more patriotic than the more comfortable classes, would be content with "la Glorie" of victory, even though it would not put food on their tables or mend the moldering roofs over their heads. But if Bismarck and the Prussians won? She could imagine a convulsion of rage from these "patriotic poor" sweeping Paris, as it had in 1789, and again only about twenty-five years ago, in 1845.

21

But no matter what the future might hold for this beautiful and volatile city, she was glad to be here. Glad to be well-fed and well-dressed, and riding through the moonlit night in a comfortable carriage, even though the purpose of her journey was to lie in the bed of still another man—a prince, in this case, but still just another bed partner.

It was not that she enjoyed whoring, she thought bitterly. As a young and innocent girl, she had felt confident of a very different life from the one she now led. But uncontrollable events had destroyed not only that young-girl innocence but her optimism as well. By the time she left New York she had made up her mind that in the future men would pay for the use of her body, and pay well.

The only child of a young couple, Dan and Rose MacNeil, who had fled Ireland's potato famine, Maggie had been born in that decaying section of New York known as Hell's Kitchen. She had a few bright memories from her earliest years; times when her parents had seemed not only at peace but even happy, beaming at each other across the table in their sixth floor flat, or strolling with her small self between them along the Hudson River, or—joy of joys—taking her on the horse car up to the Central Park Zoo.

But far more vivid and numerous were the memories of shouts and screams, and blood pouring from her mother's nose or split lip, and then the receding clatter of her father's footsteps down the long flights of uncarpeted stairs. And after, her mother, with the blood staunched, sullenly pouring herself another drink from the bottle on the kitchen table.

Sometime after Maggie's fifth birthday, her father moved out of the flat. At intervals he would reappear, bringing a few dollars from the money he earned, intermittently, as a long-shoreman on the Hudson River docks. Sometimes he stayed for a day or so, or even a week. Maggie's small heart would swell with hope. Maybe now they would not fight anymore. Maybe now Mama would bother to make good suppers for the three of them, and the kitchen, with herself seated between them, would be a wonderful place, warm and safe and filled with love. But sooner or later the angry voices would again erupt. While Rose screamed her defiance, Dan's big fists would batter her face. Then again he would plunge down the stairs to the street.

His visits grew briefer and less frequent. The sums of money he contributed grew smaller. By the time Maggie was seven and a half, his visits ceased entirely.

"I guess we won't be seeing his lordship from now on," Rose said one hot summer night. Glass in hand she sat in the kitchen rocking chair. Its runners squeaked as she rocked angrily back and forth. "I heard today he's living over in Hoboken with another woman."

Soon after that the first of the "uncles" appeared. Most of them never stayed longer than overnight. Often Maggie would be awakened by the sounds from the other small bedroom. Not really understanding, and yet feeling terribly sad, she would stick her fingers into her ears and try to go back to sleep.

But during those years she had two sources of consolation and even joy—school, and the free library some philanthropic person had set up in a vacant store in this bleak neighborhood. She felt wonderment when she heard other children grumble about going to school. Exercising her young mind on an arithmetic problem brought her much the same satisfaction she felt when she stretched her young muscles skipping rope. In fact, she was loath to see Saturday afternoons and Sundays roll around, because then there was no school, no escape from that perennially disordered flat.

At nine she discovered the free library. After that she did

not mind Saturday afternoons and Sundays. She would join Rose in the weekly effort to bring some sort of order into the flat. Then she would retreat with a book to her room or, if the weather was good, to the tarpapered tenement roof. Very soon, she was floating down the Mississippi with Tom and Huck and Jim, or riding with Ivanhoe beneath the giant beeches of an English forest. She would forget that there was even such a place as Hell's Kitchen.

Because her teachers had decided that she could skip the seventh grade, she was graduated from grammar school at the age of twelve. Her mother had said she would be present at the ceremony in the school's assembly hall. Maggie was sure she had intended to. But the night before, Rose had quarreled loudly—and as it turned out, disastrously—with the latest of the uncles, a dock foreman who had supported her and Maggie quite generously for the past six months. He had packed his suitcase, said in a grimly convincing tone that he was "through," and left the flat. For consolation, Rose had turned to the bottle, with the result that she was still sound asleep when Maggie left for her last day of school.

Clutching her rolled-up diploma, she returned to the flat at four o'clock to find her mother seated, white-faced and with deeply circled eyes, in the kitchen rocking chair.

"Mama, I want to go to high school." Because she was afraid of what Rose's reply would be, she spoke swiftly and loudly.

"High school!" Rose stared at her. "Who goes to high school?"

"Lots of people. And, Mama, the teachers say that with my grades—"

"Next you'll be wanting to go to Yale College."

Maggie checked the impulse to say that girls did not go to Yale. That would be considered "sass," and would ruin whatever chance she had of winning her mother over.

"Maggie, you're thirteen now, almost grown up."

"Twelve."

"You'll be thirteen in September. It's time you earned a living. You weren't born with a silver spoon, you know."

As sometimes happened, Rose's face and voice suddenly became gentle, sorrowful. "Honey, I know you're a smart girl. And there's nothing I'd like more than to have you go to high school. But we have to look at things as they are. Your father's no good to us. And I know that Chet won't be back." Chet was the uncle who had taken his angry departure the night before.

Her voice turned bitter. "Maybe if I'd guessed he might walk out on me, I'd have tried to get more money out of him while he was still here. I might even have gone through his pockets now and then." Again her voice had changed, this time to a tone of conscious virtue. "Lots of women do that, but I never did.

"It would be different if I was well enough to work, but I'm not." Probably that was true, although how much of her chronic ill health had its origin in the bottle, neither of them could have said. "And lord knows how much longer I can—"

With her voice trailing off, Rose threw a glance at the small wooden-framed mirror above the sink. Maggie's father had shaved himself in front of that mirror. So had other men who had shared this apartment for a few hours or day or weeks.

Inwardly cringing, Maggie understood her mother's quick glance at that mirror. With newly apprising eyes Maggie looked at the puffy face. Rose was thirty-two and appeared forty-two, a not very attractive forty-two. How much longer could she count on financial support from men?

"So you've just got to go to work, my girl." Rose's voice was loud and firm now. "I mentioned you just the other day down at the Jews'.'" That was how the whole neighborhood referred to the delicatessen store, run by David and Sara Koppel, on the corner of Forty-seventh Street and Ninth Avenue. "They'll hire you. Four dollars and a half a week and your lunch free. That's as much as you'd make in a factory, and you won't have any carfare to pay."

Maggie stood there with the look of someone who, in her mind's eyes, has just seen a steel door clanging shut.

"Oh, honey!" Rose cried. "Don't look at me like that! You'll still be able to read those books you're so crazy about. And pretty soon there'll be plenty of fellows wanting to marry you, a pretty, smart girl like you."

She went to work for the Koppels the following Monday. She realized it was a good job compared to those of girls who labored in laundries or at knitting mill looms. The Koppels were warm and kind, often insisting that she take home food for her and her mother's supper table. She even enjoyed the blend of smells in their small shop, smells of pickles and lox and freshly ground coffee.

But the hours were long, six in the morning until six at night. Each evening after supper she tried to read from the books she continued to draw from the free library. Now they were not novels, but histories and even an algebra text, with which she hoped to gain at least part of a high school education. But soon after she started to read, she would find herself falling to sleep.

Still, she did manage to absorb some American and European history, and to solve some of the easier problems in the algebra text. At noon, when she sat over lunch in the Koppels' back room, she also furthered her education with their copy of the New York *Times*. Always the front page was filled with news of the clashing Union and Confederate armies at places with names like Antietam and

Chancellorsville. To Maggie, eating bagels and lox in the rear room of a Hell's Kitchen delicatessen, the war seemed very remote.

Then, when she had been working for the Koppels a little more than a year, the war was suddenly close, terrifyingly close. In July of that year, Washington began drafting New York men into the Union Army. Prosperous men could stay out of uniform by paying other men two hundred dollars each to take their places in the ranks. Such a course was not possible for New York's slum dwellers, most of them Irish immigrants. Gathering in infuriated mobs, they burned buildings and battled police and soldiers until subdued by clubs or rifle bullets.

It was a Sunday morning when a helmeted policeman appeared at the door of the sixth-floor flat. "Hello, girlie. Is this the MacNeil flat?"

Maggie nodded.

"Your mother home?"

After a moment Maggie said, "Wait here, please. I'll see."

She walked back through the kitchen to her mother's bedroom. But even before she opened the door, the knotted snores from beyond it had told her that Rose could not be awakened by anything short of having a pitcherful of cold water dashed into her face.

She went back to the policeman standing in the hall. "I'm sorry. My mother's too sick to see anyone."

He hesitated, and then asked, "How old are you, girlie?"

"Almost fourteen."

"Well, I hate to ask this of someone your age, but unless you want him taken to Potter's Field—What I mean is, we've had to set up a morgue in the back of the Forty-seventh Street Police Station. We've got a man there that the desk sergeant is almost certain is Dan MacNeil, a guy who used to live at this address. I guess you're—you're his kid."

Feeling oddly numb, she said, "That's right."

"You want to try to identify him for sure? As I said, we've been taking all the unidentifieds to Potter's Field. And it won't be so hard on you as it would be if his face—I mean, he was shot through the heart."

"I'll try to identify him."

A few minutes later she stood in the police station's back room while an officer turned down the sheet covering one of a long row of motionless forms. Still numb, Maggie stared at the waxen face. He looked older, much older, but still enough like her seven-year-old memory of him that she could be sure. Besides, there was the scar along his jaw. She remembered sitting on his lap and listening, fascinated, while he told her of how, when he was ten years old and fishing from a boat on Galway Bay, one of his companions had snagged his jaw with a fishhook.

"Yes, that's my father."

She still found that she did not feel anything much. And when she returned to the flat, Rose, awake now, received the news with seeming stoicism. But she dressed immediately, took the one bit of jewelry she owned, the garnet-and-seed-pearl brooch inherited from her grandmother, went over to Seventh Avenue, and haggled with a jewelry store proprietor until he bought it for enough to give her husband a decent burial. Two days later, she and Maggie stood beside the grave in a Catholic churchyard in Brooklyn. Rose wept, puffy face buried in her hands. It was then that Maggie realized that once, perhaps when they were very young back in Ireland, her mother and father had loved each other deeply. And it was then, too, that Maggie found that underneath her numbness there was grief for the man to whom she owed her existence.

Chapter 3

It was also on a Sunday, a warm Indian Summer Sunday morning two months later, that the man known as Baldy came calling at the flat. Knowing that her mother would not wake from sodden sleep until at least noon, Maggie had spent the morning at the kitchen table, reading a Greek history text from the free library, and wondering how words like "Anaxagoras" were pronounced. When the knock came, she went to the door.

A man stood there in the hall, a heavy-shouldered man with a bald head that gleamed faintly in the light filtering through the grime-encrusted window at the hall's end. He had been drinking. She could smell the whiskey on his breath.

He said, "Oh! Guess I got the wrong place." His speech was slurred. "Wanted to see Rose MacNeil—"

He broke off, and then said, with a wide grin spreading over his face, "Well, I'm damned! You're Maggie, skinny little Maggie, almost grown up. You remember me. Sure you do. Baldy MacIntyre?"

She did remember him then, dimly. He had stayed here for several weeks—or was it months?—when she was eight.

He walked past her into the kitchen. "Where's Rose?" he asked loudly. "I want to see Rose!"

Quickly the girl closed the door, lest the cranky old couple in the flat across the hall heard him. "My mother can't—can't see you now. She's asleep."

Again he flashed a wide grin. "Dead drunk, you mean. Know where I've been these past few years, Maggie? Out west. No fooling. Punching cattle in Kansas and Nebraska. And all the time you was growing up into a fine young lady."

"I'm sure you must have had some wonderful adventures, and I'd like to hear about them. But right now I've got things to do, and so why—why don't you come back when Mama is awake?"

He laughed. "Wonderful adventures! Kid, where'd you learn to talk like that?" He moved toward her. "And to hell with Mama. Give us a kiss."

Too late, she realized that moments ago she should have retreated into Rose's room or at least moved away from the table. He had her pinned against its edge now. She shoved her palms against his shoulders, twisting her face away. "No! Please!"

"Don't act that way, kid. What's a little kiss?"

Thumb and forefinger biting into her cheeks, he forced her face toward him. She felt his lips, rubbery and moist, covering her own. Blind with panic and revulsion, she somehow got one hand free and raked her fingernails down his cheek.

"Why, you little—" He stepped back from her and stood motionless for a moment, with the white marks of her fingernails slowly reddening. "You shouldn't a done that, kid." He wasn't grinning now. "How come you're so uppity? How come Rose MacNeil's kid thinks she's too good for old Baldy?"

Something had come into his eyes now, something that terrified her. She opened her lips to scream. His hand clapped over her mouth. With his other arm tight around her, he dragged her, struggling, across the linoleum floor and into her tiny bedroom. Kicking against his shins, she broke free of him for a second or two. This time she did manage to scream, but his open hand, slamming against the side of her head, making her ears ring, quickly silenced her. Hands on her shoulders, he shoved her backward onto the bed.

"Little bitch," she heard him mutter. "Probably drops her drawers for every kid in the neighborhood."

She thought, "He's going to kill me. With Mama right in the next room, he's going to kill me."

Ears still ringing, vision blurred, she saw that he was unbuttoning his pants. Then he was on the bed, his body weighting hers, his hand pulling at her underclothing. Head throbbing, half-paralyzed with horror, she did not resist as he thrust her legs apart with his own. Then she felt pain, a grinding, tearing pain. Again she screamed. This time, his body lunging back and forth on hers, he did not bother to stop her screams.

Then, with a final convulsion, it was over. For a few moments his body remained on hers, heavy and motionless. Then the bed creaked as he got to his feet. Eyes squeezed tight, she nevertheless knew that he stood there looking down at her. She felt the warm trickle of blood down her thighs. "He's hurt me terribly," she thought. "Perhaps I'll bleed to death."

"Kid, I'm sorry." His voice was heavy now, and almost sober. "When I came here I never meant—But you shouldn't a scratched old Baldy, kid. You shouldn't a done that."

Conscious of a sense of violation more terrible than the pain he had dealt her, she did not reply.

He stood silent for a moment. Then: "Oh, hell!" She heard him cross the kitchen, heard the door to the hall slam. She opened her eyes and stared at the yellowish rectangle of light coming through the paper window shade. She was still bleeding. She knew that she should get up and try to rouse her mother. She didn't want to die, not even after this, and maybe Rose would know what to do about the bleeding. But she still felt too weighted down with that terrible sense of violation to even get up off the bed.

And then Rose, in camisole and petticoat and a soiled blue wrapper, was standing in the doorway. "Honey? You all right? I dreamed I heard you yelling—" Then, "Oh, my God!"

She came into the room, sank onto the foot of the bed. "Who was it?"

Maggie told her.

"And all the time I was just in the next room—Oh, my baby! My poor little one!" She began to cry with great, tearing sobs, her hands covering her face.

After a moment Maggie said, "Mama, the bleeding."

Rose took her hands down. "Don't be scared, honey. It'll stop. Cold water will help stop it. I'll get some. And then you go into my room while I clean up your bed."

Half an hour later, as Maggie lay on the wider bed in her mother's room, Rose came in and sat down in a straight chair against one wall. "Now listen to me." Her voice was no longer thick with tears, but calm, even a little hard. "You've got to get over this. I guess something like it was bound to happen, sooner or later. And anyway, for your own sake you've got to get over it. I'm going down to the Koppels now." Maggie's employers had a flat above their delicatessen store. "I'll tell them you won't be in tomorrow. I'll say you're sick. Then in the morning maybe you'd better go to the German woman, in case he—in case he did hurt you so bad you'll need some doctoring."

"The German woman," Miss Hildegarde Hoffman, was not German, but Austrian. And although she ministered to the needs of those too poor to go to a doctor—delivering babies, nursing measle-stricken children, treating black eyes and contusions suffered in Saturday night domestic arguments—she had no medical degree.

Maggie said in a toneless voice, "All right."

The carriage was traveling through the Bois de Boulogne now. The full moon, bleaching the road white, cast upon it the inky black shadows of trees, and sent shafts of radiance slanting down between the giant beeches and oaks. The effect was magically beautiful. Here it was hard to believe that there had ever been such a place as that sixth-floor flat or that waiting room of Miss Hildegarde Hoffman's on Eighth Avenue.

Maggie went there on Monday morning and waited among the crowd of shawled women and whining children until it was her turn.

In the inner office Miss Hoffman, a tall, handsome woman with gray-blond braids wound around her head, listened to Maggie's halting account of what had happened to her. Angry pain flickered in the woman's blue eyes. But when she finally spoke her voice was brisk and matter-of-fact.

"All right. Go behind that screen and take off everything except your petticoat. Then get up on that table."

A few minutes later she said, as the girl lay stretched on the table, "Now try to relax. That way it will be easier and quicker for both of us."

In wretched embarrassment, Maggie stared at the ceiling. Finally Miss Hoffman said, "I think there are no internal injuries. You can get up and dress now."

When she emerged from behind the screen, Maggie saw that Miss Hoffman sat at a small desk, writing something in a notebook. Maggie looked with a kind of awe at the woman and at the big room with its glassed-in medicine cabinets.

And despite the knowledge that many others were waiting, she could not resist blurting out, "Miss Hoffman, how did you get to be—who you are?"

The woman looked up, smiled. "A nurse, you mean? Well, I don't suppose you've heard of a woman named Florence Nightingale."

"I've read about her. She nursed English soldiers during the Crimean War."

With a raised eyebrow Miss Hoffman registered her surprise. "That is right. But she also organized a small hospital on Harley Street in London. I went there to study nursing."

"But how is it you started this place?"

"I came to this country to visit friends. They're wealthy people who support a soup kitchen on Ninth Avenue. When I saw the conditions in this part of the city—well, I decided to stay in New York and open a clinic."

Again she smiled. "At first I was afraid that the doctors might try to close my place and charge me with practicing medicine without a license. But I send any serious cases over to a municipal hospital. And the doctors seem just as pleased that I can take care of minor illnesses and accidents among people who can pay little or nothing for treatment."

"Speaking of that—"

"You work at Koppel's Delicatessen, don't you?" Miss Hoffman interrupted swiftly. "I've seen you through the windows."

"Yes."

"And you furnish your own and your mother's full support?"

Maggie said, after a moment's hesitation, "Yes." No uncles had visited for many months, except of course for—

She turned the thought aside. "I was going to ask what the charge was, Miss Hoffman."

"No charge. Just come to see me a month from now."

The girl asked in swift alarm, "But why? You said that I was all right!"

Miss Hoffman contemplated evading the child's question. Then, looking at the intelligent gray eyes under the beautifully arched brows, she decided not to.

"It's rare that pregnancy is the result of—of a first episode. But it is possible. So please come back a month from now."

Maggie did not become pregnant. And when Hildegarde Hoffman examined her the second time, she was able to reassure her that she would suffer no physical ill effects from her experience. The effects on her young spirit were, of course, quite another matter.

Maggie went on working at Koppel's. Hildegarde Hoffman began coming into the shop. Maggie was always glad to see her, so much so, in fact, that she felt real dismay when, almost a year after Maggie's first visit to the clinic, Miss Hoffman told her that she was going to close the clinic temporarily so that she could go back to Vienna for a prolonged visit with her ailing mother.

"In fact, I may not be back. My mother is aging. I hate to leave her all alone on the other side of the ocean."

Only four months after Miss Hoffman's departure, the Koppels, too, left New York. Their son, who had married a Chicago girl and settled down there, had a chance to buy one of that city's largest delicatessen shops. He wanted his parents to help him run it.

Fond as she had become of the Koppels, her heart leaped up momentarily when they told her they were leaving. With her job gone, perhaps she could go to high school after all. Then she realized what a childish reaction that had been. With herself and her mother to support, she

35

still would have to work somewhere.

She found a temporary job in a bakery a few days after the Koppels left. She lost the job, though, as soon as the woman she had replaced was well enough to return to work. After that she was employed for two months in a factory that made army uniforms. But with orders decreasing as the war wound down, the factory dismissed most of its workers, including Maggie.

Again she looked for work, but jobs were becoming scarce. Soldiers whose enlistment was up, and others who had suffered partially disabling wounds, were returning to take back the factory and clerical jobs from the women and young boys and girls who had held them during the war years. Many men, unable to find work, were drifting to the western states and territories. But that was scarcely an option for a not-quite-fifteen-year-old girl with an alcohol-addicted mother.

Working for a few days or weeks in a bakeshop or restaurant or grocery store, she managed to pay the four-dollars-a-month rent on the flat and keep food on the table. Despite her mother's protests, she kept charge of the money she earned for them. Otherwise, she was grimly sure, it would have gone for whiskey. Grumbling but helpless, Rose had to depend on the uncertain generosity of a drinking companion on the tenement's first floor, a longshoreman's wife who sometimes welcomed her with boozy warmth, and other times shut the door in her face.

By early spring of 1865, the jobs Maggie could fill seemed to have dried up entirely. On a bright April morning, two days after New York church bells had rung jubilant thanksgiving for the end of the war with the Confederacy, Maggie realized that she had a few cents less than a dollar left. Trying not to wonder what she would do when that sum was gone, she walked ten blocks to an Eighth Avenue laundry that had a

"Help Wanted. Female" sign on its door.

The manager looked her up and down. "Sorry, sister. This is no fancy hand laundry. Our girls have to push hand trunks loaded with sheets and tablecloths from the hotels. A half-grown kid like you wouldn't last a day."

When she got home, she found Rose sitting in the kitchen, a look of mingled hope and trepidation on her face. She said, "Al Summers was here awhile ago."

Sunk in her anxiety, Maggie asked listlessly, "Who?"

"Al Summers. You ought to remember him. He used to come around sometimes when you were ten, maybe eleven. He's coming here tonight." She went on swiftly, as if afraid of losing her courage, "He's coming to see you, not me. He says he's seen you a couple of times on the street lately."

Maggie stared at Rose, unable to believe what her mother seemed to be proposing.

Rose cried, "What else can we do? You told me just this morning we didn't have enough to buy more than a couple of days' food. And you didn't get the job, did you? No, of course you didn't. Do you want us to go to the workhouse? You've heard what those places are like. Old people, sick people, crazy people. You want your mother to be in a place like that? And even if you don't care about me, you ought to care about yourself. Some of the men who work in those places—attendants, they call them—they wouldn't leave you alone for even the first day."

Her voice became pleading. "Honey, I know what you must be feeling. But it isn't like it would be if you were still—" She broke off and then said, "And it won't be like that other time. Al's a nice fellow."

Al. She couldn't even remember him. Maybe it was better that she couldn't. He would seem less—real. All of it would seem less real.

She knew then that she was going to do as Rose asked.

It was not, her mother had started to say, as if she were still a virgin. Maybe those nightmarish few minutes with Baldy had made it inevitable that later on there would be men like Al Summers in her life. Or maybe this moment had been inevitable from the day her father rushed down the tenement stairs for the last time, leaving his weak-fibered wife and small daughter to cope with the world as best they could.

"All right," she said dully, "I'll see him."

For a little more than a year Al Summers and a few other men occasionally shared with her the bed in the room that had once been Rose's but was now hers. Sometimes a man would stay there all night, but never longer than that. Almost frantically, she insisted that the flat be empty of everyone but Rose and herself during the daylight hours. That way she could read books—books that had become more important to her than ever—at the kitchen table or up on the roof. That way she could almost pretend that it was some other girl who, once or twice a week, prostituted herself to men two or even three times her age.

On a late afternoon in August, unable to bear the stifling heat of those rooms directly under the tarpaper roof, she left the flat for one of her rare walks. She was moving down Ninth Avenue through the comparative coolness of the street's shady side when someone said, "Why, it's Maggie MacNeil, isn't it?"

Startled but pleased, Maggie looked up into Hildegarde Hoffman's face, smiling warmly beneath a green hat that matched her bombazine-walking suit. "Miss Hoffman! You came back!"

"Yes." The woman's smile wavered. "You see, my mother died."

"Oh, Miss Hoffman! I'm so sorry."

"Well, hers was one of those cases where death really was a mercy. She'd been in dreadful pain." She paused. "So I decided to come back to New York."

"Are you going to reopen your clinic?"

"I already have. Oh, it's not in actual operation yet. But I started refurbishing it more than a week ago, and now I'm almost ready to open its doors. Hadn't you heard?"

"No. I—I don't go out very much."

That was an understatement. Her mother did all the grocery shopping these days. Maggie preferred it that way, even though it meant inevitably that some of the money men paid her went for liquor. She herself almost never went out, except up to the tenement roof. On the street she had a sense that everyone, even strangers, knew about her, and that women stared at her scornfully and men lewdly. Worst of all, she twice had seen boys of her own age snickering, boys who had known her when she stood at the head of her grammar school class in almost every subject.

Hildegarde Hoffman peered at her more closely. "You certainly look as if you don't get much sunlight. Child, have you been ill?"

"No."

"Then perhaps you are working too hard. I see that the Koppels' store is gone. Where are you working now?"

Struck dumb, Maggie looked up at the woman with pain-filled gray eyes.

After a moment Hildegarde said, "Oh, my God. Oh, my poor child." She tucked the girl's unresisting hand into the crook of her arm. "Come with me to the clinic, so that you can tell me about it."

A few minutes later in the clinic, with its strewn packing cases and shadeless windows, Maggie did tell her about it. Hildegarde got up from the packing case on which she had been sitting and began to pace the floor so furious she was afraid to speak lest her voice shake. Damn men. Damn weak women like Rose MacNeil. Damn a society which could take a beautiful and intelligent child like Maggie and turn her into this shamed and broken creature, dark head drooping as she sat on a packing box.

But what to do about her?

Hildegarde took a couple of more turns about the room and then stopped in front of the girl. "Maggie, look at me. Was I mistaken or did you at one time feel an interest in becoming a nurse?"

"Once I had met you, there was nothing I would rather have—I mean, during that time I told you about, while I was still looking for work, I went to Bellevue Hospital. I thought maybe they would give me some kind of paying job and let me train as a nurse at the same time."

"And they must have told you that you were too young. You must still be too young for regular hospital training. Just how old are you now?"

"Sixteen. I'll be seventeen next month."

"Well, how would you like to work here?"

Maggie said, astounded, "You mean here, at the clinic? After all I've told you about those—those men, you'd let me—" She broke off.

Hildegarde thought of telling her that, until the time of Florence Nightingale, nearly all nurses had been aging ex-prostitutes. Thinking better of it, she merely said, "Yes, here at the clinic. As my assistant, you'll sooner or later learn everything I know. And I will pay you six dollars a week."

It was an excellent wage. Many male workers made less than that.

Hildegarde really couldn't afford to pay the girl that much. Most of the money she had inherited from an aunt had gone into the clinic here and into one she had founded earlier in Vienna. But she still had some income. And there were luxuries she could forego. She did not actually need, for instance, soap imported from England and wines from France. And she could live without those steel engravings of Italian scenes she had planned to buy from a Fifth Avenue gallery.

"Oh, Miss Hoffman!" Maggie said, and burst into tears.

Hildegarde waited until she was sure her voice would sound matter-of-fact and then said, "I gather that means you'll take the job."

Chapter 4

The next two-and-a-half years were the happiest Maggie had known so far. She still lived with Rose in the sixth-floor flat, but she spent long, exhausting, exhilarating days at the clinic, learning everything from how to diagnose chicken pox to how to deliver a child.

Rose showed a proud delight in her daughter's new situation. No matter what the state of her head, she rose each morning in time to prepare a stout breakfast to fortify Maggie against a long day at the clinic. Maggie lost the bitter suspicion that had haunted her from time to time, a suspicion that her mother had taken her daughter's degradation lightly. She knew now that was not so. Poor Rose, not too intelligent to begin with, and with brains further addled by drink, had been unable to think of any other means by which she and her young daughter could obtain food and keep a roof over their heads.

As she walked back and forth to the clinic, Maggie was aware that some women still looked at her askance, and that some men still spoke softly to her from shop doorways. But it mattered less now because she had an increasing sense of her own worth. Every day she was learning how to better comfort the frightened, encourage the despairing, and ease the pain of the suffering.

Too, because of her work she was meeting men of a sort she had never known before. Not one, but three young interns who had come to the clinic to acquaint themselves with Miss Hoffman's methods in the fields of first aid, diagnosis of minor ailments, and clinic administration, had returned several times. Each of them, too, had said that he would be delighted if Miss MacNeil and Miss Hoffman would lunch or dine with him. Even though Maggie declined the invitations, she felt flattered, especially by the fact that each of the interns had felt it incumbent upon him to ask Miss Hoffman along as a chaperone. Apparently her earlier experiences had left no lasting mark upon her appearance. Apparently men who did not know her history could think of her as a "nice" young woman.

The attentions of one man, though, were not so flattering. He was a middle-aged man named Danson Hayworth. He and his rich, charity-minded wife were the two friends Hildegarde had mentioned when she and Maggie first met, the friends who had introduced her to this slum area when they took her to inspect the soup kitchen they had founded on Tenth Avenue. Squeezing Maggie's arm at every opportunity and looking deep into her eyes, Danson Hayworth had made it plain that he was attracted to her. The girl was glad that he never behaved indiscreetly when Hildegarde was around. She admired the Austrian woman more each day for her good-humored courage, strength, and selfless dedication. The last thing Maggie wanted was to be even an indirect means of distressing her friend.

Maggie had been working at the clinic for about a year when Rose died. The girl awoke one morning to realize, with puzzlement, that something was amiss. After a moment she identified it. No aroma of boiling coffee. Stomach already knotted with dread, she went into the larger bedroom her mother had reclaimed. Without saying anything about it, Rose had moved her things back into that room when Maggie went to work at the clinic. Now she lay motionless, curled up like a child in the middle of the sagging bed, her face looking almost as young and peaceful as it had in Maggie's dim memories of her early childhood.

Maggie discovered that it did not matter what one's mother had been. Her grief for Rose could not have been more deep and wrenching if Rose had been the most loving wife and protective mother who ever existed.

Maggie went on living at the flat, but during the next several weeks she spent little time there. She worked, not ten or twelve hours a day, but sixteen, returning to the clinic after her solitary supper. Hildegarde, realizing that there are few forms of pain which hard work can't help, did not protest, even though she worried about the girl's weight loss.

Gradually, Maggie returned to a more normal work schedule. Again she was able to speak cheerfully to the crankies of the clinic's elderly patients, trade silly riddles with the children, and treat the young doctors, who persisted in dropping by the clinic, with a carefully impersonal friendliness.

One noon as she and Hildegarde sat over milk and sandwiches in the little room at the rear of the clinic, the Austrian woman said, "When are you going to start encouraging one of those fine young men?"

"I've just turned nineteen." Maggie's tone was light. "Why be in such a hurry to marry?"

Hildegarde's face remained grave. "I'm just afraid you'll make a mistake. I'm afraid you'll come to feel you should devote your whole life to nursing, just because I have. Such a life is right for me. It is all I ever wanted. But it is not for everyone. And there is no reason why you should not have what most women want, a husband and children."

Oh, yes, there's a reason why not, Maggie thought. What if she let herself become interested in one of those young men? What if she fell in love with him, and he with her? What would happen when he learned of Al Summers and those other men with whom she'd shared a sagging bed under that tarpaper roof? And the chances were excellent that he would find out, sooner or later. Probably she herself would tell him.

Sometimes she wondered if Danson Hayworth, older and more sophisticated than those interns, had sensed the truth about her. Perhaps that accounted for his furtively amorous approaches.

But she said nothing of all that to Hildegarde. The Austrian woman carried enough burdens without Maggie adding her dark thoughts to them. And so she smiled and said, "I'm still several years from spinsterhood. And I'm happy just as I am." That was true. She was happy most of the time, at least more so than she had been since her very earliest years. "Aren't you pleased that I can say that?"

Hildegarde nodded. "Considering the sad state of the world, I ought to feel gratified that anyone can say that she is happy, especially someone I'm fond of."

Maggie's hardworking, satisfying days stretched into another six months, then a year. Shortly after six on a crisp fall night, the last night she was to see Hildegarde Hoffman alive, she left the Austrian woman still at work and set out for home through the cool dark. She had gone a block and a half when Danson Hayworth fell into step beside her. Light from a shop window showed her his lined face, thin and smiling under his hat brim. He grasped her arm.

"I have to talk to you!" His voice held excitement.

She resisted the desire to pull her arm free. After all, he was Hildegarde Hoffman's friend, or at least his wife was.

"Talk to me? What about?"

"I'm going to Paris next week. I'll be gone two months. Fay's father left her some business interests over there, a carpet factory near Paris, and a couple of vineyards not far from Rheims." Fay was Danson Hayworth's rich wife. "I've persuaded her it would be a good idea for me to make an extensive survey of the whole lot."

"I see. But I don't understand what all this has to do with me."

"I want you to come with me." His voice was feverish. "Paris is where you belong, a beautiful girl like you, not grubbing away in a New York slum."

She did pull her arm free then. "Mr. Hayworth, have you gone out of your mind?"

"How many times have I asked you to call me Danson? And I'm not crazy. We can work it out, somehow."

His tone became earnest. "Don't you know that I would give anything in the world if I could ask you to marry me? But if I managed to get a divorce from Fay, you and I would have nothing to live on. Maybe at one time I could have been a successful business man, but from the day we were married, she's blocked everything I've tried to do on my own."

Maggie felt a desire to laugh. The presumption of him, so certain that she would jump at the chance of marrying him if he were free.

"When it is time for me to come back here," he rushed on, "I swear I'll give you enough money so that you can stay on in Paris. After all, as Fay's business manager, I've been able to—to put a little aside. But I'm hoping that by the time I have to come back to New York, you'll want to come back with me. I'll set you up in a nice little flat, and *not* in Hell's Kitchen!"

She said, "Of course, I won't go to Paris with you. What

on earth ever gave you the idea that I might?"

A certain flicker in his eyes then told her that he had indeed found out, one way or another, about that period in her life when she had supported herself and her mother with money obtained from men. But he was not going to throw that in her face, not as long as he hoped to persuade her to run away with him.

He said, "I think you'll go when you realize what I'm offering you. Think of having dinner in really fine restaurants. Think of wearing Paris clothes. This is the kind of chance you'll probably never get again in your whole life."

Fighting down her resentment and disgust, she managed to speak calmly. "I'm sorry, but the answer is no."

"I won't accept that. You'll change your mind. I'll ask you again tomorrow or the next day."

"It will do you no good."

"We'll see. Goodnight, Maggie." He turned and walked away in the opposite direction.

Frustrated anger kept her from enjoying her supper of sausage and eggs purchased at the shop that had replaced the one run by the Koppels. She longed to tell Hildegarde about Danson Hayworth's behavior! The Austrian woman surely would order him to stay away from the clinic. But Maggie must not and would not precipitate trouble between Hildegarde and the husband of her best friend.

She did not get to sleep until almost midnight and as a consequence overslept. It was nearly seven o'clock when she approached the clinic.

A small crowd of shawled women and of men in work clothes had gathered on the sidewalk. Alarmed, she pushed through the crowd, and saw two uniformed policemen and a man in civilian clothes standing in front of the clinic's closed doors.

She cried, "What's happened?"

The man in civilian clothes said, "You can't go in there, miss."

"Why not? I work here! What's happened? Where's Miss Hoffman?"

"So you work here." The plainclothesman looked down at her for a moment and then turned to one of the uniformed officers. "Take her inside, Tim. Get her statement."

She went with the policeman across the empty waiting room and then halted in the doorway to the examining room. Shattered glass from the medicine cabinet door lay glittering on the sinkboard. Talking a step forward, she stumbled over pieces of a chair smashed into kindling. She noticed then, the ledgers and papers swept from Hildegarde's desk onto the floor.

Maggie clutched the policeman's arm. "What happened? Where's Miss Hoffman?"

After a moment he asked, "Was she a relative, miss?"

Color drained from her face as the implication of that "was" sunk in. "No, she was—a dear friend." Her only friend. "Then she is—"

"At the morgue, miss. It happened around ten o'clock last night, even though people around here say that the clinic's usually closed by nine."

Unable to speak, Maggie nodded. Sometimes after the clinic officially was closed, Hildegarde stayed on to file medical histories and make entries in those ledgers now scattered over the floor.

"Anyway, this drunk fellow came in and smashed up the place. The he attacked Miss Hoffman or tried to." Maggie realized that by "attack" the policeman meant rape. "She must have put up a real battle, but finally—I'm sorry to have to tell you this, miss—he finally strangled her. Someone had heard the noise and run to the police, so he was nabbed just as he was leaving here.

"His name is Jim Callahan," the officer went on. "We know he did it. He admits it, and besides your friend Miss Hoffman scratched up his face pretty good. But so far we haven't been able to get him to say why he did it. Could you throw any light on that?"

She could. Callahan's wife, Mary, three times had appeared at the clinic so badly beaten that she could scarcely walk. Each time her frightened children, a boy of five and a girl of four, had been with her. The third time Hildegarde had realized that something drastic would have to be done. Appealing to the authorities would have been of little use. Unless domestic brawls ended in actual death, the police felt it was not their place to interfere between "man and wife." And so Hildegarde had given Mrs. Callahan train fare, so that she and her children could find refuge in Yonkers with a friend she had known since schooldays.

Maggie felt sure that Jim Callahan had come here last night to demand that Hildegarde tell him where his wife had gone. When she refused, he had smashed up some furniture and the medicine cabinet door and swept her ledgers from her desk. Then he had directed his violence toward her. Perhaps at first he had not meant to kill her. He had wanted only to show this uppity, interfering female that this was a man's world. But she had fought back—

And so now she lay in the morgue, that fine woman who, forgoing her own chance of family happiness, had dedicated her intelligence, energy, and what money she had to helping people like Mary Callahan and her children.

Maggie felt not only grief, but also a blind fury. In that instant, she gave up all ideas of following in the footsteps of the woman she had so loved and admired.

If this was a man's world, and it certainly seemed to be, then she would play by its rules. But not in Hell's Kitchen, and not with the sort of men she had entertained in that sixth-floor flat. Coldly and shrewdly, she would make use of the physical assets nature had given her, until she had the means to live comfortably and securely, and to tell everyone to go to the devil.

She said to the policeman, "Yes, I'm sure I know why he did it. And I'll give you a statement."

When she left the clinic about fifteen minutes later, she saw Danson Hayworth standing white-faced in the crowd. She turned toward home, knowing that he would catch up with her. When he did he said, "God, what a terrible thing!"

"Yes. Are you still going to Paris?"

He looked startled. "Why, yes. In fact, I had come down here to ask you again—"

"You don't have to ask. I'll go with you."

The carriage had nearly reached the western end of the Bois de Bologne now. She leaned back against the cushion, aware not only of the summer night's beauty, but of the comfortable sway of the carriage on its expensive springs, and of the caress of silken and scented undergarments against her skin. How far she had come from that flat under the tarpaper roof!

It must be some sort of perversity, she told herself, which kept her from enjoying to the full all that she now had. Or perhaps it was just that, despite all her grim, cool-headed resolutions to make the most of her own desirability, she was still something of a fool. Why else were there times when she would have given anything to be able to relive those exhausting, soul-satisfying days in the clinic? Days when she had soothed squalling babies, and bandaged small knees, and distributed free bottles of cough syrup to the elderly poor?

She looked out of the carriage window, trying to concentrate on the fragrance of green, growing things, and on the sound of a nightingale pouring out its heart somewhere in the moonlight.

Without warning, the carriage came to a halt so sharply that she was thrown forward onto the luxuriously carpeted floor. She heard the coachman shouting something in French, heard the jingle of harness and the creak of the singletree. She imagined the pair of sleek bay horses, rearing in terror of something—a rabbit, a blown newspaper—which must have crossed the road in front of them.

Then the carriage hurtled forward. She heard the pound of galloping hooves and the continued shouts of the coachman. One hand clutching the edge of the carriage seat, she pictured him standing up as he pulled at the reins. On this curving road, there was a good chance that at any moment a wheel might part from its axle or the carriage tip over.

The vehicle began to slow. Someone else was speaking now, in American-accented English. "Easy, there. Easy!" The thud of hooves grew less rapid.

She managed to get back up on the seat. Putting her head out the window, she saw that a man clung to one of the horses, arms encircling the powerful neck, one leg, crooked at the knee, resting on the wide back.

The horses came to a halt. Then the man was walking back toward Maggie. He called out, in atrociously accented French, "Is everyone all right in there?"

She answered, in English, "There is only myself, and I am not hurt."

He opened the carriage door. "You had best get out, just to make sure."

His outstretched hand helped her to the ground. She saw

that he was perhaps six feet tall. If he had been wearing a hat when he leaped from the roadside to stop the runaways, he had lost it. His hair was curly, and somewhat lighter then her own. Dark brown, perhaps. In the moonlight it was hard to be sure. But she could be fairly certain about his features, from the prominent brow ridges and aquiline nose to the well-defined mouth and square chin. She judged him to be in his late twenties.

"You're still sure you are all right?"

Before she could answer, the coachman called down, *"S'il vous plait, mademoiselle, un moment."*

In anxious French, he asked her if she was indeed all right. She could understand his concern. When a coachman is employed by a prince, even one traveling incognito, he had best make sure that nothing untoward happened to His Highness' vehicle or his young ladies.

"Certainement!" she called up to him.

She smiled at her rescuer. "Perfectly, thank you. And thank you for stopping those horses. I expected to land in the ditch at any moment."

He leaned a trifle closer to peer down into her upturned face. "Say, aren't you Maggie MacNeil, the actress?"

"Yes." At least she had been billed as such for a few weeks more than a year ago.

"I saw you in 'The Olympian Revels,' at that theatre on the Left Bank. You were wonderful."

She had known that he must have seen her in that foolish musical play about the Greek gods since it was the only production she had ever been in. "Thank you. Although I can't see what was wonderful about walking down a flight of stairs."

"It was the way you walked, and the way you looked in that costume. Gauze, or whatever it was."

She had been cast as a nymph who had caught Jupiter's ever-roving eye. Her costume had consisted of a robe of pink gauze, with a band of heavier pink material across the breasts and pelvis.

He added, "I remember thinking that a fellow would never see anything like that in Dayton, Ohio."

She found that she liked the frank appreciation in his voice. "Is that where you're from, Ohio?" He had a sort of middle-western look, she realized now, like that of a young and handsome Abraham Lincoln, if one could imagine such a thing.

"Yes, I was raised in Dayton. But I've lived in Paris for two years. I'm a newspaper artist."

"What exactly—"

"I make drawings illustrating the current news."

"For Paris papers?"

"For the Paris office of the International Press Syndicate. They sell my sketches not only to European papers but to ones in New York, Chicago and Atlanta."

"You must be very talented."

He laughed. "Unless you're the kind of artist who gets hung in galleries, you don't call it talent. You call it knack."

She knew that she should get back into the carriage and continue on to that rented house in Passy. But she wanted to linger a moment more, here on the moon-whitened road. It was pleasant to talk to a compatriot. And after Madame Theraux's customers, most of whom had lived long enough to acquire a paunch as well as considerable wealth, it was pleasant to talk to a man only a few years older than herself.

He said, "Tell me what production you are in now, so that I can come to see you."

After a second or two she said, "I'm not in any production at the moment."

She was aware of the sudden flatness in her voice. Plainly this young man did not share the bluenoses' opinion of actresses, even ones in gauze. But what would he think of her if he knew how she made her living now?

She stretched out her hand. "I must go. Thank you again, more than I can say."

With his warm hand clasping hers, the young man from Dayton handed her into the coach. It moved forward. He said, running beside it, "I didn't tell you my name! It's Glover, Richard Glover."

She smiled at him and said, before the carriage gathered speed, "Good night, Richard Glover."

The rented mansion in the chic suburb of Passy was typical of those that rich men had erected there in the past few years for their families or, in some cases, their mistresses. Just before the carriage reached it, the trap door in its roof opened and the coachman's round face peered down at her. "Mademoiselle, I beg you. If the—if the monsieur hears that I lost control of the horses—"

"Don't worry. I will not tell him about it."

Leaving the carriage, she went up the broad walk to the house, a three-story one with a mansard roof. Warm light came through the door's fanlight. A footman in dark red livery bowed a welcome and then led her across the wide marble-floored hall to another door.

The prince rose from one of the two high-backed chairs flanking the fireplace and crossed the room to greet her. She caught the impression that although the room was large and attractively furnished with brocaded sofas and chairs and marble-topped, gilt-ornamented tables dating from the era of the First Napoleon, it was by no means palatial.

"Come sit beside the fire," he said, taking her wrap. "The night has turned a bit chilly, don't you think?"

When they had sat down opposite each other, he said, "My dear, I must apologize. That reception was so dull and exhausting that I am no longer, shall we say, in a romantic mood. Too, a rather irksome dispatch from England arrived a few minutes ago."

She wondered if it had been a message from the redoubtable Victoria, demanding that her son come home at once. Although the Prince of Wales had come of age nearly a decade before, everyone knew that his mother still treated him as a boy, far too young to be permitted a role in the English government, and too naughty to be allowed to escape her surveillance.

His next words seemed to confirm Maggie's guess about the sender of the message. "Besides, I must start back to England early in the morning."

"I'm sorry. Perhaps I had best leave."

Courteous as always, he said, "Please, don't go. A glass of brandy and a little chat would be pleasant, don't you think?"

He himself poured the brandy from a bottle on the small table beside his chair. Glasses in hand, they discussed the last racing meet at Longchamps, the state of Louis Napoleon's health ("I heard he suffers dreadfully from gallstones," the prince said,) and, inevitably, France's month-old war with Prussia.

Maggie said, "In view of the unsettled conditions, perhaps it is just as well you are leaving Paris."

"Oh, I don't know. What if the Prussians do win? The Parisian leaders will just wine and dine them at the Maison Doree, take them to the latest Offenbach opera and to Madame Theraux's, and in no time at all turn them into proper Frenchmen."

Maggie laughed. But she felt that no war could ever turn out to be an amusing operetta, not even war in which

France's gaudy Second Empire was a participant. To her war meant the field at Gettysburg where, she had heard, you could still find bullets with teeth marks on them, bullets bitten by agonized men while surgeons sawed away at their shattered arms and legs. War was the rage and fear, which, just like the pall of smoke from the burning buildings, had shrouded New York's slums during those riots which had cost her own father his life.

An hour later, the prince kissed her cheek in farewell. Out in the entrance hall his equerry, the same one who had accompanied him to Madame Theraux's, rose from a straight chair against the wall. Bowing, and with eyes discreetly lowered, he handed her an envelope. She went out through the moonlight to the waiting carriage. It carried her back toward the Bois de Bologne.

Without opening the envelope, she knew that the prince had been just as generous as he would have if they had gone to bed. That meant that there was at least three hundred francs in the envelope, more than she could have earned in many months as a shop girl, or many weeks as a nymph in transparent gauze.

Her theatrical career, if it could be called that, was not something she had planned. In fact, if Danson Hayworth had behaved differently, she might never have thought of trying to become an actress.

On the way across the Atlantic in the steamer—he in a first class cabin, she in a second—he had spent only a few hours with her during the entire trip. After the ship sailed, he discovered that some people who knew both him and his wife were aboard. As a consequence he had made only two furtive visits to her cabin, both of them in the early morning hours. If Maggie had desired him, she would have found him distressingly ineffectual. As it was, she felt grateful for the fact that he could sustain lovemaking for no more than a few minutes.

She had thought that the nervous fear of being found out by his friends on board might have been affecting him. But when he had installed her in three modest rooms near the Place des Vosges—he himself stayed at one of the city's better hotels—he was no more effectual in bed. In fact, she came to feel that he really was not much interested in sex.

However, he did seem to take great pleasure in showing her off in restaurants and during strolls along the boulevarde. Maggie decided that from the first he mainly had wanted to use her to make himself appear, in the world's eyes, as manly and successful. Perhaps, too, he felt he was revenging himself on the rich, civic-minded wife whom he resented and yet could not afford to leave.

Whatever his reason for wanting her to accompany him to Paris, she increasingly was glad that she had agreed. Busy with matters concerning his wife's carpet factory outside Paris and her vineyards miles away near Rheims, he left her alone much of the time. She was free to wander through the magnificent public gardens, and to browse among the book-stalls along the Seine. She spent at least two hours a day studying French. During the time when she was trying to make up for a missed high school education, she had bought a used French grammar for ten cents. She had found it rough going back then. But now, surrounded by French-speaking people and newspapers and street signs in French, she found herself speaking and reading the language a little more easily each day.

She and Danson had been in Paris about two months when he said one night, as a hansom cab carried them from a restaurant toward her rooms, "I've decided to book our passage for New York on the *Olympia*. It's sailing twelve days from now."

After a moment she said, "I'm sorry, but I shall remain here in Paris."

"Remain! How can you stay here? What will you live on?"

She thought, not on the money you've handed out to me so far. Although reasonably generous when he accompanied her to restaurants and shops, he had never given her more than a few francs at a time.

She said aloud, "Why, until I can find other means, I will live off the money you will settle on me."

"Settle on you! Why, why should I settle—"

"Because you promised me!" Her voice rose. "Back in New York you said that if I chose to stay on here, you'd give me enough money to support me for—"

"Keep your voice down! How do you know the driver doesn't understand English?"

"You promised me!"

His tone was grim. "Even if I did promise, I don't intend to do it. You take me for a fool? Why, that would be like paying for a dead horse."

When she didn't answer, he went on, "If you want to stay here, then stay, but not at my expense. If you come back to New York with me, though, I'll furnish you a nice little flat somewhere uptown."

She wondered if he really would. Or would he, on the way back across the Atlantic, decide that he did not want to run further risk of losing his wife.

Well, what he might or might not decide did not matter. What mattered was that she had no intention of returning to that city where her friend Hildegarde had been so brutally slain, and where she herself had suffered so much as a young girl. By now she had seen enough of Paris to know that it was the right place for women like herself, women who, for what-ever reason, had resolved to use their physical attractions to make themselves rich and invulnerable.

"It's up to you," he said.

She made no answer. As if to emphasize his indifference to her decision, when they reached the building that housed her rented rooms he said good night to her on the sidewalk and then got back into the hansom cab. She felt no regret at his departure.

The next morning she went to a nearby kiosk and bought all the newspapers available. In the first one she opened she found the sort of advertisement she was looking for.

"Young ladies! Monsieur Armand Martell, the noted theatrical producer, needs actresses for a forthcoming production. He will interview applicants today, Wednesday, at the Justine Theater on Boulevard St. Germaine."

Heart beating hard, Maggie had torn the advertisement from the paper. Many women of the Paris half-world, women who were showered with money and jewelry, had first displayed their charms on the Paris stage. Some actresses had even become the wives of rich men.

That afternoon she had crossed to the Left Bank. Monsieur Armand Martell turned out to be a portly, dignified man with a monocle and the sort of pointed beard, which because the Emperor wore one, was called an imperial. After talking to her for a few minutes he announced that she would play a nymph in his upcoming production.

A week later she vacated the quarters Danson Hayworth had provided and moved into a small room near the theater on the Left Bank. She never knew whether Danson, in the few days remaining before his ship was due to sail, had tried to find her. If he had tried, he had failed.

Her acting career turned out to be in no way a success. True, the theater was almost filled every night. True, men applauded wildly when she descended the staircase in her diaphanous costume. And true, several men came backstage after the performance to see her, each of them with a bouquet in hand. But none of them seemed to offer what she needed. One of them, a rather seedy man of forty-odd, had the look of a husband hoping to embark upon an adventure he could not afford. Another one, probably a university student, had to be nineteen at most. Still another, bracing himself with a cane as he bared his false teeth in a smile, should have been sitting by the fire with a glass of warm milk, not tottering about a draughty theater corridor.

The play had been running more than three weeks when the stage door attendant came to the dressing room after the night's performance and handed her a card. With surprise, she saw that it bore the name of a woman, a Madame Celestine Theraux. On it there was a message written in a neat script: "If you will see me for a few moments, I think you will find it well worth your while. My carriage is waiting about ten yards east of the theater entrance."

Intrigued, Maggie changed to street clothes, walked down an alley to the front of the theater, and turning left began searching for the carriage. As she approached a gleaming yellow carriage a coachman got down from its box, opened the door and let down the steps.

"Please come in, Mademoiselle MacNeil," invited a low voice.

Maggie hesitated, then climbed into the carriage's warm interior, and sat down in the near corner. The woman in the opposite corner said, "Mademoiselle, do you know who I am?"

There was enough light from a nearby street lamp to show Maggie that the woman had a buxom figure and a handsome face beneath high-pilled hennaed hair. "Only your name, Madame."

"Well, I shall remedy that in a moment. But first, I hope you will forgive me for asking an impertinent question. Mademoiselle, do you have a protector?"

Maggie suppressed a momentary impulse to bristle. After all, when she joined Armand Martell's production, was that not exactly what she had hoped to acquire, a rich "protector" or perhaps a series of them?

"No, I have not, Madame."

"Don't let it undermine your confidence. Not every actress can become a Hortense Schneider."

Starting out in Offenbach's light operas, Hortense Schneider had become the mistress of so many rich men, including royal ones, that she had been nicknamed *le passage des princes*.

"It is largely a matter of luck," the woman went on, "being seen by the right sort of man at a moment when he is susceptible. But I can help you to be lucky."

"How, madame?"

"I manage what might be called an introduction service. At my house you will meet only rich men, because that is the only kind I admit. In return for a fee of one hundred francs a visit, I guarantee that they will meet young ladies who are lovely, refined in dress and deportment—and willing."

Maggie said, "You will forgive me if I, too, am blunt. What you are suggesting is that I enter your brothel?"

Celestine Theraux appeared unruffled. "Call it that if you like. For my clients, though, I try to create the impression that mine is a less crass establishment. That is why my young ladies neither live on the premises nor entertain clients there. The client must either provide the setting for his little adventure, or persuade the young lady of his choice to admit him to her own apartment.

"The young ladies' apartments," she went on, "are provided by me. I pay each of them a small fee for attending my nightly receptions. The rest of their earnings—and you would find them considerable—are made up of gifts from clients."

When Maggie did not reply, the woman continued, "I am sure you would make a great success in my salon, Mademoiselle MacNeil. You are not only extremely attractive in appearance, but I can see that you are also intelligent, intelligent enough that you will not take to drink or squander your money on some handsome young layabout. In a few years, you could become a rich woman."

"Thank you, madame. But I prefer to remain in my present situation." Better, far better, to have some choice where men were concerned.

Madame Theraux said dryly, "If by your present situation you mean your employment by Martell, then I predict that you will not remain in it long."

"I don't know what you mean."

"I mean that Armand Martell is a crook. Tell me, has he paid you as much salary as he promised you?"

Maggie was surprised. "How did you know?"

"Then he hasn't paid you in full?"

"He did for the first week. Then he called the cast together and said that expenses were much heavier than he expected, and that if he is to keep the production going, we would have to accept lower salaries for awhile. Now he says that it will not be long before he can make it up to us. After all, the theater has been almost filled every night."

"Let me tell you what will happen, mademoiselle. Quite soon now Martell will announce that his assistant has run off with all the money in the theater's safe, and that therefore he must close the production. Or perhaps this time it will be the head dresser who has disappeared, or some minor member of the cast."

She paused, and then went on, "Anyway, after the police have made their investigation, Armand Martell also will disappear. Somewhere outside Paris, or maybe even over the border in Spain, he will meet with his confederate, and they will divide the loot."

"How on earth do you know—"

"It is common knowledge. He has done it at least twice before."

"But if that is the case, surely the police—"

"The police know what he does, but so far they have been unable to prove it."

"Forgive me, madame, but what you say is hard to believe. If this man has cheated his actors before this, how is it that he was able to hire actors for this production? True, I am a newcomer to Paris. But if you are right about his reputation, others in the cast must know of it."

"People are fools, my dear, particularly young women. For a variety of reasons, they long to be on the stage. They desire it so much that they will take almost any risk."

"Perhaps everything you say is true, madame, but if so I prefer to find out for myself."

"Very well. But if at sometime in the future you decide to accept my offer, you will find me at Number Fourteen, Rue de Adele. Now, can I take you to wherever you are going?"

"No, thank you, madame. I prefer to walk between the theater and where I live. It is good for the figure."

The woman nodded. "As I said, you are intelligent. Good night, mademoiselle."

One night a little more than two weeks later, Maggie came to the theater to find the ticket seller's cage dark and a large "closed" sign on an easel in the outer lobby. She went around through the alley to the theater's side entrance and, after a few words with the porter, climbed to the stage. From halfway up the flight of steps she had descended each night in her pink gauze robe, Armand Martell was addressing the cast.

"—cannot express my sorrow," she heard him say. "Let us hope that the police catch that rascally ticket seller and recover the money that belongs to all of us. But in the meantime, my children, this beautiful production of ours must close."

Someone called out, "Hasn't this happened to you twice before, Martell?"

"Alas, yes. My luck is very bad. And the worst of it is that both times the police failed to find the culprit."

"Could it be that *you* managed to find him, Martell?"

"You, yourself do not believe what you are implying," Martell said with an air of wounded dignity. "Otherwise you would not have joined this company. Goodbye, my children, at least for now."

For more than a week Maggie made the rounds of the Paris theaters. She received only one offer, a walk-on role as part of a group of "attendant lords and ladies" in a production of Shakespeare's Henry the Fifth. If she had been under the delusion that she possessed any theatrical talent, she might have taken the part, in the hope that it would lead to speaking roles. But she knew that her only qualification for the stage was her looks, looks that might attract a rich man. And rich men in search of seductive young women did not devote their evenings to Shakespeare.

What little money she had, dwindled daily. She began to have confused dreams of being once more a girl in her early teens, searching for work in New York's shops and factories. In one dream she was climbing the tenement stairs, aware that she had less than a dollar in the knotted handkerchief pinned inside her coat pocket, and somehow knowing, too, that in the top-floor flat a man—someone who was a combination of Baldy MacIntyre and Al Summers and a number of other men—was waiting for her.

She awoke from the dream with her stomach knotted and her heart pounding. As her pulses slowed she felt a hardening of the resolution that had brought her to Paris, a determination that never again would she be penniless and helpless, selling herself for bargain-basement prices in order to stay alive.

A few hours later she called on Madame Theraux at Number Fourteen, Rue de Adele. That was a year and a half ago. She had been attending Madame's "evening receptions" ever since.

The coach had reached the stretch of road where Richard Glover had stopped the bolting horses. She thought of his lean, athletic body clinging with arms and one bent leg to the frightened animal. She thought of his smile—not a leer, just a healthy, appreciative smile—as he said, "It was the way you walked, and the way you looked in that costume—gauze, or whatever it was."

She checked her thoughts. What was the point in thinking about a young man like that, a man who would recoil in disgust if he learned about all those aging libertines who supported her?

The carriage left her before a house of gray stone on a pleasant street near the Sorbonne. She climbed a flight of stairs and then unlocked the door of the furnished flat, which Madame Theraux provided for her, rent free, as part of her compensation. Even though Maggie was determined to save money, she had added a few touches to the flat—a gilt-framed mirror in the little entrance hall, a pretty rosewood writing desk in the parlor, and floor-length blue silk window draperies in the bedroom.

She undressed and went to bed. Lying there, she found that she could not keep Richard Glover out of her thoughts. What would it be like to be loved by such a man, not just desired, but cherished and protected?

Suddenly her throat ached with tears.

What was wrong with her? She deliberately had chosen the life she led. And she was making a success of it. She already had the equivalent of fifteen thousand American dollars in the bank. Before she was thirty she would be a rich woman, able to have anything she wanted.

Except the love and respect of the sort of man *she* could respect.

Still, that was no reason to cry. Her life was turning out just as she had visualized it when she took up Danson Hayworth's offer. Besides, she hadn't cried over anyone or anything since Hildegarde Hoffman's brutal death almost two years ago.

Still, what would it be like to be in love and to lie in bed in your beloved's arms? What would it be like to have his child—

She turned over then, encircled the pillow with her arms and let the harsh, racking sobs come.

In a richly furnished room of a flat on the other side of the river, the thin, nervous-looking architect, stripped to the waist, writhed on the Persian rug. "Oh, please!" he bleated. "I know I'm helpless. But can't you show a little mercy?"

Feeling nothing but amused contempt, the woman whom Madame Theraux's clients knew as Diane Gautier looked down at the writhing figure.

"You're not going to use that awful whip on me! Are you? Are you?"

She lifted her arm and brought the whip's lash down across his bony back.

Chapter 5

At midnight Jeanne-Marie went back to a little cubbyhole next to the butler's pantry. She took off her maid's uniform, hung it on a hook, and put on a plain brown dress and bonnet. Then she crossed Madame Theraux's empty salon, said goodnight to the ancient porter, and went out into the brilliant moonlight. She walked with shoulders drooping and head slightly lowered, partly because she was tired, and partly because she wanted no one to leap to the conclusion that she, a very young woman out alone past midnight, was in search of masculine attention.

She crossed the bridge and then walked for several minutes in the inky black shadow of the southern wing of the Louvre. When she turned into the Place du Carrousel she saw that even at this hour a group of singing men and women stood near the Carrousel Arch, with its triumphant bronze chariot gleaming in the moonlight. They sang the *Marsellaise*. Ever since the war against Prussia had been declared, excited men and women, often strangers to each other, had been gathering at almost all hours and places to sing that song. Jeanne-Marie hoped that they would not be bawling it out anyplace on her street that night. She needed as much sleep as she could get before sunrise. Those first rays striking into her room always woke Marcel. Standing in his crib, he would begin to talk in his own language, a collection of gurgles, splutterings, and bird-like trills. If that failed to wake her, he would start to cry.

She crossed the square where the uncompleted opera house stood, its girders washed by moonlight, and then turned down a street that slanted off to her right. Soon she was in a fairly poor neighborhood, made up of warehouses and small factories as well as multi-family dwellings. Despite her tiredness, she quickened her pace to hurry the moment when she would have her small son in her arms.

When she reached her house she tapped on a ground-floor door, which the concierge opened. She was as aged as most of her kind, but less surly. She opened the door wider and said, "He has been sleeping ever since you brought him down to me, madame."

Jeanne-Marie lifted her son from a pallet on the floor and then carried him, still sleeping, up five flights of stairs. On each landing a gas jet burned feebly in its wall socket. Weary as she was, she enjoyed the relaxed, warm weight of Marcel in her arms.

Just as she reached the top floor Monsieur Lamartine opened his door. Obviously he had been listening for her step. He came out into the hall, a paper bag in his hand, a smile on his thin face.

"My sister paid me a visit today." His sister and her husband had a small farm less than a mile from the city's northern wall. "She brought me some newly-laid eggs. Permit me to give you and the little one a few."

She said, freeing one hand long enough to grasp the folded top of the paper bag, "You are so very kind, Monsieur Lamartine."

Henri Lamartine, a forty-year-old widower who ran a watch repair shop in the neighborhood, was indeed a kindly man. He not only shared with her his sister's gifts of farm produce. Several months earlier, when the concierge had been sick for almost a week, he had allowed Jeanne-Marie to leave Marcel with him each evening before she went to Madame Theraux's.

He was so very good to her that she grew ashamed about deceiving him. For a while she had referred vaguely to her place of employment as "a restaurant" on the Rue de Adele. Finally she had told him the truth. "But all I do," she said earnestly, "is to serve people food and drink. Please believe that, monsieur."

He had said, with his warm smile, "I wish it were some other sort of place. But no matter where you work, you don't have to assure me that you are a good girl."

Now he said, "Let me unlock your door for you. You'll find it hard to manage the key when you're carrying both Marcel and the eggs."

"Thank you."

He fished in the reticule that dangled from her wrist for the large iron doorkey. Then he moved beside her along the hall.

As they passed Charles Maubert's door, she heard several young voices, male and female, singing to the accompaniment of an accordion. A student at the Sorbonne, Charles obviously was giving a party for some of his classmates and for the pretty young *midinettes* who brightened their leisure hours.

At her door, the one at the hall's end, Monsieur Lamartine inserted the heavy key in the lock. As she looked down at his thinning red-brown hair, she thought with a familiar stab of longing, I wish Charles was the one who felt kindly toward me.

But she had long been aware that Charles felt nothing for her. He seemed to scarcely know that she was alive.

69

Henri Lamartine swung the door back then dropped the key into her reticule. He smiled at her, not just with his lips, but with his brown eyes. They did not have the opacity of dark brown eyes. In fact, they were what Jeanne-Marie always thought of as "brook-brown" eyes. The clear waters of a brook near the farm where she had been raised appeared to be of that same warm brown shade because of the fallen oak leaves lining its depths.

"Goodnight, monsieur, and thank you again."

She went into the one big room that served her as kitchen, bedroom, and living room. Moonlight flooding through the windows lighted her way first to the table, where she placed the bag of eggs, and then to the crib beside the fireplace with its unlighted charcoal brazier. Tomorrow morning on that brazier she would boil eggs for the baby and herself. She placed Marcel in the crib, covered him with a blanket, and then put the eggs away in the wall cupboard above the wooden sink. Then she locked the door.

The sounds of revelry from Charles Maubert's apartment had upset her, enough so that she knew that if she went to bed, she would not fall asleep right away, despite her tiredness. Still not lighting the oil lamp, she carried a chair over to an open window and sat down. From this height the city appeared like a sea of moon-gilded chimney pots. After a year in Paris she still was not used to all those roofs, all those chimney pots, all those people.

She had been born in a tiny village about sixty miles east of Paris. Her handsome young father, the village apothecary, had chosen as his wife the inexplicably beautiful daughter of an otherwise quite ordinary peasant family. When Jeanne-Marie, their only child, was four, the young husband's army unit had been called up to take part in the Crimean War. He was one of the thousands who died, not from enemy bullets, but from typhus. Within a year his widow, her always-delicate health undermined by grief, succumbed to consumption. Jeanne-Marie went to live with her mother's sister and the sister's husband on a farm two miles from the village.

As almost any child would have, she sensed immediately that her Aunt Therese did not want her and did not even like her. Jeanne-Marie was seven, though, before she realized why her aunt did not like her. The grownup Jeanne-Marie could not remember how her seven-year-old self had found out. Perhaps she had gained the knowledge from something her Uncle Claude had said during one of his frequent sullen exchanges with his wife. Anyway, from her seventh year on she had known that Aunt Therese had hated her sister, Jeanne-Marie's mother, for two reasons—first, because she was lovely, and second because she, Therese, had hoped to marry the young apothecary herself.

Somehow—perhaps because she was sustained by half-unconscious memories of the love which had enwrapped her during her earliest years—Jeanne-Marie managed to be a fairly happy child despite the gloom of her aunt and uncle's house, and despite the rough tasks assigned to her from the age of six on, such as slopping the pigs and scrubbing the farmhouse floors. She liked the farm animals, even the jostling pigs and the squawking, silly chickens, and mourned them when they were slaughtered. She loved running through the fields early on summer mornings when drops of dew shone like jewels in the rising sun. She enjoyed the school, a free school run by nuns, which she attended from the age of eight through eleven. "You've had as much school as is good for you," her aunt had said to her eleven-year-old niece. "Men don't want to marry girls with too much book learning. And you'll certainly have to find a husband. *We* certainly don't intend to support you for the rest of our lives."

71

Her aunt and uncle needn't have worried. When she was sixteen, she and nineteen-year-old Phillipe Perrault, a farm boy she had known all her life, discovered that they were in love. Phillipe's mother, a widow, had no objection to their marriage. Sons and daughters of peasant families often married young. Besides, she liked Jeanne-Marie.

After the noisy wedding celebration—held at the home, and at the expense, of the bridegroom rather than the bride—the young couple settled down in the Perrault farmhouse. It was larger than most such houses, and quite comfortable, despite the fact that it had been built, peasant fashion, over the stalls of the oxen and the mulch cows. Phillipe's mother turned her bedroom over to her son and his bride and moved to a smaller one.

The proximity of Madame Perrault had no inhibiting effect whatsoever on the young couple. In the shortest time possible Jeanne-Marie became pregnant.

Marcel was born when she was still two months short of her seventeenth birthday. Looking down at her son, with an immense sense of accomplishment as well as love, she thought, *Why, by the time I'm twenty-one I'll probably have had four children.*

The winter following Marcel's birth was one of the coldest France had ever known. Pneumonia of a particularly virulent type broke out not only in the cities but in rural regions. Jeanne-Marie and little Marcel remained healthy, but Madame Perrault contracted the infection. While she was still convalescent, her son fell ill. Terror in their hearts, the two women listened to his wheezing breath, put damp cloths on his flushed forehead, and coaxed him to swallow the medicine the overworked village doctor had left for him.

The night after the doctor's last visit, Phillipe became delirious. Madame Perrault looked down at her son lying scarlet-faced, head turning on the pillow, and cried to Jeanne-Marie, "Go fetch the doctor! Tell him he has to come!"

With a shawl over her head, Jeanne-Marie descended the steep staircase to the farmyard. She glanced in at the stalls where the oxen stood. By the light of a half moon, she could see the cloudy condensation of their breaths in the icy air. Should she yoke them to the cart? No, it was only a mile to the village. She could get there faster on foot. Half running, she moved past a loaded hay wain and then hurried down the road so deeply frozen that it seemed hard as iron underfoot.

When Jeanne-Marie reached the village, the doctor's wife told her that he was out visiting patients. Yes, yes, she would tell him as soon as he came in that he was needed at the Perrault farm. Jeanne-Marie started home.

She had gone only about a quarter of a mile when she saw the glow in the sky.

She ran the rest of the way, heart thudding. Soon there was a pain in her side, but she ignored it and ran on. The wavering glow mounted higher and higher. By the time she reached the farmyard, the house was a gigantic torch. Screaming her husband's name and her infant son's, she ran toward the stair entrance, now marked by just a tall black rectangle of timbers as yet not consumed by the seething flames. Heat forced her back.

Then, through the crackle and roar of the fire, she heard another sound, a baby's crying. It came not from the doomed farmhouse, but from the hay wain standing in the yard.

Stepping onto one of the wheel hubs, she grasped the top of the wagon's high wooden side and pulled herself up. There on the deep-piled hay was Marcel in his flannel gown, small face distorted with outrage, fists waving in the fire's red light. She scrambled over the wagon's side and, kneeling, gathered her child into her arms. Swiftly her hands went over the small body. He seemed to be uninjured.

She could visualize almost surely what had happened. Still weak from her own illness, Madame Perrault must have dozed off as she sat beside Phillipe. By the time she had become aware that the farmhouse was on fire, it must have been too late for her to get her delirious son, or even herself, down the flaming staircase. And so she had chosen to try to save her grandson. She had lifted him from his crib and tossed him from the window into the hay wagon.

As Jeanne-Marie clutched her son, staring in grief and horror at the blazing house, its roof collapsed, and a huge spiral of flame roared toward the sky.

In mid-morning of the next day, an unemployed farm worker was found asleep in a ditch not far from the farmhouse ruins. He still smelled of the calvados he had stolen from someone's kitchen, and one sleeve of his ragged coat bore scorched spots. He soon confessed that he had a dim memory of crawling into an empty stall at the Perrault farmhouse and curling up on a pile of straw. He did not remember lighting his pipe, but probably he had, because he could recall waking from a doze to find the straw on fire. He had left the stall then, and staggered down the road in the opposite direction from the village.

By the time she heard of the man's confession, Jeanne-Marie and her baby were at Aunt Therese and Uncle Claude's house. Still stunned with grief, she wondered if the drunk had been in that stall, curled up on already-smouldering straw, when she set out to fetch the doctor. Perhaps, she had been too agitated to notice the smell of something burning.

When she appeared at their door in the middle of the night carrying Marcel, her aunt and uncle had had no choice except to take her in. But the next afternoon her aunt had made it clear that as soon as the funerals of Madame Perrault and Phillipe were over, she would be expected to leave.

"As you know, your uncle's rheumatism was so bad last fall that he got in only part of the harvest. We scarcely have enough food for ourselves. You and the child will have to go elsewhere."

Jeanne-Marie cried, "But where?"

"You could go to work as a housemaid."

"You know there is no work like that around here!" That was true. The few families in the district well-off enough to hire a domestic worker already had one.

"Then go to Paris. It's only sixty miles away."

"Paris!"

"Why not? There must be all sorts of work there for a strong young woman."

"But how can I get there? And how can I support the baby and myself while I'm looking for work?"

"You forget you are an heiress. The Perrault farm belongs to you now. Even though the house burned to the ground and the livestock are dead, you've got the land."

"It's mortgaged. You know it's mortgaged!"

"Still, it should bring you something." After a moment she added grudgingly, "You can stay here until you sell your land. After that you'll have to leave."

It took her three months to sell her property. The purchaser drove a hard bargain. After she had paid off the mortgage-holder and the tax collector, she had a little more than a hundred francs. But at least it was spring by then. Peasants were taking their produce to Les Halles, the vast market area in Paris. Jeanne-Marie had no trouble securing transportation for Marcel and herself in the wagon of a farmer taking a load of chickens to the city. It was he who told her where she could find cheap and fairly clean quarters.

75

"Try the Rue de Meubles. A cousin of mine lived there once."

Madame Blanc, the concierge at the tall old house on the Rue de Muebles, said that yes, there was a vacancy. "It's on the top floor, but that shouldn't matter to a strong young girl like you. And the air is good up there."

Marcel in her arms, Jeanne-Marie followed Madame Blanc as she toiled up five flights, stopping frequently for breath. They had just reached the top floor hall when a door opened and a young man came out.

When she had lost Phillipe, Jeanne-Marie had thought that even though she would remarry if she could—her peasant practicality ruled out the idea of lifelong widowhood—she could never again be strongly attracted to a man. But at first sight of this young man, she felt the impact of his good looks—his curly, light brown hair, dark blue eyes, well-cut features, and the lithe grace of him in his well-tailored suit of dark brown broadcloth. He gave a smiling nod to the concierge, glanced casually at Jeanne-Marie, and then clattered down the stairs.

Madame Blanc showed her into a big room. It was indifferently furnished with a double bed, a worn table, and two straight chairs. But it looked clean, and its four windows made it light and airy.

"There's a crib in the basement," the concierge said. "You can have the free use of that. And you can leave your little boy downstairs with me every day, if you like. Don't worry. I've raised six. Of course, I'll have to charge you for my trouble, but not much. Ten centimes a day, perhaps."

"That seems more than fair, madame."

"Now you'll have only two neighbors on this floor. There is Monsieur Lamartine. He's a watch repairman, and he and his wife moved here fifteen years ago. She's been dead for five years now. The other tenant on this floor is Monsieur Charles Maubert."

"Is he the one we saw in the hall?"

"Yes, that was Monsieur Charles." Something in her tone seemed to add, *and the likes of you had best not be setting your cap for the likes of him.*

Nevertheless, Jeanne-Marie asked, "What does he do?"

"He's a student at the Sorbonne. His family has a lace factory in Lyons. I'm sure he could afford lodgings in a better house than this one. Probably, though, he wants to spend as much of his allowance as possible on wine and parties and pretty girls. A lively one, Monsieur Charles is."

She spoke with no disapproval whatsoever. After thirty years as this building's concierge, she had become used to the behavior of tenants, especially student tenants. Besides, although a fairly kind woman, she was, like most concierges, a snob. It pleased her that she had a tenant who was not only twenty years old and superlatively handsome, but also a member of the upper bourgeoisie.

"Then do you wish to rent the room, Madame Perrault?"

"Yes, I'll rent it."

The very next morning she was lucky enough—at least at the time she thought it good luck—to find work only a hundred yards or so from Madame Blanc's house. Her employer was the proprietor of a bakeshop, a stout man of about fifty. Her duties, he told her, would be simple. She was to wait on customers, watch baking loaves of bread lest they burn, and remove them from the oven when they were done.

That first week she told herself that his calling her his little sparrow or his little cabbage meant nothing. Perhaps that was just the way Parisian men talked. As for his putting his arm around her waist, perhaps he was just being friendly in a fatherly fashion. As for the times when his hand brushed across her *derriere*—well, that could be accidental. There was not much room for two people to move about in the area between the ovens and the wall.

But at seven on Saturday night as she was hanging up the apron he had provided for her, he said, "Good night, little one. Try to be back here by noon tomorrow."

"Tomorrow! Why, you said nothing about working on Sunday."

"We don't. On Sunday we lock the shop door tight and then we play." He winked at her. "I must accompany my wife to church in the morning. But you and I can spend all afternoon back there." He jerked his head toward the open door of the room at the rear of the shop. It contained not only a tall desk, but a couch where he sometimes rested after he had put a batch of bread in the oven.

Looking into his jovial-seeming face, she felt humiliated, hurt and disappointed, until indignation swept through her. "Monsieur, what reason have I given you to think I would behave in that fashion?"

"Reason!" His face, no longer jovial, looked uglier then she had realized it could. "You took the job, didn't you?"

When she just looked at him, speechless, he continued, "Don't you know that this is a comfortable, easy job? Not like a factory job, let me tell you. There are at least three girls looking for a job as good as this one. Now wouldn't I be a fool to pass up an advantage like that?"

Still speechless, Jeanne-Marie stared at him.

"The point is, mademoiselle, that if you do not come here tomorrow afternoon, you need not come here Monday morning."

Her voice shook. "Then I will not be here Monday. Now, please pay me one week's wages, monsieur."

He turned on his heel, went into the rear room, and

opened the drawer of his desk. Then he came back to her and counted four francs into her hand.

"You are a fool, mademoiselle. Almost anywhere you work, there will be someone expecting you to go to bed with him. And believe me, compared to some of them you'll meet, I'm not so bad."

Stomach knotted with anger and humiliation as well as the fear that what he had just told her might be right, she put her shawl around her and went out into the lingering spring twilight. She longed to rush home and hold her little son's comforting warmth close to her breast. But no, he would sense her distress. She would wait until she was calmer. Besides, when she went out to look for work her first morning in Paris, she had seen a "shop assistant wanted, female" sign in the window of a chocolate shop near the Place de l'Opera. Because she had thought that the place looked far too chic to employ a girl fresh from the country, she had not applied for the job. But now—

She hurried on, through a neighborhood which became more prosperous looking as she neared the incompleted opera house. Yes, here was the shop. It was still open, and the sign was still in the window. She went inside.

A woman with graying blond hair and a face that combined sophistication with warmth stood behind the counter. She said, "Good evening. May I serve you?"

"No, thank you, madame. I came to apply for the—the position."

The woman looked at her appraisingly. "Have you ever worked in a sweet shop?"

"No, madame. Until eight days ago I had lived all my life in the country."

"Then you've never held any paid employment?"

"I worked all this past week in a bakeshop."

"But you left? Or were you dismissed?"

"I left, madame."

"Why?"

"Oh, madame!" Near tears, Jeanne-Marie told her.

A kind of wry, sad amusement came into the woman's eyes. "I fear he is right about one thing. In Paris, if a girl is young and poor and alone, she may find that employers expect more from her than just her work." She paused. "The best course for such a young woman is to marry."

"I was married, madame. My husband died. Now I must raise our son. Perhaps I am wrong, but I fear that it is not too easy for a woman with a child to find a young man willing to marry her."

The woman said, in that same wry tone, "No, I don't think you are wrong about that."

A well-dressed couple had come into the shop. She sold them a box of almond creams and then, when they had gone, asked Jeanne-Marie her name, age, and address.

At last she said, "You may have the position. I think a girl with your fresh, wholesome look should please chocolate shop customers. I will pay you five francs a week, which is what your bakeshop friend should have paid you."

"Oh, thank you, madame! Thank you."

"My name is Madame Aimee Colbert. This shop opens at nine in the morning. I will see you then."

It was pleasant to work in such an attractive place, filled with aromas from the kitchen in the rear, where Madame Colbert supervised two women who made delicious concoctions out of melted chocolates, nuts, and fruits and poured them into candy molds. It was pleasant to wear an all-pink uniform—pink dress and apron, and ruffled pink milkmaid's cap. It was pleasant to wait on well-dressed people who, for the most part, were polite to her.

But the evenings were lonely. True, after she became acquainted with Monsieur Lamartine, the watch repairer twice asked her out to supper, "just to keep me company." She enjoyed his stories of his youth in a small town in southern France, where he had learned watchmaking from his father. He talked, too, of the happy years he and his wife had spent here in Paris before she became mortally ill.

Once, in the late summer, he invited both Jeanne-Marie and Marcel to share an omelet with him in his quarters. Unlike Jeanne-Marie, he had not one room, but three. From the cellar he carried up a highchair in which, long ago, the concierge's offspring had sat. Thus Marcel, obviously delighted, was able to sit at the supper table. As she looked from the crowing child to their host's smiling, sensitive face, she thought of how Monsieur Lamartine must be about the age her father would have been if he had returned from the Crimea.

As for Charles Maubert, he always greeted her with cheerful politeness when they encountered each other in the hall or on the stairs but then moved on.

Well, she reminded herself, what else could she expect? He was a university student, a superlatively handsome young man from a wealthy family. He could have his choice of any number of girls, all kinds of girls. Pretty shop girls to laugh with, drink with, and, she had little doubt, go to bed with. Fashionable demimondaines who might grant their usually expensive favors for nothing to a young man like him. *Bien elevee* girls of his own class from among whom he would eventually choose a wife. Why should he bother with an ex-farm girl, a widow with a young child?

In September, though, she forgot her loneliness in a new concern. Aimee Colbert was about to close her sweet shop.

"It is because of my sister." The sister, a widow fifteen years

81

older than Madame Colbert, lived with her. "She's not well, and Paris is too damp for her. I want to take her to a little cottage we own near Nice. With the money left to her by her husband, and the money I have made, we can live comfortably."

Jeanne-Marie felt too dismayed to speak. "I am sorry, my dear," Madame Colbert said, "but you had best start looking for another position. I shall make inquiries among my business associates too. Perhaps one of them can offer something suitable."

But it seemed that none of her associates had need of Jeanne-Marie's services. Despite her distasteful experience with the bakeshop proprietor, she was about to embark upon a search among the neighborhood's shops and small factories when, one morning, a tall, buxom woman with henna-dyed hair came into the chocolate shop.

"Good morning, mademoiselle."

"Good morning, Madame Theraux." Jeanne-Marie knew not only the woman's name but her profession as well. One of the two chocolate-makers in the shop's kitchen had told her about the mansion over on the Left Bank. But Madame Theraux had always been pleasant to Jeanne-Marie, and so the girl was pleasant in return.

"A pound of almond-paste chocolate, please."

While Jeanne-Marie was wrapping the pretty yellow satin box in silver paper tied with silver ribbon, the woman said, "I have heard that this shop is to close."

"I am afraid so, madame."

"A pity. It is my favorite chocolate shop in all of Paris." She paused. "And what will you do, mademoiselle?"

"What can I do except look for another place?"

"Would you consider accepting employment from me?"

Jeannie-Marie stiffened. Warm, indignant color flooded her face.

Madame Theraux smiled and said, "I see that someone has told you about me. But believe me, my dear, I am not proposing that you join my staff of—young ladies." As a matter of fact the girl, although pretty, was not the type one could turn into what Madame Theraux tried to offer her clients— reasonable facsimiles of somewhat depraved young aristocrats. The girl was too young, too awkward, and too obviously not long off the farm.

She went on, "I will ask you to do nothing distasteful. That is, unless you would find it distasteful to carry trays of food and drink around each evening." She hesitated, and then decided to be completely frank. "You see, my dear, it is because you so obviously are a chaste young woman that I would like to hire you. In a proper uniform, you will look exactly like the sort of parlor maid one would expect to find in some titled family's chateau.

"And I feel sure you will be honest," she went on. "A woman in my profession finds that so many servants try to cheat her. They pilfer small objects, or pad the kitchen bills, or take expensive liquors for their own consumption. My instincts—and my instincts are usually sound—tell me that you are not like that.

"Well, mademoiselle?"

The outraged color had left Jeanne-Marie's face. "I—I don't know, madame."

"Think it over. And if you decide to accept my offer, come to Number Fourteen, Rue de Adele, anytime before five in the afternoon. Can you remember that number?"

"Yes, madame."

An hour later Jeanne-Marie told her employer that she would like to ask her advice about something. They went to a neighborhood café for lunch. Over *croque monsieurs*—toasted, open-faced sandwiches of ham and melted cheese—the girl told of Madame Theraux's offer.

The older woman sat in thoughtful silence for several moments. "You're thrusting a terrible responsibility upon me," she said at last, "but I don't feel I have a right to evade it. And so I'll tell you that if I were in your place I would accept her offer.

"I don't have to remind you that the world can be an unkind place for a young woman alone, particularly if she must fend not only for herself but a child as well. At Madame Theraux's, I am sure, you will receive good wages, and more than likely, generous tips now and then.

"What is more, whatever one may think of her occupation, Madame Theraux has a reputation as a woman who keeps her word. If she promised you that you will be just a serving maid, and that she will never try to induce you to become anything else, I think she will keep her promise.

"Well, there it is, Jeanne-Marie. I have given you my honest advice. I can only hope that it is also wise advice."

"Thank you, Madame Colbert."

The next day she called on Madame Theraux at the house on Rue de Adele. For nearly a year now she had been crossing each evening to the Left Bank mansion and then starting home at midnight through the dark streets.

As she sat there looking out over the city's moon-washed rooftops, she could still hear, faintly, the strains of an accordion and the sound of young voices singing. At the moment they sang, not a French song, but an Italian one, the yearningly romantic *O, Sole Mio*. She sang along with them, very softly.

In spite of all its ugliness, how beautiful the world could be with its flood of moonlight and the young voices singing. But the beauty could hurt when you were alone.

Not that she would have traded places with any of those

girls in Charles's rooms, not if it would have meant that she would no longer have her son. But still, when you are only eighteen, it is hard to sit alone and listen to the carefree laughter and singing of other young people.

The singing had stopped now. She heard a door open, heard voices calling goodnight. Then there was the clatter of footsteps down the stairs. Charles's door closed. But probably one girl had remained with him. Jeanne-Marie pictured him taking the girl into his arms—

Marcel whimpered. She rose from her chair and tiptoed to the crib. By the time she reached it she could tell from his even breathing that he had gone back to sleep. And so it was not to comfort him, but herself that she lifted his small, sleeping body from the crib, went back to her chair beside the window and held him warm against her breast.

Chapter 6

As an American, Maggie MacNeil was able to observe the behavior of the excitable French during those waning days of summer with a certain detachment. The rattle of drums and the strains of the *Marsellaise* continued to echo along the narrow, winding streets and broad boulevards. Wild and joyful rumors circulated. Bismarck had gone insane! The Crown Prince of Prussia had committed suicide! A great French victory had sent the panic-stricken Prussians fleeing back toward Berlin!

Flags would bloom in almost every window. When it became obvious that the latest rumor, like the ones before, was untrue, the flags would disappear.

Then, early in September, the inevitable happened. In a battle near Sedan, ill-trained, ill-discipline French troops under the inept leadership of an ailing Louis Napoleon, were soundly beaten. Louis Napoleon surrendered to the Prussians and became their prisoner.

When the news reached Paris, the self-deluded city exploded with rage. Mobs surged through the streets, shouting defiance of the Prussians. Other mobs invaded the palace of the Tuileries to smash furniture and ornaments, and to search for the Empress. Fortunately, she had escaped out a side entrance, entered a waiting carriage, and been whisked out of Paris by a friend, an American dentist. Still other mobs toppled statues of Louis Napoleon and threw them into the Seine.

The news that Prussian armies were encircling Paris and would soon declare a state of siege only increased the rioters' defiant fury. Political leaders, meeting hastily in the Hotel de Ville, Paris's ancient City Hall, declared that France was now a republic. They also vowed to carry on the war. If they had not, the mobs howling outside no doubt would have invaded the building and hung them from the ornate chandeliers.

Despite the fact that the disorder lasted for several days, Maggie managed to get to Madame Theraux's salon each evening. There the champagne was as dry as ever, the gowns and coiffures of the young ladies as exquisite, and the talk as light hearted—except when it turned to the war. Even after the rioting subsided, the sleek, prosperous businessmen and politicians obviously were less afraid of the Prussians than of segments of their own people, particularly the denizens of Paris slums. If the Prussians won, as seemed likely, there was no telling what the National Guard might do.

As she listened to this uneasy talk, and sometimes even as she lay in some man's bed, feigning a response to his lips and fumbling hands, she found herself thinking of Richard Glover. She knew it was folly to do so, and yet she kept wondering where he was. Had his news syndicate assigned him to drawing sketches of the French armies still in the field? Perhaps, but as a neutral with press credentials, he could just as well have gone behind the Prussian lines. Or he could be right here in Paris, sketching those new political leaders who met in stormy sessions each day at the Hotel de Ville.

Several times she thought that she saw him walking down a street or seated at a café. But each time, after a moment, she would realize that it was some other man.

Then one mid-September afternoon when she was in her

flat she heard a knock. She opened the door to find Richard Glover standing in the hall carrying a bouquet of white roses partially wrapped in shiny green paper.

His hair was dark brown, she saw now. As for his eyes, they were as gray as her own.

He held out the flowers, and she, still feeling stunned, took them. "I hope I chose the right color. It seemed to me that white roses suited you."

"They are my favorite kind. Thank you very much." Her initial surprise had given way to a pleasure she was afraid showed in her voice. She opened the door wider. "Come in."

He stepped past her into the little entrance hall, with its pretty guilt mirror, and then into the small salon. "Please sit down," she said, "while I put these in water."

When she came back from the kitchen, she put a rose-filled crystal vase on the small table beside the chair in which he sat. Then, facing him and said, "I have some Moselle."

"That sounds very pleasant."

From the liquor cabinet at one end of the sofa she took out a decanter and small glasses. It wasn't until she had seated herself and they had both taken a sip of the wine that she asked, "How did you find me?"

"It was simple. When I got back to Paris yesterday I went to the theater where I'd seen you in that musical production. The old doorman there remembered you'd had an address on the Right Bank, and finally he found it in a cubbyhole of his desk. I went over there, and the concierge told me that she had met you on the street some months ago, and that you'd told her that you lived at this address."

In other words, he had gone first to the flat where her married American lover had paid the rent—if you could call Danson Hayworth a lover—and then to this one, where a brothel keeper paid the rent.

She realized her own folly then. She must get rid of him, this man who could mean nothing in her life except the destruction of her peace of mind.

But she could not show him the door, not right at this moment, and so she asked, "You say you've been out of Paris?"

"Yes, I was on the train that took the Emperor to Sedan. After he surrendered, I went behind the Prussian lines and made some sketches of General Sheridan."

She nodded. She had heard that the American government had sent the noted Civil War general to Berlin so that he could observe the methods and armament of the formidable Prussian war machine.

He said, "And you? What production are you in now?"

There was no way she could lie about it, not when he could so easily check on her answer. "I haven't obtained another part yet."

She saw his eyes flick toward the fireplace with its black marble mantel, then at the little rosewood desk with its gilt inlays. His thought was obvious. How could an unemployed actress afford a nicely furnished flat in a fashionable neighborhood?

He said, "Oh? Well, I'm sure you'll find a part soon. Anyway, I was going to ask you to have supper with me after the performance. We can have supper earlier. That is, if you'll be kind enough to say yes."

She must not see him again tonight, or anytime, not unless she was prepared to tell lie after lie, lies which he would eventually discover.

She heard herself saying, "Thank you. I'd like very much to have supper with you."

He left not long after that. She waited a few minutes and then walked through the still-summery warmth to Number

Fourteen, Rue de Adele. "Madame is in her study," the old porter said. Maggie crossed the empty salon. With its draperies drawn lest the sun fade the rich satin and brocade furniture, the room was almost dark. The smaller, much less ornate room off the salon, the room where Madame Theraux kept her accounts and spent much of her time, was filled with sunlight.

She lay on a black leather couch, holding an opened novel of George Sand. Laying the book aside, she said, "Sit down, Maggie, and tell me what brings you here at this hour."

Perched stiffly on a straight chair, Maggie said, "I would like to—to take some sort of holiday for ten days or so." She was aware of her racing pulse.

"Are you ill?"

"No."

"Then you want to be free to devote all your time to a man."

"Yes." Her voice was nervous and yet defiant.

"Maggie, I thought you were intelligent, far too intelligent to take up with a handsome good-for-nothing who will spend all that money you've been saving."

"He's not like that in the least. He's an American, a newspaper sketch artist employed by a syndicate. I'm sure he makes a respectable amount of money and—and that he comes from a respectable family too."

After a moment Madame said, "Then you really are a fool. A fling with a wastrel would cost you nothing but money, but a man like that! A man you'd never dare tell—You haven't told him have you?"

"No."

"Of course you haven't. And when you do—Maggie, you're going to get your heart broken." The brown eyes, which had seen so much, seemed to hold genuine concern.

Maggie said stubbornly, "I want just a little while to pretend I'm like—other girls."

"And after that?"

"I'll break with him. With one excuse or another, I'll break with him."

Madame Theraux sighed. "Very well. This is not a white slave establishment. You are free to take as long as you like."

Hours later darkness descended upon Paris, but the air remained balmy. A little after eight Maggie and Richard Glover sat at a sidewalk table on the Champs-Elysees. Now that she had made her reckless decision, she was determined to enjoy everything about this evening. The chicken lisette and its accompanying dry white Chablis, the glow of the gas lamps on the trees still in summer green, bordering the broad boulevard, and most of all, the presence of the gray-eyed young American across the table from her.

He described Louis Napoleon's tragic last hours at Sedan. "The poor fellow was so sick that his aides had painted his face, trying to hide from the troops just how badly off he was. Even though he could scarcely sit a horse, he kept riding up and down wherever the fighting was hottest. Plainly he hoped that he would at least be granted honorable death in battle. But he wasn't that lucky."

"Did the Prussians take him to Berlin?"

"So they say."

"And will the Prussians lay siege to Paris?"

"They certainly seem to be preparing to. And obviously this new French government thinks they will. That's why they've brought those thousands of head of cattle into the Bois de Bologne. Have you seen them?"

"No."

"If you like, we could go and look at them. I know you must spend a lot of time calling on theatrical producers, but if you're free tomorrow afternoon—"

"I am. And I don't spend much time looking for parts."
She paused, and then launched into the lie she had decided
upon that afternoon. "You see, it isn't necessary for me to
work."

With a quizzical look in his gray eyes, he waited for her to
continue.

"Perhaps I had best explain. Both my parents are dead."
At least that much, she reflected wryly, was true. "But they
left me fairly well provided for. About a year ago I came to
Paris with this aunt of mine who had been my guardian while
I was growing up. I fell in love with the city and decided to
stay here after she returned home."

She added, "I'm sure that my parents, if they had still been
alive, would have objected strenuously. But my aunt is quite
advanced in her views."

As she spoke she could almost see that fictional aunt, a
spinster of impeccable background but with radical views on
Women's Rights.

A certain relief in his eyes told her that he had felt a puzzled unease about that comfortable apartment with its
touches of luxury. But now she had explained it.

He said, "If I remember correctly, the program notes for
that play you were in said you were from New York."

"We lived in Brooklyn, actually."

One Sunday when Rose was in the midst of one of her rare
stretches of sobriety, she and Maggie had taken a ferry ride to
Brooklyn. Then eight years old, Maggie had looked with awe
at the tree-shaded streets, and at the big houses set back on
spacious lawns. On one such lawn a little girl of her own age
had been giving a tea party for about half a dozen dolls.
Hands clinging to spokes of the iron picket fence, Maggie had
stared with wonder at the blue ribbon binding the other

child's blond curls and at her blue muslin dress with frilled white pantalettes showing beneath its hem.

A well-dressed couple and a stout woman in a maid's uniform had appeared on the broad veranda. The couple came down the walk and the little girl, running to them, was kissed by both her mother and father. "We'll be home right after Sunday services. Now you do everything Bridget tells you to while we're away."

The couple continued down the walk, went through the gate in the picket fence, and got into a waiting carriage. Rose grasped Maggie's arm. "Come on, or we'll miss the ferry."

As Maggie walked away beside her mother, her small heart had ached with a misery she could not quite understand.

Richard Glover said, "I've heard that Brooklyn is a lovely place."

"Yes, lovely."

He took her home around eleven o'clock. With the key she handed him he unlocked her door and swung it back. Then his eyes, smiling down at her, asked a tacit permission, and her eyes granted it. He tilted her chin with one hand and brought his warm, firm lips down on hers.

His kiss, brief and restrained as it was, seemed to send warmth all through her. It was with difficulty that she restrained an impulse to throw her arms around his neck and cup the back of his brown head with her hand, prolonging the pressure of his lips.

He raised his head and smiled down at her. Oh, God! How wonderful it was to have a man touch you, kiss you, not as something bought and paid for, but gently, even tentatively.

"Then shall we go to the Bois de Bologne tomorrow afternoon? I can call for you about three."

"Please do."

"Goodnight, Maggie." He turned away.

On Wednesday a hired carriage took them across the Place de la Concorde. Despite that stunning defeat at Sedan, fashionable regiments of the National Guard still marched back and forth in their opera bouffa uniforms, and citizens of all ages still gathered at various points in the vast square to sing the national anthem, heads flung back as they shouted their defiance of the Germans who, miles away, were slowly drawing their iron ring around Paris. Just as their carriage entered the Bois de Bologne, a group of horses and their impeccably dressed riders of both sexes cantered past.

"They must be going to Mount Valerian," Richard said. That was one of the French forts beyond the city walls. "Viewing the forts seems to be the latest fad."

A moment later he added, echoing her own thoughts, "A strange people, the French. So frivolous, so irritatingly sure that other people, including the Germans, are clumsy and inept compared to themselves."

He told her then of how this past month several units of the French army, on their way to the front, had become lost for lack of proper maps. "Oh, they had been issued maps, all right—maps of Germany, designed to guide them to their victorious assault on Berlin!"

"And yet," he went on, "you can't help admire a people that brave and that convinced, even after the defeat at Sedan, that sheer French dash and gallantry will bring them final victory."

They turned a curve and there before them were hundreds upon hundreds of cattle and sheep, cropping the grass beneath the ancient oaks and beeches.

Maggie said, "Siege or no siege, Paris won't go hungry."

"I'm not so sure. Paris has over a million people, you know. And more of them are coming in from the countryside every day."

This afternoon they had passed a number of such country people moving toward the center of the city, some on foot, others in carts filled with their household goods. They had not appeared frightened or even troubled. Rather they had seemed to be in a holiday mood, as if they thought the coming siege of Paris would be an exciting new form of entertainment.

Richard went on, "If the siege lasts into the winter, I fear the French are going to run out of their food supply as well as their celebrated élan. Maggie, please lay in as much food as you can.

"I really ought to urge you to go back to the States, but I don't want you to go."

She said, a trifle unevenly, "And I don't want to go. No matter what happens, I don't think foreigners will be in any danger. Why, English people are still coming here! In *Le Figaro* this morning some rental agency advertised that 'English gentlemen in Paris to attend the siege' were looking for suitable quarters to rent."

He laughed. "The English have their own brand of élan. Which reminds me, I must go to London in a couple of weeks to sketch several political leaders. My syndicate is running stories on them. Since I may not be able to get back here for awhile, I want to be sure before I leave that you've laid in plenty of food."

So he would be gone in two weeks. Then that was the length of time she would allow herself to pretend that they could be together always. Before the two weeks were up she would have thought of some way to break with him. She did not know what the way would be. She only hoped, pray God, that no matter how much it might distress him, it would leave him thinking well of her.

The enchanted days passed. Each morning she awoke with

a sense of tingling joy, aware that in a few hours she would be with Richard. She, born and bred in a New York slum, and until recently, one of Madame Theraux's young ladies, was just as deeply and tremulously in love as if she really had grown up sheltered by loving and well-to-do parents.

And Richard continued to treat her as if she had been that gently reared girl. At the end of their evenings together, she sensed when he kissed her goodnight that he was finding his self-imposed restraint more and more difficult. And she was finding it harder and harder to check her own desire, harder and harder not to press her body against him in an embrace so ardent that he would forget everything except his need for her.

All through those waning days of September she was dimly aware that the Prussians, a few miles beyond the city's walls and outlaying forts, were completing their encirclement of Paris. But in her bemused state, she really could not comprehend what a siege might mean to the city's inhabitants, at least not until the day she accompanied Richard to the working class neighborhood known as Belleville.

His purpose was to sketch the sort of small hospital, called by the French an ambulance, which the government and a few private individuals had set up in various parts of Paris. Maggie saw that even here in the poorer districts, National Guard units also drilled. In ill-fitting uniforms, they marched up and down in the Place de la Bastille, where less than a hundred years before a blood-thirsty mob had ushered in the French Revolution. Along Belleville's streets, individual guardsmen, obviously drunk, reeled in and out of the numerous wine shops set between the moldering tenements.

She said, aghast, "Are these the sort of men who are going to defend Paris?"

Richard shrugged. "These men will do as well as any other

sort of French militiamen or maybe better."

"But they're drunk! And I've heard that a lot of them have no income except the one franc a day the government pays them. How can they afford to drink so much?"

Richard's voice was dry. "When you're that poor and miserable, maybe you feel you can't afford *not* to drink. Wine, after all, is very cheap. For a few centimes a man can get drunk enough to forget for a few hours that he'll probably never be able to make a decent living for his wife and children."

Yes, Maggie reflected, it was like that in Hell's Kitchen too. Except for the traditional Saturday night drinking, longshoremen with jobs would stay out of saloons for years and years. But when they found themselves unemployed for a considerable time, they would spend every cent they could scrounge in saloons, just because they could not face the reproach and anxiety in the eyes of their families.

Richard smiled at her. "Your problem is that you haven't been around the poor enough to understand *their* problems."

Maggie said nothing.

For another minute or so they rode on through the smells of drains and mildewing wood and cheap wine, past the sidewalks filled not only with guardsmen but shawled women, gaunt men in workmen's rough clothing, and ragged children. Then the carriage stopped before what looked like a warehouse. With Richard carrying the flat case that held his drawing paper and folding easel, they went inside. The building's ground floor, Maggie saw, was filled with rows of empty cots, each covered with a cheap blanket. A tall man of middle age, thin and balding and with an unmistakable air of good breeding, opened a door in the rear wall and hurried toward them. He introduced himself as Jean-Paul Ducrot, the administrator of this particular ambulance. Richard, in turn, introduced Maggie.

The administrator showed Richard where he might set up his easel. Then he said, "Would you care to go up to the next floor, Mademoiselle MacNeil? We have transferred the children up there. Until now this has been a children's ambulance, you know."

As she and Monsieur Ducrot climbed wide wooden stairs, she asked, "Why are there no patients on the ground floor?"

"Those beds are being reserved for the military. Soon units of the National Guard will be sent out to try to break through the Prussian siege lines and join up with French forces elsewhere. There are bound to be casualties."

With an inward shudder Maggie thought of those illnourished wine-soaked Frenchmen going up against the sort of Prussian troops Richard had described to her—supremely confident soldiers, whose military-minded Fatherland had supplied them with the best in food, weapons, and leadership.

As they reached the landing, Monsieur Ducrot said, "Most of the children are suffering from typical slum diseases, consumption and rickets."

Maggie nodded. Just so had it been in Hell's Kitchen.

But when they entered the ward, resided over by a coarsefeatured young woman in a dark blue blouse and full skirt, she saw that there was a difference between these children and ones she and Hildegarde Hoffman had treated. These children were so quiet. Except for the whimpering of one small boy with a bandaged arm, they lay silent. Only their turning heads and their eyes, big in their thin faces, acknowledged their visitors' presence. Maggie wondered if they were so listless because they somehow sensed their hopelessness, sensed that they were the ultimate victims of the accumulated folly of their elders. The weak folly of Louis Napoleon, the corrupt folly of his court, and the bombastic folly of those French street crowds demanding a war for which their country was not in the least prepared.

And if, as Richard feared, besieged Paris did find itself short of food, it would be these already ill-nourished slum children who would suffer the most.

On the way back across the city to her Left Bank apartment, Richard asked, "That place depressed you, didn't it?"

It had been more than the children, of course. It had been the reminder of the Hell's Kitchen clinic, and the brutal death of the fine woman who had founded it.

Richard clasped her hand. "I shouldn't have taken you there. But perhaps over dinner tonight I can make you forget it."

They went that night to her favorite place, the Champs-Elysees sidewalk café where they'd had their first supper. And seated there in the open air, with gaslights silvering the leaves of the chestnut trees, and a sidewalk accordionist playing a love song, she did manage to forget everything except the man opposite her.

Chapter 7

That was the night when the young woman known to Madame Theraux's customers as Diane Gautier saw Maggie and Richard Glover together. Riding in her private carriage from her chic flat near the Etoile, she looked at the largest of the Champs-Elysees outdoor cafés. The attractive man with Maggie, who also had an American look, was holding both her hands across the small table and smiling into her eyes. And to judge from the look on Maggie's face—what was her last name? O'Neil? No, MacNeil—to judge from the look on her face, she was deeply in love.

That amused Diane. She had pondered vaguely a few times over the past week why she no longer saw the American girl at Madame Theraux's "receptions." But her curiosity had not been strong enough to induce her to mention the matter to any of the other young women. As much as possible, she avoided talking to them. She found them silly and dull, not because they were whores, but because they were women. Diane had never taken much interest in members of her own sex.

True, the American girl seemed to be different from the others at Madame Theraux's. Diane had read intelligence in Maggie's face, and heard it in her precise and fluent French. But that was all the more reason for Diane to keep her distance. Even if she felt the need of a friend of her own sex, she would not have chosen Maggie. Someone as bright as the American might guess that Diane came to Number Fourteen for other purposes than financial gain or even sheer amusement.

When she reached the salon that night, she asked Madame about the American girl, just to see what the woman would say.

Whenever one of her young ladies told her something of a confidential nature, it was Madame's policy not to relate it. Besides, there was the odd emotion this titian-haired Diane awoke in her, a blend of dislike and uneasiness.

So she said, "Maggie MacNeil is taking a holiday. Some woman relative of hers is spending a short time in Paris. An aunt, I believe she said."

Diane smiled, thinking, what an extraordinary looking aunt. "I see," she answered. Over Madame Theraux's plump shoulder she watched the thin, nervous-looking architect hurrying toward her across the salon.

How often had he come here, paid his hundred-franc entrance fee, and then paid Diane an even larger amount to "punish" him? Four times? Five? She was not sure. And she was even less sure of the number of men there had been in her life.

She remembered the first one, though. She had been fourteen. He had been sixteen, a stableboy at Graytowers, a vast stone pile fifty miles southwest of London that had been built during Mary Tudor's reign by John Weston, first Earl of Braithwaite. Simon Weston, Diane's father, was the ninth earl.

The stableboy's name was Jed. She never knew his last name. He was big for his age, with heavy shoulders and thighs. Brown-haired with a broad, freckled face, he was not particularly good-looking. What attracted her the first time he led her saddle horse out to her, was the impression he conveyed of a young male so charged with sexuality that he was like a ripe seed pod ready to burst.

Not that he had made any advances to her, then or ever. He had given her a swift look from light blue eyes and then directed his gaze at the ground. Even when he linked his hands so that he could put his palm beneath her booted instep and hoist her onto the sidesaddle, he did not look at her.

Three days later she came back from a ride on Damask, the small bay mare her father had given her. Jed was waiting to unsaddle the mare and lead her back to her stall. No one else was in the stable yard. Diane had been quite sure that would be the case. The head groom and the other attendants would be down at Graytowers's private track, watching the new thoroughbred Diane's father had bought with the intention of racing him at Ascot.

Jed helped her to the ground, then turned to lead the mare away. She called sharply, "Jed!"

He turned around. "Yes, miss. I mean, your ladyship." Although he had been a stable boy since the age of eleven, this was the first time he'd had a titled employer. It was hard for him to remember that this young girl, because she was an earl's daughter, was to be addressed as your ladyship.

"Are all of the stalls in use?"

Startled, he lifted his gaze to her face for an instant, and then looked down. "No, your ladyship. There's two empty ones toward the back."

"You take girls there at night, don't you? Kitchen maids or girls from around here."

Color rushed into his face then ebbed. Lor' love us! How had she known a thing like that?

She tapped his shoulder with her riding crop. "Take me back there."

Rooted to the spot, he just gaped at her.

"Don't be a ninny." Her voice was impatient. "They'll still be at the track for quite awhile. When I rode by, they hadn't even finished setting up the barriers. Now come on."

She started down the dim aisle between the stalls. One gelding, a gray, reached out to nudge her shoulder as she passed. The others merely looked at her with soft, incurious eyes. For a moment Jed stood frozen. Then he hastily secured the mare's reins to a hitching post. Feeling a dazed incredulity, he followed the slim figure in the green velvet riding habit.

She entered the last stall. By the time he too reached it she was lying on the straw. She had removed her tall, veil-swathed hat, also of green velvet, and laid it down beside her. Still not quite able to believe what was happening, he looked down at her with a blend of terror and bewilderment and awakening lust.

She said, "Are you going to just stand there?"

For a moment more he looked down at the slender body with its budding breasts discernible beneath the velvet, at her cool greenish eyes and her red-gold hair pulled back from her perfect face. Then he dropped to his knees.

She said, in that same impatient tone, "Go ahead."

Tentatively, he reached out toward the top button of her bodice. "No!"

He drew his hand back as abruptly as if he'd found the button red hot. "We will not risk undressing," she said. "Some of them may come back soon, after all. Just take off my drawers."

Expecting that at any moment the riding crop, lying close to her hand, might lash across his face, he reached up under her skirt with both hands. He discovered that a ladyship's drawers, just like a kitchen maid's, buttoned in front at the waist. Trembling all over now he drew the garment down her legs and over her small booted feet. Dimly he was aware that the drawers were white, with a narrow blue ribbon running through the lace band that cuffed each leg. He dropped the garment onto the straw and then, still shaking, turned back the green velvet skirt.

At sight of her slender thighs, lust overwhelmed his fear. He fumbled with the closure of his breeches and then threw himself upon her. As he lunged back and forth, he was aware of greenish-hazel eyes looking up at him with cool curiosity.

In two or three minutes he reached a shuddering climax and rolled away from her. Now that his desire was slaked, the fear was returning. From the corner of his eye he saw her sit up, straighten her skirt and lie back down again. After a moment he ventured a direct look at her and saw that she had turned her face toward him. He gave her a tentative smile.

Not smiling, she said, "I have heard that losing one's virginity can hurt a great deal. You hurt me scarcely at all. Why was that?"

"Well, your—" He broke off. Surely he shouldn't call her your ladyship now. "If a girl's kind of active like, puts horses over jumps and so on, sometimes she breaks it."

"It? What do you mean by it?"

Did she really not know, or was she teasing him? "There's names for it, but maybe I shouldn't tell you."

"The real name for it, you oaf, is hymen."

Her tone, unlike her words, was reasonably amiable. He felt emboldened enough to ask, "How do you know that's the real word?"

She smiled. "Because I'm a listener."

She had been since she was eight. A listener at doors, both in the family's and the servants' quarters. During summer house parties, when there was much coming and going between bedrooms in the after-midnight hours, she became a listener on the terrace that ran past a long row of guest rooms.

And in the past two years she had become a prowler in her father's library. She was not quite thirteen when, about to enter the library one day, she saw him atop the tall ladder which moved on a track around three sides of the book-lined room. He was placing something behind books on the top shelf. She had withdrawn from the doorway before he could see her. And the next time he was in London, attending a session of the House of Lords, she had climbed the ladder in the library and found the little cinnabar box with the key inside it. Even before she tried the key she had been sure that it opened the always-locked wooden cabinet beside the huge stone fireplace.

The cabinet was filled with pornographic books, most of them illustrated. Not just English books, but translations of books from China, Japan, and India. Each time the earl went to London, Diane entered the library and, with its double doors barred, read her father's forbidden books. Her favorite remained an Indian one, with its detailed drawings of different ways for a man and woman to couple.

Now, with her gaze traveling down Jed's sturdy frame, she thought, next time I'll make him try out at least four of those positions.

He sensed the direction of her thoughts. Grinning, he cupped a hand over one of her small breasts. She said coolly, "I won't risk it. Someone might come back. Now help me up."

She got to her feet. With him supporting her, she drew on her underclothing. She put on her hat and tied its veil under her chin. "Now brush me off. Be sure you get all the straw."

Together they walked back to the stable yard, where her

unsaddled horse stood at the hitching post. She turned to face Jed.

"Do you know that clearing in the woods about a quarter of a mile beyond Gebe Pond?"

Sure of what she would say next, he grinned and nodded.

"I want you to meet me there tomorrow afternoon at two o'clock. Tell the head groom you're sick or have to see a relative in the village. Tell him anything."

His grinned widened. "I'll be there."

When she again spoke her voice was so cold and vicious that he paled.

"You just can't wait to tell the others here in the stable, can you?"

"Oh, no, miss—your ladyship. I'd never tell!"

"You won't if you have any sense. Because if I even *suspect* that you've told, do you know what I'll do to you? I will tell my father that you raped me. And do you know what would happen to a stableboy who has raped an earl's daughter?" She herself was not sure, but she went on, "If they didn't hang you, they'd shut you away in prison for the rest of your life."

He said, meaning it, "I'll never tell. So help me, I'll never tell." He was white to the lips now.

"You meet me tomorrow. If you don't, I'll suspect that you've told."

She walked out of the stable yard and then up a tree-bordered lane toward the sprawling stone house on the hill.

Jed did meet her in the woods the next day. But terror had overwhelmed all his adolescent lustiness. Frustrated, Diane tried to arouse him, using her hands and mouth in ways depicted in those books of her father's. He remained limp. As he saw the growing anger in her eyes, terror grew in his.

He disappeared that night from the quarters he shared with three other grooms in the stable loft. The head groom, who had considered him a likely lad—a hard worker and good with the horses—went to his parents's house in the village to see if he was there. Jed had been there and left, they told him. The previous night he had come to their cottage before midnight and told them that he was going to walk the thirty miles to Weymouth and find a berth aboard an outbound ship. Despite all their protests, he had packed his few belongings in an old hand trunk and left.

The head groom knew that the earl preferred him to act on his own in such inconsequential matters, and so he merely waited until someone else, an undersized boy of twelve, came along to fill the job.

Diane, coming to the stable for her daily rides, of course noticed Jed's continued absence, and drew—correctly—her own conclusions.

More than a year passed before she found another sexual partner. It was no use for her to hope to find one among boys of her own class. The parties and picnics attended by sons and daughters of the local gentry were too well chaperoned for that. But at Graytowers it was a different matter. Her mother had died shortly after giving birth to Diane, the youngest of her three children. Her father was often away and even when at home was too occupied with other matters to pay much attention to her. Her brothers, who might have become aware of her proclivities, were both at Oxford. Her Parisian-born governess, who had taught Diane her flawless French, was aging now, and stayed on at Graytowers only in the hope of receiving a nice pension from the earl. She seldom ventured out of her own quarters, even taking most of her meals in her own comfortable sitting room. Thus when Diane took her second lover, no one with any authority over her was aware of it.

He was William Crane, a newly-hired footman. He was

twenty-four years old and a Cockney. He was thin, had straight black hair, and was handsome in a sharp-featured sort of way, although not as handsome as he considered himself. He was quite aware that good-looking servants sometimes caught the eye of women of the middle and upper classes. In London he had been, for six months, the bed partner of one of his employers, the widow of a rich tea importer. And so he was pleased, but not astonished, when the fifteen-year-old daughter of the ninth Earl of Braithwaite began to look at him with unmistakable invitation in her eyes.

They held their trysts in the late mornings, when the rest of the staff was busy on the lower floors. There in his tiny room in the servants' quarters up under the ancient eaves, bodies gleaming with sweat in the light that came through the one narrow window, they experimented with various couplings pictured in the books in her father's locked cabinet. More than once, William was shocked by her suggestions, enough so that if she had been a girl of his own class he would have "told her off, and not by 'arf." As it was, he kept quiet and did as she asked.

Their relationship lasted for about eight months. Then he began to make excuses not to see her. As they dressed after their lovemaking, he would say that for the next day or so the major domo would be expecting him to do certain tasks in the morning. Once he said that the estate carpenter would be in his room the following day, mending a leak around the window frame.

One day Diane climbed to the third floor, where various upper servants—the major domo, the housekeeper, and Diane's elderly governess—had their rooms. She moved to the rear staircase and waited.

Finally she heard a door open and close on the floor above. Then she heard William's low voice and a girl's giggle. Retreating several feet down the corridor, Diane flattened herself against the wall. She saw William and a coarsely pretty brunette girl, probably a new kitchen maid, since Diane had never seen her before, appear on the landing and then continue on down the backstairs.

Half an hour later in her sitting room, Diane rang for Daisy, her personal maid, a most undaisylike seventeen-year-old with freckles and flaming red hair. "Find William and send him here."

"William, your ladyship!" Daisy was not very bright, which was the main reason Diane had chosen her.

"You know him. He's a footman, the one from London."

"You want him to come *here*, your ladyship?" Daisy found it incomprehensible that Lady Diane should want to confer with a footman anywhere, let alone in her own sitting room.

"Yes, here. Immediately."

When she faced William a few minutes later she knew, from the look in his eyes, both uneasy and defiant, that he had guessed why she had sent for him. She said, without preamble, "Pack your things and get out."

"Now look 'ere, my girl. *You* can't give me the sack."

"I see. You would prefer to have my father do it."

He grinned. "Don't try to bluff me. You don't want 'im to know what you been h'up to."

"You're the one who would be blamed. You're the one who would go to prison."

But William was older and far more sophisticated than Jed had been. "I'd 'ave to go to trial first. You think 'is Lordship would want to h'it known 'is daughter's been in a footmen's kip? Not bloody likely!"

"Perhaps not. But it's more than bloody likely that he would hire men to horsewhip you within an inch of your life, and perhaps a little beyond."

William paled. Then he took a step toward her and said, "Aw, don't take that h'attitude. You think that bit 'o fluff meant anything to me?"

"I don't know. I only know, miserable as you are, you've belonged to me. And I don't share with anyone, let alone a slut from the scullery. Now get out."

Without giving notice, William left the next morning.

The next of her lovers did not arrive at Graytowers until Diane was seventeen. Even though her governess had long since abdicated all but nominal authority over her charge, it was she who suggested to the earl that he hire someone to develop "Diane's very real artistic talent." The earl did not see that his daughter's watercolors of flowers and of weeping willows beside ponds looked any better than those painted by other young gentlewomen. But he also, on the rare occasions when he was with her, sensed a disturbing quality in his daughter, something that he chose to think of as "a certain restlessness." Now that she apparently had absorbed all that her governess could give her in the way of an education—an education that had consisted of the French and German languages, English history, and English and French literature, or at least the morally acceptable novels and poetry in both languages—now that she had completed all that, perhaps it would be well to have something to take up her energies until she was safely married.

Accordingly, he gave the governess permission to engage an art instructor. Of the several individuals who answered the advertisement she placed in the county's weekly newspaper, she chose Gilbert Bakewell, nephew of the curate in a village four miles away. Thin and blond and with a sensitive face, he looked considerably younger than his thirty years.

The first time he came to Diane's sitting room to give her a two-hour lesson, she made it quite clear—smiling into his

110

eyes, brushing against him as they stood at the easel—what she wanted of him. Even though his hand holding the paint brush trembled, he managed to continue instructing in the art of draughtsmanship, perspective, and color values. Before he left he resolved to write a note to the governess, saying that he no longer would be available to give lessons to Lady Diane Weston.

He did not, of course. Instead in the several days interval his fantasies about his pupil grew more and more heated, until he felt he could not wait for the moment when he would hold her naked body in his arms. Within ten minutes after his arrival, Diane had locked the door to the hall and they had retreated from the sitting room to her bedroom. From then on, that was where they spent most of his allotted two hours at Graytowers.

Gilbert's middle class background was not the chief difference between him and the predecessors in Diane's life. The chief difference was that he loved her. He wrote poems, not only to her hair and eyes and lips, but to her ears and wrists and feet. ("That high-arched foot that treads upon my heart.") He wanted desperately to marry her, and when she kept telling him that her father would never allow it, Gilbert began to talk of various legendary lovers who had chosen to leap hand-in-hand from volcanoes, or from cliffs into raging seas. Perhaps, Gilbert suggested, if they could not be together always in life, they should seek eternal union in death—

Amused, Diane let him talk.

They had been lovers for about five months when, one afternoon, a key rattled in the lock of the hall door. Footsteps crossed the sitting room. Then the earl stood tall and gaunt-faced in the bedroom doorway.

He glanced at his daughter and then fixed his gaze on the

curate's nephew. "Get up and get dressed. Then come down to the library." He turned and walked out.

How was it, Diane wondered, that her father had become suspicious? Probably because of something one of the servants had told him. But she was sure that her father would never tell her which one it had been.

Stumbling in his haste, Gilbert got dressed. "Don't worry, my darling. Perhaps this is all for the best. He will have to let us marry now."

Sure that she would never see Gilbert again, she watched him with regretful eyes. She would miss him.

When the earl returned to his daughter about an hour later, she was looking out one of her sitting room windows. She turned to face him.

"What did you do to him?"

"I gave him his choice. I told him that if he stayed in England I would make life difficult for him in every way I could. I also told him that his uncle would have to surrender the curacy of the village church. I control that living, you know."

"I know. But you said you gave Gilbert a choice."

The earl nodded. "I told him that if he would leave England I would pay him a thousand pounds, immediately. He's going to Australia. It seems he has relatives there."

After a moment she asked, "What do you intend to do to me?"

His voice was grim. "You're going to marry, just as soon as I can arrange it. Then no matter how outrageously you behave, your conduct will no longer be considered my responsibility."

"Have you selected a bridegroom?"

"You'll marry Sir Ralph Harding."

"Ralph Harding! Why, he doesn't like women."

"So you know that, do you?" He had a feeling that there

was very little that this appalling daughter of his had not managed to find out in her seventeen years. "It is true that Harding is not interested in women. But he's interested in money. In fact, he needs it desperately. He's up to his ears in debt."

"Father, you can't force me to marry Ralph Harding or anyone else."

"That's true. But it is also true that I can cut you off without a cent. I am a very rich man, Diane. Of course, the bulk of my estate, including Graytowers, will go to Clarence." Clarence was the elder of her two brothers. "But even so, there will still be eight hundred thousand pounds to be divided between you and your other brother. That is, if you marry Harding."

Diane had no great objection to Sir Ralph, a pleasant, balding man in his late thirties. And she did have a great objection to being penniless. "All right. I'll marry him."

With great pomp, they were married in one of London's most fashionable churches two days after Diane's eighteenth birthday.

All in all, it had been a successful marriage. With the allowances the earl had granted them, she and Sir Ralph were able to travel where they liked, sometimes together, but more often separately. In the fourth year of her marriage, her father died. After that they were able to indulge in almost any sort of extravagance, including a multiplicity of dwellings. Besides their house in London, they bought a villa near Rome, and acquired a ten-year lease on a flat in Paris.

Whenever they were together, she and Ralph got along famously. Ralph took an interest in her clothes and helped her to select them. They exchanged malicious anecdotes about the people they knew, and intimate details about their lovers. Once to their amusement they discovered that a man in Rome with whom she had gone to bed the previous May had been Sir Ralph's bedmate two months later.

She was twenty-three when something happened to her that she had not known was possible. She fell in love.

It happened in Berlin, at a large house party in a mansion on the city's outskirts. Nominally, the man was a French citizen. He had been born in Alsace-Lorraine, that province, currently in French hands, over which Germany and France had squabbled for generations. But his name, Karl Schiller, was Germanic, and so was his appearance. More than six feet tall, he had yellow hair, eyes the deep blue of summer seas, and a square-jawed face.

It was a glittering house party, made up of beautiful women and of men who were handsome or distinguished or both. Karl Schiller was not only the handsomest man there, but he was the most devastatingly attractive man Diane had ever seen.

From the time of his arrival early in the afternoon, she tried everything, short of resorting to blunt words, to make him aware that she desired him. At supper she kept smiling at him across the long table laden with hothouse flowers and silver candelabra and crystal wine glasses. Later, in the ballroom, where an orchestra played German and Austrian waltzes, she kept smiling up at him as he whirled her about the floor. What, she wondered with growing frustration, was wrong with him? In spite of his appearance, in spite of her instant and instinctive response to him, could it be that he was homosexual?

By one in the morning she was in her room. In a sheer green nightgown she sat at her dressing table, brushing her hair with strokes made more vigorous by her sense of rejection.

The door opened behind her. In the mirror, she saw Karl Schiller walk toward her. She leaped to her feet and turned.

She said, past the pulse pounding in her throat, "I don't remember asking you here."

"It's odd that you don't remember. You've been asking me in a number of ways for hours now."

He reached out with his right hand. None too gently, his thumb pressed into one of her cheeks and his forefinger into the other.

"But let us get one thing straight at the beginning. I did not come here because you wanted me to. I came here because *I* wanted to. Do you understand that?"

She felt a sense of weakness, almost faintness. "Yes."

He let go of her face then. He took a step backward, pushed her gown off her shoulders, and let the garment fall. She stood there, face pale now, and glad as she had ever been before that her small breasts were high and firm, her waist small, and her legs slender and tapering.

As easily as if she had been a child, he lifted her and carried her over to the bed. Aware that her body was already melting inwardly with its need for him, she lay with closed eyes while he undressed. She, who had always found it amusing to watch a new and sometimes rather embarrassed lover take off his clothes.

The bed gave to his weight. She opened her eyes then, and saw that his face, with its cool blue eyes, rested on his elbow-propped hand. She looked at his powerful shoulders, the skin gleaming with good health, at his broad chest with its curling hair, then at his erection, which gave proof of how much he wanted her. She heard her own soft moan. His hand, probing between her legs, found moist evidence that she was ready for him. Then he was upon her, thrusting deep. Within only moments she was shuddering with released tension and simultaneously feeling the throb of his own climax.

He left her and lay with his hands linked beneath his head.

Looking up at the ceiling he said, "Next time we will take it more slowly, much more slowly."

Minutes later, she found out what he meant by slowly. Lips closing warm and moist around one of her nipples and then the other, hand brushing her inner thighs and fastening over the red-gold triangle where her legs joined, he soon had her moaning for the release that only his thrusting body could bring her. But he denied her that release, pushing her back onto the pillow when, in her desperation, she tried to draw his body onto hers. He went on, teasing her erect nipples with lips and tongue, thrusting a finger into her only to withdraw it, raising her desire to a pitch that was not pleasure but torment. She had a feeling that he played upon her body, her senses, as he might have upon a musical instrument. Even when he at last was inside her, he stopped moving just as she was about to find release.

She moaned then, and called him a bastard, and he said, "All right. All right, now."

He thrust into her again and again, until the very core of her seemed to open like a flower, letting the shudders of satisfied passion ripple down her body in a more ecstatic release than she had known was possible.

When again he lay beside her she said, "Why—why did you keep denying me—"

"Because I find it fun that way. And because I wanted you to know which of us is the master. Besides, you enjoyed it, didn't you?"

She said faintly, "Yes. Oh, God, yes." Then, after a moment: "This house party will break up day after tomorrow. Where will you go then?"

"Back to France. Rheims, to be exact. I'll be there a few weeks."

"I'm going with you."

"That would be awkward. I will be traveling with three other men, business associates."

Right then it did not occur to her to ask him what sort of business he was in. It was only later that he told her that he was the traveling representative of a wine company. She said, "I'll meet you in Rheims."

"Why? From what I've heard, you've never lacked for men."

"You know why I want to be with you, why I'll always want to be with you."

He laughed. "Are you suggesting that we marry? According to my information, you are already married to an English baronet."

"I just mean I want to be with you." After a moment she added, "You are not married, are you?"

"No. But when I do marry, it will be for the sake of having children. And you don't strike me, Lady Diane, as the motherly sort."

She said again, "I just want to be with you."

"All right. Come to Rheims, if you like. But not until two weeks from now. I want to devote my first days there entirely to business."

For the next few months she was with him every moment he allowed her to be. She followed him to Vienna, Geneva, and Paris. Even when she was not with him she did not sleep with other men, although she realized that to Karl it was a matter of indifference whether or not she did. It was just that she knew that, after Karl, she would find other men irritatingly inadequate.

In the late winter of 1869, in Paris, he told her that he was going to the United States for perhaps as long as a year, and that she could not come with him. "I will be traveling all over the country, taking orders for wine. America is a puritanical country, Diane, probably because it was founded mainly by lower middle class Englishmen. In Europe, at least in certain circles, a relationship such as ours is tolerated. In America it would not be."

"We could travel separately! In hotels we could occupy separate rooms."

"My dear, no matter how careful we were, the chances are overwhelming that we would be found out. I can imagine the outraged Presbyterian owner of a hotel in Philadelphia tearing up his wine order in front of my face. I shall not risk that, my dear, just because you are unwilling to endure a temporary separation."

Because she did not know what else to do, she stayed on in Paris after Karl sailed for New York. Feeling like a ghost, she went to restaurants where she and Karl had gone, and sat for hours on a bench beside the Seine because a few times they had sat there. Used to unbridled sensual indulgence, she found chastity not at all to her liking. At the same time she was sure that going to bed with other men would only increase her longing for Karl.

One afternoon in her private carriage, she found herself passing Number Fourteen, Rue de Adele. Her husband, one time when they drove down this street, had told her about Number Fourteen. "I've heard that the tarts there are trained to look and act like young peeresses. Customers can imagine they are at one of those chic English house parties, where it is considered positively gauche to sleep with your own wife rather than someone else's."

Sir Ralph had giggled. "Perhaps you should try working there. That is one experience you haven't had." His voice became wistful. "I wish I could work there."

She had laughed and thought no more about it. But now the idea lingered in her mind. It *would* be a new experience, one so novel that it might distract her from her obsessive thoughts of Karl. Never mind that even Karl might be shocked by her taking such a course. It would serve him right for having left her here alone.

She began to think seriously of the idea. True, she was well known in some international circles. It might be that she would find herself face to face with a customer who had known her as Lady Diane Harding, nee Weston, daughter of the ninth Earl of Braithwaite. In that case she would say blandly that others had commented upon her striking resemblance to a titled Englishwoman. Yes, that would be a good idea. She might even say, too, that she had hennaed her hair slightly so that it would be closer to the Englishwoman's reddish blond shade.

On a bleak February afternoon, with the outbreak of the Franco-Prussian war almost half a year in the future, Diane sat in Madame Theraux's small office off the salon, silent and empty now and with its rich velvet draperies drawn. She could tell that something about her made the Frenchwoman uneasy. Perhaps it was Diane's manner, her air of self-assurance usually observed in those born to privilege. But Madame Theraux did not challenge Diane's assertion that her last name was Gautier and that her father had been a railway clerk in Nice.

And anyway, Madame Theraux was too good a businesswoman to reject someone who, with her beauty and her air of breeding, could become the establishment's leading attraction. And at last she said, "Very well, Mademoiselle Gautier. You may come here for, let us say, three nights. If by then we are both satisfied with the arrangement, it will continue."

Even before the three nights were up, her clients' comments about the new young lady made Madame Theraux realize that she had been wise indeed not to reject her. As for

Diane, she wanted to continue coming to the salon, not every night, but as often as she chose to. True, the men she met there never came close to arousing her sexually, let alone satisfying her. But having them pay her, and pay well, for her favors brought her another sort of satisfaction. She could feel that she was taking revenge upon them for being foolish and inadequate—for being, in short, not Karl.

And she could feel, too, that in doing something of which he probably would not approve she was revenging herself on Karl. Revenging herself for his having turned her, who had always dominated men, into a helpless creature he could do with as he liked. Revenging herself on him, most of all, for not taking her with him.

Perhaps men sensed that her willpower, challenged and subdued by Karl, was reasserting itself in his absence. Whatever the reason, she found herself especially sought after by those of Madame Theraux's clientele who needed to experience humiliation or even a certain amount of pain in order to find sexual release. Such clients paid her exceptionally well. And that pleased her, too, even though she had no need for the money, even though, in fact, she was probably richer than all but a few of the men who visited Number Fourteen, Rue de Adele.

Then one spring night, when she had been coming to Madame Theraux's a little more than three months, she looked across the salon and saw Karl Schiller making his way toward her through the crowed of middle-aged and elderly men and bare-shouldered, perfectly coiffed women.

Rigid, face drained of color she waited for him. Oh, God! How was it he was back in Paris so soon? She had intended to stop coming to this place well before the year of his absence was up.

What would he say to her? He would say something shatteringly cruel, and then he would walk out and she would never see him again. She was certain of it.

He bowed slightly and said in a low voice, "Get your cloak. We are leaving."

Moments later, as they stepped into the cool night, he asked, "Do you still have that flat near the Etoile?"

"Yes."

She became aware that the driver of a carriage, which stood at the curb, had gotten down and opened the door for them. Doubtless it was the carriage in which he had arrived. Had he asked the driver to wait because he had known he would find her at Madame Theraux's? Or had he, when he entered the establishment, intended merely to select a woman quickly and leave with her? The thought brought her an almost physical pain in the region of her heart.

"Then we'll go to your flat," he said.

In the cab's dark interior a few minutes later she asked, "Did you know you might find me there?"

"Yes."

She wanted to say, "And what do you intend to do about it?" but she was afraid to. Instead she asked, "How did you know I was there?"

"After my ship docked at Calais last night I took the train to Paris. In the smoking car I met a man I know slightly. He told me that there was now a French girl named Diane something-or-other at Madame Theraux's and that she was supposed to have a remarkable resemblance to a notorious English peeress."

They were crossing the bridge. Vaguely she was aware of the gas lamps' wavering reflections on the Seine's black water. "Why—why did you cut your stay in America so short?"

"I had good reasons."

121

She waited a moment and then found she had enough courage to say, "Karl, you must tell me! What are you going to do about my being at that place?"

"I will tell you, but later. I want to deal with first things first."

When they entered her flat, she learned what he meant by first things first. Arm around her waist, he drew her into the bedroom. Swiftly and expertly he undressed her. Then, on the bed, he soon brought her to such a state of desire that she cried aloud when, at long last, his big, lunging body brought her release.

After awhile, lying there in the room illuminated only by the refracted glow of the gaslights in the flat's salon, she said, "This must mean that I am—forgiven. It does mean that, doesn't it?"

"Forgiven? For what?"

"Why, for going to that house on the Rue de Adele!" She added swiftly, "I'm not really sure why I started going there." That was a lie, of course. She could recall very well what had sent her to Madame Theraux—the loneliness, the desire for some sort of secret revenge on the man who now lay naked beside her. She added, "But of course, tonight was the last time."

"No, it wasn't. I want you to keep attending."

For a moment she lay stunned and silent. Then she cried, "You *want* me to go? You actually like the idea that other men—"

"Do you expect me to be jealous? Oh, I might be if I thought you enjoyed those men. But I'm sure you don't, at least not the way you enjoyed yourself with me a few minutes ago."

He paused, and then added, "And your presence there can help me. I realized that almost as soon as the man on the train began talking about the new girl at Theraux's.'"

She said dazedly, "Help you!"

Head resting on his elbow-propped hand, he looked down at her. "It's time I told you something. It is quite true that I am a sales representative for a large wine company. But I also have another employer, the Prussian government."

She said, after a long moment, "Do you mean you are spying for the Prussians?"

"Exactly."

"But you are a Frenchman!" It was not a reproach. She merely was trying to understand.

"I am a French citizen, yes. But only because Alsace-Lorraine is, at the moment, a French possession. In every other way I am Germanic—my name, my ancestry, and my loyalties."

He went on, his voice hardening, "And Alsace-Lorraine will be German again, just as it was for most of the time from the fifth century to the French Revolution. When the coming war ends, France will have no territory on the other side of the Rhine."

"There's—going to be a war? Between the French and Germans?"

"Yes, and soon. I don't know just when, but soon. I hear that Bismarck hopes to trick the French into declaring war first. That way Prussia will have the sympathy of the rest of Europe, right from the beginning." His blue eyes held an intensity she had never seen there. "And out of the war will come a united Germany, ready to fulfill her destiny."

She said, feeling chilled and yet excited, "What destiny?"

"Why, to become the most powerful nation in Europe, of course."

She was silent for several moments. Then she asked, "Does all this have anything to do with your returning from the United States sooner than you expected?"

"It does. I was in Milwaukee when a letter reached me, asking me to return to Paris as soon as possible."

"A letter from—"

"From the Prussian agent who is my direct superior. It was in code, of course, and appeared to be a request for the prices of various vintages of wine."

She said, after an interval, "And there is some way you want me to help you?"

"Yes. Will you?"

Looking up at him, she knew that even if she had been born French rather than English, she would have done as he asked. "What do you want me to do?"

"Many of the most important men in France frequent Theraux's. Among them are army officials, armament contractors and politicians. Learn what you can from them. From time to time, I'll give you instructions as to specific information we need. For instance, the French army has a secret weapon called the *mitrailleuse*. It is a kind of French version of the American Gatling gun, a bundle of twenty-five barrels. By turning a crank, the gunner can fire the barrels in rapid succession. We want to know how many of those weapons the French have, and how many gunners have been trained to fire them. But more of such matters later on. Right now I want to know if you will do this for me."

"Do you have to ask?"

He leaned over and kissed her mouth.

She said, "How long will you be in Paris?"

"Several days. Then I must go to Berlin. But I will be back from time to time."

During the next few months he had visited Paris frequently. Sometimes she came home to find he had let himself into her flat with the key she had given him. Other times she did not know he was back in Paris until she saw him at Madame Theraux's. The most exciting aspect of her evenings there was the thought that at any moment she might see him moving toward her with head and shoulders rising above the crowd.

Almost always she had information for him. A procurement officer for the French army had told her that a crooked uniform manufacturer had substituted flimsy cloth for the sturdy material called for in his government contract, with the result that French troops would be shivering in anything but the mildest weather. From her architect friend, he of the nervous blushes, she learned that sub-standard concrete had been used to repair some of the defensive forts beyond the walls of Paris. And only days before the vain-glorious French obliged a gleeful Bismarck by declaring war on Prussia, she was able tell Karl that the *mitrailleuse* was indeed a secret weapon, so secret that in all of France only a handful of men had been trained to fire it!

And in the days since France, overthrowing the government of poor, defeated Louis Napoleon, had declared itself a republic, she'd had even more information to pass on to Karl. Information about the squabbles in the Hotel de Ville and of the men who now governed France. Information about the likelihood of the "unreliable" working class regiments of the National Guard being allowed arms. Information as to which of Madame Theraux's clients, in Diane's opinion, might be willing to take a Prussian bribe.

By design, Karl had been in Paris when its encirclement by the Prussians became complete. She was glad indeed. Perhaps now he would leave the two rooms he maintained in Montmartre for his stays in Paris and move into her spacious flat. But when she suggested it he said, "No, Diane. I will

125

have callers from time to time."

She could guess what sort of callers. Supposed neutrals—Swiss citizens, for instance, or Italian or English—who were actually in Prussian pay. Such men could pass freely back and forth through the Prussian lines and in and out of the French-guarded city gates.

Disappointed as she was that he would not live with her, she felt that at least now she would see him more often.

On this late September night, as out of a kind of half-bored curiosity she tried to extract information from Madame Theraux about the continued absence of the American girl, she kept glancing toward the salon entrance, hoping to see Karl walk in. Instead it was the architect moving purposefully toward her. "Excuse me, madame," Diane said and turned to greet him.

He kissed her hand. "You look especially lovely tonight, mademoiselle."

She thanked him then moved with him to a settee covered in red brocade. She knew that, as always, he would want to spend at least half an hour in polite conversation before suggesting that they leave. It was as if he found it hard to face that other self, the self that would soon lie whimpering false entreaties on the floor, while the hand he had just kissed grasped the handle of a whip.

She looked around and then signaled to one of the tray-carrying maids. As the girl approached, Diane noticed fleetingly that she was the very young one, surely still in her teens, with a round, pretty face that gave an impression of baby fat.

Diane and the architect removed champagne glasses from the silver tray. He said, looking around him, "That rather plump girl with the red hair. I don't see her."

"Helene? Madame had to dismiss her. I gather she had become too fond of the bottle."

"But surely that was not the case with the American young lady with the dark hair and gray eyes, and yet I don't see her either."

"You mean Maggie MacNeil." Diane thought of the girl sitting at the Champs-Elysees café, her smile a little tremulous with love as she looked at the rangy man opposite her.

Diane laughed. "Mademoiselle MacNeil is entertaining her aunt from America."

Chapter 8

Two nights after that evening when Diane had seen them at the Champs-Elysees café, Richard Glover told Maggie that in the morning he would catch the boat train and then cross the channel to make sketches of the English Parliament's opening ceremonies. With helpless dismay she realized what a cowardly procrastinator she was. Desperate in her love for him, she had not as yet devised a way of forcing him leave her.

When he took her home to her flat at the end of their last evening together, he lost some of his self-imposed restraint. Feeling the ardor of his arms and lips, Maggie longed for him to lose all his control, longed for him to be lying with her in her bed. But if that happened, she would surely find herself telling him that which she would almost die rather than have him know.

She broke free of him. He caught her hands. "Please, Maggie! I love you. Surely you've guessed that."

Heart swelling with tormented joy, she looked up at him silently. He said, "I want to marry you."

Hating herself for not having sent him away long before this, she withdrew her hand.

"What is it, Maggie?" Anxiety and hurt were in the gray eyes in the ruggedly handsome face. "Somehow I had gotten the feeling that you cared for me, too."

Helplessly, she nodded.

"Then is it just that I have spoken too soon? I realize we haven't known each other long."

"Yes," she managed to say, "it's too soon."

A relieved smile lit up his face. "Then we'll talk about it again around ten days from now, when I'm back from London."

He kissed her again, very gently, and went down the stairs.

That night she lay awake until dawn. Thank God, she kept thinking, that he would be gone as long as ten days. Maybe he would believe her story that right after he left she had met another man, a man with whom she had fallen swiftly and utterly in love.

And once she had ended her relationship with Richard completely, what would she do with the rest of her life?

Stoically, she resolved that she would do exactly what she had planned to do when she left New York with Danson Hayworth. She would pile up money, enough of it that she would be rich and invulnerable by the time she was thirty. And the quickest way to add to her already sizable savings was to continue at Madame Theraux's.

But she found herself unable to go there the next night, or the one after that. In fact, nearly a week passed before she finally appeared, dressed in a plain black velvet evening gown which made her beauty all the more startling, at Number Fourteen, Rue de Adele. Madame Theraux, who seldom showed any warmth whatever, said, "I am glad you are back, Maggie." Jeanne-Marie, the round-faced little maid, said, "I have missed you, mademoiselle."

"Thank you, Jeanne-Marie. How is your little boy?"

"He is splendid, mademoiselle." Jeanne-Marie spoke as little as possible to the other young ladies and never would have dreamed of telling them of Marcel's existence. But one night she had found herself confiding to the American girl that she had a son more than a year old.

Carrying a tray laden with triangular pieces of toast and a crystal bowl of caviar on a bed of ice, Jeanne-Marie turned away. Maggie went to the high-backed settee where she often sat. She looked around. Helene, the plump redhead addicted to brandy, was not there and Maggie assumed that she had been dismissed. All the other girls seemed present, though, including Diane Gautier. She stood talking to a tall, extremely handsome blond man who had visited Madame Theraux's a number of times, always taking Diane Gautier away with him. Always, too, the blond man's presence seemed to bring to Diana's usually cool, aloof face the same intensity it had now as she stood looking up at him.

Then Maggie, turning her head, saw that portly Monsieur Chalon, a frequent client of hers, was moving toward her and she forgot everything else.

With horror she recalled how his paps hung down, almost like a woman's breasts. She recalled that in bed he insisted upon calling her Rachel, because that was the name of a girl, a friend of his daughter's, whom he lusted after, so far to no avail. And she recalled now, after his brief and grunting possession of her body, he would insist that she still lie there and listen to his troubles. His extravagant wife, his two worthless sons-in-law and his son who wanted to be an opera singer—an opera singer!—instead of joining his father's bank.

And suddenly she knew that she could not go through that again. Not ever again. Not after those wonderful, bittersweet days with a man she loved.

She sprang to her feet. "Forgive me, Monsieur Chalon, but I am feeling ill, frightfully ill."

Stomach knotted, gaze lowered, she hurried toward the cloakroom—and almost collided with someone. Looking up she saw that it was the tall blond man with Diane Gautier clinging to his arm.

"Oh, forgive me, monsieur!"

Dark blue eyes scanned her face appreciatively. Then he said, "Not at all, mademoiselle. In fact, it was a pleasure."

Maggie moved on toward the cloakroom. When she emerged, wrapped in an ermine-trimmed black velvet mantle, she found Madame Theraux standing a few feet away.

"Madame, I am sorry, but I must leave. I am not well."

The older woman looked at her coldly. She had seen Maggie's reaction to the banker and had realized its significance. It was not the first time that a protégé of hers, a girl capable of a really brilliant career in harlotry, had ruined everything for herself by falling in love.

But there was no point in talking to the girl now. She was too distraught. "Very well, Maggie."

In Diane's private carriage, which they had entered only moments before, Karl Schiller said, "That girl in the black dress, the one who ran into me. Who is she?"

"You must have seen her there other nights."

"That is not an answer to my question. Of course I have seen her before, but not close up, so to speak. Now, who is she?"

"Her name is Maggie MacNeil."

"American?"

"Yes."

"She has an extraordinarily lovely face, really extraordinary. And there is something there—oh, maybe a hint of tragedy—that makes her all the more appealing."

In the darkness, Diane clenched her hands until her pointed nails bit into her palms. Was he really attracted to the

American girl, attracted enough that he might—

The possessiveness she had always felt, the possessiveness that had made her threaten her footman-lover with horse-whipping because she had seen him with the scullery maid, rose like gall into her throat. But there are differences now. In the first place, her jealousy was ten-fold greater. In the second place, she dared not threaten Karl with horsewhipping, or displease him in any way, lest she lose him.

But she need not bottle up her jealous rage entirely, leaving it to fester inside her. Surely she could think of some way to make the American girl pay for having caught Karl's attention.

Moving through the unseasonably warm darkness, the carriage passed the dark bulk of the Tuileries and turned onto the Rue de Rivoli with its long arcade of shops. Suddenly she smiled. Of course! Unless she was badly mistaken, *that* was the way to punish Maggie MacNeil, punish her enough that she might slink back to wherever it was she came from in America.

Karl said, "What did you learn from Delescluse the other night?" Delescluse, a client of Madame Theraux's, was an army general.

"The government is planning what it will call a 'grand sortie' out of Paris. French troops will try to break through the Prussian lines and link up with French army units in the provinces."

"When?"

"I couldn't learn any definite date. But probably it is not to be until December. And they will use just regular troops. They are still too afraid to arm the National Guard."

"The fools. They should make their grand sortie as soon as possible and use every man they've got. The Prussians are strengthening their lines every day. By December not even a

French field mouse will be able to get through."

He lapsed into silence. After awhile Diane said, "Will you spend the night with me?"

"I'm sorry, but I can't. In fact, I was about to ask you to drop me off at my place in Montmarte. A Swiss friend is coming there to see me tonight, in about an hour."

So his only purpose in coming to her tonight had been to learn whatever she had found out from the French general so that he could pass it on to another agent.

On a steep Montmarte street she said goodnight to him at the curb in front of his house and then rode to her own flat. As soon as she entered it, she went into the bedroom, opened the door of a little rosewood cabinet beside her bed, and took out a bottle of laudanum and a glass. She measured the laudanum into the glass and diluted it with water from a carafe atop the stand. Karl, who despised any kind of weakness, had warned her against laudanum. But tonight, frustrated and angry, she knew that she would not sleep without it.

Glass in hand, she sat on the bed's edge, brooding over the girl Karl had admired and the Swiss "friend" who was keeping him away from her right now. Well, there was nothing she could do about the Swiss, but Maggie MacNeil was quite a different matter.

Beginning to feel relaxed she continued sipping from her glass.

Chapter 9

Hurrying home across the city, Jeanne-Marie, too, thought of the American girl. Strange how she had rushed away tonight, only minutes after she arrived. Her white face had held a look of revulsion, as if she might be literally sick if she did not leave at once.

But come to think of it, Jeanne-Marie had never felt that Maggie MacNeil really belonged among Madame Theraux's young ladies, anymore than she herself would have. Often she had wondered what sort of earlier experiences had brought the American girl to such an establishment.

She crossed the Place de l'Opera and turned up her street. A few minutes later a man said, as he pushed past her, "Good evening, pretty one."

She said nothing, just kept moving ahead. Then he was walking along beside her. She caught the odor of brandy. "Don't you want company? Pretty girl like you, out alone this time of night—"

She was not frightened, her house was only a few steps away. Besides, this sometimes happened to her, even though she wore the plainest of clothing, and when alone, never looked at men she passed.

On this warm night the outer door of her house stood open. Still not looking at the man she went into the lower hall, knocked at the concierge's door, and was admitted. Marcel, used to these nightly transfers from a pallet on the floor to his own bed, did not even wake as she carried him up the long flights of stairs. Nearing the top floor she knew, from the silence, that Charles Maubert was not giving a party tonight. Perhaps he had gone to some other student's party. No, he was home. As she passed his door she heard the scrape of a chair over the floor.

At her own door she shifted her son's relaxed weight onto her shoulder so that she could fish her key out of her reticule. She unlocked the door and closed it behind her. The big room was so sparsely furnished that she had no fear of colliding with a table or chair as she walked across it. She laid the sleeping child in his crib, moved to the table, and lit the oil lamp.

Someone knocked.

Monsieur Lamartine? Perhaps. But he had mentioned to her that he would be having supper at his sister's farm just outside the city walls, and might spend the night there—

Then could it be that for some reason Charles Maubert—?

Heartbeats rapid, she crossed to the door and opened it.

A man stood there, thin, middle-aged, and reeking of brandy. He grinned. "Thought you'd gotten rid of me, didn't you?"

She realized then that he must have entered the house while she, herself, was in the concierge's apartment. Probably he had waited back in the shadowy reaches of the ground floor hall until he saw her start up the stairs. Then he had followed her.

"Get away from here!" she spoke softly for fear of waking Marcel.

"Man climbs all those stairs, you ought to let him in."

He tried to move past her. Still not frightened—she felt he

135

was too drunk to be dangerous—she put her palms against his chest and said loudly, "Go away! Go away!"

Marcel woke, sat up in his small bed, and began to scream. Charles Maubert opened his door and emerged into the hall. He caught the man's arm and spun him around. "What is all this?"

Jeanne-Marie said quickly, "He's just drunk, that's all. But if you could make him go away—" She turned around toward her frightened child. "It's all right, Marcel. It's all right."

She heard Charles say, in a pleasant but firm voice, "You had best find your way home, my friend." She turned back to see him propelling the stranger to the head of the stairs. "Keep moving."

With his hand on the rail, the man began a weaving descent of the stairs. Jeanne-Marie's handsome young neighbor looked after him for a moment and then walked back to her. "You should keep your door locked at night, Madame Perrault."

"After this, I will." She looked back over her shoulder and saw that Marcel, quiet now, stood in his crib, his eyes wide with curiosity. She turned back to Charles. "But you see, I had no idea that he would follow me up here."

He looked down at her. She noticed how the glow from the lamp on the table brought out the golden highlights in his curling, light brown hair. He said, "You should not be surprised, madame, that a man follows you."

Feeling color in her face, she realized that this was the first time she had seen frank admiration in his eyes. Then his gaze went past her and she knew that he was looking at Marcel. When his eyes returned to her face, she saw a hint of ruefulness in their blue depths. What was he thinking? That it was too bad she was burdened with a child, because otherwise he and his young neighbor might have very pleasant times together indeed?

He asked, "Then you are quite all right, madame?"

"Yes, thank you."

Carrying a bag of fresh eggs from his sister's farm, Henri Lamartine emerged onto the landing. The sight of Charles Maubert and Jeanne-Marie together at her open door was like a blow. Well, he had realized all along that the Sorbonne student would not remain indifferent permanently to Jeanne-Marie's soft prettiness.

He said, "Good evening."

Charles Maubert turned around. "Oh, good evening, monsieur. We've just had a little excitement here."

"Excitement?"

"Some drunk followed Madame Perrault right up to her door. You must have passed him on the stair."

"Yes, I did meet a man like that as I was coming up the first flight."

So that explained Maubert's presence in Jeanne-Marie's doorway. Relief mingled with his alarm at the thought of what might have happened to her. "You are sure you are all right?"

"Perfectly."

Charles said, "Well, goodnight, madame, monsieur." He went into his apartment and closed the door.

Lamartine still lingered in the hall. Jeanne-Marie said, "So you didn't stay the night with your sister."

"No, her husband was not well and so I thought it best not to put them to any trouble." He paused. "You should keep your door locked at night."

"I know. Monsieur Maubert told me the same thing." There was self-consciousness in her voice when she spoke the student's name. "Well, goodnight, monsieur."

She went into her room and closed the door. As he walked toward his apartment he heard her key turn in the lock.

He entered the square, plainly furnished sitting room in which he also took his meals. He left the bag of eggs on the oilcloth-covered table long enough to light the lamp. Then he carried the eggs back to the pantry.

Returning to the front room, he sat down in a straight wooden chair. Not really seeing it, he looked around the room, which he had changed scarcely at all during his five years of widowhood.

He would have slain dragons for Jeanne-Marie. And yet he had not been lucky enough even to be on hand to keep a drunk from bothering her. No, that privilege had been young Maubert's.

He loved Jeanne-Marie. He loved her the way he had loved his wife during the first years of their marriage. It was absurd, of course. He would be forty his next birthday. Jeanne-Marie was eighteen. The girl might have been his daughter and her child his grandson.

Old fool, he thought.

To make his emotion for her all the more foolish, she was obviously smitten with Maubert. The Sorbonne student, who already had everything—youth, good looks, a well-to-do family—also had Jeanne-Marie's heart.

Did Maubert know that? Probably not. Probably he had been too busy with his university classes and his friends and his girls and his parties to notice.

And even if he did realize what she felt and decided to take advantage of it, he would think of her as just another girl. The young idiot would never appreciate her gentleness, her courage, or her simple *goodness*. He would never see that she was worth more than all his lax-moraled shopgirls put together. Yes, and worth more than whatever prim bourgeois maiden he someday would marry.

Blind young fool.

Now look who was calling whom a fool.

He got up, went to the pantry and brought back with him an empty paper bag and the one filled with eggs. Carefully he transferred six of the large, lightly freckled brown eggs to the other bag. He would take them to her early in the morning. Early enough that she could cook them for her breakfast and the child's.

Chapter 10

The balmy weather, which was warm for early fall, continued the next day. Around eight that evening Diane walked from her flat to the sidewalk café on the Champs-Elysees. The table where she had seen Maggie and the young man with the American was filled, but the one next to it was empty. She sat down.

When the waiter appeared, a tall, dark man with a prominent adam's apple, she asked, "Do you service that table"—she inclined her head—"as well as this one?"

"Yes, madame."

"Do you recall a young woman, brunette, very beautiful, who sat at that table one night recently? She was with a young man. He was tall, brown-haired, probably an American."

The waiter's eye held a gleam of interest. "So many people come here, madame. One can scarcely be expected to remember—"

She took a ten-franc note from her reticule and laid it on the table. "But I do expect you to remember."

The banknote disappeared swiftly into the pocket of the long white apron he wore. "Yes, I think I do recall them. In fact, they have been here several times. I happened to have overheard enough of their conversation to be able to tell you that they are both American."

"What else can you tell me?"

He waited. She put another banknote on the table. It, too, disappeared. "Thank you, madame. Unfortunately, I do not know their names. But I did gather that the man is a newspaper artist and that he works for some sort of syndicate. I imagine it is the International Press Syndicate. That's the only one I know of with offices here in Paris."

Now that she knew where he was employed it would be quite easy to learn his name.

"I can also tell you," he said, with the air of a man who gives good value for money paid him, "that he probably is in England now but will return shortly. I overheard him talking about such a trip."

She felt like saying, "You have missed your vocation. You should have been a spy." But in this Paris of 1870, he might well be just that.

"Thank you," she said and arose. She walked along the magnificent boulevard, under the still-leafy chestnut trees, to her flat.

For three abjectly miserable days, Maggie did not stir from the small, comfortable flat which Madame Theraux had provided for her. Sometimes she almost wished that Richard Glover had not been in the Bois de Bologne that night. She almost wished it, but not quite. She still could not help being glad that she had been able to love a man like him and be loved in return.

But she still must get through that final meeting with him, that and the years beyond it.

She had decided not to tell him that she had fallen in love with someone she had met during his absence in England. She feared he would not believe that. It would be better to say that she had encountered an old love, someone she had known in America. They had decided that they would marry and return home. Yes, surely that would sound more convincing.

And would she in fact return to America? She did not know.

About eight o'clock, on the evening of the third day after she had walked out of Madame Theraux's establishment, Maggie's door knocker sounded. Heartbeats both rapid and faint, she crossed to the door and opened it.

Richard stood there, white to the lips, gray eyes blazing with accusation. She took a step backward and put one hand to her throat. Immediately she realized that her gesture and the look that must be on her face were an admission of the truth about herself.

He stepped inside the entrance hall and closed the door behind him. "You bitch." His voice shook. "You filthy bitch."

She said, "How—how did you—"

"Never mind how I found out! It's true, isn't it? I can see it in your face. How you must have been laughing at me all this time!"

She said, past the hard ache in her throat, "Laughing? Oh, my darling how could I have been laughing?"

He put his hands on her shoulders. "A harlot! A fancy one, but still a harlot." His fingers tightened, digging into her flesh. "And me treating you as if you were someone so fragile, so sensitive, that I had to keep telling myself that I mustn't—"

His voice thickened. "I loved you so. You'll never know how much I loved you."

Tears ached in her throat. "And I love you, my darling. I'll never get over loving you."

"Oh, God, Maggie! How could you have—"

"I could never make you understand." She was crying now. "You'd have had to live my life to understand. But, oh, Richard! Please, kiss me, just this once."

His bitter, suffering eyes scanned her face. A lovely face undistorted despite the tears streaming down her cheeks. He gave an inarticulate sound and then drew her close. His mouth pressed down on hers hungrily, desperately.

He lifted his head. Arms around his neck, she looked up at him with imploring eyes. "Take me, Richard. I know you are going to leave me. But make love to me now." Her throat closed up for a moment. Then she said, "You see, no one has ever made love to me."

Comprehension came into his eyes. He said painfully, "I understand. Oh, my darling, my poor darling."

He kissed her again. Then, with his arm around her waist, they went into the bedroom, dimly lighted by the glow from the lamp-lit salon. They undressed silently then lay side by side on the bed. With a blend of desire and sorrow he looked down at her lovely body. At the hollows between her clavicles and her shoulders, her full breasts, narrow waist and her long graceful legs. Gently he kissed her mouth, her throat, and the nipples of her breasts.

She lay with closed eyes, feeling a tender gratefulness for this moment mingled with a grieving foreknowledge of the lonely years ahead. Feeling, too, something she had never in her life felt before this. Desire. Desire to feel a man's body weighting her own. She, the bought bed companion of so many men, had remained emotionally a virgin.

He entered her. And for a while she forgot everything but her growing passion, her growing need to feel him thrusting again and again against the warm, melting core of her. And at last she knew what it was like, that shuddering, orgasmic release of tension. He stopped moving for a moment, kissed her mouth, and then, very quickly, achieved his own climax.

When they lay side by side, he said, staring up at the dimly lighted ceiling, "You said I could never understand how it happened unless I had lived your life. But would you try to tell me?" When she didn't speak he went on, "I mean, try to help me understand how a little Brooklyn girl, born to loving, comfortably-off parents, could grow up to become—"

"I made that little girl up. I mean, she was just someone I saw once, giving a doll tea party on a Brooklyn lawn. I wanted to be her. After I met you, I wished more than ever that I'd been raised like that."

After a long moment he said, "But you were born in Brooklyn?"

"No, not even that much is true. I was born in Hell's Kitchen. You must know where that is. My father, when he worked, was a longshoreman. My mother was always fond of whiskey, and after my father deserted us, she was drunk more and more of the time—"

She went on, telling of the "uncles" who began to appear at the flat, including the uncle who raped her. She told of how she herself, a little more than a year after that, began to entertain men in that tenement flat under the tarpaper roof.

And then she spoke of Hildegarde Hoffman. "She saved me, she and the job she gave me at the clinic. I worshipped her. I wanted to pattern my life after hers. And then, when I saw how her life ended—"

She told him of Hildegarde's brutal murder and of her own bitter decision to come with Danson Hayworth to Paris. She spoke of her first and only appearance on the stage— "That was the production you saw"—and then how, running out of money, and bitterly determined not to go back to New York, she had accepted Madame Theraux's offer.

She was crying again now. Richard held her close, stroking

her hair. Through her humiliated pain she felt a faint stir of hope. He still loved her. Perhaps, in spite of everything, they could—

He said, "Did you intend to ever tell me about this?"

"No. I planned to break with you before you found out. I planned to tell you the next time I saw you, that an old suitor of mine had turned up in Paris, and that I intended to marry him. I knew that would hurt you, but not as much as the truth would." She paused. "How did you find out?"

"A letter, an anonymous letter. It was waiting for me at the Syndicate office when I got back to Paris this afternoon. It said that I might be interested to know that a young woman named Maggie MacNeil was employed by Madame Theraux, who ran the most expensive brothel in Paris."

Who, she wondered, had sent the letter? Obviously it was someone who knew of her connection with Richard. Perhaps someone who had seen them together on the street or in a café and had managed to find out who Richard was. Could it have been Madame Theraux herself? Not likely. The woman was cold and hard, but not malicious. Probably, then, it had been one of the relatively unsuccessful girls at Number Fourteen. Someone who envied her for attracting many of the richer and more generous clients.

Maggie said, "Did you—did you go to see her?"

"Who?"

"Madame Theraux."

"No. After that letter, I couldn't bring myself to go near the place. Besides, I didn't have to. There is this man I had sketched months ago, before I'd even met you. His name is Ferdinand Artois. He's a carpet manufacturer and one of the five richest men in Paris. While I was sketching him he talked of places where you would find the city's most beautiful women and he mentioned Madame Theraux."

Stomach tightening up, she asked, "And you went to see him today?"

"Yes. I asked him if he knew anything about a Maggie MacNeil at Madame Theraux's. He said yes, there had been a brunette there. An American with the first name of Maggie and Irish last name, although he could not recall it exactly. He said that up until five months ago, when he acquired a mistress, he had gone to Theraux's quite frequently and that a number of times he had chosen the—the American girl."

Too wretched to speak, Maggie remained silent. She remembered Artois. He had been tall and balding, a self-made man who affected aristocratic manners and dress, even to wearing a monocle. As far as she knew, he had never selected any of the girls except herself and Diane Gautier, the beautiful young woman with red-gold hair and coolly classical features.

Richard asked, in a voice that sounded as if he'd had to force the words out, "Did Artois or any of the others—I mean, did you bring them to this flat?"

The answer—and thank heaven for at least that one small favor—was no. But even so, right then she began to feel that there was no hope for her and Richard. Wouldn't he, because of one circumstance or another, always be pondering fresh questions about her past?

"No. It was part of my arrangement with Madame Theraux that I could keep this place—just for myself." She paused and then asked quickly, "You are going to leave me, aren't you, Richard?"

Still holding her, he said in an equally quiet voice, "Yes. I love you, love you enough that maybe I could say, 'I forgive you,' and mean it. But I wouldn't be able to forget. All the time, beneath the surface, I would be wondering if I could trust you. And when we quarreled—and all couples quarrel

146

now and then—your past would always be a convenient club I could pick up to hit you with.

"So even though I love you more than I could ever love a woman, it's no good. Maybe after awhile we'll stop loving each other. I hope so."

She longed to say, "But maybe you'd find you could forget what I've been. Maybe I could make you so happy you would forget. And true, sometimes in anger you might remind me that I'd been a harlot. But I could bear that, just as long as I was with you."

She did not say it because she was sure, now, that it would be no use. There had been a quiet finality in his voice. She must not try to keep him for even a little while longer, or try to win him with words and with her body. She would not succeed in holding him. She would only risk spoiling this hour, which despite its bittersweet quality, had been the loveliest experience of her life.

She moved away from him, turned over in bed and placed her head on her crossed arms. Face averted from him, she said, "Please go now, Richard. No. Don't touch me. Just go, my darling."

She heard the sounds of his dressing and then his footsteps crossing the little foyer and finally the opening and closing of the front door.

Chapter 11

Madame Theraux came to see her about two weeks later. Clad in a dress of brown alpaca trimmed with jet beads and with hennaed hair showing beneath a fashionably be-plumed black bonnet, she sat in one of Maggie's armchairs and said, "I came because it is now obvious that you have left my establishment entirely."

Maggie gave a vague nod.

"It is also obvious that you haven't been out much lately. You're as pale as if you'd been in prison."

"I go out sometimes to buy newspapers, food—" Her voice trailed off.

Madame Theraux studied the girl's white face. "You've lost your lover, haven't you?"

"Yes."

"Did he find out about you? I told you he would."

"Yes, he found out." With an effort she added, "Someone wrote him an anonymous letter about me. Was it you?"

"No. Why should I have done it? To revenge myself because you'd left my place? As a business woman, I have no time for such nonsense."

"I didn't think it was you."

"I have come here about this flat. I want it. Since you are no longer in my employ, you cannot expect me to continue paying the rent for it."

"I don't. I've been meaning to write you a letter and coming to some kind of arrangement—"

"The only arrangement I'm interested in is regaining possession of this flat. A new young lady has joined my staff. I intend for her to live here."

"Oh, please! No." Because of the lethargy that had weighted her ever since her parting with Richard, she felt unable to face the ordeal of finding another place to live. "I'll pay the rent, of course. Sublease the flat to me."

After a moment Madame Theraux said, "Only if you will meet my price. I'll need to rent some other accommodations for the new girl. And prices of everything, including rent, are going up every day. Or have you been too preoccupied to notice?"

Despite her misery, Maggie had been aware, vaguely, that the Prussians had completed and strengthened their lines ringing Paris. With almost no new supplies of food or anything else coming into the city, prices were skyrocketing.

"But as I said," Madame Theraux went on, "you can have the flat if you meet my price." She named it. "It's more than twice the rent called for in the lease. But then, renting another flat is going to cost me twice what it would have last summer."

Maggie thought, I've got no income. But she did have her savings. "All right."

"I'll have my lawyer draw up a sublease for you to sign." She paused, "What are you going to do, Maggie? Look for work in the theater? A lot of them are closing, you know."

"I know." After the prolonged summer, the weather had turned bleak. Unable to obtain fresh supplies of coal to keep their theaters heated, many managers had closed their doors.

"Then what are you going to do?"

"I don't know."

Madame Theraux looked at her with something like pity. "I don't know how much money you have. I just know that it cannot be any vast sum. And it will go very quickly. Prices have only begun to rise. Except for the very rich, Paris is going to be a cruel place this winter."

When Maggie said nothing, Madame Theraux asked, "Why don't you go back to America? As a neutral, you could pass through the Prussian siege lines to the seacoast. To be safe, you could ask the American ambassador here in Paris to write a letter you could carry with you, asking the Prussians not to hinder you in any way."

"No, I want to stay here." As long as possible, she wanted to feel that she and Richard were at least in the same city. But saying that would only confirm Madame Theraux's opinion that she, because of a man, had become an utter fool.

Madame Theraux said, "Well, it is none of my affair, of course. Good day, Maggie."

The next afternoon, giving way to a growing need she had felt for two weeks, she crossed the river to Boulevard Boltaire. A few yards short of the building that housed the International News Syndicate, she saw, loitering in a doorway, a thin man in a National Guard uniform. She stopped and said, "Monsieur."

For a moment he looked merely startled. Then a look of dazed pleasure came into his eyes and she realized that she must have triggered inadvertently one of those fantasies that men sometimes recount to each other as fact. "I was just standing there in a doorway and this beautiful woman, really beautiful, and very well dressed, stopped and said, 'Monsieur, my husband is an officer manning one of the forts, and I am lonely. That is my carriage back there. Would you care to drive with me to my house for a glass of wine?' "

Maggie said swiftly, "Monsieur, I will gladly pay you two francs if you will do a short errand for me."

"Errand?" The fantasy still lingered in his eyes. Plainly he had been thinking about what would follow the glass of wine.

Reaching into her reticule she took out two coins and placed them on his outstretched palm. "Please go to the International News Syndicate. It is in that building three doors from here. Say that you are inquiring about a man named Richard Glover. Let me repeat the name. Richard Glover."

The thin man looked disappointed. Then he shrugged. After all, two francs was two francs.

"Don't ask to see him. Just ask the person who receives you whether or not Richard Glover is in Paris. Then come back here and tell me."

He returned in a few minutes. "Monsieur Glover is not in Paris. He has been assigned to accompany a writer who is reporting on the Prussian army."

After a moment she said, "Thank you." Well, at least they still were on the same continent.

Because she had nothing better to do, she walked home. As she crossed a bridge to the Left Bank, a chill wind blowing off the steel gray Seine made her shiver.

A cold October gave way to an even colder November. Beyond the city walls, French soldiers manning the forts exchanged sporadic fire with the enemy. Mainly, though, the Prussians relied upon their siege to bring the city to its knees.

Many Parisians, reassured by bombastic newspaper editorials about the invincibility of the "Gallic spirit," still believed that their city could never be conquered. But ominous signs were everywhere. Most of those cattle and sheep which had filled the Bois de Bologne last September had vanished now, consumed by the almost two million people within the city walls. The rich could still buy mutton or beef, at ten to twenty times the price of two months before. Those who were very rich could even dine sumptuously at the few fine restaurants which remained open. But for the vast majority of Parisians the siege meant standing in long lines at shop doors in order to get one's daily share of the rapidly diminishing food.

And such miserable food! Horsemeat, once consumed only in poor districts like Belleville, now was featured in butcher shops in fairly expensive neighborhoods like Maggie's. In mid-November, shops began to offer dog and cat meat.

In mid-November, too, the supply of food which Maggie, at Richard's urging, had laid in was finally exhausted. She joined the food lines, spending hours in the wind-swept streets to buy an egg, or two wilted carrots, or, if she were lucky, a bit of rabbit—real rabbit, not cat.

For her own sake she did not mind too much standing in the lines. It gave her something to do during her otherwise empty days. But despite her absorption in her personal unhappiness, she increasingly became aware of the suffering of others. What must be happening to slum children of the sort she had seen in that Belleville ambulance? There was no milk for them, no milk at all. The government, when it rounded up all those sheep and cattle to put in the Bois de Bologne, had somehow neglected to include any milk cows.

On the next to last day of November she roused herself from her apathy enough to venture over to the Right Bank. The rumor was that a butcher shop on the Rue St. Honore was offering a new delicacy, camel. Yes, camel. Paris had begun to slaughter its zoo animals for food. And camel meat was said to be more tender than elephant's and more palatable than that of such carnivores as lions, wolves and foxes.

The day was too cold and windy for walking so she took the horse-drawn omnibus to the Right Bank. Hansom cabs and the horses, which had drawn them, had become very scarce. And even if she had sighted one, Maggie would not have hired it out of her rapidly dwindling funds.

On the Rue St. Honore she stayed in line in front of the butcher shop for two hours, only to find when she reached the counter that the last ounces of camel meat had been sold. But they still had some rabbit at a bargain price only about eight times what it had been in September. She bought half a pound, even though she knew that its low price might mean that it was really cat.

The short, almost wintry day had ended by then. The horse omnibus carried her toward home through wanly lit streets. Paris was no longer the City of Light. Only every third street lamp burned. The gas, manufactured from scarce coal, was needed for the balloons.

Balloons were the besieged city's chief means of communication with the world beyond the siege lines. Launched in early morning darkness, they carried military dispatches—intended for French forces in other parts of France—as well as ordinary mail over the heads of the Prussians. Sometimes, too, the little basket beneath the highly-inflammable sphere carried one or two daring men. Many of the balloons, if not shot down by the Prussians, were blown off course and plunged into the English Channel. But others had landed safely beyond the enemies' lines.

Paris was proud of those balloons. Launching them, though, meant that there was much less gas for heating or for any sort of illumination. As the two teams of horses drew the crowded omnibus over the paving stones, Maggie noticed that many of the smart shops and cafés, once brilliantly lighted and thronged with customers, were now dark. Something else had changed too. After a moment she realized what it was. No street walkers loitered in doorways. She remembered reading in a newspaper that they had been arrested by the hundreds and put to work. Some made National Guard uniforms. Others worked in balloon factories.

The omnibus was crossing the open space in front of the Louvre when it jolted to a halt. Maggie heard swearing and the repeated crack of a whip. The conductor and several male passengers left the omnibus. She heard someone shout, "Whipping's no use, you fool!"

The conductor poked his head in the door. "You might as well get out, all of you."

Out on the paving stones Maggie saw that one of the lead horses, a dappled gray, had gone down. His side, so thin each rib showed, did not stir. She realized that probably his overworked heart had just given out. He had taken his harness mate, a bay, down with him. One of the bay's forelegs stuck out from his body at a grotesque angle.

She looked around her at her fellow passengers. Months ago, she was sure, there would have been pity in their faces as they looked at those animals, one dead and the other about to be destroyed. But now in each thin face she read the thoughts which had entered her own mind: I wonder which butcher shop they will be taken to.

A small incident, really, compared to much worse ones, that must have been taking place all over Paris. Just two fallen horses which were surrounded by half-starved humans eager to devour them. And yet somehow it broke through her emotional numbness and shocked her into a recognition of what was happening around her.

All over this beautiful city, once considered the most civilized in the world, people must be succumbing to hunger-induced cruelty, with perhaps even more savage depths yet to be plumbed. She had drifted in the midst of it, too self-absorbed to really care. Well, she would change now. She would do what little she could to assuage suffering and to stave off the barbarism that can arise out of suffering. And in doing so, perhaps she could save herself.

It was not too far to her flat. It would be better to walk than to wait for another omnibus, which might not come along for hours. Head bent against the wind that whined across the Place de Carrousel, she walked to the Seine embankment, crossed the bridge and turned down her street.

Only a few minutes earlier Diane Gautier had ordered her driver to stop her carriage—one of the few private carriages still seen on Paris streets—at the curb opposite the house where Maggie MacNeil lived. Thus when Maggie passed a gas lamp and then turned in at her door, Diane was able to get a good look at her. With satisfaction she saw that the American girl who had won Karl's admiration looked cold, pale and tired, and that her shoulders drooped.

Diane had obtained Maggie's address, not from close-mouthed Madame Theraux, who would never have given it to her, but from a pretty and empty-headed blonde name Jeanette, the latest of Number Fourteen's young ladies. Her first evening at Madame Theraux's she had confided to Diane, "Madame is giving me a lovely flat in the Rue Martine. It's on the second floor and in the front. Some girl who used to work here has it now, but Madame is going to throw her out."

"Is she an American girl?"

"Yes, Madame mentioned that she was."

Diane had felt satisfaction. So the American had not only lost her lover. She was going to lose the roof over her head—and in a city, swollen with refugees from the countryside, where any sort of housing was scarce.

The next night, though, Jeanette had said to Diane, "You know that flat I told you about? I'm not going to get it."

"But why not?"

"The American agreed to sublease it for twice the rent Madame is paying."

So, Diane thought, Maggie MacNeil must have managed to save a little money. But it wouldn't last long, not the way prices were soaring.

Jeanette went on, "So I'll just have to stay in the poky old room where I am now until Madame finds something else for me."

"Do you remember the street number where the American has her flat?"

"It's Number Thirty-five. Madame drove me past it two days ago. Such a nice house, with a mansard roof!"

Several times after that Diane had ordered her driver to take her past Maggie's house. Twice, in the early evening, she had seen lamp glow in the second floor windows. But this was the first time she had actually seen the American girl since that night when she had fled from Madame Theraux's.

She leaned out of the carriage window and said to the man on the box, "All right, Francois. Take me to Rue de Adele."

Her coachman, a man in his sixties, wanted very much to hold onto his well-paid job. Consequently he seldom dared speculate even to himself as to why an obviously rich young woman should spend so many evenings at what was really nothing more nor less than a whorehouse, no matter how fancied up.

As the carriage moved toward Madame Theraux's, Diane realized that it was her own frustration that kept her animosity toward Maggie MacNeil alive. If she had been seeing Karl frequently, Diane would have been content with sending that anonymous letter to the American girl's lover.

But she had not been seeing Karl. She had not seen him since the night when he twice had wounded and infuriated her, first by expressing admiration of Maggie and second by choosing to meet some Swiss associate rather than spend the night with her in her flat.

In the weeks that had followed that night, she had been comforted by the thought that at least he must be in Paris. After all, he was a French citizen and thus supposedly barred from going through the Prussian lines that ringed the city and its outlaying forts. If he tried to leave, he might arouse the suspicion of the increasingly spy-conscious French and thus jeopardize his work for his Prussian employers. No, he was still here in Paris, but staying away from her for his own mysterious reasons.

Again and again she'd had to fight down the impulse to go to his place in Montmarte. He had told her, with chilling calm, that she must never do that. Although he did not give a reason, she knew what it must be. He was afraid that she might encounter some other person in Prussian pay, perhaps a Paris politician who relied upon Karl to protect his treasonable activity from discovery. She realized something else too. The coldly matter-of-fact manner in which he had warned her not to come to his place told her that if she disobeyed him, the very least of the consequences would be the loss of him as her lover.

So far Diane had not been affected by the siege. True, there had been minor annoyances. Her perfume shop on the Rue de St. Honore had told her that supplies of her favorite fragrance, manufactured in Graz, had been exhausted. Her cook, who came in by the day, complained of having to stand in line to buy meat and vegetables. But because the cook, backed by her employer's bottomless purse, was able to buy even such delicacies as pheasant, Diane dined almost as well as she ever had. On the whole she was oblivious to the Paris of growing hunger and mounting disease rates of men, women and children who, in the poor districts, had begun to fell whatever trees they could find in order to heat their miserable homes. Warm and well fed, Diane was able to concentrate on her avid need for Karl.

Each evening when she went to Number Fourteen she had hoped that soon she would see him striding across the room toward her. Each night when she came home she hoped to find that he had let himself into her flat with his own key.

Then, only this morning, she had seen an item in *Le Figaro*:

> *"Now it can be revealed that several weeks ago a gallant Frenchman, Monsieur Karl Schiller, was among the first to take passage on one of our balloons which sail so gloriously over the heads of the astounded and helpless enemy. Monsieur Schiller had volunteered his services as a government courier. Although we cannot reveal his exact destination, our readers can rest assured that he landed safely somewhere in the south of France."*

So, without telling her, he had left Paris under the auspices of the very government he was betraying! All she could do was to wait, hoping that sooner or later he would return to her, or at least contrive to get a message to her.

No wonder that, as her carriage moved toward Number Fourteen, she took what comfort she could in the thought that the American girl too was alone and unhappy and, moreover, looking tired and thin and cold.

Late that night, in an upper room of a house in the rich suburb of Passy, a plump lawyer, a friend of the nervous architect, lay face down on an oriental rug. Diane ground the heel of her green satin slipper into the back of his outstretched hand. He let out a muffled cry and then gave her a reproachful look. She was not supposed to hurt him *that* much.

Chapter 12

At about that same moment, shortly after midnight, Jeanne-Marie was collecting her small son from the concierge's quarters. At the foot of the stairs Jeanne-Marie said, "I know you are sleepy. But you will have to walk. Mama is very tired. Besides, you are a big boy now. Soon you'll be two."

Slowly, she and the whimpering child started up the stairs. She looked down at the small face, wanly lighted by the feeble gaslight on the landing above. Her heart contracted. How pale and thin he was. The reason, of course, was not enough food. Would he get sick? So many children had.

She, too, was hungry. When she first went to work for Madame Theraux, one of the attractions of the position had been that Madame had not minded her taking leftover food home from the bountiful buffet offered the clients each night. Sometimes she had gleaned only a few hard rolls for Marcel and herself. Other times it had been a slice of ham or some fruit.

Now all of that was changed. By doubling, and then tripling, her entrance fee, Madame had been able to offer her clients a table almost as lavish as before the siege. There were eggs in gelatin and sliced pheasant and assorted cheeses which, per pound, cost six times the weekly wage of an average Parisian worker. But apparently she felt she could no longer afford any sort of largesse to her maids and kitchen workers. Every bit of leftover food had to be listed and then stored away in the pantry so that it could become part of the next night's buffet.

Nor was Henri Lamartine able any longer to supply Jeanne-Marie and her little boy with produce from his sister's farm. In early November a band of thieves had raided the farm and carried off everything edible, from chickens to stored wheat and potatoes. Just before they left, one of the thieves, perhaps accidentally, had overturned an oil lamp. Abandoning their fire-damaged house, Henri's sister and brother-in-law had entered the already over crowded city to survive as best they could.

Jeanne-Marie told herself to count her blessings. As a night worker, she was at least able to stand in the food lines. If she had worked days she would have had to pay some other woman to buy wilted vegetables and occasional bits of meat for herself and her son.

The top floor was quiet tonight, although a thread of light still shone from beneath Charles Maubert's door. She went into her own big room, laid her reticule on the table, and lit the lamp. With dismay she noticed that one of the large jet beads that ornamented the sides of her black reticule was about to come loose. It was a wonder she had not lost it. Her reticule, the only one she had, had been given to her mother long ago by the handsome apothecary, her father, who had died in the Crimea. Consequently Jeannie-Marie was very fond of it.

She carefully detached the bead and laid it on the table. Tomorrow she would sew it back onto her reticule. She undressed her son who, annoyingly, seemed wide awake now and bent upon chattering about Frou-frou, the concierge's dog, even after she'd put him in his small bed.

"Marcel! Go to sleep!"

161

She crossed the room, took off her blouse and shirt, and hung them from a nail in the wall beside her bed, a narrow one with a white-painted iron bedstead. She was unbuttoning her chemise when she heard a choking sound behind her. She whirled around.

Marcel stood in his crib, small hands clutching its rail. His face was scarlet. His eyes bulged with terror. And he was making a dreadful sound.

As she flew toward him, her frantic gaze flicked to the table. The large jet bead was no longer there.

She snatched him up in her arms. "Cough!" she cried. She pounded the small back. "Cough, Marcel, cough!"

Still that dreadful sound, still that imploring terror in his eyes. She heard a wild wail and after a split second realized it had issued from her own mouth. Again she pounded his back. "Cough!"

She heard a sharp knocking at the door. Still holding her son, she ran across the room, turned the key in the lock and flung the door open. Charles Maubert came into the room.

She cried, "My little boy! He's choking to death. A bead. He must have thought it was food—"

"Let me have him."

He took the child into his arms. Holding the small back against his own chest, he pressed a fist against Marcel's stomach. He removed his fist and then pressed again.

The jet bead popped out, struck the floor and rolled. Marcel drew a deep breath and then began to howl.

Jeannie-Marie took the child and hugged him to her. "Oh, monsieur! Thank you, thank you!"

Charles smiled. "It was nothing. I saw a medical student, a friend of mine, do that for a stranger in a café one night. He'd gotten a bit of mutton lodged in his throat."

Jeanne-Marie carried the little boy, who was crying more

quietly now, over to his crib and laid him down. "You're all right now, my darling. Go to sleep. Go to sleep."

She hung over the crib, soothing the child. Charles watched her. She still had not realized that she was wearing a petticoat and a half-unbuttoned chemise. How pretty her bare arms were, he thought, as he continued to admire her partially naked bosom, her slender waist and the flare of her hips under the white petticoat.

It was far from the first time that he had been aware of his young neighbor's appeal. What was more, he had known—from the slight breathlessness in her voice when she spoke to him and the soft color which came into her pretty round face—that she found him attractive too. But also he realized that this very young widow was a "serious girl." Even after he gleaned, from something the concierge had said, that Jeanne-Marie worked as a parlor maid in Madame Theraux's establishment, he still could not doubt Jeanne-Marie's seriousness. Not until he was several years older would he be ready for that kind of girl, the kind you did not take to bed until you had placed a wedding ring on her finger. And when he was ready for such a girl, she would be someone of his own class.

But what a temptation Jeanne-Marie was, especially since he had been celibate these past three weeks. A quarrel with his last girl, a milliner's assistant, had left him too disgruntled to start looking for someone else. Besides, he had been affected by the pall of gloom that the siege had brought to all but the very richest.

But here she was in gloomy Paris, this pretty, half-dressed girl, this chaste girl who had not been able to hide the fact that she liked him—

The child was quiet now. She turned and walked toward Charles, smiling tremulously. "He's asleep. Oh, monsieur! How can I ever even begin to thank—"

And then she became aware of her undressed state. She said, "Oh!" and covered the soft swell of her breasts with her hands and started to turn toward her blouse and skirt hanging from a hook.

He caught her upper arms, quite gently, and turned her back toward him. "Isn't it rather late for that? I've been staring at you for at least five minutes."

He bent and kissed her lips briefly. Then he straightened and smiled down at her.

Jeanne-Marie looked up at the handsome young face, the blue, smiling eyes and the curly brown hair with gold highlights. How often, in her imagination, had she lived a moment like this!

Dimly she was aware that her crossed hands had fallen away from her bosom. He drew her close against him and kissed her, a long kiss this time. She felt the sweet shock of it all through her.

He said, lips close to her ear, "Will you come to my place for a little while? We can leave your door open and mine too. If your little boy wakes up, we'll hear him."

Prudence bade her say no. But it was prudence also that had kept her alone night after night, listening to the sounds of the young man she'd fallen in love with entertain his friends, and often just one friend, a girl.

If she did say no he might try for a few moments to persuade her. Then he would smile, say goodnight, and go to his own quarters. After that he would speak politely whenever they met and she would never again, ever as long as she lived, feel his arms around her and his lips warm on her own.

If she said yes, though, she might gain more than the satisfaction of her aroused young body. He might see how much she loved him and thus begin to love her. Why, they might even—

She said faintly, "All right."

In his small bedroom he took off the rest of her clothing gently, but with the expertness of a man long used to coping with the buttons, hooks, and eyes of feminine undergarments. And when they lay naked in bed, his lovemaking was a revelation to her. She had loved the young peasant she had married, but his hands had been work-roughened and awkward. Sometimes he had taken her with scant preliminaries, and she, too shy to complain, had lain there frustrated while he fell asleep.

But now she learned the exquisite pleasure of a man's sensitive fingertips stroking the insides of her thighs, a man's lips caressing her throat and breasts. He did not enter her until, involuntarily, she had begun to rotate her hips. And even then he proceeded slowly enough to bring her to ecstatic climax well before he reached his own.

Afterwards he held her close, stroking her hair. What a darling she was. So pretty, soft and warm. And just as his lovemaking had been a revelation to her, hers had been a revelation to him. He had expected her to be stiff and awkward and prudish their first time together, not supple and responsive. Perhaps it meant that she was really in love with him. None of his other girls had been. Oh, he felt that they had liked him and had liked his body, but they had known that going to bed with him could result in nothing permanent and so they had kept a rein on their emotions.

Right now he felt that he could fall in love with Jeanne-Marie. Oh, he couldn't think of marrying her. His family would never stand for that. But she would be his sweetheart, his only sweetheart, for a long, long time. Perhaps even until the end of the university term when, with the war over—surely it would be over by then—he would go home to Lyons and his parents' comfortable home.

165

She stirred in his arms. "It's late. I must go back. Towards morning, Marcel sometimes wakes up—"

He kissed her soft mouth. "All right, until tomorrow night."

In his bed, Henri Lamartine lay staring at the invisible ceiling. About an hour ago he had been sleeping heavily, as he usually did these nights. In order to make a living now in a Paris where few people could buy adequate amounts of food let alone have their watches repaired, he'd had to keep his shop open from first daylight until after dark.

And so, when he had first heard the sounds—a woman's agitated voice, a man's soothing one and then a child's wail— he had made them part of a dream he was dreaming. It was perhaps minutes later that he woke up with an uneasy feeling that the sounds he had heard might not have been a dream. Barefoot, he padded across the bedroom and the front room and quietly opened the door part way.

He could see along the dark hall and through the opened door into Jeanne-Marie's lamplit room. Half undressed, she stood in Charles Maubert's embrace, her bare round arms fastened around his neck.

Henri closed the door and stood there in the darkness, feeling that everything inside him had knotted up. So it was happening, what he had been aware would almost surely happen.

Now, an hour later, he still lay awake in the darkness. Jeanne-Marie was so young, so alone and so vulnerable. "Don't let her be hurt," he prayed. "Don't let anything really bad happen to her."

Chapter 13

The morning after she had seen the fallen horses on the Place du Carrousel's stones, Maggie crossed in the omnibus to a stop in Belleville. She got out and walked about a hundred yards to the warehouse, which sheltered the makeshift hospital, or ambulance, which she and Richard had once visited. Immediately she saw that the ground floor ward was no longer empty. About a dozen beds were filled with men who, she realized, must be soldiers wounded in the sporadic gunfire between the French forts and the Prussian siege lines beyond. One soldier, a young one of about eighteen, who was sitting up in bed, his bandaged arm in a sling, gave her a flirtatious, gap-toothed grin. The others, eyes glazed with suffering, watched her with varying degrees of indifference as she started down the aisle between the beds.

Near the far wall a thin, very tall man in a workman's blue smock was turning the mattress on an empty bed. He straightened as she approached. She saw that he was young, only about her own age, with disordered curly dark hair falling over a broad forehead, and lustrous dark eyes set in an even-featured, sensitive face.

She said, "Good day, monsieur. Do you know where I might find the manager of this ambulance?"

"Monsieur Decrot?" His pleasantly cultivated voice was a surprising contrast to his workman's smock. "But of course,

167

mademoiselle. He is in his office."

He walked to a door in the back wall and knocked. When a voice called, "Enter," the young man opened the door and said, "A young lady to see you, Monsieur Decrot."

Bowing, he held the door wide and then closed it behind her.

A man she remembered, middle-aged and balding, had risen from his desk. He said, "Why, how nice to see you again, Mademoiselle O'Neil."

"It's MacNeil."

"MacNeil. Oh, yes. Forgive me. You came here with a Monsieur Richard Glover. Please sit down, mademoiselle."

A moment later he asked, "How is Monsieur Glover?"

She kept her voice even. "I do not know, exactly. He is accompanying a newspaperman who is reporting the war from the Prussian side."

"I see. Well, what can I do for you?"

"You can give me employment."

He said, astounded, "Here, in this ambulance? Mademoiselle! This is rough, unpleasant work and sure to become more so. As you probably know, the government is preparing a grand sortie of our armed forces out of the city. The object is to break through the Prussian siege lines and link up with French armies still holding out in other parts of France."

Maggie nodded.

"Even if our forces prevail—" He broke off and then added, "And pray God that they do, or we shall surely starve. Did you know, mademoiselle, that the Parisians have begun to eat rats? Catching rats and selling them has become a chief off-duty occupation for National Guardsmen in poor neighborhoods like this one."

Again Maggie nodded. Paradoxically, it was only the rich who ate rat, because they were the only ones who could afford the sauce, consisting of brandy and other expensive ingredients, which was necessary to make such dreadful food palatable.

"But as I was saying, even if we break the siege, I fear it will be at an enormous cost. All those vacant beds out there will be filled with wounded men. Caring for them will not be a task suitable for a delicately reared young woman."

"I am not a delicately reared young woman. And I worked for nearly two years in a place similar to yours. I was an assistant to Hildegarde Hoffman, who ran a clinic in New York."

He looked impressed as well as surprised. "I have heard of Hildegarde Hoffman's work, at Florence Nightingale's hospital in London and also at her own clinics in Vienna and New York. She met a brutal death, did she not?"

"Yes. The husband of one of her patients killed her."

"A terrible end for such a fine woman." He paused and then went on, "We, of course, would welcome the services of someone with your experience. But let me be sure I understand. Will you come to us as a volunteer?"

"If that is the way it must be," she said frankly. "But if you could pay me something, I would appreciate it." The money she had saved was disappearing fast now. And very soon she would have to renew the lease on her flat. Staggering as she had thought the amount demanded by Madame Theraux for the sublease, Maggie was sure that by now the landlord would want even more.

"I can pay you eight francs a day. Even though that is much more than we pay our nurses, it is still not nearly enough to offer a former assistant of Hildegarde Hoffman's. But it is the best that I can do."

Eight francs indeed was not much. In the food lines it would buy her four eggs, or a head of cabbage. However, eight francs was still more than the average French workman received, even though wages had risen—not nearly as fast as prices, of course, but still they had gone up.

"I accept, Monsieur Ducrot."

"You cannot know how much you are needed here. When will you be able to start?"

"Immediately, if you like."

"Splendid. You must not work in those nice clothes, of course. One of the nurses in the children's ward will furnish you with a clean blouse and skirt.

"I shall put you up there for the present," he went on. "Sadly, we have many children here. But right now there are so few ground floor patients that Monsieur Raoul Lussac, with the assistance of one nurse, can manage nicely."

"Is he the young man I saw in the ward?"

"Yes." Monsieur Ducrot smiled. "He is a poet. He is also an anarchist."

"An anarchist!" She could believe that the young man with the expressive dark eyes might well be a poet, but he did not look like her idea of an anarchist.

"Oh, he is not the sort of anarchist who tries to blow up heads of state. I suppose you would call him a philosophical anarchist. He will talk to you about it. There is no way you will be able to stop him." He paused, smiling. "What he will not talk about very much is his family."

"Why? What is wrong with his family?"

"They are the richest bankers in Marseilles. Raoul is ashamed of them. But I should be grateful for his eccentric notions, since one of them concerns the very sizable income he receives from a great-uncle's estate. He gives most of it to this ambulance."

They went out into the ground floor ward. With the aid of a middle-aged nurse, Raoul Lussac was changing a patient's head bandage. Dark eyes filled with admiration as he smiled at Maggie.

In the upstairs ward Ducrot introduced her as "my new assistant" to Louise and Imogene Duraz. Sisters, they were both short and sallow-skinned and heavy-featured. When he had gone, Maggie walked slowly down the aisles between the beds. So many beds now, placed so close together that it would be hard for a nurse to edge her way into the space between them. Heart contracting, she looked down at small faces distorted with the pain of rickets, or flushed with tuberculosis, or spotted with pox. But she knew that, as Hildegarde had said of the Hell's Kitchen children, they all suffered from the same underlying disease—bad nutrition.

At first the Duraz sisters eyed her coldly, perhaps because of her looks and her clothes, or perhaps because they suspected, correctly, that she was to be paid several times their own two-francs-a-day wage. When they saw that she dressed a little girl's badly burned leg with a gentle swiftness they themselves had not achieved, and when they saw that she did not flinch at the sight of pus draining from a small ear, or turn aside when a child vomited—in short, when they saw that skill and experience entitled her to be Ducrot's second in command, their attitude began to change. Before the morning was over she was sure that she could win their friendship as well as their respect.

When she came downstairs at noon she found Raoul waiting at the foot. "Mademoiselle MacNeil, my name is Raoul Lussac."

"I know. Monsieur Ducrot told me."

"Mademoiselle, will you allow me to take you to luncheon? There is quite a good café near the Place de la Bastille." When she hesitated he said, so swiftly that she knew he must have rehearsed his argument, "If we are to work together, would it not be well that we become acquainted as soon as possible? Would that not be best for the ambulance?"

171

She smiled. "Perhaps you are right, monsieur."

They walked a half-mile through the wintry grayness to the café. The menu offered both *coq au vin* and *tornedos* of beef. The patrons looked well fed. The prices printed on the menu were appalling. Maggie realized that he must have compromised his principles seriously in bringing her here.

When their portions of *coq au vin* arrived, they both ate in ravenous silence for a while. It seemed obvious that he, although well supplied with funds, had lived almost as spartanly as the vast majority of Parisians had been forced to.

Finally she said, "Monsieur Ducrot told me that you are a poet."

"I try to be." He looked at her for a long moment and then said, "I know I will try to write a poem about you. I'm sure it won't be good enough for me to show it to you, but nevertheless I shall write it."

Maggie felt dismay. It would not do for this intense young man to become really interested in her. She gave him a noncommittal smile and said, "I also hear you are an anarchist."

"You are interested in anarchy?"

"I know nothing about it."

"It is quite simple. Anarchists believe in a society where harmony is maintained, not by submission to legal or governmental authority, but by free agreements concluded between various groups, both territorial and professional. In such a world, governments would not be a necessary evil. Because that is what governments are in our present society, evil. Look at this cruel war. It is not the French and Prussian people who wage it. It is their governments.

"Anarchism is very old. Even in ancient Greece, Zeno opposed his conception of a free community without government to Plato's idea of a utopian state—"

He went on, talking of the Hussites ideas, and

Proudhon's, and Bakunin's. Maggie did not understand much of what she heard and what she did understand she found unconvincing. But she could not help liking him for the enthusiasm in his face as he spoke of a world without war or poverty or grinding labor. A world where "the humblest workman will have the leisure to climb mountains, or at least try, to paint, compose music, or write poetry."

As they walked back to the ambulance he was still talking.

At six she emerged from the ambulance into the early dark and turned toward the omnibus stop. A man stepped down from a hansom cab that stood at the curb. He said, "Mademoiselle!"

She saw that it was Raoul. "Yes?"

"Since this is your first day at the ambulance, I thought you might find it pleasant to ride home in a carriage rather than on the omnibus."

Coq au vin at noon and now a ride in one of Paris's few remaining hansom cabs, at lord only knew what cost. At this rate, there soon would not be much left of his anarchist principles—or of his great-uncle's estate. But mingled with her amusement was a very real dismay.

She let him usher her into the hansom. As it carried them across the city, he talked of a government official who, according to that morning's press, had taken a huge bribe from a French armament manufacturer. Lost in her own thoughts, Maggie scarcely heard him. She must tell him about herself straight away. She did not think he would tell Monsieur Ducrot, or anyone. But even if he did, or if Ducrot found out some other way, the ambulance manager would not dismiss her. He needed her services far too much.

When the carriage stopped in front of her house, she said, "May I offer you a glass of Moselle?"

Surprised enthusiasm in his face, he said, "That would be kind of you."

In her flat she asked him to sit down and then poured wine for them both. Seated on the sofa, glass in hand, he looked around the small salon and said, "What an attractive apartment."

Steeling herself, she said, "I subleased it from Madame Theraux. Have you heard of her?"

"I don't think so. Should I have?"

"No, I imagine you would not have. She runs a very expensive brothel on the Rue de Adele."

His dark eyes reflected puzzlement and then the beginnings of dismay. "A brothel keeper! How is it that you—"

"Until recently I was one of her girls."

He gave an uncertain smile. "I realize that this must be some sort of joke, but I am afraid I don't—"

"It is not a joke."

To convince him of that she began to speak, swiftly, of her past. Her childhood in New York, the bitter shock of Hildegarde Hoffman's death, and her decision to accept Danson Hayworth's offer of a trip to Paris. Her brief theatrical career, followed by a more prolonged one at Number Fourteen, Rue de Adele.

She did not tell him about Richard Glover. It would have been too painful for her to have spoken of that, and besides, it was not necessary. "I have accumulated considerable funds," she said, "and so I decided to leave Madame Theraux's place."

He had grown progressively paler as she talked. He sat in silence for several seconds after she stopped speaking, his eyes very dark in his white face. "Forgive me, mademoiselle." He tried to smile. "But I must leave now."

When he had gone she sat motionless in the lamp-lit room.

It had been a hard thing to do, but she could not let that boy fall in love with her. Not that he was really a boy. He was two years older than she. During that staggeringly expensive luncheon he had told her his age, but he seemed to her like a boy.

Slowly she got up and went into the kitchen. The previous day she had made a thin soup from a mutton bone plus a carrot and potato and eaten part of it. Tonight she would have the rest.

The next morning when she emerged from her house she found Raoul waiting for her. He stood on the sidewalk in the frosty sunlight, smiling as he beat his gloved hands together for warmth. He said cheerfully, "Hello! I thought we might walk to the omnibus stop together."

She stood stock still. "Have you forgotten what I told you last night?"

"Of course not." He took her arm. "Come on. If we miss the next omnibus we'll have to wait half an hour for another, and it is too cold to be standing around."

As they moved down the sidewalk he said, "What you told me last night upset me, until I realized the truth. I should have realized it right away."

"What truth?"

Instead of answering directly he said, "You think that you're a sinner, don't you? Well, you are not. You were a victim! A victim of the poverty in which you were raised."

She stopped and faced him. "That's just silly. If you like, you can say that things happened to me because I was an unprotected child, but not because I was poor. Lots of girls in my neighborhood were poor, but they didn't grow up to be"—she used the world deliberately—"harlots."

"Let's keep going," he said and took her arm again. "Don't you see," he went on as they began to walk, "that a decent society would not have allowed you to be neglected,

175

no matter what the shortcomings of your mother and father?"

"Listen to me! You mustn't—romanticize me, musn't idealize me."

"Why not?" he asked cheerfully. Then his tone altered. "You're not engaged to someone, are you?"

"No."

"In love with someone?"

After a moment she said, "Yes."

"Does he love you?"

"Yes. Or at least he did."

"Where is he?"

"I'm not sure. You see, we said goodbye."

"Why?" When she didn't answer he said, "Was it because of all those things you told me last night?"

"Yes."

"You mean," he said explosively, "that he let that stand between you and him? Then he wasn't worthy of you!"

Oh, yes he was, she wanted to say. The difference between you and Richard is that he is not an idealistic dreamer. He's a mature man who knows that one's past has consequences in the present and in the future, whether one likes it or not.

But there was no time to say that now, not with the omnibus horses clattering over the cobblestones, their breath like plumes in the frosty air. "Hurry," she said, "or we'll miss it."

Chapter 14

During the week that followed, neither Maggie nor Raoul had much time or energy to think of themselves. That was the week of the "grand sortie." While Paris waited breathlessly behind its locked gates, French forces advanced toward the enemy on every front.

At first there was hope of success. When word came that the French had crossed the Marne River in pursuit of retreating Prussians, Paris reacted with typical delirium. Singing, dancing street crowds were so thick one night that Maggie's omnibus could not make any progress. She got out and walked. As she crossed the Seine, its dark waters were spangled with the reflections of fireworks which someone had unearthed from heaven knew where.

But next day word came that the Prussian retreat had been only a ruse. When the French lines were sufficiently extended, the Prussians had attacked from the flanks and sent the French reeling back across the Marne. Then the wounded began to arrive in Paris, carried on river barges and in long lines of creaking carts. Wretched at they were, they were the lucky ones. Twelve thousand other Frenchmen had died in that one battle.

The wounded flooded into the city's ambulances, overwhelming the nurses and doctors. At the ambulance in

Belleville, Maggie and a middle-aged, short-tempered doctor named Villiers supervised the transfer of the sick children to cots and pallets in the building's low-ceilinged and poorly-lighted loft, thus making room on the floor below for wounded men.

Under the direction of Dr. Villiers and several more doctors who went from one ambulance to another across the stricken city, Maggie and Raoul and the other staff members worked twelve hours a day or even longer. Leaving the children in the care of the Duraz sisters, Maggie devoted herself to the wounded and often dying men.

As if the heavens themselves had turned against the city, that December was one of the coldest within living memory. In poor neighborhoods, where all the trees already had been chopped down and burnt as firewood, some people froze to death. Others, despite the vigilance of the police, invaded the wealthy neighborhoods by night to strip bark and branches from the magnificent trees lining the broad avenues.

Shortly after the middle of the month a heavy snowfall, rare for Paris, blanketed the city and snarled morning traffic. Maggie's omnibus, crossing a bridge over the river in which grayish chunks of ice floated, found its way blocked by two carts that had locked wheels. She knew she would be late, but she did not mind as much as she would have only a week ago. The ambulance was less crowded now. Many of the wounded had died. Others, with shattered limbs or with shell fragments embedded in their bodies, had been transferred to a large ambulance, financed by Americans, which maintained an operating room and skilled surgeons.

She hurried into the ambulance and then stopped short, feeling terror and incredulous joy. In the third bed from the entrance, next to an empty one, lay a young man with dark brown hair and a craggy face, very pale now. His eyes were closed.

Aware that her legs were trembling, she went to the foot of the bed and looked down at him by the gray light coming through the old warehouse's window. Richard? Was he really Richard?

Dr. Villiers came hurrying down the aisle. She followed him into the draughty vestibule. "Doctor!"

He turned. "Yes, mademoiselle."

"That new patient, in the third bed from the front. What is his name?"

He said testily, "I've forgotten. But when he was brought in here an hour ago he said he was an American and connected with some sort of news syndicate."

"How is he injured?"

"A bullet through the shoulder. A clean wound, nothing serious. He was transferred here from an ambulance in Montmarte because they are overcrowded and heard that we no longer were. Now if you will excuse me, mademoiselle, I am overdue at the ambulance in Menilmontant." Menilmontant was another working class district.

He hurried away. Even though she knew she should go to the ward upstairs and change into her cotton skirt and blouse, she sat down on the empty bed next to Richard's. As if sensing her presence, he opened his eyes.

She saw disbelief in their gray depths and then an overwhelming joy. Her throat closed up. So he stilled loved her. In spite of everything, he still loved her.

He was in control of himself now. Even though he smiled, his eyes were aloof, guarded. But that spontaneous joy had been there.

"Hello, Maggie. What are you doing here?"

"I work here." Her smile was tremulous. "What are *you* doing here?"

"I got in the way of a bullet during the fighting around Orleans."

She nodded. The grand sortie not only had ended in disaster for the men who had marched so confidently out of Paris, but in the course of the fighting, French forces who had been holding Orleans were forced to surrender the city.

"It's not much of a wound." He still smiled a controlled smile. "I'd had a bout of typhus earlier. Otherwise I'd be on my feet by now. But, anyway, it happened to be French rather than Prussian orderlies who found me on the battlefield. I showed them my card issued by the International News, so they loaded me onto a cart filled with French wounded."

He paused and then said, "So you're a volunteer. Do you come here often?"

"I'm not a volunteer. I'm an assistant to the ambulance manager. I work here six days a week from seven in the morning until six at night, and sometimes later."

She saw gratification in his eyes. Anyone working here eleven or more hours a day could not be spending her evenings at Madame Theraux's.

Oh, probably he still felt that they must keep their lives separate. The controlled quality of his smile indicated that. But still he obviously was glad, very glad indeed, that she no longer shared the beds of other men.

A middle-aged nurse with untidy gray-blond hair came down the aisle. In her hands was a tray holding a basin of water, a roll of bandages, cotton swabs, and a bottle of carbolic solution. She set the tray down on a small table in the aisle.

Maggie said, "Just leave it there. I will attend to this patient."

"But mademoiselle! You are still wearing your—"

"Never mind that. It doesn't matter."

The nurse shrugged and walked away.

Maggie removed the old bandage from Richard's shoulder and looked at the wound surrounded by reddened and puffed flesh. She had dealt with much worse wounds, not only here but at Hildegarde's clinic. The sight of his injured shoulder, though, and the warmth of his fevered flesh to her touch made her heart contract in a way that no other wound had, however grievous. It was as if her own body had received the bullet. She felt that she understood now what the Bible meant about a man and woman becoming "as one flesh."

She bathed his shoulder gently and then applied the carbolic solution. Thank God for that English surgeon who had first started using carbolic acid. Only a few weeks ago, even a not-too-severe wound like Richard's could have resulted in death by gangrene.

When she had finished bandaging his shoulder he said, "I think that after this you had better leave changing the bandage to someone else."

She knew then that he too had been conscious of their intimacy, their oneness, as she touched his injured body, and had been disturbed by it. She felt regret that there would be no more such moments and yet a surge of gladness that she still could affect him so strongly. "All right, Richard."

As she walked toward the stairs, she saw Raoul standing motionless beside an empty cot, a folded blanket in his arms. He said, "Maggie."

She stopped. "Yes."

"That American who was brought in this morning. Is he the one?"

"Yes." Seeing the pain in his dark eyes, she wanted to add, "I'm sorry," but, of course, that would have been exactly the wrong thing to say. She moved on and climbed the steps to the upstairs ward.

During the next five days she and Richard did not even speak to each other, except for an exchange of good mornings and good nights. But each day she awoke to the bittersweet thought that soon she would see him. Too, there was always that wild, illogical hope, the hope that by some miracle her whole sorry past would cease to matter to either of them. The hope that they would be as happy together as if she had been, in fact, that little girl she had once seen on a Brooklyn lawn.

Then she came in one cold, bright morning to see that Richard's bed was empty, its blanket drawn up smoothly to the turned-down sheet of coarse muslin. She stared at it bleakly for a moment. Then she became aware that Dr. Villiers stood at a bed near the far wall, bent over a soldier whose left ear had been shot away. She hurried forward and then waited until the doctor straightened up and stepped out into the aisle.

"Do you know where Monsieur Glover is?"

"Who? Oh, yes. The American. He'd already gotten dressed by the time I arrived here this morning. I told him that he should stay a while longer—he's still weak from typhus as well as his wound—but there was no arguing with him."

"Where did he go?"

"How should I know?" the doctor asked irritably. "Maybe it's in here." His hand dove into his pocket and came out with an envelope. "Anyway, he asked me to give this to you."

She murmured a thank you, then hurried out to the icy vestibule and opened the note with shaking fingers. He had written:

"Monsieur Ducrot has been kind enough to furnish me

with an envelope and paper for this note.

"I am now well enough to leave here. Besides, if there is another sortie, and all the newspapers say that there will be, this bed will be needed. I plan to leave Paris and join the reporter with whom I had been working. I rather think that by now he is somewhere around Mainz.

"I leave you with ever good wishes."

The handwriting abruptly changed, became ragged.

"Of course, the above is not my real reason for leaving. It is just that seeing you every day is too painful. Perhaps it has also been for you. And the one thing we can do for each other is not to cause each other additional pain."

R.

Throat aching, she reread the note.

"Maggie."

She turned and found Raoul standing beside her.

"He's not coming back?"

"No."

"I'm sorry."

She looked up into the handsome face with the expressive dark eyes. How very nice he was. "Thank you."

He hesitated, and then said, "Christmas is only three days away."

"I know."

"Could we have Christmas Eve supper at your flat? I've talked to a butcher in Passy. He has promised to have a duckling for me."

A duckling! How much, she wondered, would that cost him? At least a few times her weekly wage.

She said, past the hard ache in her throat, "Yes, I would

183

like us to have supper together on Christmas Eve."

Because they both spent the day before Christmas at the ambulance, it was almost ten when they sat down to the meal they had both prepared, sometimes colliding with each other in Maggie's small kitchen. Raoul not only furnished the duckling, but from a green grocer in a fashionable neighborhood he had obtained three large potatoes and a bunch of remarkably firm carrots. He also had brought a bottle of excellent white burgundy. Because of the wine and the presence of this young man she genuinely liked, Maggie found herself feeling almost cheerful.

At last he said, "Maggie." His long fingers twirled the stem of the wine glass standing beside his plate."

"Yes?"

"Will you marry me?"

"Oh, Raoul!" After a moment she said, "Don't you think you should wait until you meet a girl—"

She broke off. She had been about to say "a girl of your own age." That would have sounded absurd, since he was actually two years older than she. It was the weight of all her past experiences which made her feel she was his senior.

She said, "Shouldn't you wait until you find someone more suitable?"

"Maggie, you say the strangest things. Who could be more suitable for me than the girl I love?"

Because it was Christmas, she had lit two long-hoarded wax tapers. She smiled at him through their glow and then said gently, "But I don't love you."

"I think you would come to."

"Perhaps."

He said, with one of those flashes of practicality that always surprised her, "It would be an advantageous marriage for you. You'd never want for anything. As for the fact that I

184

could never hope that you would love me as much as I love you—well, people say that in a marriage the person who loves the least is really the lucky one."

If she had any sense, she told herself, she *would* marry him.

"Let's don't talk about it now."

"All right. I can wait."

From the towers of nearby Notre Dame the great, bronze-throated bells began to strike midnight.

"Merry Christmas, Maggie!"

"Merry Christmas, Raoul!"

They smiled and clinked glasses.

Chapter 15

About fourteen hours later, in the bright, cold afternoon of Christmas day, Jeanne-Marie and her small son were having dinner in Charles Maubert's flat. Henri Lamartine was there too. His sister and brother-in-law, with whom he had planned to have dinner, had succumbed to the grippe so prevalent in Paris that winter. Hearing that he was to be alone, Jeanne-Marie had suggested that they all pool their food for a Christmas Day feast.

The result was not bad—a small squirrel stewed with onions and potatoes. There was wine, of course, even though an inexpensive one. Jeanne-Marie sometimes reflected that even if Paris did become reduced to its last cabbage leaf, undoubtedly there would still be plenty of wine. Wine and good French bread.

Watching the two young people, Henri observed that they already had a married air. They had squabbled amiably over whether or not they should add the carrot tops to the ragout. Jeanne-Marie said that with them the dish would provide more nourishment. Charles, whose will had prevailed, had argued that without carrot tops the ragout would taste better.

Later on at the table, bored with the grownup talk, Marcel began to beat his plate with his spoon. It was Charles who, with the air of a young *pater familias,* rebuked the child quietly but effectively.

Yes, already they seemed married. Perhaps soon they would be. Perhaps there was no reason for the dismay Henri had felt as he lay awake night after night, aware that Jeanne-Marie was in Charles's bed rather than her own.

Looking at Jeanne-Marie's pretty round face, so vulnerable in its happiness, he prayed that indeed she someday would be Madame Maubert.

It was only the selfish part of him, the old-fool part of him, that made him feel desolate at the thought of her belonging, legally and forever, to the handsome young bourgeoise.

Lady Diane Harding, nee Weston, alias Diane Gautier, spent Christmas Day alone in her flat writing still another letter to Karl. From time to time she poured herself a glass of champagne from the bottle on a stand beside her desk. She had not opened the bottle because it was Christmas. She scarcely realized that it was, despite the clamor of church bells through the city. She drank champagne because she liked it and because she'd had the foresight to lay in a good supply before the siege began.

As for the letters she had written these past weeks, she did not know whether Karl would ever get them, or even if she would ever send them. She still had no idea where he was.

She had continued to go to Madame Theraux's on the average of two or three times a week. It was not just boredom and frustration, or even obedience to Karl's wishes, which sent her there. She kept hoping that from one of the generals and industrialists and government officials who frequented the establishment, she might gain further news of that "gallant French patriot," Karl Schiller, who had left besieged Paris by balloon weeks before.

Perhaps if she had questioned those important men closely she already might have gained the information she so desperately wanted. But she was afraid to appear too importunate lest she endanger him. After all, if her questions aroused someone's curiosity, and if, one way or another, he learned that she had met Karl in Berlin, he might begin to wonder if the Alsatian with the Germanic name really was a French patriot.

As she went on with her letter, pouring out on paper her loneliness, her need for him that was like a physical ache, she realized that this was going to be another letter so detailed in its eroticism that it would be unwise to send it, even if she knew where to send it.

Nevertheless, she continued writing.

Chapter 16

By late January, Paris was facing utter starvation. Even bread—that good French bread, the supply of which was supposed to be inexhaustible—had been rationed. And it was no longer good. Only the near-starving could have relished the black, heavy stuff made up of beans, rice, mildewed flour and about anything else the desperate bakers could find.

The military situation was equally bleak. Early in the month, spurred on by fire-eating leaders of the National Guard, the armed forces had attempted another sortie out of Paris, this time with the Guard taking part. The result was another smashing defeat. The National Guard, ill-trained and ill-equipped, suffered the worst losses.

A few of the very rich, like Diane Gautier, still lived comfortably, but even at Madame Theraux's, the buffet table no longer offered caviar and pheasant. And the guests, even while they consumed such remaining delicacies as pate of rabbit and eggs in aspic, exchanged worried talk, not so much about the Prussians as about the growing militancy of the starving, embittered French working class.

Jeanne-Marie, moving with her tray through the crowded salon, heard the talk. But she had more immediate and personal worries than the war or the possibility of revolution. Charles, she felt, was growing indifferent. True, as far as she knew he was still faithful to her, but often he was snappish and irritable with both her little boy and herself. And if he brought no other girls to his rooms, neither did he ask Jeanne-Marie to share his bed as often as he had in the beginning.

She tried to tell herself that it was just that Charles, like the vast majority of Parisians, was suffering from hunger and cold. What was more, he badly missed his parents, that comfortably-off pair in Lyons whom he had not seen nor heard from since the siege began the previous September.

But she feared it was more than that. What would she do if he was growing tired of her just when she needed him most?

Night after night, as she moved about the salon, she would think, if he is still awake when I get home I will tell him. Perhaps he does not feel about me as he once did, but still he will help me. She was afraid to put him to the test, though, even on those increasingly rare nights when she lay in his arms in his darkened bedroom.

As for Maggie MacNeil, she often had the wry thought that the city's desperate state had brought her at least one compensation. She was too exhausted at night, because of malnutrition as well as hard work, to lie awake thinking of Richard. His once-empty bed and all the others in the Belleville ambulance were filled now, thanks to that disastrous second sortie. She and Raoul and the nurses often worked far into the night.

Now, though, they did enjoy one additional reward for their labors. The government, realizing how desperately Paris needed its doctors and nurses, had issued them chits, good for a limited amount of restaurant food at one meal each day. Maggie preferred to cook her own supper in her flat, out of whatever ingredients her neighbor in the flat above had been able to buy for her. A widow of limited means, the neighbor charged Maggie two francs a week to take her place in the food lines.

No doubt because Maggie had chosen to use her chits at the noon meal, Raoul made the same choice. Usually they ate together at a café, a low-ceilinged one with smoke-blackened walls, a few doors from the ambulance. On a February day when a rising thermometer had set icicles to dripping from the eaves onto the sidewalk, they sat eating bowls of thin soup, the only dish offered by the café that day.

Raoul said, "You look very tired. Did the shelling keep you awake last night?"

"For awhile."

Prussian shells had been falling on the Left Bank for about two weeks. They shelled only at night, perhaps in hope of rendering the Parisians sleepless as well as ravenous. Anyway, that had been the effect. For days the Left Bank poor had been steaming across the Seine bridge to neighborhoods on the Right Bank, beyond reach of the Prussian guns. Maggie had not joined them. Like most of the fine old houses on the Left Bank, the one in which she lived was of solid stone. The Prussian shells, with no explosive charge, had proved unable to do more than dislodge a few roof tiles from such structures.

She said, "France has no hope of winning the war, has it?"

"No hope."

"When will France surrender?"

"Very soon, surely. I think the government would have sued for peace weeks ago if it weren't for their fear of the working class. But it's getting to where the government has no choice but to surrender."

"That is something I have never understood. Even in peacetime the French poor lead such dreadful lives. How is it that they are so stubbornly patriotic?"

"Perhaps because that is the only way in which they can

191

hope to feel strong, proud and in control of their fate. As workingmen, they are powerless even to feed their families properly. As French patriots they can feel that they are participating in *la gloire* of the first Napoleon, who had all Europe at his feet.

"But I think that after France surrenders," he went on, "they will turn all that furious determination in another direction."

"Against the government?"

"Yes."

"You mean revolution?"

He nodded.

She felt a chill down her spine. For her the word revolution conjured up thoughts of tumbrels rattling over cobblestones to where a mob, gathered around a guillotine, howled for more blood.

"And which side will you be on, Raoul?"

"I will do everything I can to aid this revolution, of course."

Then, perhaps because he saw dismay in her face, he said in a much lighter tone, "But let us hope that between the surrender and the outbreak of the revolution, there will be time for me to persuade you to marry me and then carry you off for a honeymoon someplace, Italy, perhaps. You've never been to Florence, have you? My family used to rent a villa every summer in the hills above Florence. A beautiful place, like something out of a Renaissance painting."

"A honeymoon in a Florentine villa! What an idea for a revolutionary to have. Raoul, I am afraid I am a corrupting influence."

He said, half seriously, "You arc, but I hope to convert you, either before or after the Florence honeymoon."

"Raoul, you are not going to convert me and you are not

going to marry me." Despite the thought at the back of her mind that someday she might feel it was only sensible to marry this wealthy and thoroughly nice man, she had decided that it would be unfair to encourage him now.

He said, "May I point out that young women often change their minds?"

"And may I point out that the only good thing about this soup is that it is not cold? We had better eat it before it becomes so."

Twelve hours later, at a little past midnight, Jeanne-Marie climbed the stairs toward that big top-floor room. Her whole body felt weighted with dread. Clasping his small hand, she drew her sleepy son up with her step by step.

On her landing she saw that no light shone beneath Charles's door. Well, perhaps he was asleep or perhaps he was not. But in any case, she was determined to talk to him tonight. She could not wait any longer. For a week now she had been sick every morning. Already her waist had thickened. Soon her pregnancy would be obvious to everyone.

Inside their big room she undressed Marcel and put him to bed. Then, leaving the door open, she crossed to Charles's door and knocked. When there was no response she called, "Charles!" and knocked again.

Finally, wearing a dark blue dressing gown, he opened the door. "For God's sake, Jeanne-Marie. Do you want to wake Lamartine?"

She stepped past him into the darkened room. "I have to talk to you. No, don't close the door! I have to be able to hear Marcel if he starts crying."

He lit the lamp. "What is it, Jeanne-Marie? Why did you wake me up?"

In the lamp's upward striking light he did not look like

193

someone who, until moments ago, had been asleep. As a matter of fact he had not been. Not wanting to see Jeanne-Marie that particular night, he had gone to bed around eleven-thirty and then lain awake in the darkness.

She said, "Since Monsieur Lamartine might hear, perhaps we had better go into the bedroom."

Not inclined to sharing his bed with her that night, he said, "We can talk here if we keep our voices low."

They sat down at the table where, only about seven weeks earlier, they had shared that pleasant Christmas dinner with Marcel and Henri Lamartine. "Well, what is it?"

"I am going to have a baby."

"Oh, for God's sake!" Then, as she stared at him, her round face white with dismay, he said harshly, "Jeannie-Marie, how could you have been so careless?"

"Careless?"

"Naturally I assumed you were taking precautions."

"Precautions?"

"Don't keep repeating everything I say! Considering where you spend your evenings, I though you knew how to keep from getting pregnant."

She flinched as if he had struck her. One of the many things she loved about him was that he had never reminded where she worked, not even at times when he was annoyed with her.

She said numbly, "You know I am just a maid there. You know I have nothing to do with—those women."

"But you must have heard them *talk*, for God's sake. You're not stupid. You must have learned *something*."

She managed to lift her chin. "Maybe I am stupid. Anyway, I learned nothing."

He sat there with a scowl between his blue eyes and the highlights in his curly brown hair glinting in the lamp's glow.

Hurt as she was, she could not help but think, he is so very handsome, my Charles.

He said finally, "Well, we'll just have to find someone."

She started to say, "Someone?" and then remembered that he found it irritating to have his words repeated.

"I don't know of anyone offhand," he went on. Except for Jeanne-Marie, all his girls had been knowledgeable enough not to require the services of an abortionist. "But I can ask around among my friends at the university. Or better yet," he said, his voice quickening, "you could ask that Madame what's-her-name. Theraux. She would surely know of someone."

Jeannie-Marie understood then. She cried, "No!"

He gave her a long, exasperated look. "Then what do you intend to do?" When she remained silent, he said, "You can't expect *that* of me. Did I ever, even at the very first, lead you to think that I might marry you?"

"No." It was her own starved heart that had persuaded her that he might.

"I simply could not marry you. My father would cut me off without a cent—that is, if the shock didn't kill him before he could change his will. The doctors say that there is something seriously wrong with his heart.

"And so you see, Jeannie-Marie, you must be sensible."

She said quietly, stubbornly, "If *that's* what you mean by being sensible, well, I won't do it."

"Then for God's sake, what do you intend to do?"

"I don't know. I'll get along some way."

Perhaps right now she thought that she could get along, an unmarried girl with one child and another on the way. But would she, after she had taken a really good look at her future? He thought of a newspaper story he had read a few days before. A pregnant woman, with her one-year-old daughter in her arms, had jumped into the Seine and ended all three lives by drowning.

Even if he had not been fond of Jeanne-Marie, and he was, he would not have wanted anything like that on his conscience. Just as Henri Lamartine had surmised, Charles Maubert was not an evil man, merely one who had been somewhat spoiled by money, doting parents and his own good looks.

He said, "All right, I won't urge you to do something which you're that set against. I'll work out some other solution. And now hadn't you better go back to your place? You look as if you need your rest."

In a filmy green nightgown, Diane stood at the window of her darkened bedroom looking down into an empty street wanly lighted by gas lamps. Her heart was beating hard with triumph and joy. Karl soon would come back to her.

Earlier that night, in a bedroom in a fine old mansion near the Place des Vosges, she had learned that France's surrender would be announced within a few days. The Prussians and French had already agreed upon the terms. All that had held up the surrender was the fear of those men in the Hotel de Ville that the Paris *cannaile* might rise.

Her informant had been one of those uneasy men, an assistant commissioner of public works named Maurice Boulanger. A sixty-year-old widower, he was so smitten with Diane that he repeatedly urged her to marry him. Tonight she had sensed from his tense manner that he knew something of importance. By various means—flattery and an insistence that he drink several glasses of champagne with her, and, finally, a withholding of her body—she had induced him to tell her what was worrying him.

Prussian victory and an end to the siege! Karl could return

to Paris. Since he had helped shape that victory, surely his Prussian employers would allow him to come to her.

The little ormulu clock on her dressing table chimed two o'clock. She had best get to bed so that tomorrow she could go early to the few couturieres still offering their luxurious clothing from houses along the Rue St. Honore. This past winter she hadn't even thought of replenishing her wardrobe. But now, when Karl surely would be coming back to her—

She crossed the room. She would take some laudanum to insure that she went to sleep promptly. She lit a lamp. Then she opened the little cabinet beside her bed.

With the room darkened again, she lay sipping the tincture of opium from a small glass.

Chapter 17

Two days later the apprehensive men in the Hotel de Ville announced the surrender. They themselves would not sign the final peace terms. The Prussians had insisted that a new government must be elected as soon as possible, one that represented all of France, not just Paris. Only then would the victors sign a peace treaty.

The sullen gloom that settled over Paris was lightened somewhat by another announcement. At least the populace no longer would face wholesale starvation. Even before the elections and the signing of the final peace terms, the Prussians would allow food into the city.

It came in a flood. Food from England, free for those who had no money. Food from the French provinces, far from free—quite expensive in fact—but at least cheaper than it had been before. The free English food soon ran out in neighborhoods like Belleville and all but the least palatable food in the shops remained beyond the reach of working class people. For those of moderate means, though, life was suddenly easier. Maggie, for instance, bought a roasting hen and invited Raoul for supper. When he arrived he carried not only two bottles of wine, but also a bouquet of golden daffodils. The lifting of the siege had brought, not only the return of food to the shops, but the return to the street corners of the once-ubiquitous Paris flower vendors.

As they sat at the candlelit table in her pleasant flat, she said, "How do you think the elections will turn out?"

"Badly, for people like those in Belleville. The provinces will be voting, too, remember. And the average French peasant is conservative to the core. Parisian workers are going to lose even the little influence they've had in the present government."

"Then you still predict some sort of uprising?"

He nodded. "It will take only a spark."

Maggie remained silent, thinking. Surely Richard will return to Paris if he hasn't already. With the war over, surely there was no reason why his news syndicate would continue to assign him to the Prussian army. The important news stories, the ones that would merit illustration, would originate here in Paris. Especially if the political situation was as unstable as Raoul thought.

She could find out about him by going to the office of the news syndicate. She would not do that, of course. Richard had been right when he had said, in his note, that the one thing they could do for each other was to stop giving each other pain. But somehow she could not keep from hoping desperately for an accidental meeting on the street—

Raoul said, "You're thinking of that American, aren't you?"

After a moment's hesitation, she nodded.

"Don't think of him." He paused and then added, "Marry me."

She shook her head. "Finish your chicken," she said gently. "I've made American apple pie for dessert."

Raoul proved to be right about the hastily called elections. Deputies from the provinces, nearly all of them conservative, dominated the new government. They chose as their leader

199

an elderly man named Thiers, a lifelong enemy of the city's working class radicals, and in return hated by them. Maggie felt dizzied by the very volatility of the French. In less than six months, their government had veered from Louis Napoleon's imperialism to a liberal republic, and now back to an ultra-conservative majority with royalist leaning.

Laws enacted by the new government soon had angry crowds surrounding radical orators on street corners, not only in areas like Belleville but in moderately prosperous ones as well. Landlords returning from the provinces, where they had lived comfortably during the war, could demand from their tenants the payment within forty-eight hours of all accu-mulated back rents. Those unable to pay could be evicted. In many working class or lower middle class districts the house-hold goods of victims of this cruel law were piled high on the sidewalks.

The terms of the peace treaty Thiers signed added to the city's growing rage. France was to lose the provinces of Alsace and Lorraine. She was to pay a sum equivalent to one billion dollars in war indemnities. And, worst of all, she must submit to a Prussian triumphal march through Paris, where the victors would spend the night, and then depart. Even the conservative-minded were outraged. The streets of Paris— Paris the proud, the beautiful—were to be profaned by the boots of the conquerors.

As for the National Guard, they were so alarmed and out-raged that they hauled two hundred cannon up to the heights of Montmarte, lest the Prussians see them and decide to take them back to Berlin with them.

Diane Gautier witnessed that brief but triumphal inva-sion. With thousands of others she stood in the brilliant March sunshine and watched the victors move down the Champs-Elysees. Her heart beat fast with excitement, pleasure and hope as she looked at these conquerors whose cause was also Karl's secret cause. How splendid it all was. The many bands playing music to which the satin-sleek cavalry horses seemed to dance over the pavement. The glittering steel helmets and the waving plumes and the many uniforms. White uniforms of the Uhlans, who rode with their spears stuck in saddle sockets and with each spear decorated by a little blue and white flag. Bavarian riflemen with their heavy uniforms and goose-stepping tread. Bismarck's own troops, in their black trousers, white jackets and square black hats trimmed with plumes. Mounted artillery men, drawing behind them the cannon, now polished to a high gloss, which had lobbed shells onto the Left Bank—shells which had wrecked a number of tenements, several of which Diane had driven past on her evening journeys to Madame Theraux's.

And the men in that victory parade! All of them well fed, most of them young, and many of them blond and handsome. (Although none of them as attractive as Karl, not nearly!)

"What are you smiling about?"

The man who had spoken to her, eyes narrow with angry suspicion, was short and middle-aged.

Others had turned to look at her and a woman had asked, "Yes, why were you smiling? Are you *glad* that the Prussians are here?"

Although she kept her face calm, Diane's heart was pounding with alarm. As she had waited for that splendid parade to reach her, she had heard a rumor that had raced through the crowd, more swiftly than that torrent of color and sound flowing down the broad boulevard. Two women near the parade's starting point at the Arc de Triomphe had exchanged admiring remarks about the handsome and splendidly uniformed young conquerors. People nearby, overhearing, had turned on the women and torn off their clothes.

Glaring at Diane, still another man said, "She could be a German herself. Look at that hair!"

With a bewildered air Diane said, "Was I smiling? Oh, yes! Perhaps I was. I know I was thinking of Victor Hugo's speech, the one printed a few days ago in the newspapers."

Someone said, "What speech?"

"Why, that perfectly splendid one! The one in which he prophesied that France would not only regain Alsace and Lorraine, but acquire even more territory along the Rhine."

Suspicion still lingered in the faces around her. But just then an approaching Prussian band struck up a spirited air and the people around Diane, unable as any other Parisians to resist a parade, returned their attention to the conquerors.

A few minutes later she slipped away from the crowd and walked down a side street. The café she entered was empty of customers, probably because almost the entire populace had thronged to the Champs-Elysees. As she sipped hot chocolate, her heart still swelled at the thought of that glorious parade. It seemed to her a fitting overture to the life she and Karl would lead from now on. As soon as he returned to her, she decided, she would persuade him to leave France and even Europe for a while. Perhaps they would go to Martinique or one of those other Caribbean islands. She pictured them lying naked in the moonlit, flower-perfumed nights, their bodies gleaming with perspiration. As always when she thought of their lovemaking, she actually ached with desire. Oh, if only he would come to her soon!

The morning after the Prussian march-through, Jeanne-Marie climbed the many stairs of her tenement house, arms laden with her purchases from the green grocer, bakery, and the butcher's. She had left Marcel with the concierge while she shopped. As soon as she had put her purchases away she would go down and fetch him.

She felt hopeful today. Oh, not that Charles had made good on his promise to work out some sort of solution for her problem. In fact, he had not mentioned her pregnancy since the night she had told him about it. And she, afraid of displeasing him, had not mentioned it either.

But at least he still occupied his rooms on the top floor. He had even made love to her several times. And yesterday he had taken her and Marcel to the Prussian parade through Paris. So that the child could see, Charles had boosted Marcel up and let him sit astride his neck. Some of the sullen-faced people around them had actually smiled at sight of the young man and woman and the little boy. Obviously they had thought that Charles was her husband and Marcel's father. To Jeanne-Marie it had seemed like a favorable omen.

On the top floor she unlocked her door and swung it back. Then she stopped short.

An envelope lay there on the floor with her name written on it. Even without picking up the note, she recognized Charles's handwriting. Several times he had pushed messages under her door. But they had always been scrawled on a sheet of paper, sometimes not even folded over. The fact that he had used an envelope this time struck her as ominous.

She placed her purchases on the table and hurried back across the room. Not even taking time to close the door, she picked up the envelope and opened it.

Money inside, as well as a sheet of paper covered with writing. She thrust the banknotes, uncounted, into her skirt pocket. Fingers trembling, she took out his note and read it:

Dearest Jeanne-Marie,

I am going to my parents' home in Lyons for a short while.
Now that people can get in and out of Paris, they must be won-

dering why I haven't come to them.

*Here is forty francs. I know it is not much, but as you re-
alize, all this winter I have had to live off what I had been able
to save previously out of my allowance. In fact, I had to sell my
watch and some books in order to have this money for you and
to buy a railroad ticket for myself.*

*Probably I will be gone only a week, but if I'm to be away
longer than that, I will send more money. Money will not be a
problem once I am in Lyons.*

Take care of yourself.

*With love,
Charles.*

There was no sensible reason for this sick drumming of her
heart, so loud that she could hear it. He had signed the note
"with love." He had said he hoped to be back within a week.
He had left her money—which he needn't have done, since
she had a job—and he had said that if he had to stay away
longer than he expected to, he would send still more money.

But why hadn't he told her all this, instead of writing it in a
note? Why had he chosen to leave while she was out, thus
making the note necessary? Surely he had known yesterday
that he was to leave and yet he had said nothing about it.

Footsteps sounded on the last flight of stairs. Pulses
leaping, note still in her hand, she went out into the hall.

But it was only Monsieur Lamartine, coming home from
his shop to prepare his noon meal.

He looked at her stricken face. "Jeanne-Marie! What is
it?"

"He's—he's gone to Lyons to see his family—" Unable to
continue speaking, she held the note out to him.

Henri read it through twice, not wanting to look at her lest
she see the angry dismay in his eyes. Would he come back,

that handsome young gentleman? Perhaps he at least halfway intended to, but would he really want to, once he was in his parents' comfortable home, miles and miles away from this rickety tenement and the young peasant girl he had seduced?

Perhaps he had no intention of returning. Perhaps the forty francs was conscience money.

And poor little Jeanne-Marie was about to have his child. Henri was almost certain she was pregnant. In the past month her waistline had thickened and her already full breasts appeared even more so.

He felt now that his thoughts would not show in his eyes. He handed the note back to her and said, "Well, he probably will be back before you know it."

Her round young face held an imploring look. "Do you think he really will come back?"

Oh, God! He couldn't lie to her. Yet he could not bear to have her know what he had been thinking, so he compromised with a question. "Why should he have said he was coming back, if he didn't intend to?"

Her face lit up. "That's right. He could just have said goodbye in his note and left it at that."

Except, Henri thought, that perhaps that would have required more courage—or more ruthlessness, if one preferred that term—than the young man possessed.

But what about his own courage? Wasn't it cowardly of him to encourage her hope that Charles would return?

Confused, aching with love and pity for her, he said, "If it turns out that you should—need someone, I—I would feel only too honored to marry you, Jeanne-Marie."

Color flamed in her face. So Monsieur Lamartine had guessed that she was pregnant. She said, "I feel sure that Charles will come back. But thank you, monsieur, for your offer. You are a very generous man."

"Oh, Jeanne-Marie!" He reached out and touched her cheek. "Believe me, there is no need to thank me."

If he stayed here for a moment more, he might indeed make a fool of himself. He forced a smile. "Well, goodbye for the moment. I had best fix my lunch."

Chapter 18

The day after the Prussians had withdrawn, Parisians began a symbolic cleansing of their city. As Maggie's omnibus carried her across the Right Bank toward the ambulance, she saw men and women scrubbing the streets where the conquerors' feet had trod and lighting bonfires to "purify" the cobblestones.

Even though the war was over, the Belleville ambulance remained filled with men wounded in the two great sorties. Some of the children in that crowded ward under the roof had been sent back to their families, but many of them still remained, victims of the various epidemics—typhoid, measles, influenza—which had swept through the starving population during the winter months.

Out of his own pocket, Raoul had hired two additional nurses for the ambulance. But he himself, since the signing of the peace treaty, was seldom there. Maggie gathered that he spent his time at every sort of meeting. Meetings comprised of workmen protesting eviction from their moldering tenements and meetings of writers and artists protesting the suppression of a number of publications. In short, all those Parisians whose bitter discontents had bound them together in what was often referred to vaguely as *la cause*.

The Cause. Seeing the excitement in Raoul's dark eyes on those increasingly rare occasions when they were together and hearing the enthusiasm in his voice as he talked of the glorious future awaiting the poor, the cheated, and the exploited—Maggie reflected, with wry amusement, that the Cause was really his love, his one true love.

Raoul had said it would take only a spark to set off the explosion, the one that would destroy the old corrupt world and usher in a new one. The day that the spark was struck, Maggie remained unaware of it for many hours. True, as she moved about the ambulance, she had heard rifle fire, but she had assumed that somewhere a company of the National Guard or of the regular French army was holding target practice. It was not until she started walking through the spring twilight toward the omnibus stop that she learned what had happened.

The sidewalk crowds seemed more animated than usual. People had gathered in voluble groups. She heard the words "Monmarte" and "Thiers" and "Lecompte." Several Guardsmen were reeling along, arms over each other's shoulders as they bawled out "The Marsiellaise."

Raoul was striding toward her. His face, blazing with excitement, looked very young. Maggie reflected that sometimes he gave the impression of having a seventeen-year-old's head attached to a grown man's unusually tall body.

He caught her arm, "Have you heard?"

"Heard what?"

He led her toward the café where they had so often lunched. "Let's have a glass of wine."

When they were seated in the café's dim interior with glasses of burgundy on the table between them, he said, "You know that some National Guardsmen hauled two hundred cannon up to Montmarte about two weeks ago, don't you?"

She nodded. "They were afraid the Prussians might seize the cannon during the march-through."

"Well, instead it was old Thiers who tried to get his hands on the cannon. He sent soldiers up there, under the command of a general almost as old and reactionary as himself. The Guardsmen protested. So did a crowd of neighborhood people who had gathered."

He paused. Maggie said, "And then?"

"The old general ordered the soldiers to fire on the crowd. They didn't. Instead a few of them reversed their rifles and shouted, 'Down with Thiers!' and 'Long live the National Guard!' The rest of the soldiers did the same. Soon the Guardsmen and the soldiers of the regular French army were embracing and pounding each other on the back."

He frowned. "One terrible thing happened, though. The crowd that had gathered was mainly neighborhood women. They dragged the old general—Lecompte, his name was—off his horse. The Guard tried to stop them by firing into the air, but they couldn't. The women killed the old man, almost tore him to pieces."

Sickened, Maggie asked, "What will happen now?"

"The Thiers government is through. Any government needs loyal troops to sustain it and it is apparent, now, that this regime doesn't have them. I hear that Thiers and his ministers have already fled to Versailles."

"Then who will—"

"Who will rule Paris? A commune. Leftwing leaders are already gathering at the Hotel de Ville to form a government."

A Commune. She thought of those history books she had read in the Hell's Kitchen free library. What horror and pity she had felt as she read of the thousands mounting the guillotine's steps.

Her thoughts must have shown in her face, because he smiled and said, "This is not going to be 1789 all over again. History doesn't repeat itself. Only fools say that it does.

There'll be no Robespierres in this commune. Its leaders will be civilized men. Many of them are literary men. Just wait. You'll see."

"But those women today—What they did to that old general—"

His smile died. "I know. What happened to Lecompte will be a terrible blot on the new regime, right at its beginning. But it wasn't the National Guard or the Army who did it. It was a mob of women—harpies, if you like—who had lived their entire lives in degradation and poverty."

Maggie thought, but the same might have been said of those terrible women in the French Revolution, the ones who fought each other to stand closest to the guillotine when the executioner held up the severed heads dripping blood.

Aloud she asked, "Aren't you going to the Hotel de Ville?"

"Of course! But first I wanted to come here. As the news spreads tonight, Paris is going to become a disorderly and even dangerous place for a young woman alone. I want to see you safely to your door."

She smiled at him gratefully. *La Cause* might be his great love, but he was fond of her, too.

Raoul proved to be right about the Commune. During the first few days of the regime the new leaders in the Hotel de Ville behaved with astonishing mildness. The most radical things they did were to abolish night work in the Paris bakeries and rescind the law demanding immediate payment of back rents.

They did not confiscate anyone's property. They even left money belonging to the Thiers government untouched in the bank, even though they must have known that their old archenemy was determined to destroy them.

Their main activity seemed to be making long and flowery speeches to each other, replete with literary and historical allusions, which filled many columns of newsprint in the daily press.

Raoul was both alarmed and disgusted by the Commune's inactivity. One day when he came to the ambulance to take Maggie to lunch at the café nearby, he said, "While they are quoting Shakespeare and the Bible to each other, Thiers and his men in Versailles are surely gathering up army units from all over the rest of France. And what do the men in the Hotel de Ville do about that? They send some of their members to negotiate with Thiers. Negotiate! He'll keep them negotiating until he's ready to strike."

"What do you think the Commune should be doing?"

"Sending the National Guard to Versailles to arrest Thiers and his deputies and bring them to Paris, where we can keep them under control!"

Maggie said hesitantly, "Maybe the Commune doesn't act because—"

"Because what?"

"Because like nearly everyone else they are enjoying what Paris has become. They're enjoying this lovely spring after that dreadful winter. And it's wonderful that there is enough food now that even the very poor aren't starving.

"And there are other things to enjoy. That band the Commune has furnished to play in the Luxembourg Gardens each evening. And daytimes in the Gardens are wonderfully different now, too. I went there on my last day off. It used to be that you saw only rich children and their nursemaids there. But the day before yesterday I saw children who appeared to be of all classes playing under the trees. And the Place de la Concorde and the Rue de Rivoli. In the past I almost never saw poor people in those neighborhoods. But recently I've seen people from Belleville there, people I recognized."

She fell silent, thinking of the delighted, dreamy look on

those people's faces, almost as if they, who loved Paris so passionately and defended her so fiercely, were seeing the full loveliness of their city for the first time.

But the very beauty of that peaceful springtime, after the horrors of the siege, had for Maggie a painful quality. Beauty can hurt when you are unable to share it with the person you love.

She knew that Richard must be back in Paris. English newspapers, including one which carried material from his news syndicate, again were on sale at kiosks along the boulevards. One of them had featured a series of stories about the Commune leaders. Illustrations accompanying the articles had been in Richard Glover's unmistakable style and with his initials in the corners. As soon as she had seen the first of the illustrations she again began to catch glimpses of him—on the street, in shops, in omnibuses. Of course, it always turned out to be a stranger. Nor did he appear at her flat, even though often, on those long spring evenings, she suddenly became aware that she had been listening for the knocker's strike.

Raoul pushed his empty soup bowl aside. "Oh, I grant you. In contrast to the last six months, the city now seems like Paradise. But let me remind you that even a Paradise needs its guardian angels. And what guardians does Paris have now? A bunch of windy philosophers in the Hotel de Ville!"

"Isn't the National Guard stationed at the city gates?"

"Yes, but the Commune has taken no steps to train them better or put an end to the widespread drunkenness."

Suddenly he smiled, "But let's talk of something else. Marry me, Maggie."

Returning his smile, she shook her head. "For the time being, hadn't you better concentrate on politics?"

Chapter 19

In the first of the new gowns Worth had made for her, a low-cut, slender black velvet with a bustle, Diane Gautier stood before the cheval mirror in her bedroom. She knew that she had never looked more beautiful. And what, she thought bitterly, was the good of it? What good was anything as long as Karl remained away from her?

She refused to believe that it was by choice that he remained away. True, hundreds of people of all nationalities passed in and out of the city's gates each day now, after only the most cursory questioning by the National Guardsmen stationed there. Still, she persisted in thinking that some external force prevented Karl from returning. For their own reasons, the Prussian secret service must have ordered him to stay out of Paris.

Which left her with no one but Madame Theraux's clients to admire her new gowns.

She was thoroughly bored with Number Fourteen, Rue de Adele, by now. But she still went at least a night or two each week. Her first reason was that she could think of nothing better to do with her evenings. Her second and more important reason was that Karl still might be counting upon her to glean whatever information she could from Madame Theraux's clients about this new radical regime.

The clients were fewer than before. Not only members of Thiers government, but any other wealthy men and their families had fled to Versailles. As for the Commune, those philosophers who spent their days making speeches, most of them had neither the money nor the inclination to patronize luxurious brothels. Still, a few of them did appear now and then, mingling with rich industrialists and bankers who had chosen to remain in Paris.

Diane put on an ermine-trimmed black velvet coat, took a last look in the mirror, and went out to where her carriage waited in the portico.

As the vehicle carried her through the early dark, she heard band music from the direction of the Luxembourg Gardens and wondered idly if the new government or a private person paid the musicians. Although she still skimmed through newspapers—mostly in hope of seeing Karl's name—she remained too absorbed in her own frustration to be fully aware of the changes in Paris. Oh, she had noticed that grubby-looking people had begun to appear shopping in streets once the preserve of the prosperous, but that was about all she had noticed.

She found that Madame Theraux's salon was even less well patronized than it had been the last time she was there. And when the little maid with the rustic accent—Jeanne-Louise or Jeanne-Marie or something like that—proffered a tray, the caviar on it was of a quality inferior to that served in the past.

She also noticed, with amusement, that Jeanne-something-or-other appeared to be pregnant. Why hadn't Madame Theraux dismissed her? Had the old bawd grown soft-hearted, or merely inattentive?

Maurice Boulanger, the former assistant commissioner of public works, had just entered the salon. He hurried toward her with a fatuous smile on his sixty-year-old face which told her that again tonight he would ask her to marry him. Boulanger was one of the few members of the former government who had chosen to remain in Paris when other once-prominent political figures fled with Thiers to Versailles. He not only had remained, but had ingratiated himself with the flowery orators in the Hotel de Ville, convincing them that all along he had been opposed to the harsh laws relative to back debts and back rents. As a result, the Commune had awarded him a minor post.

As he moved toward her, Diane had an impulse to tell him that she had promised the latter part of the evening to some other man. It would be interesting to see how quickly that fatuous smile left his face. Still, he was one of the few remaining frequenters of the salon who could give her unpublished information about the regime now in power, information that soon, pray God, she might be able to turn over to Karl. She would not to reject the old fool.

More than an hour later, she was fervently glad she had not rejected him. Unlike many men she had known, Boulanger was chatty in the aftermath of passion. As he lay beside her in his luxurious bedroom, dimly illuminated by the gaslight he had left on in the attached dressing room, he talked of how he had been one of the envoys the Commune had sent to bargain with Thiers and his associates in Versailles.

"I saw someone there that you might remember," he said. "At least, I once saw you talking to him at Madame Theraux's."

Diane scarcely had been listening. "Who is he?"

"Big, blond fellow by the name of Schiller. I don't know his first name. He looks more German than French, the way a lot of Alsatians do."

Her breath caught. At last she said, with only the slightest tremor in her voice, "Yes, I think I remember someone like that. What is he doing in Versailles?"

"I gather he's become one of Thiers' advisors. At least his office is in the same wing of the palace as Thiers' office."

So the Prussians had ordered him to attach himself to Thiers' forces. And, as might be expected, Karl had succeeded brilliantly.

He was in Versailles, only about a dozen miles away from her as she lay in this old fool's bed! She felt a sudden need to savor the joyful news all by herself. She was thankful that they had come here in her carriage, rather than Boulanger's. Otherwise he might have insisted upon seeing her home.

"Maurice, I'll leave you now. I'm tired." She made a movement to get out of bed.

"No, wait!" He caught her bare shoulder and leaned over her, smiling. "When will you be sensible, my darling? I'm a rich man. How many rich men are going to propose marriage to a girl like—to a girl in your profession?"

Smiling, she reached up and patted his jowly cheek. "Maurice," she asked in a tender tone, "are you really sixty?"

His own smile widened. "Yes, dearest. I really am."

"Strange. I imagine most people think you are at least seventy."

His hand tightened on her shoulder for a moment. Then he released her and lay back. Diane got out of bed. A robe, a sumptuous blue satin one which Maurice had bought for her use on occasions like this, lay on a chair back. Aware of his wounded and angry gaze, she slipped into the robe and walked toward the dressing room. He would want nothing to do with her from now on, but what he felt had never mattered much, and mattered not at all now.

As she dressed, she wondered feverishly how best to get

in touch with Karl. Try to go to Versailles herself? Oh, no. Karl would not want that any more than he had wanted her to visit his apartment in Montmarte. Try to send a letter? That would not do, either. Any letter posted in Paris and addressed to someone in Versailles would be opened by the Commune's censors. The best thing to do would be to send someone to deliver a note to Karl by hand. But whom could she send?

Well, she told herself, settling the black velvet cloak on her shoulders, she would think of a solution.

Boulanger, lying rigid in bed with his gaze fixed on the ceiling, did not speak to her as she crossed the semi-darkened bedroom toward the lighted salon and the foyer beyond.

During that lovely spring, Jeanne-Marie also was too distracted to appreciate that peaceful interlude or to be aware of the many signs of the new and even more terrible violence about to descend upon Paris. All her attention was centered upon her own dilemma. Each morning she found it a little harder to hope that today Charles would return to her, or that at least the concierge would hand her a letter from him. Nevertheless, she did manage to persist in hoping.

One April evening when she entered Number Fourteen by the service door, the chef said, "Madame Theraux wants to see you right now."

As usual, Jeanne-Marie had arrived fifteen minutes ahead of eight o'clock, the hour at which Number Fourteen admitted its first guests. Nerves tight with apprehension, she crossed the big, empty salon and knocked at the door of Madame Theraux's office.

"Come in."

She found Madame seated at her desk, hennaed hair glinting in the light from the gas wall fixture.

"Sit down, my girl." Then, without preamble, "You're pregnant, aren't you?"

"Yes, madame."

"Will the man marry you?"

"I think so, madame. You see, right after the Prussian march-through he went to see his parents in Lyons. I expected him to be back before this, but something must have delayed him."

"Has he written to you?"

"No. But the reason for that, I think, is that he keeps thinking he is going to be able to come back right away and so he sees no point in writing."

Not for the first time, Madame Theraux reflected upon the blind, self-deluding folly of certain members of her sex. She asked, "Is there someone else who might marry you?"

"Yes, madame."

"Some lazy no-good who'll expect you to support him as well as your two children?"

"Oh, no, madame! He's a good man. For many years he has had a watch repair shop."

"Then grab him quick before he changes his mind."

Jeanne-Marie looked shocked. "But, madame, how can I? I must wait for my baby's father."

The first clients would be arriving in only a few minutes. Madame could waste no more time on this little country mouse. Why she had given the girl as much consideration as she had, keeping her on after it became apparent she was pregnant, Madame was not sure. Perhaps the advancing years were softening her wits. She would have to be on guard against that.

"Very well, Jeanne-Marie. Do as you please, but surely you realize that you can't stay in my employ."

"Oh, please, madame!"

"There is no point in your arguing. The very idea of a pregnant serving maid in an establishment of this sort is ridiculous."

"But madame, I must have employment!"

Certain expenses during the past weeks had drained away her small savings, plus the money Charles had left. Marcel had suffered a cold so severe that Jeanne-Marie, fearing pneumonia, had twice summoned a doctor. She'd had to replace Marcel's outgrown clothes with new ones and buy new shoes to replace those so worn that the cobbler could no longer hold them together.

"There's my little boy and the coming child—Madame, I must have work."

"I'm sorry, but—"

"Couldn't you employ me in the kitchen, where I would be out of sight?"

"No," Madame said firmly, "I have an adequate staff now, and with business as bad as it is, I can't afford to hire unnecessary people." She opened the drawer of her desk and took out an envelope. "Here are your wages for the rest of this week, plus an additional week's wage. Let me advise you again to marry that watchmaker. Goodbye, Jeanne-Marie."

When Jeanne-Marie reached her house she did not stop at the concierge's door to collect Marcel. He was a sensitive child and whenever she was frightened or upset she would see a reflection of her distress in his small face. It would be better for him not to be with her until after she had allowed herself the release of tears. She climbed the stairs to the top floor.

Henri Lamartine, reading a newspaper in his small front room, heard her familiar step on the last flight of stairs. Why had she come home at this early hour? He went out into the hall just as she emerged onto the landing. "Jeanne-Marie! Is anything wrong?"

She said, "I have lost my employment," and burst into tears.

He led her into his apartment, sat her down at the table, and placed a glass of wine before her while she wept. When her tears subsided he did not ask her why she had been dismissed. He was sure he knew why. In fact, he was surprised that the brothel keeper had let her stay on as long as she had.

Instead he asked, "What are you going to do now?"

"Look for other work."

Look for work! Didn't she realize how unlikely it was that anyone would hire her? "Jeanne-Marie, you badly need someone to take care of you. Have you—considered my offer?"

"Your offer to marry me? Oh, monsieur, I cannot accept."

"You still think that—"

"That Charles is coming back? Of course, monsieur. In the first place, his note said that he would. In the second place, he left two months' advance rent with the concierge. Did you know that?"

He nodded reluctantly. "Madame Blanc mentioned to me that he had."

"Now why would he do that if he didn't intend to come back?"

Henri made no reply to her question. Instead he asked, "Will you allow me to loan you money?"

She considered for a moment. "I suppose I would have to, if I don't find employment or if Charles doesn't—" she broke off. "But I think that there will be no need. Nevertheless, I thank you, monsieur."

After a while he said, with a forced smile, "About my offer of marriage. Did the idea strike you as repellant?"

"Repellant!" Her face looked shocked. "Oh, no, monsieur. I think you are a very nice man, but it is Charles that I love. Besides, think how awful it would be for all three of us if he found me married when he comes back!"

Chapter 20

Maggie knew that it was arrant folly to deliberately seek out reminders of Richard Glover. But as that lovely spring progressed she found herself drawn more and more toward that Champs-Elysees café where they had spent so many happy hours. Finally she gave in to the temptation. One evening after her long day at the ambulance she went to the café and sat there in the twilight, sipping from a small cup of coffee and looking at the sidewalk crowd and at the chestnut trees. Last September when she and Richard had sat here the leaves had taken on the bronze tinge of early fall. Now, newly unfurled, they were the tender green of lettuce.

Her every nerve was tense with the thought that soon she might see Richard detach himself from the sidewalk crowd. Soon he might stand beside her chair and say, "So you weren't able to stay away from here anymore than I have been. Several times a week I've been passing this place, hoping that sooner or later—"

But nothing like that happened. Obviously Richard was stronger than she, strong enough to avoid places they had frequented in the past. Or perhaps—anguished thought—his memories of such places were no longer important to him.

Finally a man did come to stand beside her chair, but it was not Richard. It was the waiter who had served them several times in the late summer and in the early fall. Soon after another waiter had placed her second cup of coffee before her, he had left his own station to walk over to her.

"Good evening, mademoiselle."

Startled, she looked up. After a moment she recognized the dark hair and the prominent Adam's apple. She smiled and said, "Good evening."

"You have been well, mademoiselle?"

"Well enough. And you?"

He shrugged. "I had *la grippe,* like almost everyone else, but yesterday I felt well enough to come back to work."

He glanced at his station. Very few customers tonight and none of those at his tables seemed in imminent need of his services. And he wanted to linger here for a few moments. It was not just her beauty. It was his own curiosity which attracted him to her, that same curiosity which led him to eavesdrop on customers whenever possible. He sensed that something had happened to this young woman, something which also involved the young American man and that woman with the greenish eyes and generous purse.

He said, "And monsieur? How is he?"

After a while she said, "I am not sure, right at this moment. You see, his work takes him in and out of Paris." Which was true as far as it went. And no need to tell the inquisitive waiter that Richard's illustration of an article in yesterday's *Le Figaro* indicated that he was in Paris right now.

"And the other young lady? Did she manage to get in touch with monsieur?"

Maggie's heart twisted. The other young lady. Someone else he had brought here, someone he was with right at this moment? She managed to ask, "What lady?"

"She came here—oh, not long after the last time you and monsieur were here. She did not give me her name, but she described both you and monsieur. She wanted to know his name and where she might find him."

Maggie had become motionless. "And you told her?"

"I could not tell her his name because I did not know it. But I had happened to overhear enough of monsieur's conversation to know that he was American and that he worked for the International Press Syndicate and that soon an assignment would take him to England for ten days or so."

He paused. "I hope it was all right to tell her that, mademoiselle. She was quite insistent. And besides"—again that shrug—"she offered a generous tip. One must live, you know."

"What did she look like?"

"She was under twenty-five, I would say, and with very striking looks. Reddish blond hair, greenish eyes and she was expensively dressed."

Diane Gautier, almost certainly, but what interest could that strange, aloof woman have had in her and Richard? Why had she wanted to learn where she could get in touch with him?

Then it came to her. The letter. That anonymous letter which had brought Richard to her door, eyes blazing with fury and pain. "You bitch," he had said, "you filthy bitch." And then, fingers digging into her shoulders: "A harlot! A fancy one, but still a harlot."

Why had Diane Gautier done that to her? Why had she made sure that the one beautiful relationship Maggie had ever known would end, not just in pain—she had been prepared for the pain of letting him go—but also in shame and ugliness?

Maggie could think of no reason. But with a surge of rage that set her heart to hammering, she knew that she was going to try to learn the reason.

She, of course, did not know Diane Gautier's address, but from talk at Madame Theraux's she had gained the impression that Diane owned a lease on an expensive flat near the Etoile. Names and addresses of residents of that neighborhood would be available in the office of the district *maire*, or mayor. She would go there tomorrow on her lunch hour.

Her face had turned so white that the waiter felt a stab of alarm. "Mademoiselle, are you all right?"

When she didn't answer, he went on, "I hope that I did not—did not cause you distress."

Maggie forced herself to say, "It is all right. You couldn't know what she intended to do to—"

She broke off. From her reticule she took a coin, laid it beside her saucer, and stood up. Heart still pounding with bitter resolve, she walked toward the stop from which the omnibus would take her to her flat across the river.

Around eight the next night Diane sat in the salon of her flat, idly flipping through one of the scandal-filled weeklies that, even under the Commune, flourished in Paris. She was trying to decide whether or not to go to Madame Theraux's that night. She had just decided in the affirmative—she might learn something, and besides, it was less dull than staying home—when someone knocked.

Wild hope sent her hurrying across the room. Perhaps he had—

She opened the door and looked into Maggie MacNeil's white, set face.

"Why, mademoiselle!"

Disappointment was like a bitter taste in her mouth. Unable to resist taking a small but immediate revenge, she said, "I remember your face, of course, and I know that you have some sort of Irish name, but I can't recall it."

You're a liar, Maggie thought. Aloud she said, "My name is MacNeil."

"Oh, of course." She opened the door wider. "Won't you come in?"

By the mingled glow of gas lamps and the last of the daylight coming through long windows, Maggie caught an impression of luxury. Silky oriental rugs, eighteenth-century furniture, tables with gilded inlays, and the graceful-legged chairs and sofas upholstered in yellow stain.

When they had sat down in chairs flanking the unlighted fireplace with its white marble mantel and its huge Japanese fan concealing the empty grate, Diane said, "It's pleasant to see you again after all these weeks. Just when was the last time you came to Madame Theraux's?"

"About six months ago." Then, coming directly to the point: "Why did you write that anonymous letter about me to Richard Glover?"

After a moment Diane said, "I haven't the faintest notion what you are talking about."

"Stop that. Stop lying. You wrote it. I want to know why."

"My dear girl! An anonymous letter, you say? If it was unsigned, how can you know that I wrote it? And who on earth is this Richard Grover?"

"Glover. Richard Glover. He's the man you inquired about from a waiter on the Champs-Elysees. He told you that the man you'd seen me with was an American and worked for the International Press Syndicate. After that it must have been easy to find out Richard's name."

When Diane did not answer, but just looked at her with cool greenish eyes, Maggie said, "Why don't you admit that you wrote the letter?"

Diane thought, why not? What could this Irish-American

girl do to her? Beginning to feel amused, Diane said, "All right. I wrote it."

Maggie stared at her. "Why?" she cried. "Why did you do that to me? What had I ever done to you?"

Pride forbade a true answer to that question. "Perhaps," Diane said, "you offended my moral sense."

"Moral sense! What on earth—"

"I saw you with this obviously decent young man." Diane was really enjoying herself now. "From the worshipful way he looked at you I could tell he didn't know you were a harlot. Now really, mademoiselle, was that anyway to treat a respectable man? Why, if it hadn't been for my intervention, you might have married him!"

Maggie said, with a bitter rush, "That isn't so! I was going to break with him when he came back from England, break with him in a way that would have left him thinking well of me. But instead you wrote that letter and it destroyed everything wonderful we'd had up until that point—"

Her anguished voice broke off. After a moment she said in a much quieter tone, "But you've been playing with me, haven't you? All this talk about writing it out of a moral sense! Now I ask you again. Why did you do it?"

As Diane looked at the American girl's face, with its wide-spaced dark eyes under wing-like brows, she thought of what Karl had said of her that night. "She has an extraordinary face, really extraordinary. And there is something there—oh, maybe a hint of tragedy—that makes her all the more appealing."

A surge of jealous fury made Diane forget all about pride. She leaned forward, hands clenched on her knees. "All right! I'll tell you why I did it. You flaunted yourself before—before someone, that last evening you came to Madame Theraux's. You deliberately ran into him!"

227

Maggie said, bewildered, "What on earth are you talking about? *Who* are you talking about?"

"The man I was with! A tall, blond man. You ran into him."

Maggie remembered then, vaguely. She had come to Madame Theraux's that night, knowing that when Richard came back from England she would have to put him out of her life. She thought she had steeled herself to continue her existence as one of Madame Theraux's young ladies. But when a prospective client—Monsieur Chalon of the pendulous paps—started toward her, she had discovered that loving Richard had forever ruined her for harlotry. In a panic of disgust she had fled toward the cloakroom to get her wrap and on the way had collided with someone, a tall man. Diane Gautier had been clinging to his arm.

"And you think I intended to—Why, all I wanted that night was to get out of that place."

"Perhaps so." Diane's voice was almost sullen now. "But just the same—" She broke off.

What, Maggie wondered, had Diane been about to say? But just the same, you caught his interest?

Aloud she said incredulously, "And it was just because of *that* you sullied me and shamed me in Richard's eyes? Just because of that, you ruined any chance that we could remember with joy what we'd had for a little—"

"Oh, come off it!" Diane had regained her poise. "The truth is that you ought to be grateful to me."

"Grateful! *Grateful!*"

"You might have married him, you know, in spite of all those noble intentions of yours. And what is he? A newspaper illustrator? Thanks to me, you saved yourself for a better prospect."

Unable to speak, Maggie just looked at her.

"Sometimes I drive past the house where you have your flat."

As a matter of fact, Diane rode past that house fairly often. She wasn't sure why. Perhaps it was in hope of knowing again the satisfaction she had felt that winter night when she saw Maggie, cold, pale and tired-looking, hurrying toward her door. Perhaps it was partly out of a fear that some night she might see Karl entering or leaving that house.

"Not long ago," she went on, "I saw Raoul Lussac turning into your building. He was carrying a bunch of daffodils and he had the expression of a lovesick calf. I know he must have been calling on you, because your flat was the only one with its windows lit."

Maggie knew what night that must have been. It was right after the siege had been lifted and food had begun to pour into starving Paris. She had bought a roasting hen and invited Raoul to dinner.

Maggie did not bother to ask how Diane had known where she lived. Doubtless she had gleaned the information from someone at Madame Theraux's. Instead she asked, "How is it that you know Raoul Lussac?" It seemed to her that this woman and the idealistic young Frenchman were so unlike that they might almost have been inhabitants of separate planets.

"I don't know him, except by sight and reputation, but I've met his parents." That had been at a party she and her husband, Sir Ralph Harding, had attended in Rome several years before. "And I know that they're rich. They have banks in Marseilles, vineyards in Burgundy, and one of the finest town houses in Paris. Raoul, I hear, is an utter fool, some sort of anarchist, but he's rich in his own right. And probably he'd marry you, even if he did find out that you had been one of Madame Theraux's whores."

"He doesn't have to find it out." Maggie's voice was cold. "I told him almost as soon as we met. And you're quite right. He does want to marry me."

Diane felt angry dismay. She hadn't actually thought that young Lussac would be willing to marry an ex-harlot. And she hated the thought that someone who had caused her jealous pain had a chance to marry into one of the oldest and richest families in France. But she kept her face and voice bland.

"You see? I really did do you a favor by writing that letter to Richard Glover."

"A favor! My God!" After a moment she asked, in genuine wonderment, "What sort of woman are you?"

"I'm no 'sort' of woman! I'm myself!"

"You mean that you are unique? I certainly hope you are."

After a moment she added, "Do you know something? I've taken some hard blows in my life, but you are far worse off than I am. Why, I wouldn't trade places with you for anything in the world!"

For just an instant the greenish eyes seemed to flinch. Then Diane smiled and struck her palms together in brief, light applause.

"Brava! Reformed whore lashes out at sin. You sound like one of those Salvation Army people who have been preaching in the London slums these past few years. I hear they are beginning to appear in New York. You should join them." She paused. "That is where you are from, isn't it? Some slum in New York?"

Maggie's voice was even. "Yes."

Diane remained seated as Maggie stood and crossed to the door and closed it quietly behind her.

It was more than two miles to her flat on the Left Bank, but nevertheless she decided to walk. As she moved along through the cool spring dark, her anger began to subside. What good would it do to hate Diane? The damage the woman had done to her was irrevocable. Hating her wouldn't change her life one whit.

As she walked farther she became aware that many of those moving along the sidewalk of this splendid boulevard were working people. Some of their faces had that soft, dreaming look she had often observed since the Commune took over. She began to think of Raoul and of his fiery determination that these people would realize some of the hopes she read in their faces.

She began to think, too, of what that Gautier creature had said of him. Maybe, improbably as it sounded, the woman *had* done her a favor. Oh, not when she wrote that cruel letter, but tonight, when she brought Raoul's name into the conversation.

Not that Maggie could visualize marrying him, under any foreseeable circumstances. No, she would not do that to him, but couldn't they become lovers? He loved and desired her and she liked and respected him and needed someone to make the nights less lonely.

Yes, she would manage to talk to him about it, some way, as soon as possible.

Chapter 21

As it turned out, she was able to talk to Raoul the next afternoon. He dropped by the ambulance and took her to lunch in the nearby café.

It was near the end of the meal that she said, "You once mentioned that you were living alone in your family's house here in Paris. Are you still?"

He nodded. "My parents and my two sisters have been in Nice since just before the war with Prussia broke out last summer." Although he tried to keep his tone neutral, he could not quite hide his humiliation over the fact that his kinfolk had managed to escape the suffering that more than a million Parisians had endured the previous winter. "And, of course, they won't come back unless the Commune is overthrown."

Not until. Unless. So he was still hoping that an ill-disciplined National Guard and a group of flowery orators in the Hotel de Ville could win out over the grimly determined men of Versailles.

"Of course," he added, "two servants are still living at the house, the butler and the cook." He added quickly, defensively, "It's not because I need to be waited on. It's just that they're old and have no place else to live."

"Didn't you say that your family's house is in the Rue Lestrand?"

He nodded. "Number twenty-five."

"What time do the servants go to bed?"

He looked surprised. "Why, very early. As I told you, they are old. They bring supper to my rooms and then as soon as they have cleared away they go to their own quarters below stairs. I imagine they are usually asleep soon afterward." He paused. "Why do you ask?"

"Raoul, may I come to your house around nine-thirty to-night?"

After a moment she saw his surprise give way to comprehension. His face went rather pale. He said earnestly, "I've told you from the very first that I want to *marry* you. I still do."

"I understand that, but don't you want me, even without marriage?"

"God, yes!"

"Then I'll come there tonight at nine-thirty."

For a moment she thought he was going to say, "But wouldn't you rather I came to your flat?" He did not and she was glad. It would have been hard to say to him that Richard was the only man who had, or ever would, share the bed in her flat.

Raoul lifted her hand, turned it over, and kissed her palm. "Nine-thirty," he said.

That night she found that the Lussac mansion, with its mansard roof and ornately grilled front doors, was one of the newer ones, no doubt erected sometime after Baron Haussmann's Grand Boulevards had transformed partially-medieval Paris into the resplendent City of Light of the late nineteenth century.

She grasped the bell pull and heard a jangling sound inside the house. Immediately one half of the grill-protected glass front door opened and Raoul smiled at her. In the marble-floored hallway he kissed her and then started to lead her up curving stairs. Gas wall lamps in the lower hall threw a dim glow through wide archways into big rooms filled with dust-sheeted furniture.

His own sitting room was illuminated, not only by gas lamps, but also by the dancing flames of a fire in the grate. There were flowers everywhere. Giant red tulips and fat blue hyacinths, as well as hothouse roses. Maggie knew he must have bought them that afternoon.

A brandy bottle and two glasses stood on a small table near the fire. Standing in the glow of the flames they sipped their drinks. He smiled at her, his dark eyes lustrous, and she smiled back, but she was aware of feeling a certain numbness. Pray God, she thought, that the feeling would not last.

All that afternoon as she had moved about the ambulance, bathing fevered bodies, administering medicine, and changing bandages, she had thought of her rendezvous with Raoul. Until now she had ruled out any idea of marrying him. She could not, she felt, take advantage of his generosity, his idealistic generosity which seemed to her naïve.

But tonight she might begin to love him as he loved her and in time she might decide that it would be fair to marry him. Yes, in spite of the fact that his family and his family's friends, even if they never learned of her employment at Number Fourteen, Rue de Adele, would be horrified at the thought of his marrying an Irish-American girl of obscure background.

After all, she and Raoul would be the ones mainly concerned in such a marriage, not his family and their social circle. As for her ugly past, Raoul already had accepted it. And ex-harlot or not, Maggie knew that once she had made up her mind to it, she could be as good a wife to him as he could find anywhere.

Her brandy glass was empty. He took it gently from her fingers, placed it on the fireplace mantel, and set his own beside it. Hand clasping hers, he led her into the next room. Mingled gas light and firelight from the sitting room showed her the big four-poster bed, its brown satin coverlet, blanket, and sheet turned down at one corner. She saw the gleam of dark furniture and of heavy gilt frames, no doubt enclosing family portraits, on the walls.

He said, "I will be back in a few minutes." He walked to a door in the opposite wall, no doubt the door to a dressing room, and closed it behind him.

Like a wedding night, she thought, as she began to unbutton the bodice of her dress. As if they were bridegroom and bride, he was allowing her to undress in privacy.

She removed the last of her clothing, folded her garments on a chair seat, and slipped into the big bed. Moments later the door opened and he came into the room, youthful face pale above his dark blue dressing gown. Maggie sensed that it was the pallor, not of fear, but of the intensity of his feeling for her.

He took off the dressing gown and got into bed beside her. He bent over her unsmilingly and kissed her lips. One of his hands moved caressingly from her shoulder down her arm.

A fear that had troubled her from time to time that afternoon—the fear that he might prove to be a virgin and therefore awkward—left her. Perhaps this was the first time he had been to bed with a woman he loved. Probably it was, but he had been to bed with women, all right.

That caressing hand moved down her side to her thigh. His lips closed around the nipple of her breast. A hardness against her left leg told her how much he wanted her.

And yet she lay numb, frozen.

What was wrong with her? Raoul was young and hand-some. She liked him very much. Why, then, couldn't her body respond to him? And why couldn't she, who for money had pretended to desire so many men, why couldn't she, at least, give him that pretense?

She knew the answer to the second question. She liked and respected him too much to try to fob him off with counterfeit passion. What was more, he was too bright, too sensitive, not to see through such fakery.

At last he lay back. Hands crossed beneath his dark curly head, he looked up at the ceiling.

"Get dressed, Maggie."

"Oh, Raoul! I'm sorry, so very sorry."

"I know. I saw the unhappiness in your face and that was the last thing I wanted to make you feel."

After a moment he went on, "It isn't your fault, you know. It's because of that American, isn't it? You can't love me be-cause of him and you like me too much to act as if you do love me."

When she didn't answer he said, "Do you know what the early Christian couples used to do, the ones who had made vows of chastity after their conversion?"

"No. I never—"

"To test the strength of their vow, they would lie in bed with a sword laying between them. That's what your memory of your American is. The sword lying between us."

That was true, she realized. Probably it would be true no matter what man she tried to take as a lover.

She thought, what's to become of me? She was cut off for-ever from the one man she could love. The bitterness that had sustained her as a harlot long since had drained from her and her work at the ambulance, as meaningful and important as it seemed now, was not something to which she could willingly devote the rest of her life. Unfortunately, she was no Hildegarde Hoffman and so what was she to do with all those years ahead of her?

"Get dressed now, Maggie. I'll find a cab and take you home."

They drove across the satiny black river though the spring dark. A few yards beyond the bridge a line of wagons headed for the markets at Les Halles brought their cab to a stop at a street intersection.

On the corner, under a street lamp's glow, a young couple stood, arms around each other's waists, her blond head on his shoulder. He wore a workman's blue smock and rough trousers, she a dark cotton blouse and skirt. They were singing the national anthem!

> "Forward, children of the Motherland,
> The day of glory has arrived."

They sang the revolutionary marching song softly, almost as if it were a love ballad. And on their faces was the bemused, dreamy look she had seen on so many faces these past weeks.

She felt a pang of envy for those young lovers, followed swiftly by the thought that perhaps Raoul was feeling the same thing. Would he begin to dislike her for her behavior tonight? No, he was too fair-minded for that, but she wished fervently that there was something she could do to make up to him for this evening.

Almost as if he had read her mind, he said, "Don't worry about me, Maggie." She turned to him. Despite the dimness inside the carriage, she could see that he was smiling. He nodded toward the couple under the gas lamp. "I've still got people like those two and all that they represent."

Yes, he still had that. Not for the first time, she reflected that *La Cause* probably always would be his deepest love.

The last of the carts passed and the hansom cab rolled on toward her flat.

Chapter 22

Late in April, those first halcyon days of the Commune came to an end. Spurred on by threats from Versailles that were tantamount to a declaration of war, the orators in the hotel de Ville finally organized an armed force to go to Versailles and arrest Thiers and his deputies and bring them back to Paris.

On an almost summer-like Sunday, thousands of National Guardsmen, plus soldiers of the regular army who had remained in the city, streamed out of Paris, confident of victory. Old Thiers' troops, they felt sure, would come over to the Commune, just as the soldiers he had sent up to Montmarte to capture those cannons had come over to the National Guard.

Maggie was on duty that Sunday, but on her noon hour she managed to get down to the center of the city in time to see part of the exodus. To her dismay, she found that the soldiers Paris was sending against Versailles made her think of a horde of tipsily cheerful pioneers setting off for a day in the country, rather than an army about to attack an enemy stronghold. As for the commanders marching at the heads of the various companies, some of them looked to Maggie as if they were on their way to a fancy dress ball. Appointed by the Commune, and in many cases with no previous military experience, they had been free to design their own uniforms. One

239

commander, in above-the-knee boots that reminded her of drawings of *The Three Musketeers*, carried several pistols in the broad sash wound around his waist. Still another wore blue pantaloons and a tall shako of black fur and had a Turkish scimitar strapped around his waist.

Her anxiety deepened when, near the end of the procession, she saw Raoul in a company made up of men from various units. Taller than almost all of the other men, he marched along in the uniform of the Belleville National Guard. He was flanked by a soldier of the regular army and a Guardsman from another unit, both of them somewhat drunk. As he marched along, his boyish face, hiding whatever misgivings he might have felt, had a determined look.

She had recognized others besides Raoul in the long precession. Many of the Belleville men were known to her by sight. With a sense of shock she realized how very much she, a foreigner, had become a partisan in this war of Frenchmen against Frenchmen. She was on the side of the Belleville men, in spite of their drunkenness and ineptitude. She was for them because of their courage and their fierce love of their city and because of a hope of a better life she had seen shining in their eyes during the first days of the Commune.

Heavy of heart, she turned and went back to the ambulance.

Her anxiety proved to be well-founded. Even if the Commune forces had been twice as well-equipped and well-trained, they could not have prevailed. The Commune's indecisiveness had given Thiers time to gather army units from all over France. Always the provinces had resented, even hated, Paris for her frivolity, her sense of superiority and her political instability. These men were not the sort to shout, "Long live the Commune!" and turn their guns against their officers.

Most valuable of all, from Thiers' point of view, were the Breton Guards. They were from a part of France so conservative that it had never been reconciled to Martin Luther's Reformation, let alone the new political ideas that had been sweeping the rest of the world for a hundred years. Thiers knew that in any fight against what he called the Paris *cannaile,* the Breton Guards would be the most blood-thirsty of all.

Within forty-eight hours those men who had marched so confidently out of Paris had met shattering defeat wherever they turned. Even surrendering often had not saved them. National Guardsmen with upraised hands had been shot down on the spot. Regular army men had been even less lucky. Their captors had in many cases tortured them before putting them to death.

The remnant of the Commune's forces straggled back into Paris, bringing with them as many of the wounded as they could recover from the battlefields. Raoul, shot through the left thigh, was brought back to Paris in a wagon that carried about a dozen other wounded men. The wagon came to the Belleville ambulance, but by that time there were no more empty beds. Maggie, standing on the curb, managed to exchange a few words with him.

"Is it bad, Raoul?"

"My wound? No, it is really nothing."

She realized that probably was true. The pain in his eyes was not because of a wounded leg. It was because of a shattered dream.

The wagon trundled off in search of an ambulance with empty beds.

Two days later a mass funeral was held for a number of the dead, chosen to symbolize all those who had fallen in the battle with Thiers' troops. Hundreds of mourners followed

241

the two flag-draped hearses on foot as they moved slowly through Paris. Their destination was Pere-Lachaise, a hillside cemetery so beautiful, so filled with sculptured monuments to the illustrious dead, from Heloise and Abelard to Balzac, that it was more like an outdoor art gallery than a final resting place. As the dead were lowered into the mass grave, she heard other women sobbing and knew that she was crying too.

But she realized that she wept for more than these dead Frenchmen. She wept for all the wretched, whether denizens of Belleville or the New York slum where she had spent her childhood. And she wept for her own ineradicable past, which cut her off forever from the one man who could bring her happiness.

She went home across a strangely silent city. Its gates were closed now. The second siege of Paris had begun and as the omnibus carried her through the blue April twilight, she saw on almost every face the knowledge that this time the city was facing an enemy far more unmerciful than the Prussians.

Two afternoons later, Diane walked restlessly up and down the salon of her smart flat near the Etoile. Why had she dawdled away precious time? Why hadn't she realized that the silly French would bumble their way into another siege? Why hadn't she gone to Versailles, even at the risk of arousing Karl's fury, while she still had the chance?

Now it would be almost impossible for her to get beyond the city's gates. Those scruffy guards would automatically regard someone of her appearance as highly suspicious, no matter what plausible-sounding story she gave them. True, she might try bribery, but she had a feeling that these Communards, as they called themselves, were a new and unreliable breed. They might well pocket her bribe and then turn her over to their superior officers.

And of course she could not write to Karl. There was no mail service. True, there was talk that the besieged city might resume sending communications out by unmanned balloon, in the hope that they might eventually reach their intended destination. But naturally any letter addressed to Karl Schiller, Versailles, would never reach its addressee. It could only cause the arrest of its sender.

But there had to be some way, somehow—

Suddenly she stopped pacing. That little peasant girl, Jeanne-Louise, or whatever her name was. Yes, she might be the answer.

Less than an hour later the porter at Number Fourteen ushered her into the salon. It wore its usual daytime aspect of gloom, deserted and with draperies drawn against the sunlight. She said to the porter, "Tell Madame that I must see her. It is very important."

Madame kept her waiting for about ten minutes. Then a maid crossed the shadowy salon toward her. She was not one of the pretty maids who handed trays around in the evening, but a rawboned woman of late middle-age.

"Madame is indisposed. However, she will see you if you will come with me."

Diane followed the maid up some stairs, across a sitting room, and into a large bedroom. Madame stared at her coldly from the depths of a four-poster bed.

"That will be all, Hortense." Then, "Sit down, mademoiselle."

Diane sat. For a moment more Madame looked at her visitor with silent displeasure. Suffering from the influenza that was sweeping Paris that spring, Madame did not feel up to seeing anyone let alone Diane Gautier.

"Were you not aware, mademoiselle, that I have a rule

against receiving any of my young ladies in the daytime, unless I myself have sent for them?"

"Yes, madame. But this is a matter of importance."

"To you or to me?"

"To me," Diane said blandly. "I must have the last name and address of one of your maids. Her first name is Jeanne-Louise, or something similar."

"Jeanne-Marie. And she is no longer in my employ."

During her last few visits to Number Fourteen, Diane had not seen Jeanne-Marie, and so she had surmised that Madame had at last rid herself of the girl's embarrassing presence.

"I thought she might have been dismissed. That is why I want to see her. I lost my personal maid and I need a replacement."

"And you want to hire Jeanne-Marie? Why, the girl is five or six months' pregnant!"

Diane shrugged. "She seemed intelligent and not at all clumsy. She will do, at least temporarily."

Madame looked suspiciously at the young woman who had always made her uneasy. Something was strange here. Did Diane Gautier really want to hire the girl as a personal maid, or did she have some other use for her in mind?

Well, Madame thought, feeling her temperature rise, what happened to Jeanne-Marie was no concern of hers. She had given the girl good advice and an extra week's wages. That was enough. Besides, perhaps Diane Gautier really did want to hire the girl as a maid.

"Her full name is Jeanne-Marie Perrault. Madame, not mademoiselle. She lives on the Right Bank, on some street running off the Place de l'Opera. Go down to the salon. I will send Hortense to you and she will look up the exact address in my files."

Diane stood up. "Thank you, madame."

"Wait just a moment. Why did you say that you wanted to see me on a matter of great importance?"

"Why, it is!" Open mockery in the young woman's voice. "I find life without a personal maid quite insupportable."

Only someone born to both money and power, Madame reflected, could speak with that smooth arrogance. Suddenly Madame was sure that the rumors about Diane were true. She was no daughter of a railway clerk. She was a woman of high birth who, for some twisted reason, had chosen to join the establishment at Number Fourteen.

Madame wished she could tell this strange creature to leave and never come back, but if she did she would alienate certain clients who came to her establishment expressly because of this young woman with the greenish-hazel eyes and red-gold hair. She could not afford to do that. Business was bad and sure to get worse, as long as these damnable Communards were in power.

"Goodbye," Diane said. "I hope your health improves."

An hour later, following the directions given to her by the old crone of a concierge on the ground floor, Diane climbed five flights of stairs and knocked on the door at the left end of the hall. After a moment Jeanne-Marie opened the door and stared in blank-faced astonishment at her visitor.

"Why, Mademoiselle Gautier."

"Good afternoon, Jeanne-Marie."

The girl's pregnancy, Diane saw, was even more apparent now. Good. And dark circles, which heretofore had not been under her eyes, gave her a woebegone look. That, too, was good. "May I come in?"

Jeanne-Marie blushed from her own lapse of manners. "Why, of course, mademoiselle."

She held the door wide. Diane walked in and threw a comprehensive look around her. Bare floor, well-scrubbed, but knife-scarred table, a sagging single bed, and a child's crib. On a charcoal brazier in the fireplace, some sort of soup or ragout was cooking in a small iron pot. With an inward shudder she thought, how can a woman live like this?

A brown-haired boy of about two sat in one corner, a pile of worn wooden blocks between his chubby, outspread legs. He stared fixedly at Diane with eyes as blue as his mother's. Diane, who was almost never disconcerted by anyone, found the child's steady and unreadable gaze uncomfortable.

"Please sit here, mademoiselle." Jeanne-Marie indicated one of the two straight chairs drawn up to the table. She herself took the second one. "I am so terribly sorry, but I am afraid I cannot offer you wine, or chocolate, or any sort of refreshment."

"That is all right. I don't require anything. Now I suppose you wonder why I am here."

"Yes, mademoiselle."

"I would like to hire you."

Jeanne-Marie felt a flood of joy. Only half an hour ago she had come home, weighted with despair, after still another day's futile job hunting. No one would consider her for physically strenuous work in a factory or a laundry. And shopkeeper's preferred not to hire pregnant women to wait on trade.

She was down to her last few francs. Only minutes ago she had been trying to reconcile herself to the thought that she must impose herself upon Monsieur Lamartine's kindness and remind him of his offer to grant her a loan. And now here was Mademoiselle offering her employment.

Never mind that she had never found Mademoiselle Gautier likable. And never mind that Mademoiselle Gautier, for all her superior, slightly amused air, was a harlot.

Someone in Jeanne-Marie's predicament could not afford to be too particular.

She said, "You want me in your personal employ, mademoiselle, as a servant?"

"No. I shall require your services for not more than a day or two, but the pay will be excellent. I will give you five hundred francs, half of it payable right now, if you take the assignment, and the other half when you have completed it."

Jeanne-Marie was struck dumb. Five hundred francs! Why, that was more than she could hope to earn in a year. For a moment she turned the dazzling sum over in her mind. Then she said sadly, "You must have been misinformed somehow, mademoiselle. There is nothing I could do that would be worth five hundred francs to you."

"Yes, there is. You can carry a message to Versailles for me."

"Mademoiselle! You must be joking. The gates are closed. No one is permitted to leave Paris."

"It is true that someone like myself could not get out. But I think that you could. You have the appearance and manner—" She broke off. She had been about to say the appearance and manner of a lower class person. "You have a very appealing face and manner, Jeanne-Marie. Besides, you are pregnant. Men tend to be indulgent with pregnant women."

"But what reason could I give for—"

"I will tell you what to say to the guards. Tell them that your husband is a National Guardsman who took part in the assault on Versailles a few days ago. Tell them that you heard a rumor that your husband was left, badly wounded, in a farmhouse about a mile beyond the city gate. It won't matter if your story is a little incoherent. People would expect you to be somewhat distraught, a pregnant young woman trying to reach her wounded husband."

Jeanne-Marie considered, her pulses still racing at the thought of all that money. Such a story might work. "But after I get through the city gate, mademoiselle?"

"Start walking toward Versailles. Almost certainly there will be farm carts going in that direction and so you won't have to walk far. When you get near Versailles, you are sure to encounter patrols of foot soldiers.

"To them you will tell an entirely different story. You will say that you are the maid of a lady who is the *amie* of Monsieur Karl Schiller, now an aide to Monsieur Thiers, and with offices near his in the palace of Versailles." She paused. "Perhaps you remember seeing Monsieur Schiller in my company at Madame Theraux's. He is tall and blond and very handsome."

Jeanne-Marie nodded. "I remember."

"Good. You will tell the Versailles patrol that you and the lady who employs you, a staunch adherent of the anti-Communard cause, were caught inside the city when the gates were closed. You managed to get out through bribery, so that you could carry a message to Monsieur Schiller."

She reached into her reticule. "Can you read?"

"Yes, mademoiselle. I went to school for three years."

"Here is the note I want you to carry. Read it so that you will know it is quite harmless." She held out an envelope, addressed to Monsieur Karl Schiller.

Jeanne-Marie took the envelope, unfolded the sheet of paper inside and read:

I am still living at the same place. I still love you more than I can say. Karl, I beg you! Please, please get some sort of word to me.

D.

Feeling a little embarrassed, Jeanne-Marie read the note through twice, then restored it to its envelope and laid it on the table. She'd had no idea that someone as cool and controlled as Diane Gautier could experience the sort of desperate emotion manifested in that note.

"Now I hope that you can persuade them to let you deliver the note to Monsieur Schiller personally. But if not, at least try to secure someone's promise to deliver it to him immediately. Then come back to the city gate. Tell the stupid rascals on guard there that you were unable to find your wounded husband. Then come to my flat. I will give you my address then I'll pay you the other half of your five hundred francs."

Jeanne-Marie said slowly, "So many things could go wrong, mademoiselle. If either the National Guardsmen or the Versailles soldiers fail to believe me, it could be—dangerous."

"Of course there is at least a slight danger! Why else should I offer you five hundred francs? But the overwhelming chances are that you will be all right. Even if the National Guard refuses to let you leave the city, they won't do anything more to you than turn you away, not when it is obvious that you'll soon have a child."

She took a pile of new banknotes, bound with a paper band, from her reticule and laid them on the table beside the envelope. "Here are two-hundred-and-fifty francs. Take them or leave them, just as you like."

Diane was quite aware that this little peasant girl easily could cheat her, if the idea occurred to her and if she chose to act upon it. She could stay safely in Paris then come to Diane's flat with an imaginary account of how she had delivered the note and collect the remaining two-hundred-and-fifty francs. Diane felt sure that the girl had a simple-minded honesty that would keep her from even thinking of such a plan, let alone carrying it out.

Jeanne-Marie looked at the banknotes. With five hundred francs in her possession she would not have to borrow from kind Monsieur Lamartine. She would not have to spend weary hours walking from place to place in a futile search for work.

Most important of all, the money could take her to Charles. When she heard that the city gates again were closed, she had felt utter despair. But they would not stay closed forever. When this new war, this terrible civil war, had been resolved one way or the other, the gates would open and she could be reunited, at least temporarily, with Charles. If he did not come to her, she now would have money enough to travel to Lyons and stay there until she found him.

Of course, in spite of what Mademoiselle Gautier said, there would be some danger in what she had proposed. In these past few months, particularly in these past few days, the world had seen how beastly people could behave when war sanctioned them to give way to their worst instincts. And if something happened to her, what would become of Marcel?

She would leave those two-hundred-and-fifty francs with Henri Lamartine along with the request that if she did not come back, he would take care of Marcel. He loved her small son and would see to it that the child had the best possible future.

She said, "Very well, mademoiselle. I will take your note to Versailles."

Chapter 23

After supper that night, leaving the door open so that she could hear Marcel if he called out, Jeanne-Marie went down the hall to Henri Lamartine's apartment and knocked. When he opened the door his face lit up, as it always did at the sight of her. "Come in, Jeanne-Marie, come in."

She did not have to ask him to leave the door open so that she could hear her little boy. When they were seated at the table, he scanned her excited face and then said, feeling a faint apprehension, "What is it?"

Proudly she reached into the pocket of her skirt and brought out the bundle of banknotes and laid them on the table. "Here are two-hundred-and-fifty francs. Will you please keep them for me for a day, or two days at most?"

"Jeanne-Marie, where did you get all this money?"

She told him.

As she talked, his face grew progressively paler. At last he said, "Take that woman's money back to her! Tell her you will have nothing to do with this. It is far too dangerous."

"It is not and the money will give us a chance to—"

"Listen to me. Why do you want to leave the money with me?"

Seeing he had trapped her, she was silent for a moment, and then said reluctantly, "So that if something happens to me you will have the money to help you take care of Marcel." She paused. "You would take care of him, wouldn't you?"

"You know that I would. But nothing is going to happen to you for the simple reason that you are not going to the city gates tomorrow. Instead, first thing in the morning, you are going to return this money to Mademoiselle Gautier."

"No!"

"Jeanne-Marie, don't you realize that you could be arrested or even worse? What if the National Guardsmen on duty search you and find that note? Do you know what is the first thing they would do? They would force you to write the same words in your own handwriting. Then they would know someone else had written the note and given it to you to deliver. And then they would know that your story about wanting to find your wounded husband was a lie."

"They won't search me! They won't search a pregnant woman!"

"Is that what that—" He broke off. He had been about to say, "Is that what that whore told you?" But he had always shrunk from reminding Jeanne-Marie of the nature of the establishment that had employed her. He himself had not liked to think about that. And so now he amended, "Did Mademoiselle Gautier tell you that?"

"Yes."

"Probably she is right, but there is still a chance that she is wrong. What a cold and vicious person she must be to induce a young woman in your condition to take such a risk."

Jeanne-Marie was silent. Cold and vicious. Yes, that was how Diane Gautier had always struck her, too. Where there should have been at least a modicum of concern for other people, there was just a blank.

252

Henri had been watching Jeanne-Marie's face. "Will you return the money?"

"I—I don't know."

"Then at least promise me this. Promise me that you won't try to get that message out of Paris tomorrow. Give yourself at least a day to think it over."

After a long moment she said, "I promise."

He smiled. "Good. And when I come home from my shop tomorrow night, we can talk about this again."

"Yes, monsieur."

Although her eyes were filled with sorrow at the thought of giving up those five hundred francs, she was trying to smile. He had an almost overwhelming impulse to draw her up out of the chair and into his arms. But, of course, he wouldn't do that. Why, he was afraid to even ask her to stop calling him monsieur least she somehow guess the extent of his passion for her, a passion that surely would seem to her ridiculous.

He picked up the sheaf of banknotes and held them out to her. "Don't forget these."

She put the money in her skirt pocket. "Thank you, monsieur. And good night."

Back in her own big room, filled with the last of the twilight, she looked down at Marcel. Sleeping peacefully, he lay on his stomach, one hand curled on the pillow near his face. She took a chair over to the window and sat looking out over the rooftops. In the gathering dark, the forest of chimney pots was still visible.

She thought of all those nights late last summer and early fall when she had sat here listening to the sounds of revelry from Charles's rooms. Sometimes in her loneliness, her yearning for that handsome young man who seemed scarcely to know she was alive, she had wept. Would she go back, even if she could, to those nights before she had conceived his child? She knew she would not. No matter what her present anxiety, she'd had the joy of those weeks with Charles.

And she could have that joy again. With the five hundred francs, she could find him.

There could be so many reasons why he had not come to her during that short interval after the first siege had lifted and the second had not yet begun. He might have been conscripted into some provincial unit of the army. One of his parents might be ill, or—heart-twisting thought—he himself might be ill.

She needed that money. What difference did it make that the woman who offered it was cold and selfish? The money would give Jeanne-Marie a better chance of being reunited with the father of her unborn child.

She had meant her promise to Henri not to try to go to Versailles the following day. Now she knew that she would break that promise. If she delayed he might find some means of ensuring that she never tried to earn that five hundred francs.

She would rise in the pre-dawn darkness, before Henri Lamartine was awake and take Marcel down to the concierge. Probably the old woman would be awake. Jeanne-Marie knew that she slept very little. And even if Jeanne-Marie did have to awaken her, she could soothe the woman with the payment of a franc. After all, she had money now.

The money. Where could she leave it? Certainly not with the concierge. During the terrible winter months, nearly all the people in this house with anything worth stealing had suffered losses. The tenants suspected the concierge's grandson, a youth so lazy and so troublesome that even his National Guard would not tolerate him in its often disorderly ranks.

She would take the money with her, thrust down the front of her camisole. She was sure that even if she were searched, her possession of those bank notes would not appear incriminating. As for Mademoiselle Gautier's note, which certainly would be considered incriminating, she would make a small pocket in one of her shoes by picking out the stitches that held the lining in place and carry the note there. She hated to mistreat an almost brand-new shoe, but afterward she could have the cobbler put the stitches back in.

After she had hidden the note she would go to bed. Even though she might be too excited to sleep, she could at least get as much bed rest as possible.

A few hours later, in her comfortable flat on the Left Bank, Maggie awoke with the awareness that she had just heard a once-familiar sound. It came again, a distant whistling noise followed by a muffled crash. So again Paris was being shelled, this time by other Frenchmen. Probably the shells were being fired from Mont Valerian. One of the forts ringing Paris, Mont Valerian, just beyond the Bois de Bologne, was now in the hands of Versailles forces.

To judge by the sound, the shells were falling on one of the smart neighborhoods in western Paris. Passy, perhaps. Maggie smiled at the irony of it. Thiers' gunners were shelling the sort of city people most apt to favor their cause, but the artillerymen would soon get the proper range. Shells fired by Frenchmen would be chipping away at the chief glories of the world's most beautiful city—the Arc de Triomphe, the Louvre, and the Palace of the Tuilleries.

Frenchmen against Frenchmen. No one was freezing to death now, as people had last winter. No one was eating cats or dogs and yet there was a poison in the soft, almost summery air which had not been there at the height of the city's suffering. It was the poison of fear, suspicion, and fratricidal hatred. Coming home on the omnibus that night she had noticed that these French people, usually so voluble, were not talking to each other. Instead they sent sidelong glances toward their neighbors. It was plain what they were thinking. Adherents of the Commune were wondering if those who sat beside them were in secret sympathy with Thiers, and would join in the slaughter of working men and women if and when the Versailles forces broke through the city's gates. Those sympathetic to Thiers wondered if others might guess their hidden allegiance and bring about their arrest by the Commune.

Suddenly she thought of how, at the Carrousel stop, a tall man had gotten on the omnibus. Immediately she had attention only for him, but when he walked toward her down the aisle she saw that he was at least ten years older than Richard Glover and not the least like him in appearance.

Several miles away, two more shells crashed down. With one ear pressed against the pillow, she put her little finger in the other one. With a long day ahead of her, she had to get back to sleep.

Chapter 24

The coming sunrise was just a yellow smear above the horizon when the omnibus, on its earliest run, let Jeanne-Marie off at its Porte de St. Cloud stop, about a hundred yards from the city's southwestern gate. There was enough light that she could see that the gate stood open. A National Guardsman, rifle slung over his shoulder, patrolled slowly back and forth across the opening. Beyond it, a dirt road glimmering faintly in the dawn light, led across the countryside.

As she approached the gate, heart hammering, she saw that a second uniformed man leaned against the wall of a small guardhouse. He looked to be in his twenties. The patrolling man, who had stopped to watch her now, was middle-aged.

He said genially, "Good morning, citizeness." In imitation of the revolutionaries of 1769, some adherents of the Commune had taken to calling each other citizen and citizeness. "Where are you going?"

"I'm trying to get to my husband." She had been afraid that she would not be able to make her story ring true. Now, though, she was aware that anxiety had given her voice a convincing tremor. "He—was one of those in the march against Versailles two Sundays ago and—and he didn't come back."

The man said soberly, "We lost a lot of brave fellows as a result of that day."

She nodded. "I thought my husband was dead. But just yesterday I learned that he'd been severely wounded and that his comrades had left him in a farmhouse between here and the village of St. Cloud."

"And you want to get to him." His voice still held sympathy. "Very well, citizeness, just show me your pass and you'll be on your way. So far our fellows control the road as far as St. Cloud and a little beyond."

She had realized that she might be asked for some sort of a pass. Around midnight the night before she had decided what she would do in that event. Aware that the younger man had come over to join his partner, she gazed down at her feet.

The older man prompted, "Didn't you know you must have a pass, signed by the commandant of the National Guard post in your district?"

"Yes. But when I went there he was drunk and he—" she broke off, again aware that as she told her false story her very real fear was making her voice shake. "And when I—I shoved him away from me, he got very angry, and told me I'd never get a pass."

The Guardsman said, gruff with embarrassed indignation, "He must have been drunk indeed to behave like that with—with a young woman in your condition." He looked at the younger man. "Well, what do you say?"

"I say let her go through." His face, too, looked both embarrassed and sympathetic.

"All right, citizeness, go on. And good luck to you."

"Thank you. Thank you both!"

She had taken a step toward the open gate when a woman's voice said, "Just a moment, comrades."

Jeanne-Marie turned. Wearing the uniform of one of the

Women's Battalions of the National Guard—kepi and jacket like that of the men, but with pantaloons gathered in at the ankles rather than trousers—a woman of about thirty-five stepped through the guardhouse doorway.

"Comrades, I think I had best talk to this young woman for a moment." Then, to Jeanne-Marie: "Step into the guard-house, please."

Perhaps she outranked the men. Or perhaps they were afraid they might be accused of dereliction of duty. Whatever the reason, the older man's face suddenly became less sympathetic. He said to Jeanne-Marie, "Do as she asks, citizeness."

With the pulse thudding in the hollow of her throat, Jeanne-Marie went into the guardhouse, a small room with no furniture except a desk and two straight chairs. The woman closed the door.

"Undress, please."

Jeanne-Marie looked at her dumbly. In the gray morning light coming through the one small window, the woman's face under the visored kepi was calm, authoritative. Jeanne-Marie managed to say, "But why—"

"Do as I say, please. Start with your blouse."

Jeanne-Marie heard a faint ringing in her ears. In just seconds now, the woman would discover the bank notes, but that would be all right, she told herself. She had prepared a story to explain the money. Everything would be all right, as long as they didn't find the note.

With hands that felt numb, she pulled her blouse free from the band of her full skirt, drew the blouse over her head and held it in one hand.

"What is that you have inside your camisole?" The woman stepped forward and drew out the sheaf of bank notes. She began to riffle through them. "Where did you get this money?"

"It's my—our—life savings. You see, I don't know what condition my husband is in. He may need expensive care. Medicine, doctors, so on. So I thought I had best bring this money with—"

"Your life savings, you say? You seem quite young to have accumulated this much. When did you and your husband start saving?"

"Three years ago. We were married three years ago and we started saving right away."

"You saved these bills one at a time, eh, whenever you could?"

"That is right. We kept them behind a loose brick in the fireplace facing." That was a hiding place which had occurred to her before she decided to keep the two-hundred-and-fifty francs with her.

"So some of these notes have been behind a fireplace brick for three years." The woman pounced. "Then how is it that they are as crisp and clean as if someone had drawn them out of the bank only yesterday?"

Speechless, Jeanne-Marie stared at her.

"Well? Explain it to me!"

Jeanne-Marie still did not answer. There was something more she had planned to say if the money was discovered, but panic had driven it out of her head.

The woman thrust the bank notes into her jacket pocket. "Put your blouse back on." Numbly, the girl obeyed. The woman opened the door. Grasping Jeanne-Marie's unresisting arm, she drew her outside.

"There is something wrong about this young woman, comrades. She is poorly dressed and yet she was carrying more than two hundred francs in new bank notes. Obviously someone has bribed her to undertake some sort of mission."

Suddenly Jeanne-Marie remembered what else she had

planned to say if the money was discovered. She had intended to say that because some of the bills from behind the fireplace brick had looked so crumpled and dirty, she had taken them to the bank and exchanged them for new money. But it was too late to say that now. They would never believe it.

"One of us had best take her to the nearest National Guard post, so that she can be questioned properly."

Questioned. In no time at all they would discover, simply by sending someone to talk to her concierge, that she had no husband. And if they searched her thoroughly, as of course they would, they would find the note. They would think that it was in code and that she was a spy.

And maybe it was in code, she suddenly realized. Maybe Diane Gautier was working for the Versailles forces and had decided to use someone else to get a message through—

With cold terror Jeanne-Marie saw what might lie ahead of her. An accusation of spying, perhaps followed by summary execution. Marcel growing up, not only without her, but with the knowledge that she had met a shameful death—

In utter panic she broke free of her captor, bolted through the gate, and started running down the tree-bordered road.

She heard voices crying, "Halt!" A bullet whistled over her head. She knew she should obey. Otherwise the next bullet would slam into her back, but her terror would not let her stop. Instead she veered off the road, thrashed through a weed-choked ditch, and ran beyond the first line of trees.

It was still almost dark here in the woods. She blundered into a tree trunk, rebounded, and ran on.

And then something tripped her up. A vine, perhaps, or a fallen branch. It seemed to her that several seconds passed before her swollen body crashed to the ground.

Her forehead struck something hard. A rock? A tree's exposed roots? Whatever it was, the impact made lights flash

261

before her eyes. Then she felt another sort of pain, a dragging, intense pain that seemed to move wave-like down her body. She heard a voice crying out and knew that it was hers.

Sounds of people crashing through the underbrush, then the voice of the younger Guardsman, "Here she is!"

Then the woman's voice, no longer crisp and stern, "Oh, my God! Oh, the poor little thing!"

Jeanne-Marie felt blackness closing in around her.

Chapter 25

Laying in a bed not her own, Jeanne-Marie was aware of sunlight, and then lamplight, and then sunlight again, with no suitable interval between. She was aware of faces bending over her. The worried, guilty face of the woman who had searched her and another woman's face, round in the frame of the blue kerchief knotted peasant-style under her chin. Also, the bearded face of a strange man. She had a vague impression that someone had said the word doctor and she wondered if that was what the bearded man was.

Most confusing of all, she saw Henri Lamartine's thin face, his eyes terrified even though he seemed to be trying to smile. His presence, she realized must be some sort of illusion. What would he be doing here, in this strange place where night and day alternated with the swiftness of a clock's pendulum?

Then, after a blank period, the world steadied itself. She opened her eyes to find that she lay in a double bed in a low-ceilinged room she had never seen before. Sunlight streamed through a none-too-clean window, late afternoon light to judge by its bronze cast. And Henri Lamartine sat beside the bed.

She said, "Where—"

"You are in a farmhouse just outside the city wall." He

beamed at her. "The couple who live here are still in the fields."

"How did I—"

"You were carried here after you fell." From the swiftness with which he interrupted, it was plain that he wanted to save her as much as possible the effort of speaking. "You've been here three days."

That fall. Her right hand, lying on the thin blanket that covered her, went to her abdomen. She felt only flatness where the child had been. So she had lost Charles's child.

Tears welled in her eyes and slid silently down her face.

Henri took her hand and held it to his thin cheek. "Don't, little one! Don't feel like that. Just be glad that you are alive." He placed her hand back on the blanket.

Yes, alive, she thought dully. And apparently not even under arrest. But how could that be? Surely they must have found the note—

She said, "The note!"

"It's destroyed. I burned it." When she opened her mouth to speak, he said, "Don't talk. Just let me tell you what happened.

"You see," he went on, "I realized how much you wanted to earn that money. I was afraid you would try to get the note out of the city, even though you had said you would not. It also seemed logical that you would try to leave very early, while I was still asleep, and so I decided to stay awake all night."

He told her how, in spite of himself, he had finally fallen asleep, only to wake with a start to find early light filling his bedroom.

He had dressed and hurried down the stairs and out into the awakening city. He knew that he might have to wait an hour for an omnibus to take him to the southwestern gate and so he started walking as fast as he could, watching all the time for one of the city's still-rare hansom cabs. At last he saw one and flagged it down.

Despite her grief, weakness, and confusion, Jeanne-Marie still had room in her thrifty peasant soul to shudder at the thought of that expensive cab ride.

"Just as the cab approached the gate I heard the sound of a rifle shot. I got out and threw some money at the driver. I guess it was enough, because as I ran toward the gate I heard him turning the cab around. By that time one of the National Guardsmen and that woman from the Woman's Battalion were running down the road. I ran after them. The Guardsman still at the gate yelled after me, 'Halt or I'll shoot,' but he didn't shoot. I don't know why. Maybe he was still too upset at the thought that they had fired at—fired at you."

Jeanne-Marie felt sure he had been about to say, "fired at a pregnant woman."

Henri continued, "Anyway, just as the woman and the other Guardsman did, I heard you scream. I followed them into the woods and there you were. The guardsman and I carried you to this farmhouse. The farmer's wife and the woman from the National Guard put you to bed. Then the woman set out on foot to get a doctor.

"I left you in charge of the farmer's wife and went into the other room to talk to the Guardsman. He said they had found money on you. I said—" His face reddened.

Jeanne-Marie looked a silent question.

"I told him I was your neighbor and that you had stolen the money from me to take to your wounded husband. You see, I was gambling that you'd told the story you had said you were going to. About the wounded husband, I mean. I knew you'd hate my branding you as a thief, but that was better

265

than having them think you might be a spy."

Yes, Jeanne-Marie thought, a lot better.

"I told him that it was because we were friends that I had come after you. I said I really didn't mind the loss of the money. In fact, I was willing to donate it to the National Guard."

He smiled wryly. "Perhaps it will get no farther than the pockets of the three of them, but that's all right. In fact, it's good. If they reported this whole incident to their superiors, they would have to give up their windfall. It's obvious they haven't reported it. No one else from the National Guard has been here."

"And—the note?"

"At the first opportunity, I searched through the clothes the two women had taken off you. I found the note in your shoe. It was night then. The farm couple—that's their bed you're in—had gone to sleep up in the loft. I burned the note in the lamp flames."

After a long moment she said, "Did you say I had been here three days?"

"Yes. The doctor is coming again tomorrow. If he says it is all right, I'll take you home. You had best stay in my flat for a few days, so that I can look after you."

"Who has been paying the doctor?"

"Well, I have."

"And you've stayed here three days?"

"Except for going back once each day to make sure that Marcel was all right. The concierge knows you've had an accident and she says she will take care of him for as long as is necessary. Incidentally, I've gone back and forth when the Guardsmen who shot at you are on duty and they haven't asked any questions. I guess that with the guilt in their hearts and those extra francs in their pockets, they are willing to look the other way."

"Your shop. It's been closed. You've lost all that business."

"It doesn't matter. I've been able to save a little money over the years. After my wife died, there didn't seem to be much point in buying things."

For a few seconds there was silence. Then Jeanne-Marie said, "I wonder what they've thought about your—staying here?"

"The National Guard people and the farm couple?" Again his face reddened. "Well, I suppose they think that in spite of your stealing my money, I'm—fond of you."

And I'm fond of you, she wanted to say, but she didn't because quite suddenly she was aware that the fondness he felt for her was quite different from what she felt for him. And so instead she asked, "Where have you been sleeping?"

"There's a quite comfortable sofa in the other room. Now, just rest, Jeanne-Marie."

"I will. But first there's one more thing. That wounded husband I was supposed to be looking for. Have the National Guard people asked you about that?"

"No, because within a few minutes after we brought you here, they asked the farm couple if there was a wounded National Guardsmen in any of the nearby farms. They said definitely not and that you must have been misled by the sort of false rumors that are always floating around. Now rest. There's soup in the kettle on the hearth. I'll bring you some."

Two days later Henri placed her on the hay-filled bed of a cart the farm couple had loaned him. With a neighbor's young son beside him on the driver's seat, he turned the vehicle toward the city. As it lumbered through the gate she did not see either of the men who had been on duty that early morning five days before. They did not approach the cart, but she did hear the older Guardsman exchange a carefully off-hand greeting with Henri.

The cart rolled on, over cobblestones now. Soon she heard an authoritative voice call, "Halt!" Heart thudding with fear, sure that she was to be arrested after all, she sat up in the cart and peered over its high wooden side.

She saw grim-faced men and women lugging timbers and pried-up paving stones and chunks of cement and building an already waist-high street barricade even higher. So the Commune was preparing for a showdown fight. These past few days she had been too ill to give more than a passing thought to the progress of the war. Now she realized that an invasion of Paris, by a force far more deadly than the Prussians, could not be far off.

Henri backed the cart and went down a side street. Twice more during that circuitous journey, builders of street barricades turned the cart aside, but at last it stopped before the tall old house not far from the Place de l'Opera. The peasant boy pocketed the money Henri gave him and drove away. With her arm around his neck and his around her waist, Henri half-led, half-carried her up the long flights of stairs.

In the bedroom of his small apartment he said, "Better lie down. I'll get Marcel for you, although I don't think he should stay for more than a few minutes."

Obediently Jeanne-Marie lay down fully clothed on the bed. Despite Henri's supporting arm, climbing those steps had exhausted her. Henri left the apartment and returned a few minutes later with Marcel.

Glad to see her, Marcel ran across the room on plump legs and planted moist kisses on her cheek, but he showed no curiosity as to where she had been. Instead he began to tell her of his adventures with Frou-frou, the concierge's poodle, a dirty white beast who displayed a vile temper to everyone except its mistress and Marcel. Although she felt an absurd twinge of jealousy, Jeanne-Marie was thankful to Frou-frou. Because of the poodle, her small son would not mind remaining in the concierge's quarters while his mother regained her strength.

After a few minutes, Henri took Marcel back downstairs. Feeling drained and wretched, Jeanne-Marie stared at the ceiling.

In the past few days she had lost almost everything. She had lost Charles's child and the money she had thought might unite her with the child's father.

And now she faced the near-certainty of another loss. It was as if the terror and pain of the last few days had shocked her out of a stubbornly held illusion. She had lost Charles, not in these past few days, but weeks ago, when he had slipped away from this house, leaving her forty francs and a message which had fed her belief that he would come back.

Suddenly she felt sure that if he did come back, it would not be to her. She would love him always, but it would do her no good, because as far as Charles Maubert was concerned it was over.

Henri came back into the room. He opened her reticule, lying on the table, and took out her door key. "I'll get your nightgown, so that you can undress and go to bed."

When he came back he laid the plain white cotton gown over a chair back. She said, "Henri," and realized that it was the first time she had called him by his given name. He turned toward her.

"Henri, are—are you still willing to marry me?"

After a moment he said, in a voice that sounded as if it came from a constricted throat, "Willing! There is nothing in the world I want more."

"Even though you know I'm only—fond of you? Even though you know I love Charles?"

He flinched at her words, but his voice was steady. " 'Fond' is good enough, and so the answer is yes."

"Then—then that's my answer too."

He bent and kissed her, briefly and gently. He straightened, his eyes shining. "There is a vacant flat on the fourth floor. It has two bedrooms. We'll take it. This flat isn't big enough for a couple with a child."

Chapter 26

Late that afternoon, while Jeanne-Marie slept, Henri was moving quietly around the flat's tiny kitchen, reading the ingredients of an omelet consisting of ham and several vegetables as well as eggs when he heard noises from out in the hall. Afraid that Jeanne-Marie would be awakened, he swiftly crossed the front room and opened the door.

A woman stood in the hall and, back turned, was rattling the knob of Jeanne-Marie's locked door. In that dim light her red-gold hair, caught up in a chignon beneath her hat brim, seemed to gleam like copper. She stopped rattling the knob and pounded one fist against the panel. "Open this door! I know you're in there!"

Henri closed the door of his own flat behind him and moved toward her. He said, "What do you want with Madame Perrault?"

The woman whirled around. "Is that any of your business?"

"Very much so. You're Diane Gautier, aren't you?"

For a moment the woman looked taken aback. Then she said, "Yes, I am Mademoiselle Gautier. Now where is Jeanne-Marie?"

"I'll ask you again. What do you want with her?"

"Since you know who I am, you must know what I want

with her. Five days ago I—I gave her an assignment." The growing anger and frustration she'd felt during the last few days was plain in her voice. "I've been here four times since then. It's obvious now that she had no intention of carrying out our agreement. Either she's hiding in her room, or she's run away, taking the considerable sum I paid her."

"Oh, she tried to carry out your assignment." His voice shook with rage. "She almost lost her life trying to. And she did lose her unborn child."

Diane, the imperturbable, actually looked shaken for a moment. "I'm sorry to hear that. But of course I didn't intend for anything like that to happen."

"No, but you knew what you asked her to do was dangerous. You knew that anything might happen to her, a girl of eighteen, six months pregnant—" His voice was so thick that he could not go on.

Diane had regained her poise. "As I've said, I'm sorry indeed that things went wrong." She paused and then asked, "May I inquire what happened to my two-hundred-and-fifty francs?"

"Your money is in the hands of the National Guard. And so will you be if you don't go away from here and stay away. I still have your note," he lied. "With the Communards already building street barricades, what do you think they'd do to a woman like you, a woman who tried to get a young peasant girl to carry a message to the enemy headquarters in Versailles?"

Diane felt her face lose color. How intolerable to be threatened by this thin man, this denizen of a shabby tenement. How even less tolerable to fear him, and yet to discover that she did fear him.

She said, with as much cold dignity as she could muster, "Very well. We'll say no more about it." She walked past him to the head of the stairs.

Out in the street she got into her carriage and told her coachman to "just drive about for awhile." Despite her anxiety and her angry frustration, she was vaguely aware of the afternoon's beauty. Late spring tulips bloomed in window boxes and in pots atop courtyard walls. Except where they had been badly mutilated by people seeking firewood during the past frigid winter, the chestnut trees lining the boulevards were in blossom. But the day's loveliness did not preclude evidence that Paris was at war. Once her carriage had to turn out of its way because of a street barricade under construction, and whenever the wind was right, she could hear the dull boom of cannon and the rattle of rifle fire from beyond the city walls.

From her cursory reading of the newspapers, as well as from talk of Madame Theraux's clients, she knew there were frequent skirmishes between Communards holding forts that ringed the city and the besieging Versailles forces. What if Karl had died in one of those small battles?

No! That couldn't be. He was far too valuable for his superiors to risk his life in a skirmish with the wretched Communards. But if he was alive, why hadn't he managed to get word to her?

She should have realized the stupid girl would bungle things, and now her incriminating note was in the hands of that inconsequential-looking man who had not seemed inconsequential at all when his eyes blazed at her. She didn't believe that he really would turn her note over to the National Guard. He and that stupid girl—was she his mistress? Probably—would want to avoid any further contact with the authorities. Still, the very though of the note being in his possession was unsettling.

The light had begun to fade. She leaned out of the carriage

window and told the coachman to take her home.

The coachman left her in the porte-cochere then drove back to the stables at the rear of the courtyard. She went in, crossed an empty hall floored with squares of black and white marble, and climbed a flight of stairs.

The gas jets, which illuminated the second floor corridor, had not been lighted as yet. She walked a step or two through the dimness and then halted, the pulse leaping painfully in her throat.

At the other end of the hall, a man in National Guard uniform was fitting a key into the lock of her door.

So that hateful man in that wretched tenement *had* betrayed her to the authorities.

She stood frozen. What should she do? Stand her ground and try to bribe the Guardsman? Run downstairs and back to the stables, in the hope that she could get away and find someplace to hide?

The man straightened and looked at her. "Diane?"

Joy flooded through her. She ran down the corridor and into his arms. "Oh, Karl, Karl, Karl!"

He opened the door, drew her into the salon, and closed the door behind them. She clung to him, arms around his neck, mouth pressed to his mouth. He raised his head and asked, with a laugh, "Don't you even want me to get out of this uniform first?"

"Yes!" Then: "What are you doing in those wretched clothes? No! Don't take time to tell me now. Tell me afterward."

As he had their first night together in Berlin, he carried her into the bedroom.

Only moments later, as they lay naked on the bed in the rapidly fading light, she experienced in reality what had been only feverish fantasies these past tormented weeks. His big warm hands exploring her body deliberately, possessively. His lips and tongue caressing the inside of her thighs and closing warm and moist around her erect nipples. The sound of her own voice, pleading with him to take her, a plea he calmly ignored while with tongue, lips and hands he heightened the desire swelling within. Then at last the weight of his long body and the moment of his penetration, a moment so exquisite that she cried. And after that the slow, deliberate thrusting until—his own movements more rapid now—he brought her to a shuddering release from the desire he had created in her.

For a while they lay silent, side by side. Then he got up, drew the draperies against the last of the daylight, and with a match from the bedside table lit one of the gas jets on the wall. Her gaze devoured him. He was just as tall as she remembered, just as broad of shoulder and narrow of hip. Beneath his blond hair, cut "en brosse," his face was just as handsome, with that slight hint of cruelty—the ice-blue eyes, the square jaw, and full lower lip—which from the first had enslaved her senses.

He came back to the bed and lay down. She said, "You've been in Versailles, haven't you?"

"How did you know?"

"One of Madame Theraux's clients was sent there as some sort of envoy. He saw you at the palace."

He said, "So you've still been going to Number Fourteen, have you?"

"Of course! I thought you'd want me to go on gathering information for you."

He raised himself on one elbow and with a forefinger traced her features, from her forehead down her perfect nose and across her mouth to her pointed chin. "Such a lovely little bitch," he said, "and so cooperative. Yes, write down anything that you have learned which you think might interest me, and we will go over it. Not right now, but soon." He paused. "How is that architect who likes to have his backside whipped?"

"Oh, he's all right." Her voice was impatient. "Tell me, darling. Why didn't you manage to get back here before this?"

He shrugged. "Orders."

"And you're not getting any sort of word to me. Was that also because of orders?"

"No, just common sense. I'd have had to send some sort of messenger. He might have been arrested. It was just too great a risk."

Too great a risk! Angrily she thought of the risk she had run in trying to get in touch with *him*. But she dared not upbraid him for it. Instead she said, "That dreadful uniform! Why are you wearing it?"

He laughed. "What easier way to get back into Paris? I just presented myself at the Porte de la Villete about two hours ago." The Porte de la Villete was one of the city's northeastern gates. "I told the Guardsmen on duty that I'd been captured when the National Guard tried to make the assault on Versailles and had just now managed to escape. Maybe the men at the gate might have been more suspicious if I hadn't just happened to have two bottles of brandy with me. I told them that I had stolen them from the cellar of a house where I'd been held and then I made the guards a present of both bottles. They let me through."

"And now?"

"Unless I get further orders, I stay here in Paris until after the Versailles forces take over the city."

"And when will that be?"

"Whenever Thiers orders the assault. You know his

motto. *Ne rien brusque.* Nothing too abruptly. He wants to make absolutely sure that the French left is crushed for a long, long time to come. For that reason, he asked the Prussians to allow him to increase his troop strength beyond the limits specified in the peace treaty the two of them signed last February. Bismarck said yes, with the result that Thiers now has more than a hundred thousand men under his command."

Diane was sure that Karl, as a Prussian agent, had been involved in the negotiations between Bismarck and Thiers, but in the past he had always resisted her attempts to elicit details of his own activities and so she did not try to confirm her guess. Instead she said, "I can't understand why Bismarck is allowing the French army to rebuild itself. I should think that, so soon after Prussia's war with France, he'd be afraid to."

Karl smiled. "He's most afraid of his own German socialists. They are his archenemies at home, you know. He fears that unless the French Commune is utterly shattered, German socialists may take it into their heads to rise up."

She said, impatient with talk that did not directly concern herself and him, "Karl, will you stay with me, here in my flat?"

"No, my dear. Believe me, I'm far from being the only agent who has managed to infiltrate Paris these past few days. I will be meeting with some of them at my rooms in Montmarte."

She said, after a few moments of disappointed silence, "But why did you have to infiltrate, as you put it? Why couldn't you have come back to Paris just as openly as you left it—in that damnable balloon, I mean."

"If the Communards were going to be in power another few months, or even weeks, I might have come back openly and given those windy fools in the Hotel de Ville some cock-and-bull story about what I've been doing since I left. But it would be a waste of time to ingratiate myself with that bunch. They won't be in power long enough for it to matter. It's better to slip back into the city and be of as much service to my superiors as I can until Thiers troops flood in."

In the flat's salon, a clock chimed eight. He said, "I'd better be getting up to Montmarte soon."

"No!" She threw her arm across his chest and pressed close against him.

He laughed. Arms around her, he rolled over onto his back and held her lying at full length on top of him.

"I said soon, not right away."

Chapter 27

In mid afternoon of the following day, Maggie MacNeil had just finished bandaging a patient's head wound when she looked up and saw Raoul Lussac, in a National Guard uniform, limping toward her down the aisle between the beds. She smiled, straightened up, and started toward him.

Dizziness assailed her. She felt weakness in her stomach and in the back of her knees. She thought, I'm going to faint. For a while after that she knew nothing at all.

She came awake lying on a couch in the office of the ambulance manager, Monsieur Ducrot. He was looking down at her. So was Raoul and Dr. Villiers, the testy physician whom she'd seen, moments ago, coming down from the upstairs ward. He said, "How do you feel now?"

"All right. I don't know what made me faint." She started to sit up and then, struck by a new wave of dizziness, lay down again.

He said in a hectoring voice, "You've let yourself become rundown. Look at you. You're far too thin and you've got shadows under your eyes. It's stupid to work so hard that you get sick. What good does that do anyone?"

Maggie knew that it was not so much the hard work. It was the emotional strain of caring for sick and half-starved children, and for wounded men whose gaunt bodies, because of a lifetime of too little food and too much cheap wine, were so very slow to heal.

And of course it was not just the despair she felt when she looked at her patients. There was her own personal unhappiness, too. Working herself to exhaustion on behalf of others helped her to forget, during the day, her basic loneliness and sense of hopelessness. But it did not help her at night.

She said, "I'll be all right if you'll let me lie here for a few minutes."

"You will not lie here for a few minutes! You will go home and you will lie there for three or four days, or until you are thoroughly rested."

"The doctor is quite right," the ambulance manager said. "Much as we need you, you must go home until you are well."

Rebellious, unwilling to be alone with her thoughts for an unspecified number of days, Maggie looked from Monsieur Ducrot's face to the doctors. Then Raoul smiled and said, "You're not wanted here, Maggie. I'll find a carriage and take you home."

Through the reddish sunlight of late afternoon, they drove across Paris. Except for the distant sound of artillery fire, it was a much quieter city than in the past. Thousands of foreigners who had endured the horrors of last winter had departed as soon as the Commune was proclaimed. And in the past few days, ever since the men in the Hotel de Ville had begun to consider a draft of all able-bodied male citizens, thousands had gone into hiding or had managed by various means, such as scaling the city's walls at night, to escape into the countryside.

Maggie said, looking at the sparse sidewalk crowd, "How empty Paris seems."

"That is all to the good. The people who are left will

really defend the Commune."

After a moment she asked, "Why did you come by the ambulance today?"

"Because I am going back on active duty. I don't know where I'll be sent. Perhaps to one of the forts outside the city. Anyway, I wanted to see you once more before I was assigned."

"It's been less than a month since you received that bad leg wound. Do you think you're fit for active duty?"

"Of course. I'm fine."

She hesitated and then asked, "And you think you really should fight?"

"I know what you're thinking," he said quietly. "And I have to admit that some shameful things have been done in the Commune's name lately."

That poisonous atmosphere, made up of widespread fear, hatred and suspicion, which Maggie had noted days before, had become even more pronounced. Succumbing to it, the Commune leaders had appointed as chief of police a brutal man named Rigault, a hater of priests and admirer of the terrorists of the French Revolution. Already he had imprisoned three thousand Parisians on suspicion of being spies and traitors. Among them was the archbishop of Paris, a saintly man admired by Protestants as well as Catholics.

Raoul continued in that same quiet voice, "I pray the archbishop won't be executed. I pray it not only for his sake, but also for the sake of the Communards. His death would give the Versailles forces, especially the Breton Guards, an excuse for every sort of atrocity if and when they invade the city."

"If?" Maggie asked, in a voice as quiet as his own. "You think that there is a chance that they can be kept out?"

"I *have* to think there is a chance." Despite the seriousness of his tone, he smiled at her. "You see, *La Cause* may be a little frayed right now, but it is the only one I've got."

In the salon of her flat a few minutes later he said, "You'll go to bed as soon as I leave, won't you?"

"Yes," she said, realizing how bone-weary she felt.

He leaned down and kissed her on the lips, gently and briefly. In spite of the fiasco of their evening in his house, she almost feared that he was going to say, as he had so often, "Will you marry me?"

But he did not. Instead he said, "Get well. And goodbye for now."

Chapter 28

Jeanne-Marie's strong young body recovered rapidly from its ordeal. By the end of the first week in May she was not only out of bed, but helping Henri transfer their belongings to the larger flat on the floor below. By the end of the second week, she and Henri were married. The ceremony was performed by the chief officer—or mayor—of the district surrounding the Place de l'Opera. Then, with reckless extravagance, Henri hired a carriage to take them to a café near the Bois de Bologne, where they could celebrate with a gala luncheon.

They never reached there. As their carriage moved down Rue de Rivoli, the street traffic and the sidewalk crowed grew thicker and thicker. Jeanne-Marie said, "Why, this must be the day they are going to pull down the column."

Henri nodded. The announcement of the Commune's destruction of the column, which he privately considered a thoroughly pointless act, had been announced in all the papers. But Henri and Jeanne-Marie, busy with their own concerns, had forgotten about it.

The destruction of the huge column in the Place Vendome had been the idea of the new men in the Commune—men who, like Police Chief Rigault, looked back longingly to that phase of the French Revolution known as the Terror. Afraid that they were doomed, and determined to leave some permanent mark upon Paris while they still could, these men had decreed that the tall column erected by the first Napoleon should be pulled down and destroyed. To that end hundreds of men had been working feverishly for days, undercutting the thick stone column with wedges, placing rigging ropes around it, and strewing the Place Vendome with tons of straw, lest the falling column smash through the pavement to the sewers.

The street ahead of their carriage was not only packed with other vehicles but with people, all intent upon getting a good view of the coming destruction. The coachman lifted the trapdoor and looked down at them. "I can't go any farther. I'll have to turn back. Do you want to get out here, or shall I take you back with me?"

Henri looked at Jeanne-Marie. She said, "Let's go back."

After the carriage, with much maneuvering, had finally turned around, she said, "We do not need to go to a café. We can pack some food and a bottle of wine and walk across the bridge to the Isle de la Cite. We can have a wedding picnic in the Square du Vert Galant."

A wedding picnic? He looked into her pretty, smiling face. He wondered if, even as she said the words, she was remembering her lover. Her handsome young lover, whose child she had carried for almost six months? No! He was not going to let himself have such thoughts.

"Splendid!" he said. "No café meal could be as nice as that."

They spent the whole afternoon in the leafy little square at the prow of the boat-shaped island in the Seine. Behind them the mighty towers of Notre Dame rose into the blue sky. Ahead, the city's lovely bridges arched across the sparkling river. But Henri, far more drunk with happiness than with the wine, had eyes for little else than his wife's soft young face.

284

Now and then he was aware of the sound of distant cannonading from the city's ramparts and beyond. In the late afternoon, he heard a rumbling roar from the direction of the Place Vendome and saw dust billow up through the golden light. So they had managed to pull down the column. He thought, What a victory!

He wondered if all this madness, hatred, and senseless destruction would eventually claim Jeanne-Marie and himself as victims? No, he told himself. God wouldn't be so cruel as to grant him this much happiness and then take it away.

That night, lying in bed beside her husband, Jeanne-Marie knew by his deep, even breathing that he had fallen asleep. She lay motionless, remembering his lovemaking. It had been so different from the lovemaking of her sometimes abrupt or even rough first husband. It had been different, too, from Charles' skilled lovemaking.

Henri had combined passion with thoughtfulness and gentleness. Strange, considering that theirs had been a brief civil ceremony, but Henri's lovemaking had reminded her of that phrase from the Church's marriage rite: "With my body, I thee worship."

She had not stopped loving Charles. She was afraid she never would be able to stop, but as she lay beside her husband she was aware of feeling something she had never before felt in her often hard, young life. She searched her none-too-large vocabulary for the word. Finally she found it. She thought, I feel cherished.

Chapter 29

Standing at a salon window of her flat, Diane wondered what would be best to do. Rouse her coachman even though it was ten o'clock at night, and tell him to drive her around Paris for an hour or so? She sometimes did that when her nerves were bad. Or should she take some laudanum and go to bed?

Damn Karl, anyway! If he had been here at any time during the past few days or even sent her a message of some sort, she would not be prowling now from window to window, like a woman half-demented. But after that one time right after he returned to Paris, he had not been near her. Surely he could not be so busy that he could not spare her an hour.

She had started toward her bedroom and the bottle of laudanum in the bedside cabinet when someone knocked on the door.

Heart bounding with joy, she whirled around. Karl must have forgotten his key. She hurried to the door, opened it, and looked into the bland, middle-aged face of her husband.

She stood motionless. After a moment, Sir Ralph asked, "Is this a way to greet one's spouse?"

"I'm sorry," she said. When he had stepped past her she closed the door. "It was just that I thought you were someone else."

"So I gathered. Well, no doubt he will turn up soon. I won't be embarrassing you, will I? I mean, he knows about me, doesn't he?"

"He knows."

"Care to tell me who he is."

She hesitated and then said, "I'd rather not." Once she started talking about Karl, she might say more than he would want her to tell anyone.

"All right." He kissed her forehead. "You are looking splendid, my dear."

"So are you." As a matter of fact, he looked much as he had ever since, as a twelve-year-old, she had first seen him—thinning hair, mild blue eyes, and a smooth-shaven face that always smelled of delicately scented lotion.

She added, "And I'm glad to see you, Ralph." She was, now that she had recovered from her initial disappointment. Often she reflected that her father, without knowing it, had selected exactly the right sort of husband for her. They were apart most of the time and when they were together, he was amiable and amusing. "Sit down," she said. "Let me pour you some brandy."

When they were both seated with glasses in hand, she asked, "What on earth brings you to Paris *now*. I should think it would be the last place you'd want to visit."

"My dear, you are so very right. But remember that boy I told you about the last time we were together, the one I met in Florence."

Diane nodded. "Isn't his name Roberto?"

"Rudolfo. Well, the wretched creature took it into his handsome head that Paris would be a very exciting spot right now. I tried to argue him out of it, but he insisted that he was coming here, with me or without me." He sighed. "So, here I am."

"Did you have trouble entering the city?"

"Some, although not as much as I'd warned that wretched boy we might have. After we reached here in the coach I'd hired in Calais, some villainous-looking fellows in uniform stopped us at one of the city gates. I persuaded them to send a message from me to the English ambassador here. He sent back a request that they let us in."

For a while they sipped their brandy in silence. Then he asked, "Tell me, what have you been up to since we were last in touch?"

"Nothing new."

"You can't mean that you're still spending some evenings at that gussied-up brothel on Rue de Adele! Why, I should have thought you would have stopped finding that place amusing long ago."

That, of course, was the case. It was only in hopes of gathering information valuable to Karl that she had continued going there. But she couldn't tell Sir Ralph that, and so she merely shrugged and then asked, "What have you been doing?"

"Well, Rudolfo, the poor boy, had never been farther away from home than Milan, so last winter and early spring we went to Venice, then north to Berlin, then Vienna—Oh, by the way! Guess who I saw in Vienna last February? Not that we met, exactly. I just saw him at a large reception and because he was so enormously good looking, I asked who he was."

He paused. She said, nerves tight with an odd premonition, "Well? Go on."

"His name was Karl Schiller. I remembered your telling me that in Berlin you'd met this handsome blond Frenchman who'd been born in Alsace. Wasn't his name Karl Schiller?"

She said, from a restricted throat, "Yes. He was in Vienna,

you say?" Karl had told her nothing about being in Vienna at any time during the previous winter.

"Yes, last February."

"What on earth was he doing there?"

"Visiting his fiancée's family, apparently."

She heard her own voice speaking as if from a long way off, "His fiancée?"

"An Austrian duchess, no less. Pure Almanach de Gotha, practically back to the Stone Age. But a very young duchess."

Diane asked, still in that voice which sounded strange to her own ears, "How young?"

"Eighteen. The talk is that her parents insist she not marry until she is nineteen. I couldn't say as to that, but I do know it was announced that the marriage would not take place until sometime late in the summer."

Her voice began to tremble. "Ralph, if you're trying to play some kind of joke—Well, I don't find it in the least funny."

"Joke!" He was blank-faced with astonishment. "My dearest girl, why should I try—" Then his face changed. "Oh, my dear, I had no idea that you still—I mean, you never seemed to retain an interest in any one man for very long. It never occurred to me that you—"

"It's all right." She was more in control of herself now. "And anyway, we can't be sure we have the same man in mind. There are probably hundreds, even thousands, of Karl Schillers in the world. And surely more than one of them is both blond and handsome."

After a moment he said, "That's true. We have no way of knowing that the man in Vienna is the same Karl Schiller."

A constrained note in his voice made her nerves tighten again. "From the way you said that, I think there is a way of knowing. There is something more, something that you haven't told me."

"My dear, I swear that—"

"Don't try to be evasive." Her voice was cold. "If you don't tell me everything you know about this instantly, I'm going to be very angry indeed. And you don't want to make me angry, do you, Ralph?"

He could scarcely afford to do so. As part of the marriage agreement, the Earl had paid all of his son-in-law's debts. He also had settled a small annual stipend upon him, scarcely enough to keep the Baronet in cravats and cologne. It was an allowance from Diane that enabled him to wander around the world with his handsome young Ottos and Ramons and Rudolfos.

Reluctantly he took his notecase from an inner pocket. "Well, I do have this clipping. You see, I had no idea that you felt differently about this Karl Schiller than you've felt about all the others, so when I saw an account of the engagement in an English-language newspaper in Vienna, I scissored it out. Rudolfo was already teasing me to go to Paris, and I thought you might still be here, and if so, that you might be mildly interested in the article.

"Anyway," he said, as he held the folded column of newsprint out to her, "perhaps it is not the same Karl Schiller."

But it was. Her stomach tied in a sick knot as she looked down at a photograph of Karl's handsome face. A design made up of garlands and turtle doves framed both his picture and that of his fiancée, a girl with blond hair swept back into a cluster of curls at the nape of her slender neck. She looked not only beautiful, but dewy with youth.

Her eyes swept down the column of newsprint. Augusta, Duchess of Hess-Braustein. On her father's side, great-grandniece of Empress Maria Theresa, on her mother's side, a direct descendant of England's King George the Third. And Karl Schiller, an untitled member of an old and distinguished French-Alsatian family and a collateral descendant of Emperor Charles the Fifth.

The final sentence read: "After the nuptials, which will be held in St. Steven's Cathedral on August twenty-eighth, the newly wedded pair will make their home at Brinderwald, one of the estates of the bride's family, near Salsburg."

The previous winter while she herself played harlot—no longer for her own amusement, but only in hope of obtaining valuable information for him—he had been wooing and winning this Austrian beauty.

And a few days ago, while Diane lay half-fainting with desire in his arms, he had known that within a few weeks he would be married—married to a girl of such a powerful family that he would not dare to keep up a connection with a déclassé woman like Diane, even if he wanted to.

She crumpled the clipping in her fist.

Sir Ralph had never seen his wife look like this—lips thin, eyes glittering with rage—and the sight frightened him. He said, "My dear, perhaps I had better leave."

She nodded.

Promptly he got to his feet. "Rudolfo and I are staying at the Meurice. I shan't bother you again while I'm in Paris, but if you should need me for anything, send a message to the Meurice."

Again unable to speak, she just nodded.

When her husband had gone, she went to the window and with the clipping still crumpled in her fist, looked down at the street, barely visible in the wan glow of the gas. Vaguely, she was aware of distant gunfire.

She longed to take her revenge right now, tonight. But no. What was that motto Karl had quoted, the one he said was

Old Thiers'? Oh, yes. *Rien de brusquer*. Nothing too quickly. That would be her motto too.

She had plenty of time. With the collapse of the Commune imminent, she did not have to fear that Karl would leave Paris, and thus escape her. But just to make sure, she would have her coachman keep a watch on the house in Montmarte.

When the time was ripe, she would make Karl Schiller wish he had never met her.

Chapter 30

Maggie had just finished washing her hair that morning when the knocker sounded. Standing before the bathroom mirror, she wrapped a towel turban-wise around her head, noticing, as she did so, how pale and thin her face was. She went to the door and opened it.

Richard Glover stood there, silhouetted against the gray light filtering through the window at the end of the hall.

She felt a leap of joy, followed almost instantly by the anguished memory of the last time she had seen him standing there, eyes blazing, face white to the lips with the shock of having learned that she was one of Madame Theraux's harlots.

Now his face was tense, but controlled. He even smiled "Hello, Maggie."

"Hello, Richard. Won't you come in?"

When he had stepped past her into the flat's small foyer he turned to look at her searchingly. "They told me at the ambulance that you were ill."

"Not ill. Just terribly tired, but I am better now. I'll go back to work tomorrow."

As a matter of fact, she still felt exhausted, but anything was better than remaining alone here, as she had for the last few days, with her own thoughts.

She led him into the salon. "Won't you sit down, Richard?"

When they were seated she asked, "You've been back in Paris for quite a while?"

"Several weeks."

She said nothing. No need to ask why he had not come to see her until now. The note he had left for her with the doctor at the ambulance had made that clear. Seeing each other, he had said, could do nothing but bring them more pain. So the only question now was why, in spite of his own convictions, he had come here.

He said, as if to answer her thoughts, "I've come to try to convince you that you mustn't go on living alone in this flat."

She said, astonished, "Why not? I've lived alone here for almost two years."

"But not during the sort of times that lie ahead. You haven't lived alone, or traveled back and forth across Paris alone, during a street war."

"But Richard! What do you propose I do? Don't tell me to go back to America. I don't want to."

"I'm not telling you that. Even if you did want to go back, there might not be enough time left for the American ambassador to arrange safe conduct to the coast for you."

"Then what—"

"I want you to live in my flat."

As she looked at him, speechless, he hurried on, "It's a new flat, larger than my old one. As you know, a lot of people have left Paris, one way or another, over the past two months. That means there are a lot of vacancies. I found this flat in the Rue Rachel."

He paused. Then, when she didn't speak, he added, "The neighborhood is several cuts above Belleville, but still, my flat is only three or four minutes walk from the ambulance. There are two bedrooms, and a second entrance, up a set of back stairs through a kitchen. I'll use that entrance."

She said, incredulously, "You're proposing that I live there with—I mean, at the same time that you do?"

His voice was even. "Yes. Probably we will seldom see each other. You can have sole use of the kitchen. I take all my meals out."

"But why should you want me to do this?"

"I just told you. Unless I'm mistaken, Paris is going to become a dangerous place indeed, more dangerous for the average person than it was during the French Revolution."

She said, trying to keep her voice matter of fact, "Still, why should you be that concerned for my welfare?"

"Don't pretend you don't know why!" His voice was harsh. "I'd hoped I'd get over you, but I haven't. As soon as this grisly war is over, I'm going back to the States and find a job with one of the Dayton papers. Maybe that will end it for me, but right now I have to keep you safe if I can."

She sat silent, feeling a mixture of emotions. Poignant joy that he still loved her. Sorrow that there soon would be an ocean between them, and bitter resentment that, while loving her, he still felt that her past—all those rich men at Madame Theraux's, all those working men in the Hell's Kitchen flat—made it impossible for him to join his life to hers. It was an illogical resentment. After all, she too felt that they could have no happiness together. But still, the resentment was there.

She said evenly, "It's kind of you to be so concerned, but I would rather not accept your offer."

He said, after a long moment, "If you won't do it for your sake, then do it for mine. Please, Maggie. Maybe you feel I don't have any right to ask it, but please don't put me through the hell of wondering if one side or the other has invaded this flat, or if you've been shot down in the street."

She felt tears pressing behind her eyes. She waited until she was sure her voice would not tremble and then said, "Let's suppose for a moment that I accept. When would you want me to move in?"

"Today. The flat is fully furnished. All you would need to bring is some clothes, some linens, and whatever food might otherwise spoil. I could be back here in an hour with a carriage."

She looked down at her clasped hands, knowing that she was going to accept, and not just because of his plea, much as it had touched her. She was going to accept because she could not resist the bittersweet pleasure of being under the same roof with him, even though it would be only for a short time, and even though it would be in the midst of lord-knew-what sort of fratricidal war to the death.

"Very well," she said. "Come back in an hour."

The flat in the house in Rue Rachel proved to be much less luxurious, of course, than her own quarters. But its plainly furnished rooms were clean and quite spacious. Richard carried her belongings up two flights and placed them in the larger of the two bedrooms. Then, saying that he had matters to attend to, he left her.

Moving slowly so as to fill up the time, she spent the rest of the afternoon putting away her clothes in the bedroom wardrobe and bureau, making her bed, and storing away in the small pantry the food she had brought with her. At six she fixed a solitary supper of hard-boiled eggs and cheese and a green salad. Afterward she sat in the sparsely furnished front room, reading by the light of an oil lamp—the flat did not have gas illumination—a copy of Mark Twain's "Life on the Mississippi," which she had found on the dining table.

At ten she went to bed. Sometime after church bells had

struck midnight, she heard, even though the walls were fairly thick, the sound of Richard moving about in the other bedroom.

It was then that she realized that the bittersweet experience of living beneath the same roof as Richard was going to prove far more bitter than sweet. The fact that they lay apart, even though separated by only inches of lathes and plaster, made her realize more keenly than she ever had that the barrier between them was insurmountable.

She fell asleep finally. When she awoke, the empty silence of the flat told her even before she left her room that Richard must have gone to his office or out on an assignment. She fixed herself a cup of tea, drank it, and then without appetite for anything more, walked the few hundred yards to the ambulance.

Holding Marcel's hand, Jeanne-Marie slowly descended the long flights of stairs. In the pocket of her full skirt was a list of foods she hoped to buy in the shops, including fish for Henri's lunch. He liked light dishes—fish or an omelette—when he came home at noon from his watch repair shop. It was one of the many things she learned about him since that dreadful day when she had crashed to the ground in the woods. Before that he had been just Monsieur Lamartine, her generous neighbor. Now he was a man who ate fish for lunch, liked to talk of his boyhood in a village where his father had been the only watchmaker, and once had hankered to go to sea.

She also knew from a shyness in his manner when he undressed, that he considered his tall body too thin. And she had learned that, after making love, he was apt to lift a lock of her hair from the pillow and press it to his mouth.

She had reached the ground floor now. She started to turn

toward the concierge's door and then stood still. Silhouetted in the doorway lounged a familiar figure, wide of shoulder, and with gold-brown hair glinting in the morning light.

He straightened and took a step toward her. She could see his face more clearly now. He was smiling, but as his gaze swept down her body his smile died.

He said, "Hello, Jeanne-Marie." Then, bending, "Why if it isn't my friend, Marcel!"

The little boy made a crowing noise and stretched his arms upward. As Charles lifted the gleeful child and held him high in the air, she had a poignant memory of the day when he had perched her small son on his shoulders so that he could see the triumphant Prussians march by. That was the day when she had felt almost certain that, in spite of everything, Charles would marry her.

She said, from a tight throat, "That is enough, Marcel. You must stay with the concierge for a while."

"That's right, Marcel," he said, lowering the little boy to the floor. "I'll see you later."

It was Charles who, despite the child's wail of disappointment, knocked on the concierge's door. When the old woman opened it, she at first looked merely astonished. Then her eyes narrowed with speculation as she saw that Monsieur Lamartine's bride was in the company of her former lover. But all she said was, "Hello, monsieur. You owe me some back rent."

"I know. I'll settle with you in half an hour or so."

The concierge drew Marcel inside and closed the door.

Charles looked down at Jeanne-Marie, his handsome face grave now. "You're not—What became of—"

"I had a miscarriage."

After a long moment he said, "Jeanne-Marie, I don't know what to say."

"Then don't say anything." She was glad that he seemed disinclined to discuss it. She did not want to tell him that her miscarriage had been the result of a foolhardy attempt to earn money—money enough to enable her to go to Lyons and look for him.

He said, "I must talk to you. Will you come up to my rooms with me?"

After a moment's hesitation she said, "Yes."

He followed her up the stairs. Her derriere, he observed, still had that delicious roundness. Nevertheless, she was thinner, especially in the face. That made her more attractive. When he first saw her, she had been a pretty, ripe young peasant girl. Now her newly prominent cheekbones, and a certain shadowed look in her eyes, were beginning to give her the appearance of a lovely woman.

They climbed to the top floor. He fitted the key into the lock, swung back the door into his flat, and stood aside for her to enter. After weeks of being closed up, the rooms had a musty smell. As he moved around opening windows, she stood in the center of the small room that served both as a salon and dining room. Through an open doorway she could see the bed where so often she had lain in his arms, the bed where his child had been conceived.

After opening a window in the tiny kitchen, he came back into the front room and gestured toward the two chairs drawn up at the table. When they had sat down he said, "I suppose you want to know why I stayed away so long."

She was silent for a moment, thinking, he's just as handsome as I remembered him being. Several times she had wondered if he possibly could be. "Yes," she said.

"Well, first of all, when I reached home I found my father dying."

"Oh, Charles! I'm so very sorry."

"His death left me—dazed."

He reflected that perhaps that was an exaggeration, but certainly he had been fond of his father. It wasn't until he learned the terms of his father's will that his grief became tinged with bitter resentment. All of the sizable estate had been left in the control of Charles's mother.

"After a while," he went on, "I began to recover from my father's death. I began to think of returning to Paris. That is why I didn't try to get a letter to you. I kept thinking that in a day or two I would be here."

"But you didn't come, not until now."

"No, my mother objected. She didn't want me to return to where I might be in danger. Besides, she hated the thought of being left alone, but I've been a long way from forgetting you, Jeanne-Marie. Not a day has passed without my thinking of you a dozen times."

That was not quite true. When he first returned to his home he had thought of her only fleetingly and guiltily. It wasn't until he learned of his mother's plans for him that he had begun to think almost obsessively of Jeanne-Marie.

Madame Maubert was not content with controlling her husband's estate. She also wanted to control her son's marital future. Soon after his father's death, he learned that she had selected a bride for him. In fact, without his being aware of it, she had been resolved upon that particular daughter-in-law since a few days after her son's first birthday. It was then that a girl child, christened Lily, had been born to Madame Artois, Madame Maubert's closest friend since their schooldays. The two women had pledged to each other that they would do everything possible to unite their children in marriage. And now the two silly, sentimental women—worse than silly in Charles' view, almost perverted—were determined to fulfill the pledge they had made

300

to each other more than twenty years before.

To that end, Madame Maubert had told her son that if he married as she wished, she would settle a "generous" yearly allowance upon him. If he did not, he would have to content himself with the income from a small trust fund left to him by her paternal grandmother.

Lily obviously was eager for the match and for equally obvious reasons. She was living proof of how dangerous it is to name girl-children after flowers. Tall, rawboned and awkward, she was most unlilylike. Her one good feature was a pair of large and lustrous gray eyes.

Even so, he might have been willing to marry her in return for that "generous" allowance. After all, he could spend nearly all of it upon himself. Lily had her own money which, according to the marriage contract the two mothers had discussed, would remain in Lily's control. What was more, the average upper-middle class French wife was apt to be tolerant of her husband's extra-marital love affairs. But right there was the rub. In that respect, Lily would never be an average French wife. Like her parents, she was not only a Huguenot, but a Huguenot of a particularly puritanical stripe. Charles had no doubt that the first time he stepped out of line those large gray eyes would fill with cold fury. She would tell not only her mother but his also, with highly unpleasant results as far as his yearly allowance was concerned.

Once his mother had made her wishes known, he began to think longingly of Jeanne-Marie. He thought of her pretty round face, her voluptuous young body and her gentle warmth. Jeanne-Marie who adored him. Jeanne-Marie who carried his child.

It was his recollection of the child that started him thinking of a possible way out.

He decided not to tell his mother about Jeanne-Marie and

the child. She would only say that the girl must be a trollop. But once she saw Jeanne-Marie she would not think that. No one could.

He would risk everything on one gamble. He would go to Paris. Surely his card of identity as a Sorbonne student would get him back through the city gates with no trouble. He would marry Jeanne-Marie in a civil ceremony. As soon as circumstances permitted, he would bring her back to Lyons. He would say to his mother, "This is Jeanne-Marie, my wife, and the mother of your grandchild-to-be."

He remembered how Jeanne-Marie had looked the last time he had seen her, the day of the Prussians' triumphal entry into Paris. He remembered the excitement in her pretty face and the warm, pleased color that came into it when the smiles of strangers made it plain that in the eyes of others they were husband and wife and small son, with another child on the way.

If that memory of her could make his heart twist—and it did—then surely the sight of her would touch his mother. She would accept Jeanne-Marie and accept her grandchild. He would not only have his yearly stipend, but a gentle and attractive wife.

Well, Jeanne-Marie had lost the child, but his determination to marry her rather than Lily had grown so strong that he would still carry it out. True, a pregnant Jeanne-Marie might more surely have touched his mother's heart, but they could tell her about the miscarriage. And this new Jeanne-Marie, with her thinner face and the shadowed look deep in her eyes, and her air of something almost like dignity, had another kind of appeal. Once she saw what the girl was like, surely his mother would have a womanly sympathy for her in the loss of the child.

He said, "I've come for you, Jeanne-Marie. We'll get married and then I'll take you back to Lyons."

For one joyful moment she forgot. For one moment she thought it was all coming true, everything she had longed for since she had first fallen in love with him. She would be Madame Charles Maubert—

Then she remembered.

She said numbly, "I can't marry you."

He stared at her. "Can't!"

"It's too late. I'm already married."

"Married! How can you be married?"

"I'm married to Henri Lamartine."

After a moment he said incredulously, "Lamartine? Funny old Lamartine? I don't believe you. You're joking."

Her face flushed, but when she spoke her voice had that strange new dignity. "I'm quite serious. We are married. We live in a flat on the floor beneath this one."

He believed her then. He said angrily, "How could you do such a thing, Jeanne-Marie? You knew I was coming back." By now he felt convinced that there had never been any doubt of his coming back. "I told you so in the note I left."

"Yes. But you didn't come and you sent no messages—"

"I explained all that! God! Lamartine! And what do you expect me to do now? Just pack up the books and things I've got here and return meekly to Lyons?"

Not waiting for her answer, he shoved back his chair and began to pace the room. Then, gradually, his anger cooled. He stopped beside her and said, "I'm sorry, Jeanne-Marie. I can see why you did it. It was an awful mistake, but neither of us is to blame for it. It was just—circumstances."

He went back to his chair and sat down. "But we can't let that one mistake ruin our whole lives and we won't. Tell me, was it a civil ceremony?"

"Yes."

"Then it shouldn't be too hard to get an annulment. There's a lawyer here in Paris, a man my father went to school with. He's an expert at thinking up reasons why judges should grant annulments. I'll go see him tomorrow. No, not tomorrow! I'll go today."

Jeanne-Marie shook her head.

He asked, astounded, "Why not? Jeanne-Marie! Have you stopped loving me?"

Unfortunately, she thought, I guess I haven't stopped. But instead of speaking she again just shook her head.

"Then you can't love Lamartine! Not that you could have, anyway. So why won't you let me arrange for an annulment? Is it because you feel you owe him something? You don't. Already he's had more of you than he has any right to." Feeling a flash of jealousy, he thought of the watchmaker holding Jeanne-Marie in his arms.

"Well, why don't you answer me?"

"I can't do that to him."

"Why not?"

She wanted to say, but didn't, "Because that morning when I made a fool of myself, trying to earn money enough to get to you, he followed me to the city gates, and risked his freedom for me, maybe even his life."

Aloud she said, "I just can't hurt him that much."

"Why not?" he shouted. "Why is it all right to hurt me, but not him?"

She considered for a moment. Then the answer came to her. It's because you're still a boy, she thought. A handsome, charming boy that perhaps I'll always love, but boys can get over such hurts, fairly soon. Men don't. For them the hurts go a lot deeper and last a lot longer.

"I must stay with him." She got to her feet. "Charles, I feel I have a right to ask a favor of you. It's this. If you plan to take your books and leave this flat, will you do it today? It—it will upset me to know that you are here."

"Don't worry. The faster I leave the happier I'll be."

The cold fury in his eyes pierced her heart. How terrible to have someone you love look at you like that.

On the fourth landing, she longed to run into her and Henri's flat and weep for a while, but she didn't. She went on down the stairs, passed the concierge's door and then turned left toward the fishmonger's.

Chapter 31

Maggie worked very hard during the next few days, so hard that some nights she fell asleep soon after she went to bed, instead of lying awake in the dark listening for the sound of Richard's movements in the other bedroom, and wondering where—and with whom—he had been.

The ambulance was an increasingly grim place and not just because new patients constantly arrived, men wounded in skirmishes between the defenders on the city's ramparts and the besieging Versailles forces. In addition to caring for patients, the ambulance was making last-minute preparations to deal with victims of the expected final onslaught. Stacks of bandages were assembled, instruments were solicited from private physicians, and bottles of pure alcohol for the bathing of wounds were stockpiled. With grim amusement, Maggie heard Monsieur Decrot order that carbolic acid was to be added to the alcohol to prevent attendants and the less seriously wounded from drinking it.

Yet despite the Versailles shells destroying homes in the city's western outskirts, despite the Versailles sappers tunneling nearer and nearer to the city's walls, Maggie was aware that an incongruous gaiety was beginning to fill the air. A number of theaters, closed for lack of heat and light during the past dreadful winter, had reopened. To collect funds for the various ambulances, the Commune gave concerts for the public in the Tuileries Palace, where once Louis Napoleon and his pretty Empress Eugenie had entertained their corrupt court. And once again, as in the first days of the Commune, the grand boulevards were filled with people from the poorer sections of Paris. It was as if these gaunt masons and wagon drivers and factory workers wanted to enjoy for the last time the grandeurs of this city they loved with such fierce pride.

Wearied by her long days at the ambulance, depressed by the nights when Richard, just on the other side of her bedroom wall, seemed as distant as if he lived on another planet, Maggie had little desire to join in the city's final spasm of gaiety. But on Sunday, the twenty-first of May, she felt an impulse to attend the most ambitious yet of the Commune's entertainments. In the Tuileries Gardens, nearly every classical musician left in Paris was to perform, not the frothy Offenbach airs of Louis Napoleon's time, but the great music of Mozart and Bach. As she was leaving the house on Rue Rachel she almost collided with Richard in the doorway. He asked sharply, "Where are you going?"

She looked up at him through the lingering twilight. "To the concert in the Tuileries."

"Maggie! Didn't I make it clear to you? With all hell about to break lose at any minute, it's bad enough for you to venture out alone in the daytime, let alone at night."

Her overstrained nerves snapped. "I'm not a child. Against my better judgment, you persuaded me to leave my comfortable flat for this place, but that doesn't mean I'll let you deny me this little bit of entertainment."

She rushed on, "Don't you think that after all the sights and sounds and smells of that ambulance ten hours a day, I'm entitled to a little bit of pleasure—"

She broke off, ashamed of herself for having sounded self-pitying. He looked down at her, his face unreadable. Then he touched her arm. "We'll both go."

The sidewalks were filled with people that night, all seemingly bound for the vast pleasure garden along the Seine. As Maggie and Richard walked, they maintained a stilted dialogue which included the shortage of beds at the ambulance, the sketches he had made of buildings devastated by a recent explosion in a Paris arsenal, and an explosion which might have been the result of carelessness, although many Parisians were sure it was the work of Thiers' agents. Finally, though, as if realizing that nothing they said echoed their real feelings, they abandoned any attempt at conversation. They walked the last few hundred yards in silence.

The Tuileries Gardens were magically beautiful that night. Paper lanterns in the trees cast a multi-colored glow over the beds of snapdragons, marigolds and daisies, over the marble statuary, over thin faces wearing the soft, dreamy look which Maggie had noted at the beginning of the Commune. She and Richard had arrived too late to occupy any of the thousands of chairs surrounding the bandstand, but from a vendor Richard rented a square of canvas and spread it beneath a giant beech at the crowd's edge. As they sat there in the soft spring dark, great music rolled out over the audience in a healing flood. It seemed to say that no matter how painful their individual experiences, human life had the possibility of becoming serene and noble.

At the end of the concert a Communard deputy who, with his clean-shaven face and his dark curls falling over a broad forehead, looked more like a poet than a politician, mounted the conductor's stand. "Citizens," he said, "Monsieur Thiers has threatened to enter Paris. Monsieur Thiers has not entered; he will not enter. Therefore I invite you next Sunday, here at this same place—"

It was absurd, and yet so touching in its bravery, its defiant hope in the face of those thousands of well-armed men ruining the city. Maggie felt tears stinging her eyes.

Afterward, remembering those tears, she wondered if she had sensed something she could not possibly have known; namely that almost at the very moment the deputy was making his defiant speech, enemy forces were pouring into the city.

She descended the stairs the next morning feeling light-headed from lack of sleep. It had been almost midnight when she and Richard, after an almost entirely silent walk home, entered his flat. In the small front room he told her, with a strained smile, that he intended to stay up and read for a while. She went to her room. Even after she heard him enter into the bedroom on the other side of the wall, she lay awake, too keyed-up for sleep. Now and then, when the wind was right, she had not only heard the boom of cannon but what sounded like rifle fire. Uneasily she realized that the sound of fighting had never seemed that close.

This morning, as she descended the staircase to the lower hall, she saw a very tall, familiar figure standing at its foot. She said, "Raoul! How did you know I was here?"

"I dropped by the ambulance last night. Someone told me that you had—moved." From the constraint in his voice and manner, it was plain that he had reached the obvious conclusion. He believed that she and Richard, despite all that had separated them in the past, somehow had become lovers. Fleetingly she thought of telling him how wrong he was, but there would be no point in that. Whatever her relations with Richard, or lack of them, she could never feel more than warm liking for this tall man with the young-boy face.

She said, "You wanted to see me about something?"

"Yes. Did you know that the Versailles army entered Paris last night?"

Her hand flew to her throat for an instant then dropped to her side. "How?"

"They marched through the Pont du Jour Gate, by the tens of thousands. Some civilian, obviously someone who hates the Commune, discovered the gate was unguarded, so he climbed onto the ramparts and signaled the Versailles troops."

The wry look in his eyes acknowledged that this was only the crowning bit of carelessness in a regime, which from the very first, had been as slipshod as it was brave.

"What are you—"

"I'm going to the barricades in the western part of the city. Men and women and even children have been working on them all night. Of course, scores of barricades should have been completed weeks ago all over the city, but they were not—"

His voice trailed away. Then he said, in a firmer tone, "The wealthy neighborhoods, Passy and Auteuil, are already in enemy hands. After all, those districts are overwhelmingly pro-Thiers. But as the enemy troops move east, they're going to find that they have a fight on their hands."

He hesitated. Then: "Maggie?"

"Yes."

"Do you think he'd mind? I mean, will you kiss me?"

Oh, God, she thought. He feels sure he's going to be dead soon.

She nodded, trying to smile. His arms went around her and he kissed her, not briefly this time.

"Well," he said, releasing her, *"a bientot."*

He went out onto the sidewalk and turned right. She stood there for a moment, her hand on the newel post. Then she, too, went out into the street and turned in the opposite direction.

Richard called for her that evening at the ambulance. It had been a long, tense day. Both patients and staff had displayed the quiet grimness of those who know they face defeat, but intend to maintain their defiance until the very last. People continually reported on the fighting. Thiers' men now held all of western Paris. Yard by yard, and despite desperate men and women firing at them from behind barricades of old busses, paving stones, and even furniture, they advanced toward the splendid heart of the city—the Place de la Concorde, and Place Vendome, and the Tuileries Gardens where, less than twenty-four hours earlier, Maggie and Richard and thousands of others had gathered in the almost summery night to hear the mighty strains of Mozart.

When she and Richard emerged from the ambulance she saw that this was another evening of crystalline air. Even though the sound of cannon and rifle fire seemed much louder, it still was hard for her to realize that on such an evening Frenchmen were destroying their beautiful city and each other.

Richard said, "I have to be out in the streets. It's part of my job, but from now on until this is over, I want you to stay in the flat."

"No."

He said, sounding exasperated, "Why not?"

"You know why not. If it is your job to be out on the streets, it is my job to care for my patients."

"Well, I don't suppose I can keep you locked up in the flat."

"No, you can't."

"All right, then. But I'll walk you to the ambulance each morning and back here each night."

311

When they reached the doorway of the house on Rue Rachel, she had an almost irresistible impulse to say, "Don't go to a café tonight. Let me make supper for both of us."

But no. Probably that would bring the humiliation of his refusal. And if he accepted, the result in the long run might be even more painful for them both. They needed to keep their distance until this bloody interlude was over and they could go their separate ways.

She watched him walk away through that luminous pre-sunset light, then went in and climbed the stairs to the silent flat.

Chapter 32

Late Wednesday afternoon, Diane Gautier made up her mind. Almost seventy-two hours had passed since Thiers' troops had poured through the unguarded gate. Surely the time had arrived for her to even her score with Karl Schiller.

By then, most of her own neighborhood had been "liberated," as the new wall posters phrased it, by the Versailles troops. Near the Etoile the fierce Breton Guards, in smart uniforms purchased in part by funds from their erstwhile enemies, the Prussians, manned barricades from which the Commune forces had been forced to retreat. But further east and north, as well as on the Left Bank, the civil war raged more bitterly than ever. Almost every hour Hortense, Diane's unusually phlegmatic housekeeper, came to her mistress with a story she had heard from other servants in the building. Thiers' soldiers had invaded an ambulance in the western part of the city and, despite the pleas of the English doctor in charge, had shot the wounded National Guardsmen to death where they lay in their beds. In retaliation, aides of Chief of Police Rigault had taken the aged and beloved archbishop of Paris and five other priests from their cells and executed them.

The very air seemed electric with blood lust. So the time was ripe, Diane told herself grimly, to deal with Karl Schiller as he deserved.

She said, "Hortense, inform Armand that I want him to bring my carriage around." She waited until Hortense returned and then descended to the carriage waiting beneath the porte-cochere.

She found the air thick with smoke. All over Paris, Hortense had told her, fires were raging. As they fell back, the National Guardsmen had put the torch to the Tuileries Palace, that splendid structure set in the gardens where the Commune's last concert had been held. Other fires blazed along the Rue de Rivoli and at several spots on the Left Bank. Perhaps some of them, too, had been set. Perhaps they were the result of cannon fire. Whatever their origin, their smoke had enveloped the entire city.

Diane said to her driver, "Do you know the location of the National Guard post in Montmarte?"

The old man looked down at her with frightened eyes. "Oh, mademoiselle! Don't ask me to take you there."

Diane looked at him with cold fury. Several days ago she had ordered him to keep a watch on Karl's house in Montmarte. Each evening he had reported that yes, Monsieur Schiller was still there. He had seen Monsieur going in and out of his house. Now Diane was convinced that the cowardly old liar hadn't even been near Montmarte, at least not these past two days. Instead, he likely had just driven to a neighborhood where the fighting had ceased and waited there until late afternoon.

"There's still fighting there," the old coachman was saying. "The Communards still control Montmarte and all of—"

"Don't you think I know that, you old fool? Take me there."

"We might be arrested—"

"Both sides are too busy to bother with a woman and an old man!"

"How can I get past the barricades?"

"You can't, you idiot. When you see there's a barricade ahead, you'll have to take to the side streets to get around it. Now drive on."

They moved at a snail's pace through narrow side streets, sometimes encountering groups of Versailles soldiers so intent upon pursuing the Communards that they gave the old driver and his passenger scarcely a glance. At last they emerged onto the broad Boulevard de Clichy. Diane looked to her left and saw that they had entered the boulevard behind a barricade still held by Communards. Late afternoon sunlight, filtering through the smoky pall, cast a lurid light over the uniformed riflemen firing across the barricade, and over the scurrying old men and women and children who carried boxes and broken furniture to plug up breaks in the flimsy barrier. Diane thought, They look like figures in hell. The idea brought her satisfaction. After all, if she was in hell, surely these wretched, lowborn creatures ought to be.

Armand turned off onto a steep, cobble stone street and then, a few yards farther on, stopped at the curb. The trapdoor opened and his worried face looked down at her. "This is the neighborhood National Guard post, mademoiselle."

She left the carriage and went through an open doorway into what had once been some sort of shop, to judge from shelves lining both of the side walls. Typically, she had been able to enter unchallenged. Two men sat at a rough table strewn with newspapers and what might have been street maps. Both men, one white-haired and one bald, looked close to sixty. Apparently all the younger men were manning the barricades, but to judge from the grimness of their faces, they felt that their years would bring them no immunity from execution if they fell into the hands of Thiers' soldiers.

315

Diane's voice was crisp. "Which of you is in charge?"

The gray-haired man said, not rising, "I am. Who wants to know?"

"My name doesn't matter. I want to report a spy."

Both men looked her up and down. She had put on the plainest clothes she owned. Nevertheless, it was obvious from their expressions that they had recognized her as a member of the upper class.

The gray-haired man said, "What sort of spy?"

"He's an Alsatian and a Prussian agent. After the war between France and Prussia ended last February, Bismarck lent him to Thiers. Until very recently he used an office close to Thiers' headquarters in the palace of Versailles."

"And where is he now?"

"He re-entered Paris about two weeks ago, wearing a National Guard uniform. Unless he's slipped away sometime during the last few days, he is right here in Montmarte. I'll give you his address. His name, by the way, is Karl Schiller."

"Even if all this is true, why should the likes of you be turning him in?"

"Because he didn't betray just France. He betrayed me too. I want him punished for it."

He looked into the cold, greenish blaze of her eyes. Then he lowered his own eyes to the desk for a moment. Diane saw something like sympathy cross his face and realized that the pity was not for herself, but for Karl.

She said, "Well, do you believe me?"

He paused. "You realize what will happen to a man arrested on such a charge, at a time like this?"

She said nothing.

"Yes, I guess you do know. I guess you waited until feelings were so high, over acts like the murder of those Guardsmen in that ambulance, that someone like this

Schiller wouldn't have a chance. Well, give me the address. We'll send some men to arrest him and bring him in for questioning."

"One thing more," she said, as she wrote down the number, "I want him to know that it was I who reported him. Instruct the men who arrest him to tell him that it was on information supplied by Diane. You owe me that much."

"All right. He'll be told."

She went out to the carriage. At her direction, Armand drove for perhaps four minutes and then stopped at the curb on another steeply slanted street. About fifty yards ahead she could see the tall house where Karl stayed when in Paris.

Diane could hear distant rifle fire and smell the smoke that covered the city, but this street itself had a weirdly peaceful aspect. No one moved along the sidewalks. Every door was closed and nearly every window shuttered. It was as if the inhabitants of this street hoped that by huddling behind their walls, like rabbits in their warrens, they could escape the notice of both factions locked in a deadly struggle for the control of Paris.

Minutes passed. Heart pounding with rage and excitement, Diane waited. Once she saw a group of National Guardsmen fleeing across a street intersection some hundred yards ahead, some looking back over their shoulders as if to see whether the enemy was still in pursuit or had stopped at the barricade the Guardsmen must have abandoned. Otherwise the cobblestone street and its shuttered houses maintained its eerie peacefulness. Diane began to wonder if the men at the National Guard post had decided that the Commune, in its death throes, had something more important to do than pick up a lone traitor.

She was about to order Armand to drive back to the post when, from behind her, came the pound of running feet. She looked through her window and saw four Guardsmen, rifles carried loosely in their hands, running along the sidewalk. They passed the carriage without a glance and then, seconds later, ran up the steps of the house where Karl lived. She saw one of them knock. When there was no response, he pounded against the panels with his rifle butt. The door finally opened, and the men hurried inside.

Now that it was too late, a surge of wild regret mingled with her hatred. She could hear her own heartbeats now, like the pound of surf on a distant beach. Then they came out of the house. Hands tied behind him, Karl walked between two Guardsmen who, rifles slung over their shoulders, grasped his arms. Behind them, rifles held at the ready, walked the other two Guardsmen.

The men turned up the street towards her. She saw now that Karl was inches taller than any of his captors. Even when the group was still yards away, it seemed to her that Karl's blond hair and deep blue eyes were clearly visible through the smoky air. Had he seen and recognized her carriage, with Armand on the box?

Seconds later she was sure he had not. The concentrated look on his face told her that he was steeling every nerve, ever fiber, for an attempt to escape his fate. She thought, with a stab of almost physical pain, he's so alive, so magnificently alive!

Suddenly, almost as if she could read every thought behind those coldly alert blue eyes, she knew what he intended to do. A few yards ahead of him was the entrance to a narrow alley. If he could shake off the comparatively puny men who held him and dart into the dimness of that narrow alley—

It did not strike her as odd that she, who had brought his doom upon him, was now hoping desperately that he would escape it.

Again with that sense of complete identification with him, she felt that she could feel the tensing of the powerful biceps in the arms that so often had held her. She thought wildly, now, beloved, now! Thrusting the two Guardsmen aside almost as if they had been children, he sprang forward. Her fingernails bit into her palms as she saw him take three running strides, then four. The alley entrance was only a few feet ahead.

Rifles cracked. Karl spun half way around, went down on his face, but almost instantly rolled onto his side and tried to rise.

The four of them, though, were upon him. One of them placed a booted foot on Karl's neck and forced his head to the pavement. Hearing her own strangled scream, she watched as two others fired bullets into his body.

The firing ceased. As if to make sure that the big blond man was dead, one of them used his foot to roll Karl's body over on its back. He put two more bullets in the broad, motionless chest. Then the Guardsmen slung their rifles over their shoulders and moved up the street, their faces set. As they passed the carriage, one of them threw Diane a dully-curious look. Then they walked on toward whatever the next few hours would hold for them.

After a moment Diane leaned out of the carriage window, looked up at Armand, and cried, "Back up!" Not for anything in the world would she have driven past the spot where Karl stared with dead eyes into the smoky air. "Back up and then take me home."

That roundabout homeward journey, with the carriage often backing into a side street to avoid a barricade or flaming buildings, was like a confused nightmare. She saw fallen Guardsmen with the certainty of their own deaths in their faces. She saw groups of their exultant pursuers. She saw men in Breton uniforms shoot down five ragged youths of about seventeen whom they had lined up facing a house wall. Once something, probably a rock, struck the carriage's rear window. She turned and looked dully through the scarred glass at an old woman who, face twisted with grief and hatred, screamed at her, "Filthy bourgeois! Filthy, murdering bourgeois swine!"

None of it seemed real. The only reality was Karl, lying back there on the sidewalk.

She thought, until Karl, I had never loved anyone. Not my father or my mother or my brothers or any of those many men. Karl was the only human being I ever loved. Unless I can meet another man like him, and I won't, he is the only human being I will ever love. And I killed him.

She felt alone then, a sense of isolation from the rest of the human race, colder and bleaker than the isolation of someone fated to live out his day on a desert island.

Finally the carriage stopped beneath the porte-cochere of that fine house near the Etoile. She got out and climbed the stairs to her flat.

Chapter 33

By the next afternoon all of Paris, except Belleville, was in the hands of the Versailles troops. As Maggie moved about the ambulance wards, trying to appear calm and matter-of-fact, she was aware that she no longer heard the boom of cannon. Big guns were not needed now. With rifles, rifle butts, and bayonets, Thiers' men were dispatching the defenders of the few remaining barricades.

Around three in the afternoon one of the nurses approached Maggie. "There's a boy outside, asking to speak to Mademoiselle MacNeil."

Maggie found him, a frightened-looking child of about eleven, standing in the vestibule. "Mademoiselle, a Monsieur Lussac is calling for you. He's wounded. Some National Guardsmen brought him to our house."

Raoul! "How far is your house?"

"Not far. I will show you."

She went back into the ambulance, told one of the nurses she would be gone for a few minutes, and then, taut with anxiety, hurried with the boy down the street. Apparently some building filled with archives was burning because bits of blackened paper filled the smoky air. She kept brushing what might have bits of someone's mortgage or marriage license from her cheeks.

The boy turned into the doorway of a rickety tenement. Maggie followed and saw Raoul's long form stretched out in the narrow hallway. The boy, his errand complete, scampered up the dirty stairs.

Why Raoul was lying there, instead of inside some family's living quarters, she never knew. Perhaps no one had room for him. More likely, each family in the building was afraid to have the advancing troops discover that it was sheltering a wounded Guardsman.

Even before she dropped to her knees beside him, she was sure that he was dead. She knew it by the empty look in his dark eyes. Nevertheless, she felt for his pulse and then unbuttoned his tunic and shirt. There was a neat hole in his chest, right over his heart. With weird detachment she reflected that the bullet must have gone straight through his body, making an exit wound through which he had bled as they carried him here. Certainly there was little blood on his chest and none at all on the floor.

She closed the dark eyes. There was little more she could do for him. Burial was impossible. Those still willing to risk their lives in the Communard's cause would bend their energies to help the living.

Still, there was one thing she could do. She and Raoul had never discussed religion. She had no idea whether he was Catholic, Protestant, or indeed any religion at all, but she felt she should offer some sort of prayer. And so, kneeling there in the dim hall, she said silently, "Lord, this is Raoul Lussac. I don't know whether he ever went to church or otherwise appeared to acknowledge You, but I do know that he felt as You did about the poor, the hungry, the ones You called the insulted and injured. He gave his life for them. So please accept him, Lord." She got to her feet and went out onto the sidewalk.

But as she went back to the ambulance through the smoke, the blackened bits of flying paper, the rattle of gunfire only a few hundred yards away, she wondered if any good would come of Raoul's death. Perhaps all of him—his youth, his warmth, his generous bravery—had been wasted utterly.

She continued walking up the Rue Rampaneau. Ahead she saw figures moving through the smoky air, and soon realized that people of the neighborhood were building a barricade. She guessed, quite correctly, that it would prove to be the last of such barriers erected in the path of the victors. Speaking scarcely at all, the men, women and children worked feverishly, piling paving blocks, crates, barrels, and cheap furniture. Maggie sidled past one end of the barricade and then, at the corner, turned right toward the ambulance.

As soon as she entered the ground floor ward she became aware that something must have happened during her absence. No nurses moved along the aisle between the close-packed beds. Except for one boy of seventeen who was delirious from a festering chest wound, the other patients were silent. Almost immobile, too. Only their eyes moved, looking at her as she hesitated at the head of the aisle.

Finally one of them said, "They are all in Monsieur Decrot's office, mademoiselle."

She walked to the rear of the long room, knocked briefly at a door, and then stepped into the ambulance director's office. He sat at his paper-strewn desk. The other ambulance personnel, six women and two men, stood leaning against the wall, their faces pale and tense.

Monsieur Decrot said, in a strained voice, "I am glad that you are back, mademoiselle. I heard that you went to see Raoul Lussac."

"Yes. I found him dead."

No one said anything. With men, women, and even children dying by the thousands in this smoke-darkened city, what was there to say of the death of one man, even one they had all known?

Monsieur Decrot said, "I have been giving some final instructions. According to a report I received about fifteen minutes ago, only those of you who live in neighborhoods north and east of here, neighborhoods the Thiers forces have not yet reached can be fairly sure of reaching your homes safely. I suggest you leave at once. The rest of you may find your way cut off by fires as well as street fighting. I suggest you stay here.

"We will lock the doors of the ambulance," he went on, "and hope that the Versailles troops will pass it by. Perhaps they do not even know of its existence. But if we do hear them breaking in, all of us, including myself, will climb to the children's ward in the loft. I doubt that the troops, no matter how bloodthirsty, will harm the children or harm us for being with them."

Maggie cried, "But our patients, lying there helpless! We can't just—"

"Mademoiselle! Do you think that their fate *now* depends upon anything we do or do not do? It does not. If this ambulance is invaded, the fate of our patients will depend upon the whim of the invaders. Nothing that we could say will make any difference. If Thiers' men, in spite of the pleas of the doctors and nurses, killed all those ambulance patients in a middle-class neighborhood like Passy, what makes you think they would be any more merciful here in Belleville, which has been the Commune's stronghold?"

He added, "Incidentally, Mademoiselle MacNeil, you now live on the Rue Rachel, don't you?"

"Yes."

"Then you are one of those who had best stay here until the fighting is over. According to this report, street fighting still rages in that neighborhood and there are several large fires."

He looked around the room. "Very well. The three of you who live north and east of here—it is three, isn't it?—had best leave immediately. The rest of you, for the time being, can return to your posts."

That afternoon, time seemed to slow to a crawl. As she moved about the strangely silent ward, changing bandages, administering medicine and water, and sponging fevered bodies, Maggie found it almost impossible to look into the eyes of these men. It seemed to her indecent that, in all probability, she would still be alive hours from now, and they would be dead.

Finally, one of the patients, a gaunt-faced man of about thirty-five, said calmly, "There is no need to feel guilty, mademoiselle." As her startled eyes rose from the chest wound she was bandaging and looked into his eyes, he stated quietly, "You cannot save us, you know, if the dirty beasts decide to slaughter us. So why shouldn't you save yourself?"

There was such quiet resignation in his eyes, as if he felt he had already joined the dead. She had a sudden wild impulse to do something, anything—such as bend over and kiss his mouth—to bind him to her and to life. But no, it would be cruel to break through that indifferent acceptance he had somehow achieved. She gave him a noncommittal nod, finished tying his bandage, and moved on to the next bed.

Because of the smoky pall, daylight through the windows began to dim as early as four o'clock. At Monsieur Decrot's orders, though, they lit no lamps. Darkness and silence would give the ambulance its best chance of escaping the notice of Thiers' men. And they were very close now. The sound of rifle fire came from what seemed only a few hundred feet away. She pictured the barricade erected by women, children and old men on the Rue Rampaneau. National Guardsmen, retreating from former positions, must have fallen back to the Rue Rampaneau barrier. She could imagine them firing over that pile of paving blocks and old furniture at figures advancing steadily through the smoke.

By five-thirty the sound of nearby firing had ceased. The National Guardsmen must have been ousted from that barricade. Those still alive must be fleeing north and east, into Commune-held territory which was shrinking by the hour. By the time Richard came for her at six o'clock, perhaps the fighting would have moved well away from this neighborhood. No doubt it had already ceased in the Rue Rachel. She and Richard might be able to reach their house or at least to the ruins of it, if it was one of those that had caught fire. Probably, though, Monsieur Decrot would want them to remain at the ambulance overnight. After all, even if organized fighting in the neighborhood had ceased, there probably would be Versailles patrols looking for stray Guardsmen.

Perhaps not just for the Guardsmen. One of the ugly stories circulating during the past few days had concerned the execution of civilians suspected of firing at Versailles troops. Because rifles used by the National Guard left smudges on the fingers when fired, women and even children, including at least one chimney sweep, had been shot down on the spot because of smudged hands. Still others, including several elderly women, had been summarily executed on the charge of throwing flaming bottles of petroleum into the basements of buildings. Often the evidence was nothing more than the statement of a soldier that he could smell petroleum on his prisoner's hands. In the case of the old women, their insistence that they merely had been returning empty milk bottles to shops, had not helped them.

No, it would be better if she and Richard remained at the ambulance until some measure of sanity returned to the tormented city.

But where was Richard? Always he had been prompt in arriving to escort her to their joint shelter. But tonight six o'clock came and passed. By six-thirty her stomach had tied itself into an anxious knot. True, he had an identity card. Recently the Commune had ordered that all inhabitants of Paris carry such cards. His stated that he was an American and the employee of an international news syndicate. That should protect him from arrest by either the Communards or the Versailles forces. But no card could protect him against a stray bullet.

The little watch pinned to her blue uniform blouse told her that it was now seven. Could it be that he was in the Rue Rachel? Perhaps, knowing that something would delay him until past six o'clock, he had assumed that she would go home alone when he did not appear on time.

By seven-thirty she could stand it no longer. She explained briefly to one of the nurses, went to the vestibule, and threw her cloak around her over her uniform. Then, very cautiously, she opened the front door and looked out into what was left of the daylight, amber now from smoke mingled with the sunset's afterglow. She looked in both directions. No soldiers, thank God. No persons of any sort. The inhabitants of these rickety tenements, like helpless, unarmed people in poor neighborhoods all over Paris, must be huddling behind their locked doors, waiting for whatever the next day would bring.

She started swiftly toward the cross street, the Rue Rampaneau. No movement around that abandoned barricade, and nothing of the barricade itself remained except for smashed furniture, and boxes and barrels scattered for yards in both directions.

She moved forward. Then, from around the corner, came a sound that made her heart leap almost painfully. Footsteps. She heard the cadenced footsteps of many booted feet.

They swept around the corner, at least a dozen of them, some with rifles at the ready, some with weapons slung over their shoulders. With even sharper fear she saw they wore the uniforms of those most merciless of the Commune's enemies, the Breton Guards. She realized that they must be a "mop up" squad, looking for National Guardsmen who might have been missed during the Versailles troops' victorious sweep through this area.

She thought, thank God! Thank God she had left the ambulance when she did. If she had left even a few moments later, these men might have seen her emerge, might have investigated the building—

Automatically she had halted. The men slowed and surrounded her. A lieutenant, face young and sharp-featured under his visored cap, snapped at her, "Hold out your hands, palms up!"

She obeyed, praying that her fingers held no smudges from an improperly dusted bedstead, or from the kettle in which she sometimes brewed tea for the patients, or from any other source. Evidently the lieutenant saw nothing incriminating, because after a moment he lowered his head and sniffed at her palms.

Again her heart contracted with terror. What if this young man, as nervously excited as he must be, confused a possible scent of some sort of medicine with that of petroleum.

Straightening, he turned to his men. "All right. You have your order."

They moved on. He turned back to Maggie. "Your identity card, please."

She reached into her cloak's slanted pocket, glad that she'd had the foresight to carry her card there. Otherwise, in order to get to it, she might have afforded him a glimpse of her uniform of blue cotton blouse and skirt. She was glad, too, that her card identified her only as Mademoiselle Margaret MacNeil, American, with the word "visitor" written in after the printed word "occupation." It had been Richard who had told her that it would be wiser not to identify herself as a nurse.

The lieutenant asked, "Where do you live, mademoiselle?"

"In the Rue Rachel."

"What are you doing on this street?"

"I have a maid of whom I am very fond. She lives a hundred yards or so from here. She fell seriously ill last week and I thought, now that the fighting seems about over, I might see—"

Suddenly she heard the crash of a rifle butt against wood. Her head jerked around. Breton Guards were there at the door of the ambulance. So they had known even before they came here that there was an ambulance on this street.

The lieutenant said hurriedly, "Very well. Go home and stay there." He turned and, at a dog trot, moved toward his men.

Maggie stood rooted. She heard a louder crash as the ambulance door parted from its hinges. She saw the soldiers lunge into the building. The lieutenant, as if expecting the arrival of something or someone else, remained on the sidewalk.

From inside the building came shouts, screams, a rifle shot, and then a fusillade of shots.

It was not bravery that made her rush up the street through the dying light toward the figure on the sidewalk. It was just that she quite literally had forgotten her fears for her own safety. She could not let them die like that, those men she had struggled to keep alive day after day, week after week.

She seized the lieutenant's arm with both hands. "You can't, you can't! Stop them!"

He pulled his arm free. "What are you talking about?" he asked coldly.

Shots seemed to be coming from the upstairs ward also. "You can't shoot helpless men."

"Helpless? Wasn't the old archbishop helpless, and those other priests killed by this sort of *canaille?* Now get out of here." Then, almost instantly, "No! Wait!"

He seized the two sides of her cloak and pulled the garment down from her shoulders. "A nurse! So that's how you knew what this place—You're one of them, aren't you?"

He did not wait for her answer. One hand holding her arm, he turned and shouted into the ambulance. "Lancier! Rostand! Anyone! Out here on the double."

Running feet, and then two soldiers, faces flushed with the excitement of the kill, clattered over the fallen door and out onto the sidewalk. The lieutenant said, "Hold onto her," and then turned his attention back to the street.

Her instinct for self-preservation, in absence only moments ago, flooded back. Straining against the hands that held her, she cried, "You can't do—"

"Maggie!"

Her head swiveled around. It was Richard, standing tall in the near darkness. He said, "Let her go, you fools." Then, to the lieutenant: "Order your men to leave that young lady alone!"

The lieutenant asked coldly, "Who are you to tell me what to do?"

For answer, Richard took his identity card from an inside jacket pocket and thrust it at the officer. "If you need a match to see by—"

"I'll manage." The lieutenant held the card close to his eyes. "Richard Glover, American. Occupation, newspaper artist. Employer, International News Syndicate, Paris Branch."

"And this lady is also an American citizen. And so if you will kindly—"

Even in the thickening dark, the cold cynicism in the Breton Guardsman's face was plain. "In Tours two weeks ago, we shot three men and a woman, all with what looked like valid identification as Americans." As if to underline his words, the sound of several more shots came from the upstairs ward given over to wounded men. But as yet there had been no sound from the children's ward in the loft. Surely they wouldn't harm the children, Maggie thought. Surely they wouldn't.

"All four of those people masquerading as Americans," the lieutenant informed them, "turned out to be spies for the Paris Commune."

A man with sergeant's stripes on his sleeves and accompanied by two privates, came out onto the sidewalk. The lieutenant asked evenly, "Finished?"

"With the swine on the first two floors, yes. Up under the roof there are maybe fifty children and a few nurses and an old guy who says he's the director."

"Just station a couple of men up there to keep an eye on them. Otherwise, don't bother them."

As the sergeant went back into the building, the lieutenant turned to the two men in privates' uniforms. "Hold this man."

They seized Richard's arms. Maggie could almost feel in

331

her own body the effort it must have cost him to stand there calmly, rather than try to free himself from their grasp. He said, "You are making a mistake, lieutenant."

"So? Mistakes happen in wartime."

"You can at least release Madame MacNeil. It is absurd to think that she is a spy, or any other sort of threat to—"

"It is absurd? As a matter of fact I would far rather let you go than her. On your identity card, if it really is yours, your occupation is given. That is something that we could check, if we decide to take the trouble. But the young lady, quite obviously a nurse in this Belleville ambulance—"

"What if she is? I just heard you give an order that those other nurses are not to be harmed."

"They did not try to hide what they were. This woman did. Besides, she interfered with an officer in the performance of his duty." He added deliberately, "Just as you are doing now."

As he spoke he had turned his head toward the Rue Rampaneau. Maggie followed his gaze. A van, its arched ribs covered with canvas, and drawn by two pairs of white or gray horses—it was hard to tell which in the gathering dark—had turned the corner. The vehicle stopped at the curb in front of the ambulance. Two soldiers leapt from the van to the cobblestones and stood with rifles pointed toward the van's interior.

The lieutenant said to the men holding Maggie and Richard, "Put them both in the van." He turned toward the driver, and Maggie heard him say, "These horses are only livery stable hacks. Don't drive them too close to gunfire. They're not used to it."

Numb now, she felt herself half-led, half-dragged to the van's steps and then propelled up them. Hands on her shoulders forced her down onto a hard bench. A moment later she became aware that, in the same fashion, Richard had been forced down beside her. There were other people in the van, many others, facing each other along two parallel benches. She could hear their breathing, see the faint shine of eyes and feel the thigh of the person on her left touching hers.

The two soldiers who had descended from the van had climbed back inside. One at the rear end of each bench, they sat facing each other. There was a shout from the driver, the crack of a whip, and the van rumbled forward.

After a moment she felt Richard's hand close around hers. She whispered in anguish, "Why did you do it? When you saw I had been arrested, you could just have walked away—"

He said in a low voice, "Don't talk like a fool, Maggie."

Her eyes were becoming accustomed to the dimness. She gained the impression that there were about thirty in the van, perhaps all of them men except herself. She also gained a vague impression that all of them wore civilian clothes of fairly good quality. Now and then, as the van creaked past a guttering street lamp, a burning house, or a sidewalk bonfire kindled for heaven knew what reason, she caught a glimpse of one of her fellow prisoner's faces, or of the glitter of eye-glasses or watch chains, or of hands crossed on a cane's head.

At last someone said, from the depths of the van, "Is that you, Glover?" The voice sounded elderly. "What are you doing here?"

"Rouncenaur?"

"That's right. Jean-Phillipe Rouncenaur. A Versailles captain—he must have been a literary type—arrested me in my bookshop because I had a French translation of William Blake on my shelves."

"How about Rousseau and Voltaire?"

"Oh, I had hidden those. But who would have guessed

333

that a military man would know that Blake harbored dangerous ideas?"

One of the soldiers at the rear of the van shouted, "Silence!"

Unperturbed, the old voice rambled on, "But you, Glover! How do you find yourself in this kettle of fish? Have you been working for the Commune?"

"I've been working for my employers. As for this kettle of fish, I am not even sure what it is."

"Oh, I am sure we will be shot, but I imagine that first we will be honored with some sort of drumhead trial, perhaps lasting about two minutes for the lot of us. After all, we're not ordinary suspects—supposed snipers or throwers of petroleum bottles—to just be shot down without any ceremony whatever."

"Silence!"

Monsieur Rouncenaur said, "If I am to be shot, how can you threaten me into silence?"

"I can beat you into silence, old man. Which do you want? To be shot some time later tonight, or to be dragged out onto the cobblestones right this minute and clubbed to death?"

There was no answer.

The vehicle rumbled over the cobblestones. Maggie felt a merciful sense of unreality as the dim light of street lamps or of wavering flames occasionally entered the van, only to be replaced by almost pitch darkness. Occasionally she heard rifle shots, sometimes sounding near, sometimes far off.

Now and then light shone on the two soldiers at the van's rear entrance. The one next to Richard sat with his rifle slung across his knees. The one opposite sat with his rifle propped upright, its muzzle pressed against the floorboards. Every once in a while he bent and rested his forehead against his hands crossed on the rifle butt. The soldiers' faces, in the intermittent light, looked tired, strained, and very young. She wondered how many men, women and children each of them had shot down that day. Scores? Hundreds? Had these particular two been sickened by the killing?

Dimly she realized what she was doing. She dared not think of what might lie ahead for her and Richard. She dared not think of standing beside him while bullets smashed into both their bodies, knifing through flesh and shattering bone. So instead she was asking herself questions about these two young soldiers. Try to imagine, she told herself, what they had been before they donned uniforms. Farm boys? The big, broad hands of the boy at the end of the row where she and Richard sat, loosely holding his rifle across his lap, looked like a farmer's hands.

The van turned in at a wide gateway. The road sloped upward beneath overarching tree branches. After a moment or two, through the van's rear opening, she caught glimpses of pale objects among the dark vegetation stretching away from the road on either side, objects that looked like pillars, domes, and even human figures.

She realized where they were then. Pere-Lachaise Cemetery, at the eastern end of Paris. At the ambulance that day she had heard a rumor that several hundred National Guardsmen, doomed but still fighting, had retreated to somewhere in this vast and beautiful cemetery. So not only those gaunt Guardsmen would die here, if they had not done so already, among the tombs of France's poets, artists, musicians and statesmen, she and Richard also would die here. Along with an aged bookseller and other miscellaneous civilians, they would be lined up against a segment of the cemetery wall and shot.

From somewhere still quite distant came the rattle of the *mitrailleuses,* the rapid-fire weapon employed by the Ver-

sailles forces. It was answered by rifle fire. So the
Communards were not entirely defeated, at least not yet.

The van continued up the steeply sloping road. Almost no
sound except gravel spurting from beneath iron-rimmed
wheels, the jingle of harness and creak of singletrees, and the
occasional distant firing. Once what might have been an owl,
a darker shape against the darkness, flew across the van
opening with a faint sibilance of wings.

Then she felt Richard's breath warm against her ear. He
whispered, "When I tell you to, jump!"

Her first impulse was to whisper back fiercely, "No! It will
be too dangerous." Then she realized how absurd that was.
They were headed for almost certain death. Thus any
gamble, no matter how small its chance of success, would be
worthwhile.

So instead she squeezed the hand that held hers. He returned the pressure and then withdrew his hand.

For a while they rode in silence. Then from the corner of
her eye she saw Richard launch himself to one side. Moving
so quickly that she sensed rather than saw his actions, he
snatched up the rifle from the knees of the man beside him
and stood up. She saw him use the weapon to strike the rifle
the other soldier had propped upright against the van's floor.
It flew out through the opening, discharging as it struck the
graveled road.

"Jump!" Richard shouted.

She obeyed, throwing herself past him and out into the
night, landing on hands and knees in the gravel. Behind her
she heard shouts, the sounds of struggle, and the whinny of
the horses, terrified by the gunshot close behind them in the
road. She heard the jingle of their harness as they reared and
then the panic-stricken beat of their hooves.

Someone struck her and knocked her flat, pressing her

cheek into the gravel. Richard said, body weighting hers, "Lie quiet."

A bullet whistled above them. So even though they had not been able to prevent Richard's escape, their guards must have managed to regain one of the rifles. From perhaps fifty yards away she heard one of the young soldiers yell, "Don't shoot, you fool! Do you want these horses to kill us all?"

The sound of pounding hooves and rushing wheels died away. Richard stood up and pulled her to her feet. "Let's get off the road."

As they moved toward the road's edge, Maggie saw the dim glint of the rifle lying on the gravel. Richard said, as if reading her mind, "Leave it there! It will only weigh us down. And if they come after us in force, one rifle would do us no good anyway."

They moved into the darkness. The air was redolent of pine, cedar and wilting memorial bouquets. Even on this high ground, the smoke of burning Paris hovered in the air. Arm around her waist, he drew her along at a fast clip. Even when she asked, panting, if they could rest, he said, "No! They'll probably send a patrol back to look for us. We must run deeper."

They went on, past alabaster angels, granite columns, and elaborate marble tombs whose round roofs and columned portals were now visible to Maggie's darkness-accustomed eyes. They could still hear distant firing now and then, but mingled with it were peaceful sounds of the splash of a fountain. Once they heard a nightingale, indifferent to the slaughter raging in the city and even in this serene abode of the dead.

At long last Richard said, "We can stop." He kept his voice low.

They were beside a large tomb of some dark material,

probably black marble. Except for the narrow path that led to it, cedar trees surrounded it entirely, looking like fat black exclamation points in the darkness. Maggie slumped to the grass and he lay down beside her.

For a while they said nothing. When no sound had broken the silence for some time, he said softly, "Unless I'm wrong, this is the tomb of a rich American who died in Paris of typhoid about twenty years ago. Nice of him to provide a hiding place for a pair of his compatriots, isn't it?" As he spoke, there was the sound of distant firing, both of rifles and of *mitrailleuses*. To judge by the sound, it still came from somewhere within the vast cemetery.

She said, not answering his question, "You not only tried to keep those Breton Guards from arresting me, but after I jumped out onto the road, you covered me with your own body, so that if a bullet had struck—"

"I wasn't hit."

"That isn't the point and you know it."

"Yes, I know it. And if we get out of this alive, we'll discuss it. But first we've got to get out alive."

They heard more distant firing and then silence. Although she had not been able to consult the watch pinned to her blouse—not when even the briefest match flare might endanger them—she had the feeling that it was well past midnight. Eventually, a stray breeze carried to them the bronze voice of a church bell, marking two o'clock.

Soon after that they heard more firing. This time it was not a clash of Versailles and National Guard weapons, but fusillades of perhaps twenty rifles. There was the crackle of simultaneous fire, then an interlude of silence, then a second fusillade and a third. Maggie imagined how they must have been stood up against a wall—the old bookseller, and his companions in that van, and those people who had been brought to Pere-Lanchaise in heaven only knew how many other vans.

Maggie fought down an impulse to lower her face into her hands and weep. She must not make noise, not while she and Richard were still in danger.

Again there were three fusillades, then an interval of perhaps twenty minutes. Then the sounds of still another execution of prisoners and then still another.

After that there was silence, except for a pre-dawn breeze sighing through the cedars.

The slaughter of now-helpless Communard sympathizers and those suspected of being so, might continue for days down in the city. But perhaps here, in this beautiful and supposedly sanctified place, the killing of Frenchmen by Frenchmen had come to an end.

There was a rustle nearby in the shrubbery and the snap of a twig. Swiftly, and making no noise whatsoever, Richard threw his body across her own.

A cat, gray or white or perhaps light yellow, emerged into the clearing. It was one of those doughty street cats of Paris, ocelot-large and almost ocelot-fierce. Not deigning to look at the two humans, it disappeared around the corner of the tomb.

Maggie repressed a hysterical impulse to laugh. Richard rolled over onto his back and said softly, "Whew!"

A few minutes later a church bell—this time somewhere to the north of the cemetery, to judge by the sound—struck three-thirty.

Richard said, "It will be light soon. We might be seen leaving this place. We had best start working our way toward one of the gates."

"Do you know where the nearest one is?"

"I think so. I once drew eighteen of the most beautiful or

famous tombs here for a French publisher who was bringing out a book on Pere-Lachaise."

They moved off, threading their way through sorrowful angels, couchant lambs, and hooded marbled mourners, keeping to the grass lest even at this late hour the crunch of their footsteps over gravel reach listening ears. At last they came to a gate. Ordinarily all the cemetery's gates remained closed and locked from sunset to sunrise. But, as was to be expected in the chaos Paris had become, this gate and probably several others as well stood open.

Crossing swiftly to the opposite side of the street, they started moving north along the sidewalk. The substantial middle-class houses they passed were all dark and silent. No one else moved along the sidewalk. Maggie noticed that the air seemed a little less smoky now. She also noticed that the blackness was shading to dawn gray.

A few yards farther on they encountered their first patrol, two tired-looking boys of about eighteen in Versailles uniforms, so dirty that Maggie decided they must have put in some stints of fire-fighting during the last tumultuous hours. Challenged, Richard showed one of them his identity card.

The soldier asked, "And why are you out at this hour, Monsieur Glover?"

"Doing my job, of course. I shall go home and make sketches of what I have seen for my editor's approval."

An older and more sophisticated questioner might have asked, "What sort of sketches. Do you plan to present our forces in a bad light?"

But all the boy said, "And Mademoiselle?"

Maggie handed him her card. Richard said quickly, "As you can see, Mademoiselle is an American. She is also the daughter of Monsieur Silas MacNeil, one of President

340

Grant's special envoys to France. You have heard of Silas MacNeil, of course."

From the boy's expression one might have doubted that he had even heard of President Grant. Nevertheless he nodded and then asked, "But why is she with you?"

"She insisted upon coming. You know how the ladies are," he went on, with a man-to-man air, "when they make up their minds. Especially American ladies!"

"Very well, monsieur. You may go, but it would be wise to get indoors somewhere as soon as you can. The streets are not yet entirely safe."

Richard thanked him. At the next corner they turned onto a street that angled northeast. Twice more they were stopped by patrols, but allowed to pass each time. Maggie had a sense that these young private soldiers, at least, were losing their stomach for violence.

When she and Richard reached Rue Rachel the newly risen sun was striking along it through the smoky air, straight into their tired eyes. By tacit agreement they stopped and stood still for a moment, looking at the empty sidewalks, an overturned wagon in the street, and the blackened remains of three houses, two of them still smouldering.

Their house stood unscathed. They climbed in silence to the third floor.

Chapter 34

Standing at a window of her handsome salon, Diane looked down into the street. Even though she had not stirred from her flat that night, and even though she had drunk glass after glass of brandy, she had not been able to sleep. It was not the distant sound of fighting which had kept her awake. Why should she lose sleep over the fate of people so stupid and wretched that they were better off dead anyway? No, she hadn't slept because again and again in her mind's eye she had seen a National Guardsman use the toe of his boot to roll Karl over onto his back, so that the dead blue eyes in the handsome face stared straight at the sky.

She heard a clattering in the street. She looked down and saw a woman servant on the steps of the house opposite kneeling beside a metal bucket as she wielded her scrub brush. How quickly, after its orgy of bloodlust, the city was returning to its accustomed ways.

She wished that she could return to what had once been her accustomed ways, taking her pleasure with whatever man caught her eye, then forgetting him almost as easily as she might forget a dinner she'd enjoyed the night before. But there could be no going back to the life she had led before she met Karl. No easy, casual pleasure from now on. If she took bed partners now, she would find herself sickened by them for not being him, the man she had killed just as surely as if she herself had held the rifle.

The sunrise light hurt her eyes. Perhaps if she took a little more brandy she could sleep for a few hours. She looked at the bottle on the small table beside her. It was empty. Well, there was laudanum in the cabinet beside her bed.

She went into the bedroom, measured liquid into a glass. It was said that laudanum by itself was bad for you. Combined with brandy, it probably would kill her someday.

Perhaps not this time.

Chapter 35

Afraid of waking Marcel and yet too tense to sit still, Jeanne-Marie moved quietly around the front room of the Lamartine apartment. Sometimes she stood at the window to look down into the street washed with early morning sunlight. Other times she sat in a small armchair with a mending basket beside it on the floor. Then, after she had placed a few stitches in a work smock of Henri's she was patching, she would wander to the window again.

At dusk the night before, just after they had put Marcel to bed in the tiny bedroom adjoining their own, Henri had told her that he was going out again.

"No, Henri, no!"

"My darling, I must."

"But you've said you didn't feel you could take sides! You've always said Thiers was too cruel and the Communards too blundering for you to support either one."

At this late date, when it was plain that the Commune had been crushed, had he been seized by one of those quixotic impulses that men seemed subject to? Had he decided that he must join the National Guard in its last, losing battle?

He smiled. "No, Jeanne-Marie, I have not changed my mind. I'm not going out to defend a barricade. I'm going to spend the night at the shop."

"The shop!"

"Yes. Thieves and vandals have been taking advantage of this chaos, you know. With most of the police fighting on the side of the Versailles troops, lots of shops have been robbed. Antoine's shop was broken into last night." Antoine had the cobblery next to Henri's watch repair shop. "They not only stole all the shoes but his equipment too."

"If fighting was still going on in this neighborhood," he added, "I wouldn't leave you and the boy, but you'll be quite safe as long as you stay indoors."

"But you won't be safe! There may not be pitched battles in this neighborhood now, but you yourself said that there were patrols out looking for snipers—"

"Jeanne-Marie, if I had only myself to think of, I wouldn't go out. I would just take a chance that my shop wouldn't be harmed, but now I have you and the boy to think of. That shop is our livelihood. What would we do without it?"

In the end, despite her pleas, he had left. She had gone to bed at nine, the usual hour, but she had heard Notre Dame's bells strike midnight before she fell asleep. And, while it was still dark, she had awakened with a start, found Henri's side of the bed empty, and then lain awake, hearing occasional rifle shots—some distant, some quite close by—until the windows grayed with dawn. Finally, she arose and got dressed. With no appetite for solid food, she had forced herself to drink a cup of tea.

At seven, when Marcel awoke, she had dressed and fed him and then placed him on a pad in the corner of his room with his blocks and some wooden animals Henri had carved for him. Lest her own restlessness upset him, she had closed the door of the child's room. Since then she had been moving distractedly back and forth between her mending basket and the window.

Finally she heard footsteps at the top of the stairs, then along the hall. She flew to the door and flung it back.

Charles Maubert said, "Good morning, Jeanne-Marie." Then, after a smiling moment, "Aren't you going to ask me in?"

Dazedly she stepped back. He walked past her and then stood, looking so youthfully handsome, so out of place in this prosaic room with its table covered by a red-and-white checked cloth and its mending basket on the floor.

When they were both seated, she in the small armchair, he in one of the three dining chairs, she said, "I thought you had gone home to Lyons."

"I intended to. I tried to."

He certainly had. After his last stormy interview with Jeanne-Marie, he had packed his books, made a final settlement with the concierge, and started toward one of the city's southeastern gates, sure that as he neared it, he would encounter farm wagons about to leave for the countryside. Almost any of them, for a fee, would be willing to take him at least part of the way toward Lyons.

But by then the National Guard had begun to build, belatedly, their barricades all over Paris. Guardsmen were stopping passersby to demand that they add at least one paving block to the growing barriers. Twice Charles had to put down his suitcases, take a crowbar, and pry up a paving stone from the street. The third time he was stopped he had lost his temper. A shouting match with a Guardsman about his own age had resulted in physical combat. Taller and heavier, Charles no doubt would have won, if he had not slipped on some bit of refuse on the cobblestones. He had gone down, striking the back of his head on the curbing.

The injury had not seemed serious. In fact, he had refused the offer of the suddenly solicitous Guardsman to try to find a doctor for him. Nevertheless, his head had throbbed. He shrank from the thought of making the rest of his way across the city, encumbered by the heavy suitcases and an aching head, and faced with the prospect of being stopped by some unwashed crew of Guardsmen every few hundred yards.

It was then that he remembered that a classmate of his lived with his family not far from where he stood.

His classmate's family took him in, bandaged the small cut on the back of his head, and put him to bed. He had been expecting to leave the next day, but when he tried to stand the next morning, he found himself so dizzy that he sat down abruptly on the bed's edge. His host and hostess managed to summon a doctor who said that he had a slight concussion and should rest for several days. Charles scribbled a note of explanation to be mailed to his mother and then went back to bed.

A week later he had recovered completely, but by that time fighting raged within the city. No young Frenchman could venture out without being pressed into service by one side or the other. A refusal of such service might bring on-the-spot execution.

Charles and his classmate had stayed indoors, playing piquet and leafing through books in the family library. Most of the time, though, during those days, Charles had thought of his own situation. He was no more reconciled than ever to the prospect of spending his life under the domination, financial and otherwise, of three strong women—his mother, the raw-boned, misnamed Lily, and Lily's mother. He kept thinking of Jeanne-Marie, so pretty and gentle and biddable.

What was more, she still loved him. Remembering the pain in her face when he had flung those final, bitter words at her, he could not doubt that she loved him.

This morning he had awakened with the resolve that he

347

would see her again. A young man of obvious middle-class appearance could venture onto the streets now with little or no risk. The housemaid had brought him, along with his morning chocolate, a report that in Pere-Lachaise cemetery during the night, the last organized Communard resistance had been smashed. Defeated Guardsmen as well as civilian sympathizers had been stood against the wall and shot. What people were already calling *La Semaine Sanglante,* the Bloody Week, must be winding toward its close.

If he remembered correctly, Lamartine always left for his shop around eight. That meant that by eight-thirty Charles could be almost sure of finding Jeanne-Marie alone. This time he would not lose his temper. Quietly and reasonably, he would point out how foolish it would be for her to waste her life.

He said, "I had to see you again, Jeanne-Marie. I just can't believe that you meant what you said the last time."

She didn't answer, just looked at him with her anxiety-filled blue eyes. What was she anxious about? When she had opened the door and seen him in the hall, the joyful surprise he had expected had not rushed into her face. Instead she had looked almost—well, disappointed. But that couldn't be. She had been disconcerted, that was all.

He did wish that she would say something, rather than just look at him with an odd, distracted air.

He forged on with the words he had rehearsed. "I know how grateful you must feel to Henri Lamartine, and I admire you for it, I truly do."

He meant that. During these past few days he had been thinking of women—Jeanne-Marie in particular—in terms different than ever before. He had realized that Jeanne-Marie, in abiding by her marriage vows to a man she could not possibly love, was behaving with what in a man would be called honor. It was strange to think of a woman as being honorable in that sense. Until now he had thought of female honor only in terms of the preservation, until marriage, of virginity. Now he found Jeanne-Marie's sense of honor another reason for wanting to marry her. He wanted, all for himself, not just her gentleness, her pretty face and her softly rounded body, but also her resolute and trustworthy spirit.

"Ask him to let you go, Jeanne-Marie. You can't make him happy, you know, when you yourself are not happy. He is a reasonable man. He will see that."

She said slowly, "But I have become happy." Quite suddenly, she realized that was true.

"Happy! How can you be happy with a man you don't—"

"But I do. I do love him."

That, too, was true. When had she begun to love him? Plainly it was before she actually realized that she had. Could it have been that afternoon when they'd had their wedding picnic in that leafy little park in Notre Dame's shadow? Or perhaps it was that night, their wedding night, when some quality in his love-making had made her think of those words from the Church's marriage rite, "with my body I thee worship." Or perhaps it had been only a few nights ago, when there had been gunfire and screams not far off, and he had held her in his arms in bed, talking steadily of events during his village boyhood, until his voice and those dreadful sounds had blurred, as she slipped into sleep.

Charles reminded himself to hold onto his temper. "My dearest, I know that you're a good woman and that every good woman is supposed to say that she loves her husband. But—Henri Lamartine! Don't you remember how I used to tease you about your watchmaker admirer and we both would laugh? Why, you used to think he was a—kind of joke."

"Did I?" Her voice was serene. "Certainly, I don't now."

He shouted, "Jeanne-Marie, you must be insane! Don't you realize all that I'm offering you?"

"Yes, and it's good of you, Charles. But I don't—"

"Good of me!" He leaped to his feet. "What the hell are you talking about?"

"I just mean—thank you, Charles, but I love Henri too much to ever leave him."

He said bitterly, "This is your last chance, Jeanne-Marie. You can be Madame Charles Maubert with all that will entail. Or you can live out your life with your watchmaker in poky little flats like this one."

"I'm sorry, Charles."

"I suppose that means your final answer is no. Very well, Jeanne-Marie! When I close this door, you'll know that you've seen me for the last time."

"I realize that." She added, with a gentleness which made her words sound more final than any amount of shouting could have done, "And Charles, try not to mind too much. I think you're the sort of person who always gets much of what he wants out of life, one way or another. So don't feel too bad about not getting me."

When the door closed behind him—to his credit, he did not slam it—she wondered briefly what had made him so eager to marry her, eager enough that he had come back to make a second proposal. He had not said he loved her. Then her thoughts swung back to Henri. It was all she could do to keep from running down the stairs and through the streets to his shop. But she did not want to leave Marcel alone and she dared not take him into the streets, not when only a few hours ago she still had heard occasional firing. Bullets could go astray or they could ricochet—

It was almost nine when she again heard footsteps in the hall. She flew to the door, afraid that once more she would see

Charles. But this time it was Henri. As soon as he stepped over the threshold she threw herself into his arms and burst into tears.

"Jeanne-Marie! What is it?"

Woman-like, she turned immediately from relief to indignation. "You've been gone since eight last night! I pictured you dead in the shop, or in the streets—"

"Jeanne-Marie, I would have been back by daylight, except that the bakery a few doors from my shop caught fire. The poor woman who owns it ran from building to building, pleading for help. Several of us finally managed to put the fire out."

She saw how tired his thin face was. Paradoxically, though, it also looked younger, perhaps because the fervor of her greeting had brought a shine of pleasure into his eyes.

"Were you afraid you and Marcel were going to be left all alone?" He cupped her face in his hands. "I can understand how you might have that kind of anxiety. You lost Marcel's father and before that, when you were a little girl, your own father didn't come back from the Crimea—"

His voice trailed off. Then he said, "I imagine that if he had lived he would be just about my age now, wouldn't he?"

She felt bewildered, not only by the tangent he had taken, but by the way the pleasure in his eyes had given way to a kind of resigned sadness. She said, "Yes, I suppose he would be."

Then suddenly she understood the look in his eyes. He knew that she loved him, but he feared that her affection for him always would be more that of a daughter than a wife.

She wanted to tell him that was not true. She wanted to say that in ways that really counted he was young, as those of unembittered spirit and unhardened heart always remain young. She wanted to tell him that most of the time she had ceased even to be aware that he had been on this planet longer than she had.

Even if her love for Henri did contain an element of what she as a child had felt for her young father, what of it? In a world as brutal and destructive as this one, every kind of love was precious. Every love was a bit of the eternal flame, to be cherished and guarded against the cold winds of cruelty and death.

Even if she had not felt too shy to tell him all this, she did lack the words to express it. So instead she put her arms around his neck, kissed him lingeringly, and then said, "I will make you some breakfast, my husband, and then you must sleep."

Chapter 36

When they entered the sparsely furnished front room of the apartment on Rue Rachel, Maggie and Richard went, by unspoken accord, to a window. They looked out into what would be a beautiful late spring day once the smoke cleared entirely.

"So awful!" Maggie said, thinking of the night that had just passed. "How can human beings treat each other like that?"

"I don't know. People have been asking themselves that question for hundreds of years."

For a few minutes more they stood in silence. Then he put his hands on her shoulders and turned her toward him. "But can't we try to put all that out of our minds for a while?"

She saw a bone-weariness as great as her own in his gray eyes, in his Lincolnesque face with its prominent brow ridges and cheekbones. She also saw something that made her heart twist with a half-unbelieving joy. There was unmistakable tenderness in his tired face and an undisguised hunger. It was as if he were giving free rein to all the emotions he had tried to repress these past months. He drew her close to him and his warm lips covered hers in a kiss that sent an electric tingle all through her.

He raised his head and said urgently, "I want you now. Right now."

"Yes," she said. "Oh, yes!"

They went into her room. Swiftly and silently they undressed and lay down on the bed.

Perhaps it was because of her tiredness, which sometimes can have a more uninhibiting effect than wine, or perhaps it was because of the very dreadfulness of their past few hours, but whatever the reason, she found herself more abandoned, more open to him, than she had been the first time she lay naked in his arms. Just as his hands and lips roamed hungrily over her body, her hands and lips caressed him. Soon the need to have him within her, thrusting against the singing core of her, grew so urgent that she had a dim awareness of her fingernails biting into his back. When he finally did enter her, he brought her within moments to ecstatic heights. As the waves of gratified desire rippled through her she was conscious of the throb of his own release.

For a few minutes after, they again lay side by side, neither of them spoke. Then he said, "We'll make love again in a few minutes."

She knew what he meant. Next time it would last longer. Perhaps it would, but it would not be better than it had been a few minutes ago. Nothing could be. It seemed to her that they had celebrated a rite, not just of lust, or even of love, but of the sheer glory of still being alive.

"Richard, there in Pere-Lachaise you said that if we got out of there, you'd talk to me about—about why you risked your life for me."

"Yes, I'll talk about it," he said, and then paused. After a minute he explained. "Do you know what I was saying to myself while we were in that van? I was saying, 'You damned fool! You love this girl. You love her so much that if they are going to kill her they will have to kill you first. And yet all these past months you've been telling her and yourself that

354

you must live out your lives separately.' "

Her throat was aching. "And now?"

"Now I see that if I love you enough to die for you, I sure as hell ought to be able to live for you and *with* you. Maggie, will you marry me, just as soon as possible?"

"Richard, Richard! Are you certain?" After all, she, too, had felt that her unchangeable past was a barrier between them, one they could never surmount. "What about Madame Theraux and before that my life in New York—"

"Damned right I'm certain. In one way you can never change the past. In another way you can, by creating something to take its place."

He drew her close, and stroked her dark head as it lay pillowed on his shoulder.

"Remember how you let me think you were a loved and sheltered little girl, growing up with comfortably-off parents?"

She said, in a muffled voice, "I remember."

"Later you told me that there really had been such a little girl, but that she hadn't been you. She was just someone you'd seen on a Brooklyn lawn while you stood out on the sidewalk clutching the fence.

"Well, you and I are going to get married and go back to the States and have a little girl. She'll give doll tea parties on our lawn. And *that* will be our way of changing the past. It will be almost as if, years ago, you really had been that little girl. Do you see?"

"Oh, yes, my darling," she said brokenly. "I see."

He held her close then, while the tears rained down her cheeks and deep, healing sobs shook her body.